A BORING BOOK

The Personal History, Adventures, and
Observations of Dull Mr. John Smith

Mercifully Ghostwritten by
SETH MCDONOUGH

A BORING BOOK

or

AVERAGE EXPECTATIONS

Ghostwritten by

T.D.SETH MCDONOUGH

*For my parents, Tom & Marg McDonough, who furnished us
with an upbringing that was always dependable
and yet never boring.*

—TDSM

FOREWORD

By Ghostwriter Seth McDonough

Hello there, kind reader, I'm Ghostwriter Seth McDonough. Welcome to the fictional autobiography of Mr. John Smith.

Now, please be advised that, even though John is a made-up guy, he is entitled to possess the same weaknesses as the rest of us. In fact, John—like any real person might—was originally feeling daunted by the idea of writing his own autobiography. You see, although he's a nice fellow, John is one of the dullest personalities ever invented. Quite rightly, therefore, John decided that he would do the same thing that a non-fictional person might in his situation: he hired a ghostwriter to help him tell his tale.

So here's the deal: as with any tell-all celebrity autobiography, John is in charge of having lived his life and now narrating the details of it to you (our favourite reader so far), whereas I am responsible for providing boring John with a not-so-boring script for his narration so that you won't be bored by his boring personality.

Artistically enough, John and I didn't always get along during the writing of his story, but we hope that the friction between us will improve the dramatic tension within the sentences of this book as John stumbles along words that are too good for him.

Pleasent readings,

Seth McDonough

THE BORING TERMS

In the pages of this book, the word 'dullard' will not—as your dictionary might claim—refer to 'a person who is stupid.' Instead, it will mean what it sounds like: 'a person who is boring.'

Table of Boring Contents

Chapter 1
A Boring Beginning

Laughter is the Best Memory

Not that long ago in a small town Canadian park not that far away, I watched my five-year-old twin brother, Peter, attempt to climb the scariest part of a giant jungle gym while our mother held the waistband of his shorts.

"Led go, Mom!" Peter said, using a dialect that had not yet developed the ability to pronounce the letter T.

"Okay, just be careful, Peter ..." Mom said. "Okay, Peter, that's far enough."

"A liddle more!" my brother said, rounding his face into a magical collage of sorrow and urgency. "*Please, Mom.*"

"Okay, just a little more ... okay, that's far enough. Mommy wants you to stop now, Peter."

Peter must have realized in that moment that he'd gotten as much out of his facial contortions as he could because he immediately applied his brakes and smiled down at his mom. Something familiar in the expression invited me to suspect that my brother's sudden stillness was intended to create a false sense of obedience. My mom, apparently, did not share my unkind speculation; instead, she smiled back at Peter and unlocked her grip. Peter then doubled his smile before reviving his assent at maximum warp.

"Whoa!" Mom yelped, and she shot up her arm and caught a scruff of Per's shirt and shorts.

But Peter didn't immediately notice that he was no longer in control of his midsection, which meant that—for a tiny but permanent moment—I was treated to the sudden image of my brother pumping his arms and legs upwards while his torso didn't move. It was the funniest piece of physical comedy that I'd witnessed during my half decade of existence, and so I let out an uncharacteristic giggle.

Just before my laugh had stopped, I heard a similar one coming from my father, who was standing next to me. I looked up to see what was so amusing.

He grinned at me. "Peter looked funny there, eh?"

"Yeah," I said, beaming back.

That retort of mine—I'm honoured and proud to say—started my dad chuckling again, and so for the next few seconds we laughed together as if we were two equals with the same taste in comedy. Even though my brother soon after started up a tirade about the unfairness of climbing restrictions, the feeling of my dad laughing beside me is encased in my memory and lives independent of the subsequent tears of injustice that came from my sibling.

My mom, meanwhile, was also able to separate and discard the unwanted portions of the incident in her memory.

"Mommy's proud of you, Peter," she said, combing his hair with her fingers as we stood in line for ice cream. "You were very brave being up so high."

Luckily, our mother's edition of the memory was acceptable to Peter as well.

Chapter 2
Dullard vs. Brother

Coming Up Shy

A common boast made on behalf of young children is that they live their little lives with unadulterated enthusiasm for each moment without any deference to the judgmental preferences of those nearby. Children, the thinking goes, are 'authentic,' which apparently is a good thing.

Unfortunately, my particular brand of authenticity may not have been exactly what the framers of that blanket compliment had in mind. You see, intrigued reader, by the time Peter and I started Grade One in the fall of 1986, I had settled my personality into being at its most comfortable when I did more observing than participating. There was no child glamour to be attained by such passiveness.

In contrast, my ghostwriter and I surmise that my brother instinctively understood that authenticity required action to be most effective.

"And, um," he said to his parents one evening in regard to some toy logging he'd done for the day, "we god do make our own cabin by pudding the wood on dop of the wood. And then Norrinder forgod, and she god liddle pieces. And I didnd, and my house is bigger."

"Good for you, Per!" my mom said (using a T-free nickname that my brother had earned from our Aunty Susan in honour of his adorable trouble with the letter T). "I'm so proud of you."

"My house was *a lod* bigger," Per replied.

"That's our Peter," my dad said. "How about you, John? Did you build a house today?"

"No, John jusd build a square," Per said, chuckling. "And Norrinder forgod, and my house is bigger."

"Is that right, John? You didn't want to build a house?"

"Yeah," I said, grinning.

"His was jusd a square," Per noted.

"How come, John?" Mom said. "Why didn't you want to build a house?"

"Because he didn'd know how," Per said.

"Is that right, John?" Dad said.

"Yeah," I said with a merry shrug.

"He didn'd know *how!*" Per said, chuckling through a chew of food.

Suspiciously, I felt no annoyance during those frequent occasions that my brother outperformed me and answered my parents' questions for me. Instead, I was satisfied with listening to Per's take on the events.

PRONUNCIATION NOTE: For your consideration, phonetical reader, my ghostwriter has asked me to inform you of the obvious: 'Per' is pronounced *Pare*, not *Pur*.

The corollary of children feeling free to do as they please is that they don't often see any reason for acting *other* than according to their whims. In my case, I was content living in my introverted personality.

Admittedly, there was one unavoidable problem provoked by my non-participatory lifestyle. Sometimes—as I observed my classmates—I spotted trouble on one of their faces that seemed to indicate that they were feeling underappreciated. I recall, for instance, the day that shy Dale Rostrovich joined our class. He watched the events of his cohort with eyes swaying like a crowd to a tennis match, and, unlike me, he was clearly longing for an invitation. I remember staring at his sad mouth and wishing that someone would notice him. But my imagination could not conceive the idea that I, my very self, could have influenced the events toward the conclusion I wanted.

My brother, meanwhile, continued to seek out the centre of

the action. His muses were TV and kids from higher grades, and he studied them as though his popularity depended on it. But Per was a facilitator, not an inventor, and so—as far as my ghostwriter and I could infer—the only way he could think to replicate his observations was to mimic them *exactly*. That meant that, if nine classmates showed eager interest in a game, but the originating event called for only eight, then, by definition, one applicant had to be excluded.

"Can I play?" Dale Rostrovich asked one recess.

"No," Per said, "we only need eight."

Dale's face flushed. It was more than just the bruised feeling that comes with being left out; it was the sorrow that arises from being rejected after persuading oneself to try again. As I watched Dale's face retreat, his sadness enveloped me. But, once again, as an audience member, there was nothing for me to do about it.

The passive way I'd chosen to live my wee life must have been concerning to my mother. As far as my ghostwriter and I can speculate, she was certain that shyness was not good for a person. Yet we think her readings in non-interventionist child-rearing persuaded her to delay acting on her worries. When, however, my Grade Two personality brought the same results, my mom could wait no longer.

"John, honey," she asked me after school one day, "do you not like the other children in your class?"

I shrugged. "I like them."

"So why are you so shy around them?"

"I dunno."

"Well—"

"What's 'shy' mean, Mom?"

"It means ... quiet and maybe afraid to play with the other children."

"But ..." I said, taking in a long pause before concluding, "I play with them."

"Really? Because Miss Denton tells me you usually just watch the other children."

"Oh ... sorry, Mom."

"There's nothing to be sorry about, John. But *maybe* ... why don't you try playing with them?"

Hmm. I hadn't before considered that I *wasn't* playing with my classmates.

The next day at recess, I noticed for the first time that, when I watched my peers, they didn't watch me back. In fact, it seemed that their fun wouldn't have even been affected if I were to observe other kids instead. So I resolved that I should start participating in my classmates' adventures. *But how was I supposed to suddenly invite myself to join them?*

As you can see, patient reader, nothing came to my dull mind. I realized consequently that my mother's prophecy was right: I was indeed feeling shy. Of course, being aware that I was a shy kid made me self-conscious about it, which, in turn, made me hesitant around my peers. I continued to watch my classmates from a distance, just as I always had, but now I understood that socializing was reserved for personalities possessing charisma.

CRITICAL NOTE: My ghostwriter would like me to point out that, while my mother was the first to identify my shyness for me, she should not be blamed for the many years of shy pain that would result from my introversion. Someone was bound to have told me eventually that I was shy. And, even if no one had, surely, at some point, I would have noticed that the kids I was playing beside never asked me to go to their birthday parties.

Per, on the other side of our genetic code, continued to make up for my disappointing personality and was leading our Grade Two and then our Grade Three society with the various games he had acquired. On one occasion, I happened to be nearby, so I was among those drafted to participate.

"When you tag someone, they have to freeze—" Per was instructing.

"Can I play?" earnest Norrinder Gill asked.

"No, we only need six people."

"But I'm not very big."

"No, Norrinder. We only need six."

"But I'm only little."

"We only need six. Go away."

As Norrinder's little face slumped, I wished there were a way the rules would allow a seventh member.

"Do I go here?" Dale Rostrovich asked my brother.

"Yeah, but don't start till I say."

I was pleased that Dale had made it in this time, and for a moment that made me feel better about Norrinder. But then she sat down with a thump and rolled her neck downwards. Her sadness whooshed through my chest even harder than Dale's had previously. I looked at Dale; he was sporting an anticipatory grin. I wished he'd remember his prior pain and realize that he could save Norrinder from the same sorrow by giving up his spot up for her. I thought about that for twenty seconds.

"Norrinder can play!" I shouted as my fourth wall came crashing down.

"No, she can't. We only need six."

"She can play and not me."

Per looked me over for justification. Seeing none, he shrugged. "Okay, Norrinder can play. John can't."

Norrinder bounced to her feet. "Thanks!" she said, beaming as though her favourite cartoon celebrity had just given her a toy.

Considering how momentous that occasion was for my psyche, you might think that it would have motivated me to come up with more ways to help Per to avoid wounding our childhood colleagues during his game productions. But I lacked both the creativity and the boldness to support your noble thought, kind reader.

Chapter 3
Dullard in the Ring

Physical Comedy

Like my mom, my dad was tentative in his parenting tendencies. In his case, though, my ghostwriter and I suspect that my father wasn't so much acquiescing to the parent-help experts who demanded such passivity; instead, we estimate that he was demotivated by his own innate lack of confidence in his child-rearing instincts. According to his several-years-younger sister, Aunty Susan, my dad had never fully understood children (especially, in fact, when he was a member of their kind).

That was in evidence one Friday afternoon as Dad drove my brother and me home from school, and we passed a farm which produced a manure smell for the amusement of the two Grade Threes in the car.

"Hey," my brother said, squinting his nose at me, "was that *you?*"

"No," I said, giggling.

"Well," Per said, "whoever denied it, pried it."

"Nope," I said, delighted to remember my role in the interchange, "whoever smelt it, dealt it."

Per laughed back.

"I'm not sure either of those are fair standards of justice," Dad said.

"Whaddya mean?" Per said.

"Well, first of all: *John*, if just noticing an offence were enough to make someone guilty of it, then I'd say we'd all be guilty, wouldn't we? And, *Per*, if denying that guilt were also suspicious, then no one would ever able to defend themselves, would they?"

Per looked at me with a giggle on his face, and I laughed again.

"Oh, right," Dad said. "Sorry, *that's* the joke, isn't it? That it's a Kafkatrap."

I looked at Per with a confused face. He shrugged his shoulders in equal bewilderment, and I chuckled again.

A few minutes later, our journey landed in a library parking lot.

"What're we doing *here*?" Per said.

"Well," Dad said, "I may not be able to keep up with you boys' humour, but I know some people who can."

Per and I were understandably unnerved to be taken to a book collective to learn about comedy. Nevertheless, Dad rented three movies, one starring Charlie Chaplin, another led by Buster Keaton, and a third run by The Three Stooges.

The Smith family was soon introduced to a compilation of magic humans who somehow rivaled cartoons with their physical comedy. Per and I, for instance, were mesmerized by how the Chaplin fellow was able to successfully participate in a boxing match with a much larger foe by mirroring the movements of the referee in the ring so that the bigger boxer couldn't get to him without wounding said umpire.

Next up, to our even greater delight, the trio of stooges fought each other with electrifying creativity. They were fast and wild and yet always in sync.

The next morning, Per and I tried to choreograph our own Stooges-style fight by mixing together our favourite of their moves in a new order. But once again our dad took the comedy literally.

"Those fight moves wouldn't really work in the real world," he told us. "They're just meant to be funny. Maybe it's time I taught you boys how to wrestle properly."

"Why?" Per said.

"Because you want to know how to defend yourself if someone starts a fight with you, don't you?"

Per shrugged. "I guess."

And so our dad attempted to teach us the intricacies of wrestling.

It was very boring.

"Can't we just wrestle, like, all together?" Per said. "Like, me and John against you?"

Fifteen minutes later, our mom arrived home to find her sons giggling as we tried to pull her husband's arms behind his back.

"You all look like monkeys," she said, chuckling. She watched us for a few minutes, cheering the littler combatants on, until one of our limbs came "frightfully" close to colliding with a lamp, at which time she told us to take our games outside.

Over the next few weeks, our dad refined the rules of our wrestling matches, but our mother's instruction to hold our competitions outdoors stayed the same, which wasn't always convenient since we lived in a rainy part of the universe. So the year we entered Grade Four, my dad built a padded ring in our basement.

In that soft space, Per's and my challenge was to tackle our dad from his knees all the way to the ground while his competing task was to pin us both simultaneously. I don't know how hard Dad tried, but he made his assignment seem difficult. As soon as he had one of us subdued, the other would escape and jump on his back, which would force Dad to let the pinned pion go so that he could safely remove the other attacker from his spine. Sometimes Per or I would avoid our dad's subsequent lunge, which, in turn, allowed us both to jump on him at the same time. That usually led to a Per-John victory.

In every case, we departed the wrestling mat a little sore everywhere, but most strained in our stomachs from laughing. Our poor dad: after his attempt to influence our comedy sensibilities had led to our interest in play-fighting, his effort to teach us how to properly fight was now proving funny to us. I don't know if that bothered him, but I suspect so because, one day, he bought Per and me boxing gloves and demoted himself to referee.

"Okay, boys, I know you just like to be creative and do whatever you feel in the moment, but, in a real fight, you need to strategize."

"Yeah, whatever, Dad," Per said, grinning. "I'm just gonna win."

A sparkle of anxiety shot through me just then as I pondered competing against my brother.

"Per, don't be so confident," Dad said. "That's your first strategic mistake. Now, before you start, I want you boys to touch gloves. That's how you show respect for your opponent."

As our padded hands connected, I felt another punch of nerves.

"You okay, John?" Dad said.

"Yeah. It's just weird. We're usually on the same side."

"It's just practice," Per said, still beaming. "Once we get good, we can beat up Dad again."

The sincerity of my brother's smile relaxed me. "Okay, let's do it."

At first, Per was better at boxing than I was because he was more aggressive, and so he could exhaust me with manic flurries, but then Dad taught me how to use my brother's wildest lunges against him. Soon I was winning more than I was losing, so Dad showed my brother how to time his flurries so that they took advantage of lapses in my defences. That cycle of improvement continued throughout our childhood.

Yet, despite the sport's significant influence on my upbringing, when I reflect on it now, my first smile always goes towards its Three Stooges' origins and our dad's earnest concern that we might learn the wrong way to fight.

Chapter 4
Dullard in Conversation

The Grand Apparent

Per and I were also well matched in the competitive sport of tidiness. You see, intrigued reader, our parents had a talent for keeping our home sharply organized at all times, and so my brother and I—whether by genetic advantage or by parental inspiration—became obsessively neat as well.

For a few months in Grade Four, for instance, Per and I played *Monopoly* every day after school. Following each competition, we efficiently put the pieces back in their cozy box before transferring it to the games closet.

"Thanks for cleaning up, guys," our mom often said to us as if there were anything else to do with a mess.

One strange day after school, though, our parents sat and watched us play and then offered us unnecessarily supportive comments regarding our strategies and rolls of the dice.

"Yeah!" Per said, laughing, when he collected my last fake dollar, "that means I've won two out of the last three."

"Although," Dad said, "doesn't that also mean that you've *both* won two of the last four?"

"I guess," Per said, with a *What's he talking about?* look on his face.

I laughed at that and began putting the evidence of Per's victory back in the box.

"Actually, boys," Mom said, "just for tonight: don't worry about cleaning up, okay?"

"Why?" Per said, utilizing the same incredulous face he'd

performed on our dad and, in turn, drawing the same laugh from me.

"Well, because we have some sad news to tell you."

"What?" Per said, smirking at me.

"Your Grandma Chevelier passed away this morning."

Per and I were appropriately horrified to find out, especially since Grandma Chevelier was the last of our grandparents. But we would need a few more years before we would understand the full significance of our loss.

That evening, Aunty Susan came into town and stayed with us for a few days. At the time, that seemed to me to be an appropriate show of respect for my grandmother. But, upon telling the tale to my ghostwriter, I've come to realize that my favourite aunt and her brother's mother-in-law had only met each other once or twice. So I now suspect that Aunty Susan joined the mourning to give my parents a break from their sad but not yet grief-comprehending children.

Aunty Susan had always been one of my favourite adults, but—with the departure of my grandparents—she took over as the *leading* doting, spoiling, always-fascinated-with-Per-and-me grand persona. Once a month, she visited us from an hour's drive away, supplying hugs and enthusiasm for whatever was going on. Per and I were always delighted by her attendance, and we both wanted to sit next to her during dinner. Aunty Susan received our applications for her attention gracefully: along with playing with us as a pair, she took us each out for individual attention. I consistently felt honoured when it was my turn.

"How'd you like school this year, John?" she asked one summer afternoon as she drove me to the mall to pick up cake supplies for my dad's birthday.

"It was okay," I replied, relaxed in the conversation she was directing.

"So what'd you do during lunch hour and recess?"

"I watched them play games and stuff."

"You watched the other kids?"

"Yeah."

"What kind of games?"

"King of the castle and dodge ball and Star Wars and, um ..."

"Did you have fun?"

"I guess."

I'd never really thought of fun as being part of my responsibility at school.

Aunty Susan smiled. "You know you're a very mature little boy, John?"

"Is that bad, Aunty Susan?"

"No, no, no, *mature* means that you see things that other children don't—no, that's not quite right. It means you treat people—it kind of means you're less childish than other kids. Does that make any sense?"

"Yeah," I said, not wanting to hurt my aunt's feelings by admitting otherwise.

"So you're probably wondering what my point is …" she said. "The thing is it's nice that you're so considerate and respectful of others. You remind me of your dad at your age. But sometimes it's fun just to be a kid."

"But I *am* a kid."

My aunt laughed. "Yes, of course you are. Just ignore your Aunty Susan. She's having trouble making sense today."

"Okay, but I don't *want* to ignore my Aunty Susan."

My aunt smiled. "Okay, then let's change the subject. Let's see, have you and Per got anything for your dad for his birthday yet?"

"No," I said, surprised by the question: I hadn't realized that adults got presents too.

As we arrived at the bakery section of our grocery store, Aunty Susan and I were still reminiscing about the above discovery.

"How's it going?" the bakery man said with a smile.

"Oh, we're fine," Aunty Susan replied, smiling back. "We're looking for a cake for his dad—my brother—and we'd like to write something nice on it. Any ideas?"

"On what cake to buy or what to write?"

"*Both*," Aunty Susan said, laughing with unusual enthusiasm.

"Okay," the man said, "well, I'd say something creative, like, 'Happy birthday, dad and brother.'"

Aunty Susan laughed some more. "That's not bad, but, um, you know, he's also a husband. His wife might feel left out."

"Okay, so go with, 'Happy birthday, dad, brother, and husband.'"

"Not bad, except—"

"You think it sounds like he's playing dad, brother, and husband to the *same* person?"

Aunty Susan laughed her loudest yet. "Wow, no, I wasn't thinking *that*."

"What's the problem, then?" the man said with a grin.

"Well, I was just thinking it sounds like a tombstone, like: 'This cake was made for a devoted husband, father, and brother.'"

"Good point," the bakery man said, now adding his own laugh.

"It was a good idea, though," Aunty Susan said.

"Well, does he have any hobbies? Maybe we can create a cake to match his interests."

"Okay, great, yeah," my aunt said, "um, he likes to read. How about a book? No that's silly. Um—"

"Is he a golfer?"

"No."

"Too bad. I do a great golf ball."

"Oh, well, I'm sure it's great, but, you know, he's just not into golf."

So, as you can detect, observant reader, it took a significant while to pick out a cake; and I noticed that the further into the discussion Aunty Susan went, the more verbally clumsy she seemed to be. For instance, she continually corrected herself in the middle of sentences. That was something she did in general, but, with Cake-man, she second-guessed so much of what she said that I wondered if she wasn't feeling well.

We finally settled on a soccer-ball-style cake—since Aunty Susan had corrected herself that her brother wasn't really that big a soccer fan but then corrected herself again, noting that he certainly liked it enough to have it on his cake. In fact, she decided it would be funny to give my dad a kid's cake.

Aunty Susan was then oddly silent as we left the grocery store in pursuit of shops in which to pick out a birthday present from Per and me.

And then she began giving me unnecessary instructions.

"Stop for this lady," she said, even though I'd already slowed on my own for a woman and her stroller. "Okay, we can go again."

"Are you okay?" I asked my aunt.

"Of course. Why would you think I'm not okay?"

"Oh, sorry, Aunty Susan. I didn't mean to hurt your feelings."

"No, no, you *didn't*. But I wonder what made you think that. You know, you're actually right: I *am* a little distracted."

"How come?"

"Well, your Aunty Susan sometimes talks to people and then replays what she said in her mind to see if she could've said something better."

"Oh…how come?"

My aunt smiled at me. "Your Aunty Susan's very silly for doing this, John, so—*if I tell you*—you shouldn't copy me, okay? Do you promise not to copy me?"

"Okay."

"Well, I shouldn't make you promise not to do something if that's how you feel—just don't *purposely* copy me, okay?"

"Okay," I said with no idea to what I was agreeing.

"Okay," my aunt said, "so your Aunty Susan sometimes wants to make friends with people, but she gets nervous—which means she's not herself—but that makes her *even more* nervous, and then she second guesses herself. Pretty silly, isn't it?"

"No," I said, still confused but recognizing that, shockingly, my hero did not seem to feel good about herself. "Aunty Susan, can I tell you something?"

"Of course."

"You're my favourite aunty."

I would have said that she was my favourite non-parent-based adult, but I wasn't sure how to word that. As it was, I hadn't given my aunt much of a compliment since I had only one other aunt (whom I rarely saw). But Aunty Susan didn't seem to notice the insignificance of the compliment; instead, she told me that it made her feel better.

Chapter 5
Dullard at School

Mirror Imaginations

For the next few months, I pondered my aunt's idea that I try to be more of a kid, but I couldn't think of anything to do differently. *Perhaps her suggestion was related to my mother's continued hints that Per's way of playing with our peers was a model I should consider adopting.* But, as I watched my brother dominating Grade Five lunch hour discussions, I realized that I had neither the courage nor the school yard credibility to copy my sibling. So my mom and I could only hope that one day I might get a new personality in the mail.

My motivation to hope for such a delivery was encouraged, conveniently, by Per's and my Grade Five teacher, Mrs. Holmstead, who was strongly in favour of children being free and always themselves—so long as those selves were expressive and imaginative like children should be.

"Now, my darlings," said Mrs. Holmstead, "this is one of those times that we've talked about—one of those occasions that you have an opportunity to be creative. You get the joy of using your wonderful imaginations." She paused to smile at our confused faces. "Many years ago," she continued, "I had a student named Kallie, and Kallie was given the same assignment that I'm giving you children now—which, you'll soon learn, is to make a presentation to the class about an important historical figure—and do you know what Kallie did?" Mrs. Holmstead paused as if she thought we might want to offer a guess. "Well," she said when no hands were raised, "Kallie decided to do her project about Cleopatra, and do you know how she brought Cleopatra to life?"

I sheepishly shook my head.

"What Kallie did was she took a scene from a movie about Cleopatra, and she acted it out for the entire class." Mrs. Holmstead sighed at the memory. "Your teacher was very, very impressed with Kallie. She had taken my assignment and made it her own. It was such a wonderful surprise. Does that make sense, children? Just remember to let your wonderful imaginations be your guides, and you'll do wonderfully. And, don't forget, I like to be surprised."

Per decided to let Kallie's imagination be his muse, and he set to work on finding another historical character who'd starred in a movie.

"That's a great idea, Per," Mom said after school. "We'll have to get you a costume."

I, meanwhile, did not have the imagination to borrow from Kallie's prior genius; instead, I focused my research on the Smithhouse encyclopedia.

"John," Mom said when she and Per returned from costume shopping, "I'd like you to help Per with his mini-play about Horatio Nelson. You're going to play his second-in-command, okay?"

I accepted my commission and tried to memorize my lines. Luckily, my brother hadn't altered my words from the original movie text, so I was able to watch the borrowed-from scene repeatedly until it formed an accessible pathway in my brain.

"Won't John need a costume *as well* if they're in the same scene?" Dad asked that evening.

"Good point..." Mom said, pausing for contemplation. "Yeah, but it's delicate because, if they're both in costume, it'll look like a group project, and John's already got his *own* project. Hmm..."

After giving the matter some due thought, my mom decided that I would sit at my desk, like the rest of my classmates, during Per's presentation. Lord Nelson Per would then yell at the class as if we were his crew, and then my second-in-command replies would come from off stage on behalf of the group.

My ghostwriter claims that that decision ought to have made me even more nervous about my role in the pending production.

CLARIFYING NOTE: My condescending ghostwriter explains that, by sitting inconspicuously among the rest of the audience, no one would know in advance that I was to be a speaking part of Per's play. Instead, my voice was to come charging into the scene from behind without warning, leaving my peers no choice but to swivel probing eyes in my direction in a quest to figure out why the heck I was talking in the middle of Per's project. Of course, they would soon recognize that I was working on director's orders, but, for the eternal second that it would take them to realize so, I would endure some displeased looks.

Luckily, I was not sufficiently sophisticated to appreciate the consequence of performing from inside the crowd, so I became no more excessively nervous than I already was.

When performance day cruelly arrived, Mrs. Holmstead had us present our projects in alphabetical order, which meant the Smith boys had many presentations to consider before we would take our turns. In my experience, watching others' versions of the same assignment that one is about to offer generally produces one of two reactions, (A) renewed confidence as Per realizes that his presentation is indeed going to be the best, or (B) renewed lack of confidence as John recognizes that he would have been best off not getting out of bed that morning.

You see, it turned out that Per wasn't the only student who had taken Mrs. Holmstead up on her request to surprise her. Various posters and even musical accompaniments were brought out to remind me that a mere words-based report would not do.

Thirty minutes into the torture, Carrie Richards walked to the front. Several of my male classmates and I were confident that Carrie was the prettiest girl in the world, and so we would have been entertained even if she had spent the presentation talking about a famous poet. Instead, though, she whispered something to our teacher, received a grin of approval, and stepped out of the room, carrying a duffle bag.

We all looked at Mrs. Holmstead to see if there was something we should be doing while we waited.

"I think you're going to like this," she replied.

Two minutes of awkward anticipation later, the hallway door reopened, and Carrie returned wearing a simple ballet outfit.

"Ladies and gentleman," she said, staring at her notes, "my project is on Alexandra Danilova. She was a prima ballerina born in Russia in 1904. She's my favourite ballerina because she was my teacher's teacher. Her friends called her *Coura*. This is the dance she did in *Swan Lake*—my favourite ballet—at the New York Met Opera House."

Carrie put her notes down and clicked on her music player.

"Wonderful!" Mrs. Holmstead whispered.

As pretty Carrie pointed her toes and began to glide around the presentation space, I was stunned by her sophistication. She wasn't a kid like the rest of us: she was a star as competent as any hockey player on TV. A few minutes into that fascination, it struck me like a heart palpitation that I had acquired a crush on my dancing classmate.

PRETTY NOTE: My ghostwriter says I shouldn't get any respect for having finalized my crush on Carrie as a result of her artistic skills; instead, he contends that my readiness to appreciate her dancing brilliance was the result of the fact that her prettiness had long subconsciously made her my favourite female classmate. I have no defence against that accusation other than that my ghostwriter is obnoxious in his delivery of it, so I leave it to you to break the tie, fair-minded reader.

When the Mrs. Holmstead-led applause for Carrie dispersed, you might have thought that Per and I would have increased our nervousness out of respect for Carrie's performance, but, luckily, we didn't feel much need to compare ourselves to pretty girls. Had she been Andrei Vishnevski—Per's rival for the most appreciated boy in the class—we may have had to reconsider, but, as it was, I sat in my desk with no extra butterflies on board as I waited to hear my name called.

"Okay," Mrs. Holmstead said, "I can't wait to see what we have in store next. We have, let's see …John S., you're up next."

There was a burning feeling in my forehead as I carried my cue cards to the front of the watchful class. When I arrived at the centre of attention, I noticed that a few of my cards seemed to be sticking together in deference to the glue I'd used to attach them to my notes.

"Um," I said, trying to talk through the malfunction, "Charles John Huffam Dickens wrote books in the 19th century—that means the 1800s." My hands then succeeded in separating my speech, but two of the cards were now out of order, so, with sweat swirling around my forehead, I focused my attention for a never-ending second on rearranging them. "Um," I returned, "he wrote lots of famous books, including *A Christmas Carol*—that's about Scrooge from the Canadian Tire adverts ..." (Mrs. Holmstead laughed at that; neither the class nor I was sure why) "... *Oliver Twist, David Copperfield, Great Expectations*—my dad says it's the best book ever written—and *Nicholas Nickleby*. His first book was *The Pickwick Papers*. He was born Friday, February 7th, 1812 in Portsmouth, England, and ..."

As I continued listing, in no particular order, the facts that I had transcribed about Mr. Dickens, I was too focused on my cue cards to notice that the yawns of my classmates had awakened from their slumber.

"Lovely, John," Mrs. Holmstead said with a forced grin when I finished. "That was a lot of useful facts. Thank you, John. Next, I'm sure Peter has something special for us."

Like Carrie before him, my brother excused himself to go into the hall to prepare. I was pleased at that point to notice that I was less nervous about my supporting role in Per's play now that I had carried a presentation by myself.

A Horatio Nelson arm soon reached around the doorway to start Per's tape player. Some trumpet sounds were heard, and Per reentered the classroom, English accent blazing. If I didn't know better, I might have thought that he was anxious too, but Per's impressive Admiral-flavoured costume overshadowed any suspicion.

"Oh my," one could hear Mrs. Holmstead saying with a grin in the background as Peratio Nelson strolled around the room.

I performed my supporting role punctually but with a lack of eloquence as I accidentally ran some of my words together. Not to worry, concerned reader, Per's subsequently crisp retort helped his audience to retroactively realize what I had said.

"Wonderful, wonderful, wonderful," Mrs. Holmstead said,

leading the class in applause again when Per was done. "You children's imagination never ceases to amaze me. Thank you, Peter. You just made your teacher's day."

After a few more not-up-to-Per's-level presentations, Andrei Vishnevski stepped up to the scrutiny. Andrei had joined our class a month into the year, and he was surprisingly un-shy for someone who spoke with an accent caused by a non-English first language. Strangely, though, as he gave his presentation, he continually took his eyes off his cue cards to peek at those of us watching. As I observed Andrei bobbing back and forth between us and his notes, I also noticed that he had put the details of his subject, Mahatma Gandhi, into an order that made it seem like he was telling us a story. In fact, while half of my concentration was nodding along with the Andrei bobbing, the other half was inadvertently becoming interested in the Gandhi fellow's history.

"Thank you, Andrei," Mrs. Holmstead said when the presentation was complete. "Some interesting facts."

The blandness of the commendation seemed odd to me. Andrei had received the same low compliment that I had, and yet Andrei's performance was clearly superior to mine. I felt bad about that, and I hoped that Andrei didn't conclude that I believed that my project was as good as his.

Chapter 6
Dullard vs. Sociopath

The Popularity Polarity

As Per and I grew out of Grade Five and into Grade Six, my brother's popularity expanded with us. Even when our class mixed with our French Immersion rivals at recess and lunch hour, there was still no one possessing sufficient charisma to challenge my brother's leadership on the boy-side of the playground. If he wanted to spend a break playing football, his associates were so sure that it was the right thing to do that they may have even thought that they had an influence in the decision.

Meanwhile, as far as I can intuit, my mom was attempting to resist her inclination to prefer one son over the other. She tried to be interested in my Grade Six Science project—a chart on the nutritional content of various cereals—in spite of the fact that, with her help, my brother had put together a spectacular volcano display.

HELPFUL NOTE: You might already be aware of the volcano to which I'm referring, well-informed reader: there was a time that, at almost every Grade Six Science fair, at least one superstar kid created one.

About my cereal graph, my dad was heard to say, "Nice work, son: very informative."

"Yes," Mom said, "that's really good, John. I'm really enjoying reading it. Oh, by the way, you should check out the final version of Per's volcano before he turns it off."

As Per and I arrived in Grade Seven, our mother tracked our social affluence carefully. My ghostwriter smugly claims to be amused by that news. He contends that Mom recognized that the Grade Seven year was an important time for kids to finalize their personalities and reputations for high school. If Per could hold onto his classmates through Grade Seven, then maybe he could take a following with him into the ruthless popularity wars of the large high school for which we were destined. But our mother soon had a challenge to her serene hopes: at the beginning of that final elementary school season, we acquired two new classmates, Ashley Anonti and Jake Richport.

Ashley was sent to us from a far away, impoverished land. The resulting girl did not immediately connect socially with her elementary school colleagues. Not to worry, concerned reader, Ashley did not seem at all traumatized by the notion of being an outsider. In fact, her lack of anxiety in the face of social segregation made it appear that she might be enjoying her exile. That bullied into submission any thoughts her peers might have had of picking on her. Indeed, Ashley's confidence seemed to cause many of her classmates to crave her attention. It wasn't so much that they liked being around her; they just seemed to feel that her approval would mean that they'd achieved a certain level of maturity. It was that aspect of Ashley's personality that my ghostwriter and I suspect concerned my mom: if Ashley's non-standard comfort-fit into her own skin were ever to persuade the rest of the class to go for non-conventional existences, then Per would cease to be the best person to lead them.

Jake, meanwhile, was donated to our school by his previous school, which had suspended him so many times that his parents had apparently decided that he was misunderstood and needed a fresh set of teachers. Like my brother, Jake had spent his life traveling the centre of attention, so—when the two landed in each other's lives—they both seemed convinced that it was their duty to take the lead.

"Why do you wanna play baseball?" the newcomer said with a chortle as Per was counting out teams.

"Uh, because it's fun," Per replied.

"Right on," Jake said, "and, while you're having fun, I'm gonna go talk to the girls."

"I talk to girls!" Per later yelled to the enthusiastic agreement of his mother. "But I'm not going to talk to them *all the time*."

"Exactly," Mom said, "and I bet sometimes the girls watch you play sports, so that'll impress them more than Jake rambling at them all lunch hour."

Unfortunately, in reality, the girls never seemed to be that interested in observing boys' sports, and so I suspect that Mom's speculation only worried Per more. *Was it dangerous to be spending so much time playing sports, leaving Jake unfettered opportunity to convince the girls that he was the graduating class's most eligible colleague?* Perhaps it was time to beat Jake up to set the hierarchy straight.

One rainy afternoon, though, with several followers gathered around a Per-run *Dungeons & Dragons* tournament, Jake wandered into the area and imitated how the principal might react to the indoor activity.

"Now, boysh and girlsh," he said, using the administrator's iconic lisp, "jusht becaushe itsh raining doeshn't mean there ishn't plenty of adventuersh for you to dishcover outshide."

A couple of the game players laughed but then glanced at Per to make sure it was okay.

Per grinned. "Holy hell! That's an *aweshome* impression. Can you do Ellings?"

Jake could indeed impersonate Ms. Ellings, the Vice Principal, and he mimicked the condescending floweriness of her tone so perfectly that Per evidently realized that this was not the sort of person with whom he could be enemies. Jake, in turn, had clearly already recognized that my brother's prior claim on the class gave him valuable influence.

The merger was soon complete, and it was apparent that my brother and the newcomer were an excellent match. Whereas Jake had a multitude of ideas for creating original fun, Per had the conviction and leadership qualities to get them carried out.

Beauty in the Eye of the Distorter

Within a few months, 'Per and Jake' became a common expression as the twosome had come to represent the pinnacle of elementary school power.

"Hey," I saw Jake whispering to my brother one recess, "help me start a prettiness database."

"Sure," Per said. "Wait, what you do mean?"

I discovered the answer to Per's question that afternoon during science class. A piece of paper was passed around among the male classmates. At each stop, it was examined and either smiled at and filled in or glanced at and passed on. Tragically for Jake, the sixth guy in the paper trail, Andrei Vishnevski, tore it up.

Jake sent Andrei a glare but didn't linger on it since Andrei now had a reputation for being the biggest kid in the school. A new form was drafted and reached me a few minutes later. At the top it said:

PRETTINESS DATABASE: FOR GUYS IN GRADE SEVEN D. NO GIRLS OR ANDREIS ALLOWED ACCESS. FILL IN YOUR PRETTINESS RATING FOR EACH GIRL IN OUR CLASS OUT OF TEN.

The form included a column for each of the girls in the class, squared off into rows for every boy (minus Andrei) and a final average score line for each girl. I scanned the marks and noted that there seemed to be three types of result so far: (A) tens for the girls recognized as pretty and popular, (B) sevens or eights for the girls whose reputation was pretty *or* popular, and (C) zeroes for the girls diagnosed as neither popular nor pretty.

I admired and wanted to copy Andrei's sabotage efforts, but I wondered if I was more impressed by our classmate, Tony, who had given *every* girl a ten. That was clearly going to annoy Jake because it would artificially move the lower marks closer to the elite.

So which classmate was I to copy? Andrei the destroyer or Tony the digit spinner? It would break my heart to give legitimacy to the process by filling in the scorecard—even with all tens. Plus, the thought of one of the contestants finding my imprint on Jake's cruel production damaged my heart again. But my insides were wounded a third time as I imagined one of the uncelebrated girls finding out just how disproportionately she was ranked. At least, with Tony's system, her average score was nudged up.

I then realized that, if Math 7 had taught me anything, I could improve the not-pretties' relative scores by bringing the pretties' totals down. My calculator was called into service, and I determined the average up to then for each girl, and I gave them the opposite score in my slot. Consequently, poor beautiful Jessica received a zero while not-so-pretty-or-popular Hillary got a perfect ten. My heart was beating as I filled in each ugly number.

But, when I arrived at the name of beautiful Carrie Reynolds, the crush of my life, I couldn't persuade myself to inscribe the zero that my calculations demanded. Instead, with a stutter in my pen, I completed her row of tens.

At the end of lunch hour that day, I found myself near the highly pretty Jessica as we arrived in the classroom. As usual, I pretended not to see her.

"Hey, Jess," Jake said, startling us from behind. "I asked John how pretty he thinks you are on a scale of one to ten, and you know what he gave you?"

"Ah, I have no idea," she replied with a healthy rolling of her eyes.

Jake smiled with raised eyebrows. "Zero! As in not pretty at all."

Jessica turned her eye-roller to me. "I love you too, John."

"No, but, *Jessica*," I blustered as she turned and walked to her desk, "my scores actually meant, like, the opposite!"

Jessica did not look back at me; instead, she presented me with her middle finger as she sat down.

Jake laughed.

I put on my grittiest glare. "What'd you do that for?"

"Just doing you a favour. You think she's a dog, so now you don't have to worry about her liking you."

No response was available to me at that point. I wish now that I'd just let my boxing experience speak on my behalf. Not aware of the persuasiveness of violence at the time, though, I decided that, in the future, I would need to be more vocal in my response to Jake's slander.

To my disappointment, I would soon get another opportunity to respond to the tyranny of my new classmate. At recess the next day, Jake and Per interrupted me while I was reading in the library.

"Come with us," Jake said.

"Why?" I said, looking at my brother

Per shrugged. "I don't know what he wants. He says it'll just take a second."

I was led to Ashley Anonti, who was sitting on a swing and reading. Ashley was to my eyes nearly as pretty as Jessica, but her lack of recognized popularity had cost her a dominant score on the prettiness scale.

"Hey, Ash," Jake said, "so I asked John how pretty he thought you were out of ten, and do you know what he gave you?"

"I don't care."

"Oh, no worries: I'll tell you anyway. He gave you a two! As in—"

"You did?" Ashley said, looking at me.

I grimaced back. "Yeah, but not because—"

"Why the hell'd you tell her that?" my brother said.

Jake raised his eyebrows in congratulations to himself.

"What exactly is going on?" Ashley said.

"We created a prettiness database," Jake replied.

"It was Jake's idea," Per said. "I didn't wanna do it."

"You actually ranked all us girls?"

"Yeah, Mr. Dupreve told me I had to practice my math."

"How is *that* math practice?"

"Because I had to work out your average scores."

"That's so stupid. You're a sexist pig, Jake. Go away."

"*So?*" Jake said. "You can rank us guys too, if you want. I don't care."

"No thanks. I'm not that immature."

"It was Jake's idea," Per said again.

"*Bye*," Ashley replied.

Jake and Per walked away, but I stayed, staring in the direction of our victim. This time, I had to clarify myself.

"You're such an idiot," I could hear my brother telling Jake. "Now all the girls are gonna hate us."

"Hey, Per's brother!" Jake yelled back. "She meant you *too*."

Ashley looked up at me. "No, he can stay."

"Suit yourself," Jake replied with a forced laugh. "Just don't forget: he thinks you're ugly."

"Sexist pig," Ashley muttered again before turning to me. "So you really think I'm a two out of ten in his stupid ranking thing?"

"No, I promise I don't."

"So why'd you give me a two on his stupid scale?"

I explained to Ashley my rob-from-the-popular-to-give-to-the-less-popular system.

Ashley nodded. "I would've just thrown it away if I were you."

"I wanted to, but Andrei already tried that, and Jake just started another one."

Ashley sighed. "I still would've thrown it away."

"Yeah, you're right. I'm sorry. I didn't mean to hurt your feelings."

"It's okay," Ashley said, smiling her pretty smile, "you didn't hurt my feelings. I know I'm gorgeous."

I nodded blankly, not sure if Ashley meant for me to laugh at the apparent joke, but definitely sure that I didn't have the courage to agree with her. The awkwardness of my non-retort was clearly not lost on Ashley.

"See you, then," she said.

"Okay, see you."

I walked away wishing that I were the sort of boy who had the courage to pull up a swing next to a girl. In fact, I was strongly considering betraying beautiful Carrie Richards and transferring my crush on her to Ashley.

The Rumour Spill

The growth of my affection for Ashley was matched only by the progression of my dislike of Jake. Per sometimes brought the demonic preteen to our place after school. That would have been fine if I had been allowed to hide in my room, but my mother saw no reason why I couldn't learn something from Per's involvement in the cool crowd.

"Why don't you three go downstairs and hang out, and I'll bring you down some homemade pizza?" she would announce whenever Jake came over.

Within our forced trio, Jake and I would have been content ignoring each other, but my brother decided it would be best if we interacted, so he made jokes about me for Jake to enjoy. I didn't mind the funniness because I was confident Per was just being playful, but the vehemence with which Jake laughed made me feel that he was chuckling more at me than the humour.

Meanwhile, I received the honour of overhearing Jake designing his malevolent schemes. For his latest, he had decided to follow his advice to Ashley and start a looks database for the girls to rate the boys. It did not have the same success as its forebrother because most of the girl judges were disinclined to fill it in. So, after making refinements as to where he sent the survey, Jake had only three responses from which to calculate the visual status of the boys. Among the less favoured was our old Grade One colleague, Dale Rostrovich, who had an extra layer of softness on him, which earned him a unanimous zero in the contest.

---

*CREEPY NOTE (**Optional Reading**):* My ghostwriter says he suspects you're wondering how I did on the analysis, curious reader. I wouldn't be so presumptuous to think you would care, but, since my ghostwriter contends that you want to know, I did surprisingly well. I got an average 5 out of a possible 10 'handsomeness' points, which I guess makes sense. I was neither attractive nor memorable enough to be specifically *un*appealing. My brother, meanwhile, was both memorable and handsome and so he averaged 9.7. Second place went to the growth-spurting Andrei Vishnevski with 9. Jake, further meanwhile, seemed fascinated to discover that he was in sixth place (out of thirteen) and seemed pleased to calculate himself to be 6.3 points more appreciated by the adjudicators than Dale.

Now, officially, in that time and society, it was easier for boys to get away with obesity than girls—so long as they were loud and opinionated enough to get respect from the other boys. Dale, unfortunately, could not match his physique's extroversion.

So, one dull lunch hour, Jake scanned the spatter of students in the field, and—upon spotting Dale in the vicinity of Carrie Richards (my long term crush and the top scorer on the female looks scale)—he smiled to his evil self.

As the lunch bell yanked us back into class half an hour later, the sounds of rumours suddenly rang in my ears.

"Yeah, Carrie Richards totally has a crush on Dale Rostrovich," one rumourist said to another.

"Not likely," the receiver replied.

"Someone heard her telling Jessica she's like *in love with him* or something."

With my ears pointed in the direction of that discussion, I collided with a sprinting by Grade Two student.

"Sorry," I said, peering down at my wee victim.

The felled munchkin looked up at me skeptically, jumped to his feet, took another stare at me, and then returned to full sprint.

By that time, the important gossip had passed me by, so I was forced to discuss it on my own. *Beautiful Carrie in love with Dale?* For a moment, I was jealous; but, as I glanced around for a view of Carrie, I noticed Dale still deep in the gravel field, trudging back to class. I couldn't resist a hopeful smile. *Perhaps the news of Carrie's love for him would cheer him up.*

I entered the classroom to find a gathering around Carrie.

"Um, I don't think so," she said. "Dale's not exactly my type. Thanks anyway."

Oh.

"You're lying," Felipe said, grinning. "You've got a huge crush on him. Somebody heard you telling Jessica."

"Um, *no they didn't,*" Jessica said.

Carrie nodded at her friend. "Dale's like the last guy I'd want to be my boyfriend."

In spite of the compliment towards me—that I was *not* the last guy that Carrie would go for—I was sad for Dale.

At that same moment, I heard the not-so-faraway door to the school open and close; a slow-sounding walk was now travelling in our direction. I stepped into the hallway to find Dale drudging towards us.

I rushed back into the classroom. Carrie was still talking about her approaching classmate. I stared at her, silently pleading for her to change topics, but, instead, she was now telling a humiliating story about Dale from Grade Four.

"Um, Carrie," I blustered, "can I borrow a pencil for math?"

"You don't have a pencil?"

"Yeah."

Carrie stared at me. "Um, I don't really carry extra pencils with me, John."

"Oh. Okay."

"Why don't you ask *Dale*?" someone said, smirking past me.

I turned around.

And there was Dale, looking confused.

"Oh, hi, Dale. Um, yeah, can I borrow a pencil for math?"

"Okay," he said softly. "I've got one in my desk."

The gathering giggled at Dale.

"What are they laughing at?" he whispered.

"Um, I don't know. They're weird."

"Is this some sort of joke?"

"No, I just need a pencil."

"Okay," he said.

Dale, my ghostwriter and I suspect, was accustomed to people laughing at him for no reason that he could pick out. His desk, meanwhile, was crammed with school supplies, which he slowly removed in pursuit of a pencil.

"Actually," I said, "don't worry about it if you can't find one."

"No, I've got one."

Several teeth-clenching moments into Dale's search, I heard our teacher's voice.

"John," Mr. Dupreve said, "please return to your seat."

"Oh, okay, I'm just borrowing a pencil."

Half the class laughed.

Dale was sweating now as the books on top of his desk seemed to be more voluminous than the space from which they came.

I felt my neck muscles burning.

Dale stretched his arm to the back of his desk, felt around, and finally pulled out a perfect, newly sharpened pencil complete with bonus eraser nub.

He reached it over to me.

"Thanks, but what are you going to use?"

"Right," Dale said, pondering.

Those nearby giggled.

"Okay, John," returned the voice of Mr. Dupreve, "you've got your pencil now. Back to your seat, please."

"Um—" I tried.

"Let's go, please," Mr. Dupreve said.

"It's okay, thanks," I whispered, handing the pencil back to Dale.

He seemed to still be contemplating our situation, but then—smacked by a smile—he broke the newborn pencil in two. He examined the product for a moment before adding the bonus eraser nub to the sharpened half pencil and giving the result to me.

"John, I'm not going to tell you again."

"Thanks," I whispered, and I sped back to my desk.

"Good, thank you for joining us, John. Now, as promised, it's time for your quiz. You won't need your calculators for this; you'll only need a pencil and your brain."

I glanced back to see Dale locating a pencil sharpener in his desk. I was nervous on his behalf: the tests were being passed out while his work surface was still covered in books.

"There's nothing on this test that you haven't seen in your homework," Mr. Dupreve continued, "so, if you've been doing your homework, there's no reason you should have any trouble. John, no calculators."

"Oh, sorry."

As I put my technology away, I checked back on Dale again, which was not good news for my hand-eye coordination; that is to say, I knocked one of my own pencils out of my desk. It cruelly dropped to the floor and made an enormous pencil clattering. I stomped on it to shut it up, before sending panicked eyes back to Dale to see if he'd noticed the not-borrowed-from-him-pencil aspect of my noise. But he was still absorbed in the inspection of his pencil mitosis.

So, in short, the math test produced many painful moments, which required meditative analysis on my walk home from school. My thoughts were so locked into my grimaced reminiscing that I didn't hear the running steps of someone coming from behind me until they were within a metre. I swiveled to find Ashley.

"Hey, John."

"Oh, hi Ashley."

"How'd you do on your math test?" she said without expression on her voice or face.

"Um, okay, I think."

"Me too. So what was the deal with that pencil you borrowed from Dale?"

I explained to Ashley that I was attempting to create a diversion so that Dale wouldn't have to witness some harsh analysis of his personality.

She nodded when I finished. "Oh, okay, then ... you're a good guy, then."

"Thanks," I said "you too."

Ashley giggled just enough to make me realize my error.

"Sorry, I meant—"

"It's okay," she replied with a wave of her hand. "My ride's here—I've gotta go. See you," she said, returning at a sprint from whence she came.

Obviously, my walking-home introspections were now taken up by Ashley. I quickly realized that, somewhere during our interaction, Ashley had officially bumped Carrie to second place in my personal crush rankings.

When I arrived home, I was sent down to the basement to join a Jake and Per meeting already in progress. Jake was giggling when I entered the room. Strangely, my arrival did not decrease his festive presentation.

"Ahah, it's the guy *without the pencil*," he said.

Per laughed.

"*Um*," Jake said, furnishing an ugly impersonation of my voice and face, "*Carrie—I'm an idiot—can I borrow a pencil?*" Jake giggled again as he turned his sinister eyes directly upon me. "What, do you have a crush on her?"

"No. I was ...she was talking about Dale, and he was coming."

"So? What do you care?"

"She was saying mean things about Dale. I didn't want—"

"So ...what ...do ...*you* ...care?"

"You ruined Jake's plan," Per said.

"Well," Jake said, "don't you worry your pretty little head about that, Per's brother. You only got in the way at the end."

"What plan?" I said.

Per rolled his eyes. "Jake started the rumour about Carrie and Dale, you idiot."

"What for?"

Jake smirked. "Same reason you asked Carrie for a pencil—to entertain me."

"I didn't do that to entertain you."

"Could've fooled me."

Per laughed.

"Let me repeat," Jake said, "it's not your fault that you screwed everything up."

Now, I understood that Jake was intending sarcasm in that remark, but I could think of no way to disarm the snarky sentiment, so, instead, I pretended he was sincere.

"Thanks," I said.

And, of course, Jake and Per laughed.

Fortunately, Jake moved on from my stupidity more quickly than I was used to because he was distracted by a new plan he had in evil mind for a more developed rumour-mill production. Apparently, while Jake had indeed been entertained by Carrie's hostile reaction to the reports of her romance with Dale, he felt that he could produce better. This time, he was going to *massage* a rumour into the greater consciousness, utilizing subtler rumour-creating techniques that, in the long run, would produce sturdier gossip that would be harder to refute.

"Do what you want," Per said. "I want no part of it."

Jake rolled his eyes. "Is that all you care about? Protecting your rep so the girls'll like you?"

"Yup," my brother replied. "What the hell else is there to care about? Girls like me, so me happy."

At school a few days later, I was in a pondering mood during lunch hour; consequently, I was the last to finish my meal. When I finally left the then empty classroom, I spotted—in the adjacent cloakroom—a pair of papers spooning. All alliteration aside, they grabbed my curiosity as I leaned down to retrieve them. The top sheet was a beautifully aligned piece of social studies homework. The mixture of blue penmanship with red title underlining gave the document sophistication. The round but sharp printing added precision. And the 10/10 mark at the top gave it elite respectability. But most impressive of all was the name on the top right corner; it was Ashley Anonti's work.

There was a jolt in my stomach as my eyes absorbed her name.

My fingers tingled knowing they were holding a parcel of Ashley's estate.

With my heart maintaining its pounding pace, I pulled the second sheet of paper out from behind. The new page was drenched in little hearts and pictures of Cupid. My eyes sprinted around the paper and discovered the initials 'D.R.' within one of the hearts. *Who the hell was D.R.?*

Somebody was coming! I put the papers back together and swiftly walked to Ashley's desk and pushed the red-hearted evidence inside.

Pretty Jessica entered the room and looked at me. "Hi, John," she said with a *Why aren't you outside like normal people?* expression on her face.

"Hi," I said with a *Please don't tell Ashley I was near her desk* look on my mine.

"I just came to take my jacket off," Jessica said, squinting her eyes at me as she stepped out of view into the cloakroom and then resurfaced one layer less. "See you," she said with a continued *You're weird* look.

"See you," I copied with a *You're even prettier without your jacket on* expression.

With the intruder gone, I returned to the more significant matter. *Who was D.R.?*

I scanned the seating chart on Mr. Dupreve's desk... D.R. was ...*Dale Rostrovich! So now* Ashley *loved Dale?*

I stared at Ashley's desk. You'd think I would have noticed that the only things inside it that weren't perfectly in order were the two papers I had just deposited. I should have asked myself how it was that someone so organized would have dropped two incriminating papers out of her well-shut binder in the middle of the cloakroom.

More obviously, I should have noticed that the hand printing within the love paper did not quite match the rounded form in Ashley's homework. If only I had seen the heart-filled sheet first, I would have naturally assumed that Dale was being sucker punched again. But, since Ashley's authentic notes were on top, my mind had fixed itself on the notion that I was holding papers that were a part of her collection. Jake had brilliantly given me directions to my own false inference.

In the weeks following, Jake found many ways to trick individuals into thinking they'd made their own deductions. Soon I heard whisperings of an Ashley to Dale crush.

"I think it's because she's from a Third World country," Carrie suggested thoughtfully. "She's like used to guys being all malnourished and stuff, so Dale probably doesn't even look that bad to her."

The rumours soon got louder and the voices more confident. Any time Dale and Ashley were in the same area, giggles surrounded them. On one occasion, Mr. Dupreve naïvely put the unofficial couple together for a partner-based project.

"Whooo," the class sang.

Dale traded his facial colour in for red.

But Ashley just smiled at him.

And Dale smiled weakly back.

"Whooooo," the class sang louder.

Dale stayed red as he looked again at Ashley; she shrugged with another smile as though they were the first to board a great adventure. My pencil provider shrugged back and took his seat beside my crush.

That evening at the Smith house, Jake could no longer keep his guffaws hidden from my overhearing.

"Did you see the look on Dale's face?" he said to Per. "It was awesome."

Jake's smirk immediately told me what I should have realized earlier.

My brother smiled back at his friend. "Yeah, Dale's got no idea."

"No, no, no," Jake said, "he's heard the rumours *too*. He's just playing dumb."

Per chuckled. "And I bet he believes it too."

Jake laughed as well and returned to reminiscing about Dale's various awkward facial displays.

"So what are you gonna do to end it?" my brother said.

Jake shrugged. "Nothing. I'm just gonna sit back and let it play itself out. There's no way a chick as hot as Ashley'd go for Dale the Whale. And someone's gonna ask her about it sometime. I just pray to the comedy gods that I'm there to see it."

Now, considering how angry I was about the manipulation of both my pencil-providing classmate, Dale, and my new lead crush, Ashley, you'd think I would have yelled at Jake or got up and punched him in the nose or *something*! But I didn't have the courage to be rude and interrupt the assumed agreement in the room (that evil is fun).

After not much sleep on it, I decided that I had no idea how to terminate Jake's malevolent plot. My attempt to save the day the last time Ashley was involved had not measured up to her approval. If only she had told me in advance the save-the-day plan that she would accept, I would have done it without argument.

That thought eventually led me to realize that there *was* a way to get a heroic plan pre-authorized.

The next day at lunch hour, I kept an eye out for Ashley's availability. A few girls were talking to her, so I waited. (I wasn't about to interrupt her while she was socializing.) The girls eventually left, and Ashley picked up her book, so I waited some more. (I wasn't about to interrupt her while she was reading.)

At the lunch hour bell, I spotted my theoretical sweetheart standing up with a yawn; she was finally without the distraction of classmates or book, but there wasn't time now for her to give the necessary attention to our plan for me to save the day.

Oddly, for about a week, that basic pattern continued to get in the way of my discussion with Ashley. On a rainy morning, I finally decided that nothing would stop me. At recess, I took in a long and deep sigh and readied myself to follow Ashley wherever she went. But, with the playground soggy that day, Ashley and a few others decided to stay in our classroom during the break.

Felipe stepped onto his chair and sat on his desk. "So, *Ashley*," he said, with an ugly smirk, "what's with you and Dale? Are you totally like in love with him?"

My head swiveled furiously to take in Ashley's reply, but then I heard a scurry in the cloakroom. I swiveled again, and I spotted Jake's and Per's eyes peeking around the corner. They saw Ashley looking inquisitively at her interrogator.

"Um," she said, "that's between me and Dale."

"So that's like a *Yes*, right?" Jessica said.

Ashley rolled her eyes amidst a row of giggles. "You guys are so immature."

The cloakroom shuffled again.

Ashley turned to look.

Jake and Per were now looking into the hallway.

One beat.

And then Dale drudged into the room.

Ashley smiled at him.

Dale smiled with a skeptical lip quiver.

"There's your man," Felipe cheered.

Ashley kept her eyes on Dale, and she walked towards him. "Do you wanna go to the library and read?"

"Okay."

"Great," Ashley said.

But Dale stopped and looked at her. "You mean ...together?"

Ashley laughed. "Yeah, *together*. Let's go."

As they left, I could hear Dale apologizing for being confused. "But," he explained, "I thought maybe you just meant you wanted *me* to go."

Dale became annoyingly inaudible after that. I tried to turn up his volume, but, tragically, the alleged couple was out of range.

That evening, evil plot headquarters were in a somber mood.

"I can't believe she likes *Dale the Whale*," Jake said, glaring at his pizza.

At school the next week, I noticed that Ashley and Dale were sharing each other's company more often than chance. That garnered some ogling from passersby who, in turn, were greeted with an *Is there a problem?* look from Ashley. My sweetheart's lack of embarrassment seemed to force those who were judging her to reconsider their assumed superiority.

Meanwhile, returning to class early one lunch hour, I spotted on the floor another two-page edition of Ashley's social studies homework. I flipped immediately to the second page and found various epithets of rage against Dale, accusing him of betrayal.

In spite of my full-strength confidence that Jake had once again ghostwritten Ashley's alleged emotions, I couldn't let myself tear up the evidence on her behalf. Its attachment to Ashley's genuine social studies work made it her possession and so was hers to discard. Besides, maybe she would be glad to have a preview of what stories would be next told about her in the press, so I once again put the documents in her desk.

At the Smith house a few days later, Jake boasted to my brother that he'd decided to break up his couple. I wanted to question him about why he was contradicting his month-before promise to let the story grow without further interference, but, as ever, such a snarky question would have awkwardly trampled on the social niceties of our club.

In any case, as Jake had instructed, the gossip did start to wonder if Dale & Ashley were breaking up, but the gossip was not stupid: it noted that its favourite couple were hanging out just as much as ever. *Perhaps*—the gossip contemplated—*Dale & Ashley* had *broken up but had remained friends.* But that didn't seem right. In our Grade Seven world, the difference between a boyfriend/girlfriend relationship and a boy & girl friendship was not much more than some occasional handholding and maybe a few controlled kisses. *Would it really be worth the nuisance of breaking up for such a small reduction?*

Moreover, the gossip had assumed that the only logical explanation for Ashley's lack of panicked denial of the initial accusation that she was dating Dale was that it *had* to be true. *But why then was Ashley not now* rushing *to announce the alleged breakup? Was she so misled by growing up in an alternate culture that she really saw no reason to urgently redeem her name from Dale-affiliated shame?* If so, then it could now be retroactively seen that maybe the reason she hadn't denied her alleged love for Dale *originally* was simply because she actually saw no reason to be mortified by such speculation. In which case, the gossip further contemplated, it was perfectly plausible that Dale & Ashley had never really been a couple at all!

The gossip thereafter transformed into a sophisticated debate as people called into evidence their various encounters with Dale & Ashley:

"This one time, I saw them totally laughing, and Dale's not funny, so it's like, *why is she laughing?*"

"Yeah, but maybe she's just, like, being nice. I totally do that with my little brother—and it's not like I'm in love with my little brother."

"That's *gross*. Well, *I* heard someone found, like, Ashley's diary, and she's like, 'I love him so much. He's so handsome.'"

"Yeah, and I heard she had, like, 'I love Dale' notes all over her binder."

"Yeah, but you know what I've been thinking?—Remember when everyone thought *I* was in love with Dale?"

"Yeah, that was so disgusting."

"I know, but someone totally just made that up. So maybe somebody made *this* up too."

I almost piped in my support for that notion, but, luckily, I remembered that I was eavesdropping and so not entitled to comment.

Meanwhile, although I continued to fantasize about telling Jake that his greatest rumour was losing its power, I realized that it did not make sense for me to act on my dream: if I told him about the skepticism enveloping his fiction, he might have been inspired to do something about it.

ARTISTIC NOTE: Even though Jake had decided to break up Ashley & Dale, it seemed clear to me that he still wanted his classmates to believe that the failed relationship had happened. After all, as a rumour creation artist, he had worked hard to build the sculpture of Ashley & Dale. Just because it was no longer the piece he was working on, didn't mean he didn't want to keep it in his portfolio.

Many subsequent weeks then went by without any worried discussion at all from Jake on the breakdown of his rumour mill. Eventually, though, the skepticism became so pronounced in the public discussion that I was sure Jake had to know about it. Per confirmed my hypothesis one evening between bites of macaroni.

"Hey, Jake," he said, "are Ashley and Dale still going out?"

Jake rolled his eyes. "Don't you ever think about anyone else? I'm so bored of them now."

My brother laughed, and a bit of cheese flew onto his shirt.

Apparently, he and I were both embarrassed on Jake's behalf for his convenient boredom. I'd always wondered how people like Jake could be so unwaveringly confident, but now I could see that it was easy to focus on one's greatness when all other thoughts were *boring*.

Regardless, Jake was going to have to be bored for a while because, with no one officially opposing the Dale & Ashley romance skeptics, they began to have greater sway over public thought.

"If they want me to think they ever went out," one observer informed another, "they're going to have to prove it. I totally don't care anymore."

Before the end of Grade Seven, almost everyone was tired of all gossip and no confirmation, and so they moved onto other topics.

Chapter 7
Dullard vs. Regret

One Dance Step at a Time

Somewhere near the end of her elementary school career, my new top crush, Ashley, decided to become an active member of the school community, signing up for any organized club available to her. Those of her classmates who were already involved in such groups soon discovered that my dream girl was a good leader—not in that loud *Do what I say* way, more in the *I'll be logical in showing you that my way is better* sense.

The most powerful group that Ashley helped lead was the Grade Seven grad committee, who—against my nervous judgment—convinced the teachers to help us organize a dance finale to our elementary school careers. Of course, the teachers were persuaded every year to facilitate such a party, but my ghostwriter contends with his usual smugly smirk that they wanted us to think it was our idea.

"Now, don't be nervous, John," Mom said to me as Per and I finalized our outfits for the cruel event. "If you want to ask a girl to dance, you just need to be confident. Girls like confidence. That's a big reason why they like Per so much."

Unfortunately, I was not confident in my ability to be confident, and so—since my mother was insistent that confidence was related to success—I became less confident.

"Your mother's right, John," my dad said, "confidence is good … but also … you don't have to pretend to be someone you're not."

"But," I said, trying to be funny, "I think the girls would rather I *was* different from who I am."

Per obliged me with a chuckle, which reduced my nerves more than any wisdom could.

"*Maybe*," Dad interrupted, "but you don't need *all* the girls to like you, John. The girl who's interested in you will want you to be you."

"Gag," Per said, still chuckling.

Mom shook her head with a smile at Per. "No—your dad's right, John: you're not trying to impress everyone. But, if you're confident in who you are around the girl you *are* interested in, she's much more likely to be interested back."

"I guess," I said, letting out a grand sigh before looking at Per to see what he thought.

He shrugged. "Yeah, they're probably right, bro."

Now, there was—as was standard with Grade Seven dances of the early 90s—an unwritten initial segregation of the boys and the girls. Suddenly, these opposite-sexed people who, just a day before, may have been sharing conversation and homework answers, were potential dance partners. It was to be an exploration of strange new social interaction; whereas, previously, flirting could have been interpreted as boisterous friendliness, there was no hiding from the romantic implications of dancing together in front of all of one's peers.

SOCIO-TEMPORAL NOTE: In our particular time and place, there was an unwritten assumption that boys only coveted girls and vice versa.

As we boys leaned against our wall, trying not to look like we were scanning the pretty dress wearers on the opposite wall, I spotted the nicest dress owner of them all, Ashley Anonti.

She didn't look at all nervous. Made sense. *What would a perfect dream girl be worried about?*

I glanced around her for comparison's sake and discovered that some of the non-dream girls were also lacking any apparent anxiety. It seemed, for primary instance, that beautiful Carrie and Jessica were calm observers instead of participants in the event.

Anyway, back to Ashley. She looked our way with her brilliantly inquisitive eyes. Her stare was traveling along our wall, which is to say that her gaze was headed straight for me! I lengthened my posture—as if that would help—took in a deep breath and faked a smile. Just in time because she was now looking at me. And she smiled back!

For a mini-moment, I didn't question Ashley's intentions; instead, I increased the sincerity of my own smile (it might have even looked natural). In response, my crush half-raised her hand as if to wave, and then she continued on her visual tour of the boys.

The butterflies in my stomach were suddenly being overwhelmed by an oddly euphoric enemy. In fact, you may not believe this, skeptical reader, but I was actually considering breaking the gym-length barrier between the boys and the girls and going to hang out with Ashley.

Now, don't be too mad at me, soon-to-be-disappointed reader, for not actually following through with my consideration. It was a breakthrough for me just to contemplate the idea. And, if—like my ghostwriter—you don't believe me that I was sincere about it, I submit into evidence the fact that, while I was discussing the wild plan with myself, my heart was beating as fast as it knew how. That sort of high-speed internal anticipation could only have been the result of genuine consideration; otherwise, my insides—which were familiar with my passive nature—wouldn't have fallen for it.

But, before my speeding heart could prove its reason for beating, time was up. Per and Jake traveled across that squeaky floor and into Carrie and Jessica territory. Instantly, all four of them were smiling as if there were nothing to be nervous about. That result, of course, provoked me to realize that such a journey was out of my league. My ghostwriter says that that's proof that I was never really planning on making the trip at all, but I don't see *why*. Just because I happened to come to rationality after witnessing Per and Jake eclipsing me, doesn't mean I wasn't genuine in my previous thought of doing something crazy.

Big Andrei Vishnevski was the next to make the long trip over the gender divide. His recipient giggled at something he said; and, a minute later, before the dance floor knew what had stepped on it, two of my Grade Seven classmates were dancing *together* on its premises.

A few girls then jumped aboard and began practicing some complicated-looking moves. If they were trying to inspire male partners to join them, they were doing an intimidating job of it. Not to worry, I hadn't really come to the dance expecting to dance.

I looked back at Ashley. Oh my horror. She was talking to Jake!

Ashley seemed to be speaking to him with far more politeness than was deserved by the world's most evil human. She even smiled while she spoke to him. In response, Jake's head was bobbing in such a way that it was clear that he was trying his stupidest to be funny. But my Ashley just nodded at him; she did not laugh. *Well done, Ashley!* And now, if my long-distance sensors didn't deceive me, she was shaking her head at Jake. He again bobbed his head in reply. But then, clearly, there was another shake of the head from Ashley. Jake's head bob was now joined by some hand gestures. He was obviously trying to talk Ashley into something, but—like the dream girl she was—she turned him down! And then, thank ghostwriter, Jake walked away. I couldn't have been more charmed by Ashley if she had asked me to be her boyfriend.

Now, I don't want to get your hopes up again, fragile reader, so let me preface my next thought by noting that I didn't go through with it. That warning said, I can tell you that I was so inspired by Ashley's good taste in rejection that I again considered walking over to visit her. Tragically, when I was only ten minutes into motivating my moxie to undertake said invasion of privacy, Andrei Vishnevski—who had already had three more than his share of dance partners—approached my love and started his own head bob. This time, neither Ashley nor I could think of a reason to turn my rival down, and so off she went to the dance floor without me.

Andrei danced two full songs with my favourite before he left to steal someone else's beloved. By that time, Ashley's mood seemed to be intertwined with the music, and she remained with some other girls to practice their intricate steps. Meanwhile, Andrei ruined my plans to resent him: he found, along the wall opposite me, a girl named Desantra who, according to Jake's vicious database, was the second least appreciated girl in the class. But Andrei—the second most admired boy—was asking her to dance.

Within twenty minutes, a majority of my classmates were trying their best to step to the music. From my observing wall, I determined that it was mostly Andrei's doing—which made me wonder if the girls found him appealing because he was kind, *or was that merely a bonus gift that came along with his good looks?*

The answer, I quickly recognized, could be found back in Jake's database. The one boy who had scored higher than Andrei in the girls' assessments was my brother, which meant that Per's looks/elementary power had beaten Andrei's looks/kindness. Power, therefore, must have been more important to girls than kindness.

UNNECESSARILY SCIENTIFIC NOTE: My ghostwriter would like it pointed out that I seem to have forgotten that Jake's database of girl preferences was not the most scientific of studies, considering that it was based on the opinions of only three of my female classmates. But, in my defence, I would like us to remember that those three girls were some of the most socially respected students in our class.

Meanwhile, you might have thought that I would have been inspired by Andrei and tried to assist him in his goal to get the shyest of the girls dancing. But clearly that would have been a selfish act: after all, Andrei was having no trouble provoking the girls to dance; if I'd endeavoured to help, I would have replaced a great compliment to the girls' egos with a lowly one.

However, there was one girl whom Andrei hadn't gotten to yet, but she travelled to the dance floor anyway and stepped side to side by herself. I didn't recognize her. She must have been a friend or sister from another school. And she must not have realized who I was either because she smiled at me. It was a pretty smile: while I had never found braces to be attractive before, on that day, her mouth glittered sweetly.

I smiled back at her just to be polite, but—before I could clarify what I meant—she walked towards me. Thankfully, the fact that we would probably never see each other again took the sting out of my nervousness as I prepared myself for conversation.

"Hi," I said, without even stuttering.

"Hi," she said, pausing for awkwardness.

"Would you like to dance?" I said as if I hadn't dreaded asking the question all night.

"Okay."

Before I knew what song I was dancing to, my feet were shuffling from side to side. The girl with the braces smiled some more at me. I smiled back, and—noticing the movements of those across from me—I added a tiny arm swing to my repertoire. The arm that swung collided with the person dancing beside me.

"Oh, sorry—"

It was Ashley—dancing with Dale!

"Oh hi, John," she said as if there were nothing for me to be afraid of, "this is fun, isn't it?"

"Yeah ...*dancing*, you mean?"

"Yeah."

At that point, brace-face started to steer our dance away from Ashley.

Ashley smiled and nodded in the direction that I was supposed to go. "Have fun."

Well, how was I supposed to have fun with the metal-mouthed freak when she was trying to pull me away from Ashley?

But not all goodness was lost. If it hadn't been for that girl of metal face, I wouldn't have bumped into Ashley on the dance floor. In turn, I wouldn't have realized—by virtue of my love's casual tone of voice—that this dance didn't have to be a momentous last chance to get to know her. It was our final elementary school function, but there was no reason I couldn't still adore her in high school.

Chapter 8
Dullard vs. Sociopath II

A Study in Cool

The night before Per and I were to undergo our first official day of high school, our mother again tried to increase our confidence.

"Per, just be yourself. Kids've always liked you. High school won't be any different."

"What makes you so sure?" Per said, more, I suspected, for the fun of having our mother rush and gush to answer than from genuine nervousness.

"*What makes me so sure?*" Mom replied on cue. "Remember, Per, I once had a first day of high school *too*. And," she added with a laugh, "I was one of the kids that the other kids *didn't* like, so I would know if there was anything that they wouldn't like in you."

"Kids are kind of different now, Mom."

Our mom laughed again. "Yes, their clothes are different. Boys in my day used to wear their baseball caps facing forward, and *Ms. Pac-Man* was the arcade game of choice instead of *Super Mario Brothers*."

"Nobody plays *Mario Brothers* anymore, Mom," Per said, rolling his eyes in my direction.

I was honoured to be included in the comedy, so I faked a laugh even though I still occasionally enjoyed hanging out with Mario and Luigi.

"So that's my point," Mom said. "What's *cool* is always changing; that's what makes it cool—it's current. But the *types* of people who are cool: that doesn't change. The cool kids in my day were outgoing like you are."

"Sorry, John," my brother said.

"Be nice," Mom said, sending me a sympathetic smirk. "But, John, Per's right: you could show a little more personality. It's important to make an impression on the other students in high school. I know you've got lots going on in your mind, but your fellow students won't be able to see that if you're so quiet and shy all the time."

In reality, of course, there was no way I was going to be able to de-shy myself in the belligerent world of high school, but I appreciated my mother's comments, nonetheless; at least she hadn't lied to me and told me that *being myself* would get me liked.

Mini Skirts & Longitudinal Studies

Our high school brought the graduates of several small-town elementary schools together to create one mega school. That reunited evil Jake with a former scamming mate, Gaton Galleau, whom Jake had many semesters before renamed 'Gator.' The long-lost classmate lived up to Jake's nickname prophecy and had grown into a chiseled chunk of adolescent swagger. That was good news for Jake who had forgotten to have his own growth spurt; Gator's extra cells gave Jake's antics security. You see, curious reader, high school status at that time and place demanded more acquiescence to cool doctrine than Jake was willing to give. To qualify for the cool leadership in the early stages of our high school, one needed to offer oneself fully to the rules of dress code, attitude, and music taste. Jake was far too creative and didn't care enough about his reputation to be fully cool. Yet, with Gator and Per at his side, he was respected.

My sibling association with Per helped me as well: for the most part, the bullies left me alone. Of course, I was a *nerd* who had no life, but it was generally agreed that I would be allowed to live my lack of a life without being picked on for it.

Meanwhile, Gator was well-liked for his intimidating build and sense of humour; he had a good sense, that is, for when it would be most fun to laugh at people. If you were the one mocking someone, Gator would make you feel *pretty good* about yourself with his rapid-fire chuckles. Indeed, I believe that Gator's voluminous laughter was the primary basis for his friendship with Jake who clearly enjoyed receiving Gator's ready amusement as much as Gator appreciated feeling it.

The thrill of Gator, though, also came from the fact that he was loyal only to his own entertainment. Jake surely knew that, if he ever ceased being the funniest guy around, there would be no incentive for Gator to stay his friend. But, so long as Jake continued to entertain with both humour and scheme, Gator seemed to be convinced that riding Jake's creative genius was his best chance at making the most of his high school years.

Similarly, I believe my brother saw Jake as a visionary who would take him to the top of popularity once *cool* started to be more discriminating. By Grade Nine, however, Per must have realized that plan Jake—while not detrimental to his official image—wasn't yet producing the popularity gains he'd anticipated. Nevertheless, having invested so much in Jake already, he didn't give up on him yet. That meant my brother was forced to lead a double cool life whereby he split his hangout time between (A) unique and entertaining conversation with Jake & Gator and (B) more tedious fraternizing with the respected cool yet dull leaders.

In that Grade Nine year, Jake tried to start a movement to inspire the girls to wear shorter skirts. Whenever the teachers weren't looking, he taped on school walls magazine pictures that did a nice and short job of illustrating his point. Each day, thereafter, he checked the length of the first five skirt-wearing girls he came across to see if he'd made a subliminal impression.

After two weeks, Jake hadn't noticed a statistically significant skirt shortening, and so, during their usual after-school meeting, he discussed with Per and Gator the option to recruit some of their male peers to subtly suggest to the girls that short skirts were the ideal form of female dress.

"Why are you doing this?" my brother inquired. "It's so retarded."

"What, are you gay?" Jake said, chuckling.

"No."

"Then what's wrong with having a little something nice to look at between classes?"

"Well, I think a chick in tight jeans is just as hot as one in a short skirt."

Gator laughed cheerfully as he watched the debate, perhaps hoping it would turn violent.

"Fair point," Jake said. "But I'm just trying to shorten the skirts that are already out there. We can do the tighter pants campaign next time."

"You're such an idiot," my brother said, raising his volume over Gator's continued chuckling. "You're going to make all the girls hate us. I wanna go out with them, not tell them what to wear."

"Good one," Gator said, turning his grin on Jake. "Who's gay *now*, Mr. Fashion Designer?"

Jake seemed to ponder that seriously. "Why not do both? I'm not trying to *design* their outfits. I just want to see them picking out clothes that'll give their fine bodies a chance to show themselves off."

"He makes a good point," Gator said.

Per sighed. "Right now, girls like me. I'm not gonna screw that up."

"Well, the girl *I* like hates me," Jake said.

I smiled at the unnamed girl's good taste.

Per shrugged. "It's your own fault Ashley hates you."

Oh my ghostwriter. *What was Jake doing having a crush on Ashley?* Indeed, I was so mortified to learn that I had the same taste in girl as Jake that, for a moment, I second-guessed Ashley, *herself*. But I quickly realized that Jake could not possibly like Ashley because he liked her; surely, instead, he liked her because she disliked him, and so he wanted to conquer her rightful opinion of him.

"What's your point?" Jake said. "Just once, I wanna see her in a miniskirt."

"Fine," Per said. "You go piss her off again. Don't make me piss off the girls *I* wanna go out with."

Sadly for Jake, he quickly determined that most guys were as boring as my brother and so would likely be unwilling to risk the company of girls just for the small chance of shortening their skirts. As a result, Operation Minier-Skirt was cancelled.

Chapter 9
Dullard vs. Brother II

Caught Between a Snitch and a Cheater

Two months later, my parents received a call from our nosy principal, claiming that Per was becoming a disruptive influence at school. My brother's mother was not fooled by the busy-body administrator's attempts to repress her son and his friends, and so she continued to encourage Per to be himself.

Coincidentally, right around that time, Per began dropping certain social niceties from his personality catalog. 'Please' was deemed an unnecessary member of his vocabulary, and all expressions of gratitude were either similarly exiled or used only ironically. And sarcasm, itself, changed from playful and teasing to biting and humourless.

But, even more significantly from my perspective, Per came to the epiphany that his contribution to keeping the Smith household compulsively clean and orderly was no longer to his taste. That troubled me as I was concerned that his lack of cleanliness might disappoint and hurt his adoring mother's feelings. Our mom, by then, had invested so much time boasting to her friends about Per's tidiness and its proof of his status as a perfect young gentleman that it seemed to me that she would be wounded if she found out that she was no longer justified in such claims.

For my own sake, too, I dreaded my mother's discovery. I had watched Per in his pedestal perch for so long that the thought of him being removed from it saddened me. So I came to a simple unspoken arrangement with Per: as long as he agreed to create clutter, I consented to clean it up for him before his mother-directed parents could discover the evidence.

The arrangement worked well for both Per and me. There was rarely a time that Per was home, but I was not, so I was able to monitor and remove his mess before it officially became mess. School days were trickier because Per always created his first helping of clutter just before we left for the day, and so there was generally no time for me to exterminate it before we set out. Consequently, I created a policy to always get home before the rest of my family so that I could have some time alone with Per's mess before anyone else could witness it.

One day during that symbiotic pattern, I waved *Good bye* to a healthy mess and travelled to school with an impending French midterm heckling my mind. A few uninteresting hours of school later, the test was on, and I sat aggressively over my desk, retrieving the various vocabulary words that I had implanted in my memory in the weeks prior. Next to me sat a small-time bully by the name of Gilbert Burghardt, who had very few French words in his memory. Clearly, I had an unfair advantage, so Gil tried to remedy the situation.

"Pssst," he whispered, "what's 'poisson' mean?"

I knew the answer, but I didn't want to be an accessory to cheating, so I shrugged to indicate that I wasn't going to say.

"What's poisson mean?" Gil said again, with stronger emphasis.

"I don't want to cheat," I whispered back.

"Don't be a chickenshit!" Gil replied, staring at me.

I'd been in high school long enough not to be troubled by such a basic insult, but Gil's unwillingness to let me return to my own task left me aggravated and thus unusually defiant.

"Better than being a cheater," I shot back without thinking.

That was a mistake. Neither Gil nor the French teacher, Madame McNeil, seemed to enjoy my analysis.

"Monsieur Burghardt and Monsieur Smith, bring your tests to me."

Monsieur Burghardt glared at Monsieur Smith as we walked the long walk through staring eyes to Madame McNeil's desk.

"There's no talking during the test," she said when we arrived.

"We weren't cheating," Gil said, full scowl. "I just wanted to borrow an eraser."

"Is that true?" Madame McNeil said, directing her interrogation towards me.

"Um—"

Madame McNeil interrupted me just then to raise her voice in the direction of the rubbernecking classmates that surrounded us.

"Mesdames et messieurs: get back to your work, s'il vous plait."

All of the observers pretended to return their focuses to their papers.

"John," the teacher then repeated slowly as if I had not understood the question, "was Gilbert asking you for an eraser?"

"Not ... *really*," I said, my dull instincts leading me to truth.

DEFENSIVE NOTE: Before you judge my unnecessarily honest answer, rebellious reader, please keep in mind that, as a growing dullard, I had little understanding or experience with the notion of lying being a viable form of communication. As such, my attempt to deflect the question was actually my most heroic attempt to avoid *snitching* on my classmate. Unfortunately, Gil was as quick to overlook my generosity as you were, sanctimonious reader.

In that moment, I could feel Gil's eyes invading the side of my head.

"Thank you, Monsieur Smith, was he asking you for an answer from the test?"

"Um ..." I said, feeling my breath hesitating in my chest, "I think I'd rather not say."

Madame McNeil sighed. She had given me a choice between (A) alienating her by not tattling and (B) alienating Gil by not lying. But I had chosen to alienate *both* teacher and student by neither tattling nor lying. 'I'd rather not say' amounted to saying, 'Yes, he's a cheater, but you won't find it out from me.' So I was in trouble with both Gil and Madame McNeil.

The teacher offered her punishment first. "Gil, go finish your test at the table. John, finish yours at your desk. And I'll see both of you here at 3:15 for detention."

I had never been detained after school before, and so I spent the rest of the test wondering about what lay in wait for me. After class, though, I realized that my worried focus should have been on Gil who aimed himself in my direction on our way out. I saw him coming, but I had no idea what to do with him when he got to me, so I just pointed my eyes ahead and pretended I was in a rush. Just when I thought I was free, I felt a hearty shoulder collide with mine.

"You'd better watch yourself," Gil said. "Your teacher's not always gonna be around to protect you."

I stared back at him but could think of no reply.

Gil rolled his eyes and continued on his way.

I stayed where I was and watched him leave. My heart was beating so fast that I wanted to sit down. But I ignored the craving and just stared ahead.

A minute later, my autopilot had me walking to my next class; my mind was on spin cycle as I considered how a fight with Gil might go. He was bigger than I was, but perhaps I had more sparring experience. Yet Per's and my boxing practice offered gloved padding and the comforting bureaucracy of our dad's refereeing; I had no experience in the wilds of an unregulated fist fight.

One of our PE teachers, Mr. Boyko, had once told us that, if we were ever forced into a street fight, we should do everything we could to stay on our feet. He claimed there was safety there. But, if Gil got a full swing past my block and through to my face, I could become dizzy and thus less able to block another punch which, in turn, would leave me in danger of going down.

I wasn't afraid of the pain caused by such a collision, but I was weary of the damage that Gil could cause if I was on the floor and unable to shield myself. The humiliation of receiving such a beating from a classmate would surely adhere to me for the rest of my school career. That was my most insistent fear.

After my final class for the day, I put my books into my locker in preparation for detention. I wondered if there was any way I could talk Gil out of a fight. The school was already nearly empty, and so there would be few people to intervene when detention was over if that was when Gil decided to make me watch myself. Perhaps, if I could find a way to delay my departure from detention, Gil would get bored of waiting for me. I smirked morbidly at my naïvety on that point.

"What are you smiling at?" a voice arrived in the previously barren space behind me.

"Oh," I said, turning to look into the glaring face of Gil, "I guess I was just laughing at this whole thing. I didn't mean to get you in trouble—I just get nervous when Madame McNeil asks me questions. Sorry about that."

"Sorry about *what?*" Gil said, stepping into my space.

I instinctively lifted my hands to protect my face; before they were fully up, Gil shoved me against my locker.

"What's your problem?" I said, pivoting way from the metal wall.

"*You're* my problem!" he replied.

I'd walked into that one.

Gil pushed me again.

"Back off," I said, my heart now at full pump.

"You back off," Gil said, grabbing for my shirt.

I pulled away.

He pushed me in the direction I was pulling, and my momentum made me stumble backwards.

"Back off," I said again.

"Sure, I'll back off," Gil said. Then, inconsistent with his promise, he grabbed for my shirt again.

Strangely, that last case of sarcasm set me off, and I launched forward with the full weight of my anger. I tackled Gil in the middle of his grab; this time, he stumbled backwards, so I twisted my torso and drove him to the floor. If there had been anyone around, they would have heard a giant thud as we smacked the ground.

I wasn't sure what to do now that I had Gil underneath me. I was hoping Gil would take the lead and start us fighting again, but he just lay there without moving. I pulled myself up and looked down at Gil. He was gasping for air—yikes, I'd winded him. I looked around, wondering if I should get help.

For a few lengthy seconds, I felt a flurry of worry in my chest while Gil tried to suck in oxygen. Finally he found it and started to pull himself up. That didn't sound like a good idea for either of us, so I shoved him back towards the floor. He didn't put up much resistance; instead, he let himself roll back onto his hindquarters.

Mr. Boyko, the PE teacher, walked by the confrontation just then. "What's going on, guys?"

I looked over at Gil to explain our situation.

My fallen foe slowly returned himself to his feet. "Nothing," he said in a subdued voice that I'd never heard from him before.

Mr. Boyko looked at me. "What's..." he paused, apparently trying to remember my name. Without any luck, he returned to the question. "What's going on?"

"I don't know."

"You don't *know*? Do you usually shove people like that and not know why?"

"No. But I didn't plan to do it."

"Well, maybe then you can come to the gym and help me clean up the equipment room. Maybe then you'll learn to think before you act."

"But, um, I have detention right now."

"Detention as well as this?" the teacher said. "You're not doing too well today, are you?"

I shook my head in agreement.

Mr. Boyko sighed. "Gil, you may go."

Gil nodded with a grumpy mouth and walked away to meet Madame McNeil.

Mr. Boyko watched my victim leave and then he turned his focus on me. His stare transformed to a smirk.

"So what happened? Did he take a swing at you?"

"Um," I said, wary of a trick question, "well, he shoved me against my locker."

"I figured as much. What set him off?"

I sheepishly described the originating incident from French class.

Mr. Boyko shook his head. "What a little bastard. Sorry I didn't back you up there, but I only saw you shoving him to the ground, so—if I took you to the principal—the little punk would just lie, and it would be his word and my damning testimony against yours."

"That's okay," I said, "thanks for...trying."

"Yeah, of course—so, if he wants to fight again, you can tell him that I told you that, if you got caught fighting again, I'd get you both suspended. He might consider that a good enough excuse not to fight."

"Okay. Thanks."

"Unless he forces the issue," Mr. Boyko said. "If you have to fight, one punch to the stomach, and he'll go down—don't hurt him too much, though. I don't want you to really get in trouble."

"Okay," I said, honoured by the unexpected turn of advice.

"So what's your detention for?" the teacher said.

"Oh," I said, "for talking during the test—when he asked me for the answer."

"So you got detention because he was trying to cheat—the little bastard. Next time he asks you for an answer, give him an answer all right, but give him the wrong one."

I laughed. "Good idea."

"All right," my new favourite teacher said, "you better get to that detention or you're going to be in more trouble."

After my altercation with Gil, detention didn't seem so scary anymore.

"Monsieur Smith," Madame McNeil said when I arrived, "you're late."

"Sorry," I said, "Mr. Boyko wanted to talk me."

"That may be," the teacher replied, "but you had a previous engagement, so I'm afraid you'll have to stay an extra half an hour to make up for it."

Once my sentence was set, Madame McNeil recommended Gil and I work on our homework but said we could do whatever we wanted so long as we sat silently while she marked the French tests. I was too alert for homework, so I chose doodling.

Gil, meanwhile, stared at the ground and did not look at me. At first, I thought that he was giving me some sort of bully silent treatment, which meant that I was really going to get it. But, as I pondered with doodling hand how I might use Mr. Boyko's advice in response, I accidentally dropped my pencil; it cruelly bounced its way under Gil's desk. He stared down at it, but then—instead of kicking it farther away from me as was his right—he sent it back to me. It was a peculiar moment which led me to the wild but irrefutable conclusion that Gil had become scared of me.

When I'd tackled him, he must have determined that I was tougher than he was. Whether or not I was actually the stronger combatant, Gil clearly thought we had discovered my physical superiority. And so it seemed that I had inadvertently challenged my classmate's leading principle of existence that the socially inept (like John Smith) are always weaker than the bullying elite (like Gil Burghardt). *How was he to deal with the notion of a dork who seemed tougher than he was?* It was a paradox that Gil would have to deal with for the rest of his life.

But Gil had affected my life even more profoundly. While I sat detained in Madame McNeil's classroom, my parents were nearing the end of their workdays. And, after Gil was set free, and I stayed for my detention extension, my parents were on their ways home.

Half an hour later, as I walked the long trek home, I suddenly realized that my parents were likely to get there before me—before I had a chance to clean up my brother's morning mess. I switched my walk to a run, but I quickly noticed that I was tired from all the adrenalin infusions earlier, and so I decided that I was too late: there was no way I could be home in time to save Per. My brother's reputation for cleanliness—for being the perfect son—was doomed.

The Pedastall

I arrived home to find, as anticipated, my parents' cars already in the driveway. As I passed through the kitchen entrance, I noted an eerie living room murmur coming from my father. Admittedly, Dad often talked with a murmur, but, on that day, I was pretty sure it was eerie. As I surveyed the kitchen, I discovered that Per's morning mess was already gone.

"Hi, John," my mom said as I landed in the living room.

"Hi, Mom."

"Hello, Son," my dad weighed in.

"Hi, Dad," I said, keeping a peripheral eye on my mother.

"You're later than usual today. How come?"

I gave my parents as much detail of my lateness provocation as my nerves would allow (which is to say that I left out the violent incident).

"I think you did well," Dad said. "That was a tough spot, John, but he can't expect you to lie for him."

"Paul, don't encourage him," Mom replied. "John, you're not gonna make any friends that way. That teacher obviously has no idea what it's like to be a teenager. You should've just told her Gil wanted to borrow the eraser."

"But, Mary, John doesn't owe this Gil anything."

"Paul, John has no friends. Goody Two-Shoes don't make friends in high school. I know you don't like it, but that's the way it works."

"Well," Dad said, "I'd say there are better ways to make friends than helping someone cheat on a test."

Mom sighed and turned to me. "John, it's a good thing that you didn't actually tattle on Gil. That's a good start. Now you can build on that. Why don't you watch Per at school? Try to follow his lead. There's a reason everybody likes him."

If you were new to this book, you might have thought that my mother's request for me to be more like my brother would have hurt my feelings, but, of course, I was long used to losing in such comparisons. Instead, my concern was focused on that fact that— on that messiest of days—my mom still wanted me to be more like my brother. It was as if Per's morning clutter had not existed at all.

Indeed, a few minutes later, Per arrived home to a cheerful greeting from his mother.

"Hi, Per," she said, full grin.

"Hey."

"What've you been up to?"

"I just won another bet with Gator," Per said, smiling as he slumped into a chair; indeed, my brother seemed to be in a better mood than his recent standard.

"What was the bet?" Dad said.

Per giggled. "It was Jake's idea. We wanted to see who could get kicked out of Dempsey's first."

"What for?"

"We had to get kicked out without actually doing anything wrong. Jake was like, we could do whatever we wanted to make it look like we were shoplifting or whatever, but we weren't allowed to actually do it."

"But you wouldn't want to shoplift anyway."

"Obviously."

"So how'd you win?" Mom said with her intrigued voice.

Per laughed. "It was perfect! I'm like really close to the stuff in the candy aisle, and I look really guilty, and I pretend like I'm putting stuff in my pocket." Per laughed again.

"You really did that?" Mom said, smiling.

"I *did*," Per said, shrugging his shoulders. "Jake challenged us, so I had to come up with something ... So Dempsey's guy comes up to me with his tough Dempsey's-guy face, and he goes, 'Empty your pockets!' And I went, 'No! You can't make me show you what's in my pockets.' But then he's all, 'I'm gonna call the police,' so I pull out my pockets and show him they're empty. It was perfect. I totally started telling him off for falsely accusing me, and I finally got kicked out for disturbing the other customers—which isn't illegal, by the way, Dad. And I was out before Gator even knew what he wanted to do."

"Peter," Dad said, with a closed-eye sigh, "don't you think the clerks at Dempsey's have more important things to do than dealing with you and your friends' immature little games?"

Mom shook her head with a smile. "Paul, I understand you're concerned about Dempsey's guy, but I think you need to lighten up. I'm sure the Dempsey's guy forgot about Per and Gator the moment they left the store."

Per giggled.

His mother smiled at him. "So what'd Gator do to get kicked out?"

"Oh, right, so Gato' grabs a magazine, and he starts turning it sideways. He figures Dempsey's guy'll think he's looking at a skin mag' or something. But it didn't work. Nobody at Dempsey's cared. Me and Jake waited for like five minutes before Jake finally tells Gator that time's up."

As my mom laughed at that one, it was an odd time for my thoughts. I stared at my mother's grin for any sign of weakness, but there was none—not a single hint in her eye that she'd discovered something chaotic and awful when she'd returned home that afternoon. *How could that be? How could a person be so proud of a behaviour one day and then so content with its opposite on another?*

My above speculation delayed my sleep until late that night, and I decided that the next day I would not clean up Per's mess when I arrived home from school. Instead, I intended to sit and wait for my mother: I was going to witness for myself her true reaction to her son's disorder.

As planned, when I returned home the next day, I sat in the kitchen with my homework, and I ignored a Per-created mess that was calling me to clean it up. I was too nervous to work on schoolwork, but I put it on the kitchen table to explain why I was there. When my mother opened the door, she greeted me, and then—without announcing any emotion on her face—she walked towards Per's mayhem. I instantly became re-worried about her reaction to it. *Sure, Per had been excused for one horrific mess, but two days of inconsideration in a row?*

"Oh," I said, "um, yeah, Per was in a hurry this morning, and he didn't have time to clean up."

Mom smiled at me.

What was she smiling for?

"I know," she said as she took a cloth to the counter, "your brother is getting to be a pretty busy guy."

And then my mother smiled at me again!

Half an hour later, my father landed in the same location; after a brief visit with me, he moved to the living room to sit with my mother.

"Per left a mess again," my mom told my dad.

"Again?"

"Yes, Paul, and I think we have to be aware that, as Per gets busier and busier with his friends, he's going to have less time to be cleaning up after himself."

"But it shouldn't take him long."

"Paul, he's a teenage boy. Cleaning up is not going to be one of his priorities anymore."

"What about John? He's a teenager as well, you know."

"*John* ..." Mom replied, her voice suddenly removing to a whisper (which greatly hampered my listening experience). "John is WHISPER. He WHISPER WHISPER WHISPER friends. WHISPER WHISPER WHISPER WHISPER girls WHISPER WHISPER. WHISPER WHISPER WHISPER WHISPER WHISPER WHISPER WHISPER WHISPER WHISPER social life

WHISPER. But Per *WHISPER.*" And there my mother's voice returned to proper eavesdroppable volume. "We are going to have to be very supportive of Per right now. I want him to know that it's more important to us that he makes friends than that he cleans up after himself."

Baffle me. I had been protecting my brother's pedestal from a nonexistent enemy. As much as my mother had enjoyed Per's youthful cleanliness, she now, it seemed, vowed to enjoy his messiness even more because it was a symptom of his popularity.

After that epiphany, I stopped obsessing about cleaning up after my brother. I still did the job, of course—since I was always the first one home—but I was no longer trying to protect Per's reputation. Instead, I was just protecting the house from clutter.

Chapter 10
Dullard vs. Sociopath III

The Phantom Flirtation

By Grade Ten, my status as Per's brother was beginning to lose its currency in our high school community, and so my schoolmates started to treat me more like the dork I was. Per, meanwhile, continued to tease me in front of his friends for personal failings, such as my posture and fashion sense. But Per was also possessive of that mocking, and so he would sometimes discipline those who tried to join in on his fun.

"Shut up—he's my brother," was a common phrase that he uttered only moments after he had pointed out the flaw that was being celebrated.

Meanwhile, Jake decided that year to experiment with a reputation-protection club that he patterned after his favourite mafia movies.

"Hey," he'd say to an attractive and popular girl who had wandered away from her flock, "how's it going?"

"I'm okay," she'd reply skeptically.

By that time, Jake was clearly disliked by most of his female classmates, but his association with Per—who had steadily increased his popularity—and Gator—whose good looks camouflaged his cold-blooded personality—protected Jake from official contempt.

"So I hear you played naked twister with Geoff Green," Jake would say with a smile at his target.

"Ah, *no*—who the hell told you that?"

"Who cares who told me? The bigger question for you should be: *Is he going to tell anyone else?*"

"Ah, I'm not too worried about it. I think everyone knows I wouldn't give it up to Geoff Green if he was the last guy on earth."

"I believe you, but are you sure everyone else will?"

"As if anyone's going to believe that me and him—"

"You're probably right, but, just in case people *might* believe him, I can protect you if you like?"

"Um, how exactly are you gonna protect me from Geoff spreading his fantasies all around the school?"

"Well, I know the guy, so—if you like—I could talk to him and make sure he doesn't tell anyone else?"

"Oh, okay, that would be awesome, actually, thanks."

"I was hoping you'd say that because, in exchange for this small favour, I'd just like one small token of your appreciation."

"What's that?"

"You and me: two minutes in the custodian's closet."

"You're such a pervert," was the most common response.

Upon laughing at Jake's failure, Gator decided to try the protection plan for himself. To his further chuckles, the girls reacted much more positively to his offerings than they had his undersized mentor's. While no actual time was spent in a custodian's closet, Gator got several dates out of Jake's protection plan.

The distinction intrigued Jake, and so he decided to research Gator's success.

"So here's the plan," Jake announced to Per one afternoon in the Smith basement. "You and Gator are gonna ask out five girls *each*, like you're asking them out for yourself, but, really, you're asking them out for *me*. Then—"

"What for?" Per interrupted. "That's stupid."

"I want to see how they try to squirm out of it when they realize it's *me* they have to go for ice cream with and not you or Gator."

"Awesome," Gator said, chuckling.

"It's stupid," my brother said, "I'm not gonna piss off five hot girls just for one of your stupid experiments."

"So pick five girls you *wouldn't* want to go out with—I don't care."

"But *still*..." my brother said, his forehead tilting into introspection.

Gator nodded rapidly. "Yeah, yeah, and you know what'd be funny? How about Peter's actually asking them out for his brother. I'd love to see their reactions when they get stuck with John."

"*Interesting*," Jake said, nodding as though he were a college professor encountering an original perspective from a student, "*that's not bad, actually.*"

Quite rightly, my pulse quickened at the evil suggestion.

"Um," I said, "no thanks."

"Shh," Jake said, "the adults are talking."

"Yeah, no," my brother said, "girls talk. I'm not risking that."

Gator laughed. "You're such a chickenshit. I'll do it no problem."

"Good for you, Gator," my brother said, rolling his eyes. "I'm so proud of you."

Gator forced a laugh.

"All right, then, Jake," Per said, "who are the five girls you and Gato are going to mess with?"

"I'm thinking Erin McDonald, Fatema Karimi—for a cultural comparison—Jennifer Chen—for the Asian vote—Susan Luoko-wicz—for the Goth perspective—and, of course, our very own Ashley Anonti."

"*Ashley?*" I said without consulting me first.

"Yup."

"Leave her alone"

"Why?"

"Because...she's nice."

"They're *all* nice. Why her specifically? What, you got the hots for her?"

"No, she's just the only one on the list that I know well." My heart was beating at me to stop, but it was too late now. "If you wanna ask girls out, do it yourself. Don't play games with them."

Per laughed. "I'm gonna have to agree with my never-had-a-girlfriend brother on this one, Jake. You're the one being a chickenshit."

"Nope, he's just jealous," Jake said, sending an evil smirk in my direction. "Gator can ask girls out for you too if you want, Per's brother?"

"No thanks."

"What, are you gay?"

"Shut up, Jake," my brother said. But then a smile scooted across his face. "He's just saving himself for marriage."

Gator laughed with the full weight of his chest.

By the time Mom brought down our pizzas, Gator and Jake were determining how Gator would approach the targets in such a way that they would think he was asking them out on his own behalf instead of Jake's.

"So I know this guy ..." Gator said, practicing his lines on Jake. "A lot of people think he's confident, but he's actually not as confident as he looks."

"Good," Jake said, nodding, "now pause for effect, so she'll think you're talking about you."

Gator grinned as he complied. "So this guy acts all confident, but he's totally just faking it. He can fake it really great around most girls, but he can't fake it around the one girl he's really interested in."

"Good. Now smile and look into her eyes and wait for them to melt."

Gator laughed.

Jake shook his forehead. "Don't laugh when you're doing it, or it won't work."

"I agree," my brother said. "It'll give it away."

Gator raised his eyebrows. "I've scammed enough girls to know not to laugh."

"Good," Jake said, "okay, so ask her out. *You were hoping—*"

"So, Miss Hottie, I was hoping—"

"Don't say, 'Miss Hottie.'"

"*Obviously,*" Gator said with a full volume laugh. "So, sweet thing, do you want to go on a date with this guy?"

"*Okay,*" Jake said, giggling on the girl's behalf. "Yeah, I'll go out with him."

Gator laughed. "Cool, his name's Jake. I'll give you his phone number."

"What? I'm not going out with *him!*" Per replied with an exaggerated bimbo voice.

Gator laughed again.

I couldn't eat my pizza: my stomach was already filled up with those pesky butterflies. How the psychopath could I thwart Jake's evil plan? Well, I suppose I did have the list of victims. *Who were they again?* Ashley, Fatema, Jennifer, Susan and, damn, I couldn't remember the fifth person—I'd have to remember her later. *But what could I do with the names anyway?* There were no authorities to inform—except maybe the girls, themselves. But talking to girls wasn't my forté.

On the way to my first class Monday morning, I spotted Erin, the forgotten fifth victim. I followed her, hoping the parallel crowd would dissolve so we could talk privately. She led me to my math class and went in. *Oh, right, we had a shared class scheduled for that time.* I took the seat behind her.

"Um, Erin ..."

"Oh, hey, John, how are you?"

"I'm okay. I have to tell you something."

"Oh, okay, what's up?"

A pair of loud peers passed by our conversation; I didn't want Erin to be embarrassed by my news, so I muted.

"So what's up?" she interrupted.

"Just a sec. There's more people coming in."

More people kept coming in until finally the math teacher, Mrs. Neilsen, arrived and rudely moved immediately into lecture mode.

"I'll write you a note," I whispered (courageously, I thought).

"Okay," Erin said cheerfully.

SOCIO-TEMPORAL NOTE: By 'writ[ing] a note,' I don't mean, digital reader, that I was planning to gather my fingers on a mini-keyboard to tap out a text message to my classmate. Instead, since cell phones weren't yet living in most palms, my intention was to follow the pre-texting lead of my female classmates and use my pre-texing fingers to manually write my declaration on a lined piece of paper.

As I wrote my note, I felt that Mrs. Neilsen was watching me more than usual. But her surveillance would not daunt me from my task. 'Dear Erin,' I wrote, 'I'm sorry to bother you, but I have to tell you something bad.' *No, no, 'bad' wasn't quite right.*

"John, can you tell us the answer to number five?"

"Um, yeah." I could only hope that she was referring to number five from the homework. I pulled it out. "Um, it's, ah, X plus 1."

"How'd you get that?"

"Sorry, X *minus* 1."

"Good. You know, John, it's easier to follow along when you're on the right page."

The class laughed.

I nodded and forced a smile. For the next few minutes, I stared blankly at what Mrs. Neilsen was saying. Eventually, I decided it was as safe as it was going to get for me to return to my task.

'Dear Erin, I'm sorry to bother you, but I have to tell you something important. Gator and Jake are doing something stupid. And I feel really bad about it.' No, she wouldn't care how *I* felt about it. 'Dear Erin, I'm sorry to bother you—'

"John, maybe you can come up to the blackboard and show us how to do this one."

"Oh, okay."

As I walked, I looked squeamishly at the formula on the board. It seemed nothing like the homework and a lot like what I hadn't been paying attention to. There was only one thing to do: I tried to solve the problem using the homework method.

The teacher raised an eyebrow at my efforts. "John, you have to factor it first."

"Oh, um, how do I do that again?"

"By paying attention when I'm teaching it."

The class laughed again.

"Back to your seat…" Mrs. Neilsen whispered to me, "and try to pay attention."

I nodded and returned to my chair.

'Dear Erin, I'm sorry to bother you, but I have to tell you something important. Gator and Jake are going to do something really stupid. And I wanted to warn you. Gator's going to pretend to ask you out for himself, but really he'll mean Jake. Jake is doing an experiment to see how you'll react when you find out it's him and not Gator. Please act accordingly.' *Whew, good enough.* I folded the note into a two-inch square (just as I'd witnessed my female classmates doing many times), and I tapped Erin's shoulder.

Erin sent back a cupped hand, utilizing a stealth that made me suspect that she was an experienced note receiver.

Unfortunately, Mrs. Neilsen was an even more practiced note interceptor, and she was now standing over Erin. Without taking her voice off the lecture, she held her hand out.

Those who noticed laughed.

Erin grimaced back at me.

I shrugged to indicate that I realized she had no choice.

She dropped the note into the hand of the enemy.

Oh well, at least now Erin knew that I really wanted to talk to her, so it wouldn't be too awkward to commandeer her after class.

But Mrs. Neilsen thought better of that as well. "John," she said during the post-class exit time, "can you hang on for a second?"

"Oh," I said, glancing at Erin.

"I'll talk to you later, John," she said with a lovely smile.

A minute later, after all of my classmates had left the room, Mrs. Neilsen looked at me with a compassionate face.

"So," she said, "what was up today?"

"Sorry, I had to tell Erin something."

"Right," Mrs. Neilsen said, pulling my note out of her pocket and handing it to me. "Any reason it couldn't wait till after class?"

"Um, yeah. I didn't want anyone else to hear."

"Right," Mrs. Neilsen said. "You know, John, there's no rush. Girls will wait for you to find the right moment to ask."

My face went white at that suggestion. "I wasn't asking her out!"

"Oh, okay," Mrs. Neilsen said, smiling in such a way that I suspected that she didn't believe herself when she said it.

That should have been a hint to me of what was to come, but math class was over, so it was no longer my job to put two and two together.

With Mrs. Neilsen's delaying tactics, there was no time between first and second block to seek out any more of Jake's targets. Between second and third block, I found another of the victims hanging out with a pod of friends.

"Hi, Jennifer."

"Hi," she said, glancing at her companions, "do I know you?"

"Um, maybe not. I just have to tell you something."

"Ah, okay, what's that?"

I glanced back at her friends. "Um, can I talk to you alone?"

"I don't think so, darlin'. We have to get to class."

"Oh, okay, um, just don't trust Gator today, okay? If he tries to tell you something, he's just playing a game."

"Holy cryptic," one of the friends said, chuckling.

"Okay darlin'," Jennifer said with a smirk, "*will do*. I'll totally be careful if Gator tries to tell me something."

"Everybody knows Gaton Galleau's a player," her friend added. "That's like telling her to be creeped out if Henry Chu asks her out. Ah, *yeah*, I think she already knows."

"Oh, okay, good," I said. But I walked away to the sounds of a hefty laughter that made me wonder if Jennifer was as prepared for Gator as her advisors were making it seem.

"Why, what's he going to say?" Fatema said when I found her outside at lunch.

"Um, he's going to try to tell you that somebody likes you—and he's going to try to make it seem like it's him, and then he's going to try to get you to agree to go out with him. But then, if you agree, he'll say that the guy is Jake. Jake's doing an experiment to see if girls'll change their minds when they find out it's him."

Fatema rolled her eyes. "He's such a creep. He needs a lobotomy."

Fatema's friends laughed at that.

"Why does Gator hang out with him?" one of them pondered aloud.

"I know," another replied, "he's so very fine."

"And he's totally nice," a third piped in.

"Did you see what he was wearing yesterday?" a forth asked.

With the conversation firmly set on Gator's excellence, and me apparently no longer a necessary addition to the discussion, I muttered, "Good luck," and snuck away.

"You're kidding," Susan said later in the lunch hour. "What a disgusting pig. Guys are so ridiculous."

"I know," I said, rather hypocritically, considering my own membership in the gender.

Susan smiled at that. "Well, not *you*," she said, "—that was highly decent of you to say something. You're all right, dude."

"Thanks, um, so good luck."

"John," a familiar voice interrupted as I walked away.

"Oh …hi, Per."

"Were you hitting on Miss Piercings?"

"No."

"How'd you get her to smile, then? She never smiles."

"Um—"

"Oh, *shit*. Did you tell her about Jake and Gator?"

"Um, yeah, kind of."

"You're such an idiot. Jake's gonna kill you. Don't tell any of the others."

"Um," I replied.

"Who else have you told?"

"Just Jennifer and Fatema."

Per laughed. "Such an idiot. Well, you can tell Erin if you want, but don't tell Ashley—she can handle them herself."

"Yeah, but I'm gonna warn her, just in case."

"Don't be stupid, John. She'll be fine."

"Yeah, but this way, she knows."

"What, do you have a crush on her? You trying to impress her?"

"No," I said, which—in fairness to me—was true if you only counted the second question.

"Then don't tell her."

"Why?"

"Because Jake needs that one—especially since it's Ashley. And she can handle herself."

"Well, I still wanna tell her."

"Fine. And, if you do, I'm going to tell Jake that you're the one who screwed up his plans."

I shrugged. "He'll probably figure that out anyway."

Per rolled his eyes. "You're such an idiot."

Fifteen minutes later, as I peered down a hallway in search of Ashley, there was a tap on my shoulder from behind. I jumped.

"Oh, hi, Ashley. I was just looking for you."

"*Really?*" she said with a smile. "What's going on?"

"I have to tell you something about Gator."

"That he's going to pretend to ask me out, so Jake can see if I'll change my mind when I find out the invitation was actually from him?"

"Yeah, did they already do it?"

"No, your brother told me."

"My *brother*?"

"Yeah, is that weird?"

"Um, I don't know."

Ashley titled her head with a smirk. "Is Per telling me part of the greater conspiracy?"

"No, I don't think so. I just didn't think Per would tell you."

"Well, *you* were going to tell me, and you *are* brothers, so..."

"Yeah, I guess you're right."

Ashley smiled again. "I'm just teasing you. I was surprised too when he told me. I thought you were the nice one, and he was the total knob. No offence or anything."

"Oh, no—none taken. I know he can be a bit—"

"No, I meant *No offence when I called you* 'nice.' Most guys hate being called that."

"Oh."

"I'm just teasing you!" Ashley said, grinning. "I like nice."

"Oh...*why*?"

"Nice guys are the best. Life's too short to spend it with knobs."

That was not something that I wanted to argue, but—considering that Ashley had identified me as a member of the non-knob fraternity—I decided that it would be self-aggrandizing to agree too wholeheartedly.

"Yeah, I guess," I said, trying to display a neutral expression.

Unfortunately, my unopinionated face must have come across as indicating a lack of interest in Ashley's wonderful, dullard-charming point.

"Anyway," she said, "I better get going. See you later."

As Ashley walked away, I felt that I may have missed a chance to have a friendship-style conversation with her. But how I could have made use of the opportunity, I did not know. My ghostwriter contends that I should have taken Ashley's claims (A) that she liked nice guys, and (B) that she thought I *was* a nice guy, and deduced (C) that maybe she would like to date me. That, of course, is a stupid suggestion: she said she *liked* nice guys, not that she wanted to go out with one.

That evening, I decided that the best way to deal with Per's insistence that I *not* inform Ashley of something that he, himself, ended up telling her was to keep my annoyance to myself. That way, he wouldn't have to know that he had irked me, which, in turn, would make my resentment much easier on everyone. Unfortunately, Per got in the way of my low-key manner of being mad at him by bringing my anger rights out in the open.

"So," he said, arriving in the living room where I was watching TV with our parents, "did you tell her?"

"Did he tell who what?" Mom said, sitting up in her chair and muting the TV.

"Um," I said, still looking at my brother, "she told me that you already told her."

Per forced a huge Gator-like laugh. "Well, yeah, that's because I'm trying to get her to go out with me. I wanted to impress her."

Holy ghostwriter! *Per too?*

"Who is *her*?" Mom said with wide eyes.

"Ashley," Per and I replied.

"And what's she like?" our mother said, grinning at Per.

"You know, Ashley from elementary school."

"Oh, yes, I remember Ashley!"

"She's just totally not like any of the other girls," Per said.

My mom's smile was overpowering her face now.

"Perhaps it's time to invite Ashley out to see a movie?"

Per rolled his eyes. "Not yet," he said, muffling a smile, "I haven't even asked her out yet. So, John, what'd she say when you told her?"

"Um, she just said, um ...'Thanks.'"

"Yeah, and what else?"

"I guess that I was nice for telling her."

"But did she say anything about *me*—did she say *I* was nice?"

"Um, she said she was surprised you told her."

"That's a good sign," Mom said. "Maybe she's impressed."

"You think so?" Per said.

"Maybe, what else did she say, John?"

"I don't know. She said she likes nice guys."

"Well, that's encouraging—then she'll, of course, like our Per."

Per was too busy with his own thoughts to acknowledge that most recent gush.

"Well," my dad's voice entered the discussion, "maybe then ... maybe she likes *you*, John."

"Why?" my brother and mother said, clearly too startled to yet be offended by the thought.

"Because she said she likes nice guys, and she was surprised when Per did something *nice*, but John didn't say anything about her being surprised when he did the *same* nice thing for her."

Per and his mother gave pondering looks to each other.

"Well," the latter said, "I think we can assume that she would have been just as surprised by what John did, but, since his brother had done it first—"

"Totally," Per said, "he told her even though I told him not to. What, are you after her too?"

There was a creature in my throat that made words implausible at that moment, so I shrugged instead.

"John," my mom said, "there's lots of girls out there for you. Are you just interested in Ashley because she said you were nice?"

"No."

"Totally, that's what it is," my brother said. "I've liked her since elementary school. You're just being jealous."

"Per, don't be unkind," Dad said, "John's never been a jealous person."

"Oh, no, of course not," Mom said. "Sorry, John, I didn't mean to belittle how you're feeling. So have you liked Ashley for a while too?"

"Um, yeah, I think I started liking her, like, in elementary school too."

"Okay, and when did you start thinking about Ashley as a possible girlfriend?"

"Oh, well, not really *ever*." That was true, of course. I'd thought of her as the nicest and smartest girl in the world since a few months into our acquaintance, but I had never seriously imagined that she would want to be my girlfriend.

My mom smiled at me as though I'd just said something heroic. "Okay," she said. "So maybe—since Per *is* thinking of her in that way—maybe for now ... well, is there another girl that's caught your fancy?"

"No."

"Well, that's okay. Sometimes it's okay to let the girls pick you. Are there any girls who might like you?"

"Other than *Ashley?*" Dad said.

Mom laughed. "Yes, other than Ashley?"

"Nope."

"Okay, well, maybe, if you tried talking to girls a bit more—like your brother does—they might start to notice you."

"Okay."

"Good, I think you'll be surprised."

"Okay."

My mother smiled at me as though I were the family's employee of the month. "In the meantime, Per, tell us more about Ashley."

As my brother talked about why Ashley was worthy of him, I was not as sad as you might have thought, concerned reader. My parents on that occasion had shown unprecedented interest in my nonexistent dating life, and I appreciated that more than my lack of words could say.

The next morning, the only victim left to warn about Jake's evil plan was my math class neighbour, Erin. It was too risky to wait until our next class together (which wouldn't be for another day), so I searched the hallways for her during every break, but I didn't find her. Consequently, I could only hope that my failed (teacher-intercepted) attempt to deliver her a note the day before would be sufficient to make her at least aware that something anomalous was afoot. Of course, that was an unreasonable consolation, but it was the only solace I could come up with on short notice.

That evening, as my brother, his two most maniacal friends, and I waited in the Smith basement for chili dogs, Jake recounted Gator's efforts to Per.

"So," the sociopath said, grinning, "we started Operation Date Swap today, but the only one we did so far was Erin. And," he said, laughing, "it didn't go well. She didn't fall for it all."

"Why?" Per said.

Jake laughed. "As soon as Gator told her about her admirer, she said she thinks she knows who he's talking about."

"How'd she know it was you?"

"I don't know if she *did*, but Gator's like, 'Who?', and she's all weird and says she wants to talk to him personally."

"Awesome," my brother said, smirking.

Jake chuckled again. "Yeah, she's changed the rules of the experiment, but it'll still be interesting. I can't wait to see if she really knows it was me. I'll try to hang around her tomorrow in case she wants to take me aside and talk to me personally."

"So you never told Erin, eh?" my brother asked me after his friends left.

I shrugged. "I tried to, but Mrs. Neilsen got in the way."

"Awesome, I hope she dumps Jake on his ass. I wonder how she knew."

So did I. Perhaps my implausible wish had come true, and I'd gotten the message across better than I'd thought.

As I walked to math class the next morning, a hand touched me on the shoulder.

"Hey, John," Erin said, "got a sec?"

"Um, yeah."

"Good, come with me." She found us a secluded spot outside. "So," she said, smiling in a strangely nervous way, "I talked to Gator yesterday."

I grimaced. "I know; I'm sorry."

She smiled. "I didn't realize you guys were friends. I thought he was more your brother's friend."

"Well, I wouldn't say we're *friends*."

"Oh, okay, but you guys hang out sometimes?"

"Sort of: he and Jake come over to our place sometimes, and I sort of hang out with them when they're talking."

"That's what I was figuring. So, um, he told me that someone *likes* me."

"Sorry about that. I tried to stop it."

"Don't be sorry. It's okay. I didn't tell him my answer because I wanted to talk to the person, myself."

"Oh, how'd you know who it was?"

"I have my suspicions," Erin said, a sweet smile suddenly itching at her lips.

"Oh, okay," I said, amazed at her perceptiveness.

Erin continued to smile.

Holy ghostwriter! She suspected *me*. "Um—"

"So what I was going to tell Gator's friend is that I really like him, but I don't think we'd be a good match. Do you know what I mean?"

"Yeah—"

The start-of-class bell rang.

I looked towards the door.

"It's okay," Erin said with a dismissive wave at the bell. "You were saying?"

I smiled back at her generous look. I did not want to embarrass such kindness. "Um, yeah, I was just gonna say that, yeah, I think I know what you mean."

My alleged crush smiled again. "You okay?"

"Yeah, yeah, I'm fine," I said, and I felt some genuine emotion crawling into my voice. Although I hadn't really asked Erin out, her tactful rejection felt real.

"I'm just not the girl for you," she said, putting her hand on my shoulder.

"Right, thanks," I said. "I understand."

"How about a hug?" she said.

Wow, I'd never received such a gesture of concern from a girl before; if I didn't have a crush on Erin previously, I certainly had one now. But the neat thing about this crush—unlike my previous attractions—was that I wouldn't have to regret never asking her out. And I wouldn't have to wonder what her answer would have been if I had.

I was nervous as we arrived late for Mrs. Neilsen.

"Thank you for coming," she said, but noticing how close to me Erin was walking, she gave me a wink of a smile.

"So," my mother said that evening, during a commercial on TV, "did you boys have any interesting conversations with any interesting girls today?"

Wow, how the heck did she know about Erin?

"Um," I said, "maybe."

Mom laughed. "Very funny, John. I was talking about Per and Ashley. Did you talk to her today, Per?"

"No."

My mother raised her eyebrow at her son.

"I was already planning on doing it tomorrow," he said.

Our mother took in a grand sigh. "Very good," she said.

The next school day at lunch hour, I avoided all areas that could involve Per. After all, I could only conceive of two results that I would discover upon seeing him. Either (A) he would confirm that Ashley had agreed to go out with him, or (B) he would announce that Ashley had banned herself from any further interaction with *any* Smith family member. But, as long as I didn't talk to Per, then neither painful eventuality could yet be true.

Unfortunately, I miscalculated the range of Per's movement; as I entered a non-hangout hallway, I spotted him from behind. He hadn't seen me yet, so there was still time to escape. I slowly backed away so that, if he suddenly looked my way, I could change directions and pretend as if I was coming to see him.

As I backed through the doorway behind me, I breathed in a full helping of relief: I was free of his sight line. But then I heard some hopping footsteps coming down the stairwell. I turned to walk past the hopping person.

The hopping turned the corner: it was Ashley.

"Hey!" she said, grinning.

"Hi, how are you?"

"Good. Did you know your brother was going to ask me out today?"

"Um ..." (I was rush-debating with myself whether it would be a betrayal of my brother to admit classified information about him that his target seemed to already know.)

"You can tell me," Ashley said. "It would only be a betrayal of him if you'd told me *before* he asked me out, but now that I know, it's all good."

I decided that her intuitive understanding of my issue gave validity to her solution to it. "I guess you're right. Um, yeah, I knew."

"So why didn't you tell me?"

"Um, because, like you *said*, it would've been, you know, a betrayal of him."

"Yeah, normally, but what's Peter to you?"

"Ah, he's my—"

Ashley laughed. "So he's your brother. You happen to've had the same parents. You had no control over that. But we're friends *by choice*."

"Oh," I said, a grin peeking through my lips. "But, um, so why would you wanna know in advance that he was gonna ask you out?"

Ashley gave me an *Are you stupid?* look. "Ah, so I could prepare my response, obviously."

"Oh ...what'd you need to prepare?"

Ashley's eyes rolled. "It's hard enough turning a guy down without hurting his feelings."

"Oh, you turned him down?"

Are you stupid? face again.

"Sorry, you already answered that. So, um, why'd you turn him down?"

"Well, first of all, he's not really my type."

"Oh, okay," I said.

"*Well*," Ashley said, flicking a smile at me, "he's good-looking and everything, but he's just not as nice I'd like. You know my feelings about wasting my time with someone who isn't nice."

"Yeah, I remember," I said, trying to slow down time in order to ponder my options. I considered asking her what her feelings would be on wasting her time with someone who was allegedly nice, but a wee bit boring. I didn't even think about the consequence of my mom finding out that I'd asked out Per's girl. This time I was really going to do it.

Ashley smiled at me.

I smiled back. This was our moment.

"I hope we stay friends," she interrupted.

Oh. *Of course I wanted to stay friends.* But, if I asked Ashley out and was appropriately turned down, our friendship would thereafter be awkward. And so, empathetic reader, I'm sure you'll understand when I tell you that I cowarded out once again.

UNKIND NOTE: For his part, my ghostwriter says he cannot forgive my cowardly muteness; he claims, rather stupidly, that Ashley had clearly enunciated feelings in my direction; he further argues that my lack of response was an insult to unrequited crushes everywhere who are never given such an obvious *go ahead* to state their case. I cannot agree with my ghostwriter on that notion because it hurts to do so.

Oh well, at least I now had a confirmed friendship with Ashley to support my interest in her.

Strangely, though, after that friendship-building event, Ashley was rarely to bother my nerves with her conversation again; and, when she did, there seemed to be, in her demeanour, something of an *Oh, hi, I forgot about you* aspect to her voice.

I missed her a lot, but, as time moved on, I started to lose track of exactly what had made me fall for her. She was still the one I was hoping for in theory, but, in practice, not being around her forced me to develop crushes on other, less wonderful girls.

Chapter 11
Dullard in the Ring II

With Regret

Three weeks after that romantic finale, I noticed in biology class that Gator had sidled up next to a girl named Jocelyn whose intellect lived somewhere between average and in need of special assistance. She was articulate and confident-seeming (even pompous), but her social cue detector didn't always fire. That was a dangerous result in high school where an omnipresent sarcasm crackled in the air. Thankfully, given her near disability, most of Jocelyn's classmates didn't punish her for her cluelessness.

On this occasion, Jocelyn grinned as she argued with Gator during a lab assignment.

"No!" she said. "That's not where it goes. You have to read the instructions, silly. If you don't pay attention, you can't learn, Gaton."

"Thanks, Jossy," Gator replied. "I'm learning so much."

"Gaton Galleau," she said, "I've told you before that my name is Jocelyn. My parents didn't name me *Jossy*. Please don't use that name, please and thank you."

"Oh, so sorry, Jocelyn. It won't happen again."

For a tiny moment, I thought Gator might have decided to give up his Jake side to be a decent person, but that idiotic speculation was devoured as I looked over at Jake who was watching the Gator-Jocelyn discussion wearing his top psychopathic smile.

Clearly, I was witnessing another of their games. For some evil purpose, Jake had assigned Gator to flirt with poor Jocelyn. The realization left me nauseated.

I monitored the situation during the next two weeks as Gator continued to sit next to Jocelyn in every biology class. I wanted to warn her—to tell her to avoid Gator—but she seemed so happy with his pretend appreciation. He wrote her notes that made her grin, and, during lab assignments, he whispered flirtations in her ear.

"*Gaton Galleau*," she replied on one occasion, "you don't say *that* to a young lady!"

"I'm sorry, Miss Jocelyn," he replied. "It won't happen again."

"It had better not," she said, failing to hide her grin.

That should have been my cue. Whatever Gator and Per had planned was obviously coming soon; someone needed to put up some resistance to the cruelty that was plotted for Jocelyn. But I couldn't think of a way to intervene on something that was currently causing her to smile.

The next lunch hour, I arrived in the school foyer where I discovered Gator making out with Jennifer Chen. *Was this part of it?* I looked around for poor Jocelyn and instead spotted Jake watching with that smirk of evil. I continued scanning the room, but—before I could find her—I heard Jocelyn screaming.

"Oh my God, Gaton, why are you kissing her?"

Gator and Jennifer disentangled their lips and turned to face their approaching accuser.

"Um," he said, "I'm sorry, why *shouldn't* I be kissing her? She's my girlfriend."

"No, she's not! I'm your girl. You said *I* was your girl!"

"I never said that," Gator replied. "Awe, Jossy, what have your My Little Ponies been telling you? I was just being nice. You're not my type."

"You said you thought I was … you *said*!" Jocelyn screamed. "Why would you do this, Gaton? Why? You said! You said!"

My legs felt numb as I approached the confrontation. "Um, Jocelyn," I said, "there's something you should know about Gaton."

"What?" she said, tears free-falling down her face. "He said! Why would he do this? He said *I* was his girl?"

"He's not a nice person. He plays games with people. It's not you. It's—"

"What the hell, man?" Gator said. "Stay out of this. You know nothing about it. I was nothing but nice to Jossy. She's just confused because she's, you know …" He laughed.

"No, she's not *confused*," I said. "You did this on purpose."

Gator forced another laugh. "*Why?* Why would I want her to think I wanted her? She's not exactly my type, John-boy."

"Because you and Jake love to mess with people you think are weaker than you, and you know what? It's pathetic. It's like you're his puppet and he's—"

The word 'puppet' had pulled a string on something within Gator, and he launched his arm in a wide circle towards my face. His fist landed on my nose and caused my nasal cartilage to crunch inwards. I felt the impact in slow motion. It was the first time I'd been punched in the face with an ungloved hand. If you've never received such an offering, lucky reader, I must tell you: it's a surprisingly personal feeling. Someone's naked knuckles have melded with your face, which is the closest they can physically get to your brain, where you live. And so it feels as though they're trying to break in to you. The result is a kaleidoscope of pain and adrenaline, but somehow the latter allows you to temporarily ignore the former.

Before I could consider a fight plan, I instinctively grabbed Gator's punching arm with my left hand and sent my right fist straight for his own centre of operations. I didn't feel it land, but I saw Gator's head jolt backwards. I quickly zapped in two more shots, which strategically put me at risk, but I now determined—by his lack of dexterity in the matter—that Gator had never been in a fist fight before, so I decided to go with a Per-style flurry of punches. I got in four or five solid cracks while Gator swung wildly back and missed.

"Tackle him, Gator!" Jake called out.

It was the right call. Gator rushed me, and—with my right arm still firing away—I wasn't ready for him. His round and hard frame wrapped around my midsection and took me down. As my back smacked the ground, I knew I was in danger. Gator was stronger than me. And I couldn't outpunch him from the ground. I tried to grab his arms, but he knocked them away.

"What the hell?" I heard Per's voice yell.

Both hope and fear filled my chest. *Whose side would he take?*

Gator suddenly gasped. Per had kicked him in the ribs. My brother now had Gator by the neck and was pulling him off of me. A few of Per's friends joined him in the excavation.

I stood up and looked around. Fifty or sixty students from various grades were staring at us. Jennifer Chen looked at me with wide eyes.

"Oh my God," she said, "your nose."

Next to her was Jocelyn, whose face seemed to be blank.

"Are you okay?" she said.

"I'm okay," I said with a nasally clogged voice. "Are *you* okay?"

"I don't know. I don't understand what's happening."

I tried to pull in my emotions with a sigh. I walked to Jocelyn and gave her a hug.

"I'm sorry about how he treated you," I said,

She hugged me back, but I wasn't sure if she knew whether I was friend or foe.

As I was getting my face tended to at the hospital, a very nice nurse reprimanded me for participating in violence.

"You know," she said as she applied some gauze, "my brother used to get into trouble too, and it didn't do him any good. He wishes now that he'd grown up a little sooner."

"Okay, thanks," I said. "That makes sense."

"John!" my mom said, coming around the corner with my dad. "Are you okay?"

"He's okay," the nurse said. "He's got a broken nose. That's what happens when you get into fights at school."

"John wouldn't get into a fight unless he had a good reason," Mom said.

"Really?" I said, feeling a cool tingle in my stomach

"*Of course*," Mom said, smiling with a sigh. "Your poor face."

My dad smiled at me too. "You all right, son?"

Gator and I were both suspended three days for our bout. Per, meanwhile, received a one-day sentence for his participation. And he resigned his commission with Jake's sociopath club.

When I returned to school, I looked for Jocelyn, but she did not return. I had waited too long to try to help her.

Chapter 12
Dullard at Work

Affirmative Distraction

There was, in my hometown, a successful bakery called Sweet On You, which was staffed entirely by young, attractive females. Whether that was intentional or coincidental, I do not know, but it is clear that, when my male high school peers had a few extra dollars available for a snack, doughnuts seemed to be disproportionately more popular than pizza.

With the success of Sweet On You, its owner, Mr. Arthur, decided to expand: he bought the bakery of one of the neighbouring towns and called it Sweet On You Too. The entrepreneur then gave a promotion to one of his original Sweet On You employees to manage the first installment while he was activating the new franchise.

My ghostwriter's research indicates that the promoted staff member, Aryana, was pleased about her advancement because she had many ideas that she had long fantasized about implementing. Of course, her new authority was only applicable during the six out of seven days that Alex Arthur was out of the store, but it was enough for Aryana to apply her long dormant schemes.

Indeed, when Mr. Arthur took a three-week vacation with his wife and child at the same time that one of the employees of Sweet On You retired unexpectedly from the business to pursue life in the big city, Aryana had no choice but to fill the vacant position without Mr. Arthur's input. Once again, I'm told she was happy about the forced predicament because she was looking forward to hiring someone who was neither pretty nor female.

The above facts are relevant to our story, plot-preferring reader, because Alex Arthur's vacation lined up with the end of his daughter's school year, which, in turn, matched up with the graduation of my Grade Eleven career. With only a year left before college, I decided I needed a job to help me fend off future expenses, so I submitted my resume to the bakery. Most of my male peers were, I suspect, too embarrassed to apply for a job that was apparently reserved for pretty girls, but—upon acquiring hindsight—I further suspect that some of them came to notice that working amidst a crowd of attractive females would have demonstrated their heterosexuality much more effectively than working with a collection of rugged guys. Per was especially impressed.

"Nice," he said. "I gotta respect you for that one, bro."

Unfortunately, I could not claim the respect that he was offering since I had applied for the job for no other reason than that I'd spotted a HELP WANTED sign near the store's entrance.

Not knowing about the advantage that Aryana's affirmative action plan was giving my application, I arrived at my interview wishing I hadn't had the breakfast which was now bubbling around in my stomach.

"Um, hi," I said to the pretty girl at the front till, "I'm here to be interviewed."

"Right on," she said with a well-rounded smile. "It'd be great to have a guy here. I'll get Aryana."

The lady who came out of the backroom was not, on first glance, as pretty as her retriever. She was wearing, however, a business-like outfit that infused in her a mystique of sophistication that had not, in my experience, been equaled by anyone in her age range (20-25). As such, had I not felt that I was (A) too young for her and (B) a prospective employee, I might have considered starting up a crush on her.

The interviewer approached me with a serious voice. "Good morning, you must be John," she said, holding out her hand for me to shake.

I sent my own greeter in too quickly and consequently I caught more fingers than palm.

"Yes," I said, contorting my smile into a double, "nice to meet you, I'm John."

She nodded pleasantly. "I'm Aryana. Would you mind coming with me to the back?"

"Yes, no, I wouldn't mind."

"Great," she said with her first smile of the interaction.

"So, I see from your resume that most of your previous work experience is in lawn mowing?"

Ordinarily, I would have thought that she was teasing my green experience, but her serious face assured me that she was going to treat lawn mowing as a legitimate occupation.

"Yes, I've been lawn mowing for people around my neighbourhood for a few years now."

"Okay. And would you say that you've done a good job?"

"Oh, um …" I wasn't used to tooting my own lawn mower, "yeah, I guess so. I mean I think anyone could do it but, yeah, I think I got all the grass cut. I don't think I missed any spots or anything."

"Okay … and do you think that your employers would say that you did a good job?"

"Um, well, Mrs. Lalji—she was the first one who asked me to do it—I thought I was just doing it as a favour, but then she paid me and started suggesting me to the other neighbours, so I think she must've said I did a good job. But I don't know what the other neighbours would say. They never complained, but they could've just been being polite."

For a tiny moment, Aryana had a smirk on her face.

That surprised me, but I decided it would be best if I didn't ask what the joke was.

"How about punctuality? Would you say that you arrived for your jobs on time and got them done on time?"

"Oh, um, well, we didn't really set up exact times. I would just tell them that I would do the grass by the end of the weekend, and I always did—unless it was raining because rainy grass isn't good for the lawn mower. So then I would wait for the grass to dry, and I'd do it then. Nobody ever complained about it, but—"

"They might've just been being *polite*?" the smirk returned.

"Yeah, um, is that funny?"

"Oh, it's just you're very, um … sweet," she said with a chuckle. "You don't have to be so modest. You're allowed to try and make yourself look good in an interview."

"Oh, okay, sorry."

Aryana laughed. "No, it's okay. You don't have to apologize. Actually, your sincerity impresses me."

"Oh, thanks," I said, not sure if she was being sarcastic.

"Okay," she said, "so almost all of your work here will involve working with the public. How are you with people?"

"Oh ...um, I don't know, um ..."I felt myself panicking as I tried to think of an impressive interaction with the public, but I could think of none. "Um," I said, realizing that I had paused for too long now, "well, I get along well with, you know, my parents. Um," I panicked some more as I overheard what I'd said, "and, um, my brother and I sometimes disagree, but we also get along okay... sorry," I said, noticing that Aryana was fighting off another smirk, "that's probably not what you meant."

"Not really," she said, now grinning, "but that's actually a good start—believe me, getting along with your parents is a skill I haven't yet mastered. But I'm wondering more how you would be with dealing with customers ...who are usually strangers."

"Oh, I see," I said, chuckling now, myself. Indeed, I was surprised to realize that being rightfully teased for my blunder made me less nervous about further bobbles. "Right, yeah, the *public*. Well, I got along with all of my lawn mowing, um, customers, I guess."

"Good, so do you *like* people?"

I hesitated on that one. "Um, I like people who are nice."

"And how would you deal with a customer who wasn't *nice*?"

"Oh, um, I guess I'm kind of used to people not being nice, so I'd just kind of pretend like I didn't notice they weren't being nice."

"Good answer," Aryana said with a nodding smile. "All right, I think I've got a pretty good sense for what kind of an employee you'll be."

"Okay," I said, returning to nervousness.

"Don't worry. It's all good."

"Jaspreet," Aryana said to the beautiful girl who had first received me, "this is John. He's going to be your new co-worker."

"Great," Jaspreet said. "You're the first guy we've had working here since Stacy had her sex change."

"Oh, okay, um—"

Jaspreet laughed, which made me think she was probably joking about Stacy's current configuration. That was confirmed when an unambiguously female girl came around the corner.

"And this is Stacy," Aryana said. "Stacy, this is your new co-worker, John."

"Hey," Stacy said, smiling directly at me with such gusto that I felt a sparkle in my chest; surely she'd mistaken me for someone interesting. But her alleged enthusiasm for my presence lasted for only a second before she turned back to her boss. "We're out of small bags."

Hmm, her flash of smiling had been so brief that I now recognized it wasn't a case of mistaken approval, but, instead, it was simply her standard operating greeting that I had no justification to take personally.

The Customer Who's Always Right

A couple days later, after some basic but thorough training about the technical operations of the bakery, Aryana taught me how to work the customer service till. She had me watch her perform real transactions with live customers and then had us switch roles so that she could observe me pecking away at the till. It was a nerve-provoking experience as she corrected me *after* my mistakes instead of before them. Apparently she felt that I would learn more from my errors if she didn't stop me from experiencing them. I don't know whether she was right or not, but I can report that, with her system, my blunders reduced more rapidly than I'd expected.

Soon Aryana left me alone with the customers.

"Is that everything for you?" I said with a smile at one.

"That's it, thanks."

"Okay, from *twenty*…twelve eighty-seven is your change."

I poured the bills and change into the cupped hands of the customer, who had to be careful not to spill as he transferred the money to his wallet. The whole exchange seemed inelegant to me, and I wondered why I'd never noticed the awkwardness of such transactions before during my years on the other side of the customer counter.

Just after the customer left the store, I was startled to hear Aryana's voice right beside me.

"John," she said, "can I give you a hint?"

"Um, sure," I said, surprised that she thought I had the right to decline such an offer.

Aryana smiled. "It's the way you give change back to customers. It's kind of messy, don't you think?"

"Yeah, I think so too!" I said, delighted I wasn't the only to have arrived at that shocking conclusion. "I never realized how messy transactions are."

"Well, maybe just give the coins first with one hand; and then—with the *other* hand—give the bills. That way, it's not just a pile of money."

"Oh, okay," I said, sensing that, despite Aryana's patient smile, I was expected to have now mastered the mysterious change-giving method.

"John," Aryana said a few minutes later, "so you're separating the bills from the coins great now, but can I make another suggestion?"

"Sure, um, but I kinda found that putting the money into the customers' hands with two hands was just as messy as before."

I said so not because I didn't want further advice, but because I didn't want my boss to get her hopes up about its success.

"It's just," she said, "in order for it to work, you can't do both hands at the same time. You have to do one hand, wait for a sec, and then do the other hand."

"Oh, I see," I said, still skeptical. "Okay, sure, I'll try."

My boss chuckled. "Let me show you."

As she handed my right hand some coins just a tiny moment before providing my left hand with bills, I realized immediately the beauty of her method. It was an epiphany that bored my ghostwriter, but which I persuaded him to include in this book anyway because it's an ideal case study of how I learn.

As I became more confident with my till work, the customers became more confident in their willingness to treat me harshly.

It turns out that customers can be some of the most demanding creatures on earth. Clearly, I'm stereotyping, but, if you've ever worked in customer service, unfortunate reader, then you know what I'm talking about.

"Hello," you'll say to a nice customer standing in front of you, "how can I help you?"

"I was wondering—" the friendly customer will begin to say before being interrupted by a more important consumer.

"How much are these?" you'll hear from a loud voice across the store.

"Those are four ninety-five each," you'll quickly reply, hoping to return to the client who has first dibs on your service.

"How come there's no blueberry?" the loud voice will continue as though they're the only customer on duty.

"Sorry, just a second, please," you'll say with assertive sheepishness. "I'll be with you in a moment."

The faraway customer will then sigh and retreat to an annoyed stare, which articulates the unfairness of the world.

At that moment, you'll realize that certain high-confidence customers have uncanny similarities to that species of people known as children. Indeed, if such a customer is feeling particularly upset with the way things are going, they may feel obligated to start up a customer tantrum. According to the customer guidebook, they are justified in raging at a service clerk in the following conditions:

(1) Customer is not happy with how much something costs.

(2) Customer is not happy with how long something takes to prepare.

(3) Customer is not happy with their spouse (who hasn't been communicating lately).

Now, as I've said, still offended reader, I'm stereotyping. Not all customers are so childish. In fact, to be fair, most customers are perfectly adult-like. But, when you work in customer service, it's hard not to focus your introspection on the most self-empowered people.

Chapter 13
Dullard In Conversation II

Assignment of Flame

Worry not, skeptical reader, my ghostwriter doesn't want anyone feeling sorry for me for having to deal with unpleasant customers; after all, working along my side of the customer counter were an array of pleasingly beautiful girls, which was a fascinating education.

Previously, the female conversations on which I had tried to eavesdrop in high school were clearly edited for content due to the conversers' awareness of being near many male ears. But, since I was just one (shy) guy, my Sweet on You co-workers seemed to feel comfortable talking to each other as they would have if I weren't there.

EVIDENTIARY NOTE: As I'm sure you've surmised, scientific reader, I cannot say for certain that my pretty co-workers were speaking as freely as they would have when truly alone among their own kind, but I formed my above hypothesis on the basis that they clearly chatted differently when I was the only male around than how they spoke to each other when there were additional males nearby. So I think we can agree that it would have been arrogant of me to assume that they spoke one way around guys, a second way among just themselves, and a third way just for me.

"Henry is the sweetest guy ever," pretty Amy said, for instance, one afternoon.

"Oh, how so?" pretty Tabitha replied.

"Like yesterday, he said he liked the way I look in my jeans, and I hadn't even *told* him I got new jeans. He's so observant and just, like, considerate all the time."

"That's cool," Tabitha said. "Although, I suppose ... um ... it might not've had anything to do with him realizing you bought new jeans. He might've just liked how you look in them—they *are* very cute on you."

"Yeah, maybe," Amy said, beaming as though Tabitha hadn't harmed her argument.

As Amy continued her gush, I noticed that I was also unsure of the claim she was justifying. *If Henry were indeed the nicest guy in the history of the planet, then why had I witnessed him practicing a not-so-nice behaviour—being rude to his bakery server (me)—just a week before?* That curiosity was my first official inkling into the propensity that some humans have for seeing the qualities they would *like to want* in the people they instinctively prefer.

Before I get too uppity about that, confidant reader, it should be noted that I too had spent some time having my assessments of peoples' personalities distorted by red herring factors, such as how pretty they were. Not that pretty girls received automatic admiration from me in reward for their visual performances, but their symmetrical smiles were known to distract me away from noticing defective personality traits.

Fortunately, working at a place whose female dress code was *attractive* made it difficult for me to continue being so undiscriminating of pretty girls. I could now only compare my stunning companions to other visually generous creatures, and—since some of them had inner physiques that were as appealing as their outer offerings—it became increasingly difficult not to notice the cases in which the girls' personalities did *not* live up to the promise of their looks.

For instance, I noted that I was not a fan of Stacy (of the falsely alleged sex change); you see, intrigued reader, Stacy had been fortunate to discover at an early age that she found herself to be much more interesting than everyone else. Consider the following conversation:

"Hey, guys," Amy said, "what should I wear on my date tonight?"

"With who?" Tabitha replied.

"Henry."

"Oh ... I thought you didn't want to see him again after he said—"

"Yeah, I realized he was just nervous, so I decided—"

"Guys are always nervous around me," said Stacy, just arriving in the room. "I just tell them I'm not into squirmy nervous guys, but," she added with a laugh, "that just makes 'em more nervous. But I'm like, 'If you wanna get with me, you gotta prove you can keep up with me.'"

"I don't know," Tabitha said, "I kinda like it when a guy's nervous. At least then I know he likes me."

Stacy laughed. "Yeah, honey, I'm not usually too worried about whether guys like me."

Tabitha shook her head with a smile. "Yeah, well, it's a little easier when you're gorgeous."

Stacy made no attempt to deflect the compliment. Instead, she grinned unreservedly. "You're cute too, Tab. You just need ..."

And suddenly makeup advice was flowing in Tabitha's direction. That was shocking to me since I considered the pupil to be a smile prettier than the instructor.

"Okay, thanks, I'll try that," Tabitha nevertheless said with a smile at the unnecessary suggestions.

"Good girl," Stacy said. "Now, let me look at your hair."

Tabitha laughed at that. "Well, why I don't I just keep to the makeup tips for now? You don't want me to be too pretty too fast, do you?"

Stacy shook her head. "Trust me, honey: it's worth it. There's nothing more satisfying than knowing you can have any guy you want."

The pronouncement startled me; after all, for statistical purposes, I myself could be considered a guy, which meant that, according to Stacy, I had a crush on Stacy. That discovery would have been disturbing enough—but finding out about my attraction right in front of her was enough to make me blush. Luckily, Stacy didn't seem aware that I was in the room, so my alleged auto-crush didn't cause an awkward moment of eye contact between us.

When Stacy finally finished her lecture series on improving

Tabitha's appearance and left the room again through swinging doors, her pupil turned back to Amy.

"So," she said with a touch of a giggle, "you decided to forgive Henry, why?"

"Well, he's not usually that retarded. I'm pretty sure he was just nervous."

"I suppose, but …even if he was nervous, for him to treat someone like that, don't you think that shows there's something—"

"I know," Amy replied as Stacy swung back into the room, "but normally he's so sweet. I don't think he meant—"

Stacy laughed. "Come on, girl. Guys are always sweet when they're trying to get into your pants. It doesn't matter if he *means* it. It just matters if you to wanna get with him too."

I wasn't sure if I was supposed to be hearing those details. Not to worry, Stacy still didn't seem aware that I was there.

"I don't know about that," Tabitha said. "I think some guys are sweet just because they're sweet."

Stacy chuckled again. "Yeah, you keep on believing that, Sleeping Beauty. Admit it, John," she said, suddenly looking at me, "you act all sweet 'cause you think girls'll like you for it."

Tabitha snapped her gaze in my direction. "You don't have to answer that, John."

"Why not?" Stacy said, staring at my rescuer.

"Because he'll look bad no matter what he says."

"No he *won't*. I'm just saying he's no different from any other guy."

"But, actually, I don't think John is *like every other guy*. But, if he says that, he'll seem like he's full of himself."

That made me smile: not even my ghostwriter could have worded my predicament so well. Indeed, for a self-indulgent moment, I wondered why Tabitha seemed to have such a generous understanding of my situation.

Stacy let out a humourless chortle. "You're just defending him because Rander's a shy guy too."

"Yeah, I suppose he is …" Tabitha said, seeming to ponder, "… and he's also sweet and completely sincere."

Stacy upgraded her amusement to a hearty laugh at that one. "Wait till you've been with him for a couple months. Then the belching and all that guy stuff will come out."

"I don't think so. I've seen him with his sister."

"That's because he knows you're watching."

"No, I don't think so. Then *she'd* point out that he was treating her differently than usual. She's not the sort to put up with people being fake—especially her brother."

As the debate continued, I contemplated Tabitha. Although the possibility of our relationship had been cut down in its prime by the revelation of Rander, she was no less attractive to me. She reminded me of the standard of crush that Ashley had once set; and that made me smile. I was now able to conclude what I couldn't have previously: on the bizarro chance that large-egoed Stacy *were* to ask for my hand in dating, I would refuse her.

DEFENSIVE NOTE: You may think, critical reader, that it was easy for me to say that I would turn pretty Stacy down, given that it was extremely unlikely that my claim would ever be tested. I see your point, helpful reader. Nevertheless, even just out of obligation to my word, I believed I would, if called upon, be able to follow it.

Backseat Dater

A week later, I arrived for my afternoon-to-evening shift and spotted a lengthy customer lineup, which could have been reduced if Stacy weren't away from her customer service post giving an outlandishly handsome young male patron a hearty helping of advice about which was the best raisin bread to buy.

I scampered to the backroom to release my jacket; I returned to hear Stacy still giggling as she detailed the various numbers of scoops of raisins in the differing breads.

"And, trust me," she said loud enough for the entirety of the expanding lineup to eavesdrop, "the size of the raisin does matter."

"How come?" her prey replied, clearly pretending not to be aware of the extra entendre available to him.

"Because, there's more fruit in those ones," Stacy said, smacking him with a giggle. "What were *you* thinking?" she added as I rushed behind the counter five minutes early.

"Just *that*," her new friend said. "So, um, I should get this one?"

"That's what I'm saying," Stacy said, touching his arm. "So you wanna take it home with you?"

"For sure," he said. "I just wish I could take your, um, expertise home with me."

"That's easy," Stacy said, suddenly walking back to the counter, "there's a raisin bread hotline number I'll put on your receipt for you."

"Hi, Stacy," I said as she arrived at the till where I was now serving a lineup of customers.

"Hiya," she said with one of her *You find me sexy* grins, "I'm just gonna scooch in here, so I can ring this guy in."

"Oh, okay."

I suspected the rightful next customer in line was not pleased with my passivity towards her place in the queue; I concluded so because she tossed me a roll of her eyes. It was an unnecessary flogging. I was already ashamed of my easy acquiescence to Stacy's demands, but I could think of no way that I could have stopped the lineup hijacking.

An hour later, Amy and I were alone for the final closing hours of the shop. During a shortage of customers, I spent my thoughts ranting at Stacy. Her voice had become ugly to my ears, and—although my eyes had yet to achieve the same disdain—I was glad that I had no intention of ever being attracted to her.

"Hey, John," Amy interrupted my proud pondering, "I need a guy's opinion."

"Okay," I said, honoured to be considered eligible for such a request.

"So do you think, if a guy says he's gonna call you …like, how soon should he call you?"

"Hmm," I said, not certain how to answer, considering that I'd never promised a girl that I would dial her number. "Well, um, what's he supposed to be calling you about?"

"A *date*. We're like boyfriend and girlfriend now, so don't you think he should be calling before the weekend?"

"Yeah, I guess so. So have you called *him*?"

"Um, no. I don't wanna look desperate. Seriously, if a girl called you, complaining that you didn't call, you'd dump her, right?"

"No," I said, insulted that she thought I could be so callous, but complimented that she thought I could have a girlfriend. "I think, if someone was my girlfriend, I think I'd want her to, you know, tell me if I was doing something that bothered her."

"Right? That's what *I* think! So you think I should tell him?"

"Um," I said, nervous about my influence. "I don't know your boyfriend."

"It's Henry—you know Henry! Tall, stocky guy, comes in all the time."

"Right, Henry," I said, remembering the loud-voiced walking interruption whom I'd endured serving. "Well, I don't think Henry and I are that similar, so—"

"That's true. He's like always making jokes and being funny and stuff—not that you're not funny. It's just that he makes everybody laugh and stuff."

"Right," I said, scanning my memory with no success for an instance in which Henry had made anyone but himself or Amy laugh. "Well, then I guess I wouldn't tell him that you want him to call more. I don't think guys like him like being told what to do."

"So what should I do? I *want* him to call me."

"And you don't wanna be the one to call?"

"Right."

"Well...I guess you could send him a letter."

SOCIO-TEMPORAL NOTE: At that time, curious reader, email communication was still relatively new, and social media was just a glint in Lord Twitter's eye.

"Ah, *no*," Amy said as a customer came into the store. "I told you I don't wanna look desperate. I mean how's sending a letter not gonna look desperate?"

Amy, in that moment, was at the point of customer contact, and so I felt rude on her behalf that she hadn't acknowledged her patron.

"Um," I said, motioning my eyes towards the visitor.

Amy squinted at me.

"Hello," I said, smiling around her at the customer.

"Hi," the customer replied.

Amy then took on her role of customer converser as I gathered up the customer's order. The time away from the Henry discussion gave me an opportunity to come up with a justification for the suggestion I'd arrived at only by process of elimination. Now that it was on the counter, I felt that I should give it some reasoning.

"So?" Amy returned.

I paused for the customer to get out the door. "Well, I guess the letter doesn't have to be about like asking him to hang out or anything. You could just send him … or why don't you buy him a present and send it to him?"

"Really? Do guys like presents?"

"I don't know. Do *girls* like presents?"

"Yeah, but that's because we're girls. Guys are supposed to buy us stuff."

"Okay, so why do you like getting presents?"

"I guess because it means that he was thinking about me enough to, like, go out and pick something out for me."

"So wouldn't a guy like the same thing?"

"You think so?"

"I really have no idea," I said, chuckling. "That's why I'm asking. *I'd* like a present, but, like I said, Henry and I are not much alike."

Amy took in a deep, introspective breath. And then she smiled. "Maybe you're right. Why *wouldn't* he like getting a present? I'm gonna do it."

A couple days later, Amy beamed at me when she came on shift. "Guess what I did yesterday?"

"I don't know," I said, figuring it would be inappropriate to guess my hope that a breakup was about to be described.

"I bought him a CD. And I'm calling him tonight to go over there and give it to him. I was gonna send it, like you said, but then I thought, 'This way, I can get to see him too.'"

I had to admit: I was impressed with her improvement on my plan.

"Guess what?" Amy said a couple more days later.

"I don't know," I said, a wee bit annoyed with the constant requests for me to guess random news.

"He totally loved the CD, and he played it for me, and everything's totally great now."

Throughout that shift, Amy told me many details about how

music had brought rhythm back into her relationship. The information was fascinating, certainly, but, on more than one occasion, I felt that Amy could have paused her story to give more due attention to the customers she was supposed to be serving.

The next time I worked with just Amy, I was even more concerned to note that Amy continued her Henry discussions even while *I* was about to serve customers.

"Hi, can I help you?" I said loudly, on one such occasion, in hopes of indicating to Amy that it was time to pause her story.

"Yeah, can I get six of these and six of those?" the customer tried.

"Don't you think he's funny?" Amy said.

"Um, not sure. Sorry, did you say six of *these*?"

Amy laughed. "Come on, he's totally funny. Why can't guys compliment other guys?"

"Um—"

"Actually, I meant these ones."

"Oh, sorry."

"John, why can't you just admit that he's funny?"

"Okay, he's funny," I said, realizing I'd now forgotten which one was the second pastry choice. I gambled and went for glazed doughnuts."

"Actually, I wanted the crullers," the customer caught me.

Amy giggled at me. "Sheesh, John: pay attention."

The above painful experience repeated itself several times, so I finally asked Amy to hold her thoughts when customers were in the store. She agreed to do so, but, in practice, she decided it was only necessary to be quiet while the guests were directly requesting items from me. Once they'd picked their dessert, Amy apparently felt that the spirit of my request had been met and that she was thus safe to reinitiate babble. Unfortunately, I do not possess a multi-track brain, so I was unable to listen to my colleague and compile orders simultaneously. I tried ignoring Amy's commentary but then she simply raised her voice until I acknowledged her. It was from those interactions that I came to dread my shifts with Amy.

Another couple weeks later, though, I felt guilty about my

Amy-trepidation when she asked me to guess what was wrong ... *Henry had again been negligent in calling her.*

"Seriously," she said, "how long do you think a guy should wait before he calls his girlfriend?"

"Um ...two days?" I guessed.

"Yeah, that would be fine. It's been like *six*. What's wrong with me? Am I totally ugly?"

"No, of course not," I said. "There's nothing wrong with—"

"So why are guys so mean? Don't they know that girls want them to call?"

Over the next few months, Henry's lack of calling would lead Amy to have no choice but to confront him. He, in turn, would have no choice but to tell her to take him as he was or leave him as he was. Amy chose, at first, to take Henry as offered, but a few days later—after criticizing his boyfriend skills again—she was forced to give up on him after he broke up with her. Not to worry, concerned reader, two weeks later, she started dating another Henry of a different name (Terrence).

Throughout Terrence's stay, I continued to try to offer Amy my inexperienced wisdom, but I noticed that the deeper we got into trying to figure out why Terrence was so distant (during non-canoodling times), the less open Amy was to considering my ideas, and so I reduced myself to being more of an absorber of what she had to say than a participant in our conversations. Nevertheless, I felt as if we had inadvertently become friends. Admittedly, we never got together outside of work, and she didn't know much more about me than that I knew a lot about her love life, but I was still pleased to have acquired the friendship of a co-worker.

Chapter 14
Dullard vs. Pride

Bombshell Game

"Hey, John," Amy said, a few weeks later, in her once-a-week serious question voice, "can I ask you something?"

"Yeah, of course."

"Do you think Stacy's prettier than me?"

"No."

"You don't think she's totally hot?"

"Um—"

"It's just she's all like, 'Every guy wants me.' Do you think that's true?"

"Oh, well, um, please don't tell her I said this, but *I* wouldn't go out with her."

"Really? Why not?"

My instinct was urging me to declare every annoying Stacy trait, but the thought of my anti-Stacy commentary sneaking back to her was too scary. So I went with boring and said with a smile, "She's not my type."

Oddly, Amy didn't seem bored with my boring answer. Instead, she smiled back. "So maybe, when Terrence was checking her out yesterday, he really just meant," (Amy switched to a mocking deep voice to quote Terrence), "'I'm a guy, and she's hot, so I'm going to look at her, but that doesn't mean she's my type.'"

"Yeah, I guess that's possible," I said, suddenly regretting that I'd inadvertently inspired Amy to forgive her obnoxious boyfriend.

"Hi John," gorgeous Jaspreet said, grinning at me when I arrived at the bakery a few days later.

"Hi?" I said, glancing down to make sure I wasn't flying low.

"I think somebody likes you."

"Really?"

"Mmm hmm. Yesterday, somebody was talking about you a lot."

"Who?"

"Wouldn't you like to know?"

Jaspreet was quite right, of course. My curiosity was yanking at me like a young child to a parent's jacket. *Who could the allegedly affectionate co-worker be?* Currently, there weren't that many single girls at the bakery, and they all seemed too socially accomplished to consider a dullard. Perhaps my many heart-to-broken-hearts with Amy had made her realize that her latest 'nicest boyfriend in the world' wasn't even as friendly as me. That seemed unlikely, but so was the notion of *any* of my pretty co-workers ogling my personality.

So, of course, the big question was: *Would I want to go out with Amy if she was the culprit behind Jaspreet's claim?* She certainly wasn't my first-through-fifth choice; in fact, if you'll forgive the judgment, non-judgmental reader, I found her to be a teensy bit self-absorbed. Still, she had always been nice to me. And, if she was willing to be interested in me, I was in no position not to celebrate that.

"Hey, John," Amy said, smiling at me when she arrived on shift. "Guess what?"

"Um ..." I said, nervous that she was about to confirm my Jaspreet-induced suspicion, "I don't know."

Amy grinned at me. "He finally called, and we've got a date tonight! He was so sweet."

Oh. Amy was already cheating on me with her boyfriend. And the giddiness with which she described the affair made me suspect that she was not going to be feeling guilty about it.

So who else could my alleged admirer be? Or maybe Amy had merely complimented me as a friend, and Jaspreet had mistaken that for crush-like behaviour. Yeah, that had to be it. In fact, now that I thought about it, the only other currently unattached girl in my approximate dating age range at the bakery was—

"Hi, John," a loud, smiling voice arrived in the store. "You look good today."

It was Stacy.

She was wearing a grand, flirtatious smile that seemed to be directed at me. *How could that be?* I felt as if I were the naïve Dale in one of Jake's evil experiments. For the rest of the shift, Stacy seemed to forget about our personal space boundaries. If we were standing beside each other, her arms leaned against mine, and, whenever she passed behind me, she preempted the danger of us colliding by putting her hand to my back, in lieu of a standard and probably more efficient verbal expression of her proximity.

Those touching moments were not lost on my heart rate. As I sat by myself in the backroom on my lunch break, I had no choice but to double-check with myself whether I could live up to my personal promise that I would never go out with Stacy. I'm not proud to say that both sides of the debate were well represented. Nevertheless, I finally accepted my obligation: I wasn't going to help her vindicate her claim that I had an auto-crush on her!

Only a few moments after I reaffirmed that resolution, the door to my backroom sanctuary opened and revealed Stacy, looking like the girl next door's prettier sister.

"Aryana thinks I'm getting bags," she said, smiling aggressively.

"Oh. So what *are* you doing?"

"Just wanted to say, 'Hi.'"

"Hi."

Stacy laughed at that. "You're so cute. So my parents are away tonight. And some friends are coming over. Care to join us?"

Oh. Well, if her friends were there, it wouldn't technically be a date. It would be a chance to make new friends.

"Okay," I mustered.

Stacy smirked. "I thought so."

That remark led me immediately to panic that she was about to admit that she had tricked me into agreeing to go out with her just so that she could spurn me, but, before I could renounce my agreement, she placed a piece of paper on the lunch table.

"Eight O'clock," she said.

On the paper was an address that looked surprisingly legitimate.

Upon getting home after work, I told my parents that I was going to a work party (which was sufficiently truthful for my conscience). My guardians were apparently pleased to hear news of me attending a non-familial social gathering.

An hour later, I arrived as instructed at 8:00 at Stacy's address. There was no answer to my first doorbell ringing. I smiled as I noticed that twenty seconds still hadn't produced a response. It was my own fault for having believed that Stacy would want my company. I rang one more time just for protocol.

But this time I heard movement from a staircase. My heart fluttered, and the door opened. There stood Stacy wearing minimalist clothing. That was nerve-provoking but not horrifying to my eyes.

"Hi, John," she said, smiling roundly, "you're early."

"It's 8:00."

"Honey, that's early," she said with a giggle.

Soon we were on her couch sitting closer than the spacious piece of furniture required, especially considering none of her friends had yet arrived.

"So I guess your friends will be coming *soon*?" I said.

"Maybe," Stacy said, "unless this goes well. I decided I'd give you a chance to be alone with me."

"Oh."

"Don't play coy," she said. "I've seen you watching me."

That, oddly enough, was a false accusation. Not that I was opposed to glancing quietly at attractive girls, but, with so many pretty ones to choose from at the bakery, I had no need to look at my least favourite. But, in Stacy's ego's defence, most guys who came into the store *did* take a moment to appreciate her visual presence, so it wasn't unreasonable for her to generalize that behaviour to me.

"Um," I said, deciding it would be rude to deny the accusation, "well, you *are* pretty."

"Just *pretty*?" she said with a push on my shoulder that was more pleasing than any push I'd ever received before.

"Beautiful," I corrected, "um, yeah, I'd say you're quite beautiful."

"*Quite*?" Stacy said. "I think maybe you've dug yourself enough of a hole there, honey. You might want to try a different tact."

Oh. I was just meaning to be polite. I wasn't trying any tact.

As I smirked that to myself, I noticed that Stacy was scrunching in even closer than before. Wow. Close up, she was undeniably attractive. Maybe she wasn't so bad, after all.

She gave me an adorable smile.

Yikes, was I supposed to kiss her?

Tragically, I can't say that I wasn't significantly intrigued by the idea. The thought of getting that close to a gorgeous girl was not exactly the worst opportunity I'd come across all decade. And I'd like to say that I turned her down on the grounds that she was arrogant and obnoxious, but, once again, there was a more important factor weighing down my mind. Were I to accept her invitation, I would be proving her theory that all guys would like to go out with her. After all, I couldn't imagine any guy disliking her more than I did. Poor Stacy: if she hadn't claimed that all guys would go for her, she might have been right, but, as it was, her pride inspired my own.

"I have to tell you something," I said, remembering how wonderful Erin had once so nicely turned down my hypothetical crush on her. "Um," I said, trying to remember Erin's specific technique, "so someone told me that someone at the store likes me ..."

"Is that right?" Stacy said, snuggling even closer.

"Yeah, and, um, I think I know who it is."

"I think I do too."

"And, well, I don't really think we'd be a good match. Do you know what I mean?"

Stacy raised her eyebrows and laughed. *"You don't think we'd be a good match?* Ah, honey, you're not the kind of guy who gets to be choosey."

"You're probably right. But I guess I'd rather be single than go out with someone I don't feel—"

"Oh my God," Stacy said, with a *You're the dumbest guy I've ever met* look on her face. "Look, honey, I was just trying to give you a thrill. Nobody said anything about *going out* with me."

"Oh, okay. So I guess we agree?"

Stacy shrugged with a smirk.

"So ..." I said, "I guess I should *go*?"

"Yeah, you *do* that. You know you're gonna die alone, right?"

I shrugged back. "Maybe."

There was an urge in me to remark that at least I wasn't going to have to complete my existence having been proved wrong about my claim that I could acquire the devotion of any guy I selected. But I decided the point was better left implied.

As Stacy walked me to her door, I figured I should complete Erin's method of discharging a candidate, so I offered my rejected a hug. My ghostwriter laughed when he heard that and contends that I was doing so for the fun of seeing how Stacy would respond, but I assure you, fair-minded reader, that I simply felt that I had no right to question Erin's impeccable system.

"Ah, no thanks," Stacy said. "You had your chance."

"Right, um, okay," I said. "See you at work."

"Whatever," she replied, but somehow I felt that—despite her confident tone of dismissal—she knew that I had won.

Chapter 15
A Boring Development

In Charm's Way

In 1990, when I was ten, big-city resident Bertrand Hardelean II moved to our town and opened Bert's Shirts & Skirts: The Clothing Store. At the time, Bert knew little about the clothing industry, but his talents with supplier negotiation, store presentation, and customer flattery quickly turned his operation into a destination shop for several towns within a half hour drive.

Three years later, Bert hired Michael Leith, a recent high school graduate, to be his assistant. Michael, who was a relative newcomer to our town, had—according to my ghostwriter's research—fallen in love with the comfortable world of small-town values. Surprisingly, though, the small-town values were not so relaxed with Michael who possessed an inability to find his opposite sex attractive. Luckily for Michael, it didn't occur to anyone in our little redneck of the woods that a conventional-seeming fellow like himself might be gay, and so they didn't bother him about it.

BOASTFUL NOTE: For your interest, curious reader, I'm pleased to point out that, as far as I can remember, I myself have never felt any bigotry towards gay people. That may seem impressive, considering my 1980s-90s small town upbringing, but it was really just the result of the fact that my mother's university roommate, Aunty Shanna—who happened to be attracted to people of like-gender—was such a thorough adventurer of life that she had found a prime position in the stories that my mom told Per and me. Consequently, my brother and I inadvertently became accustomed to thinking of gay as a worthy way to be attracted to the world.

Now, Michael has told my ghostwriter that, at the time, his only experience with confirmed gay people (other than himself) was in movies and television. He apparently did not match up with many of the official gay characteristics presented in 1990s' Hollywood, but he says that he nevertheless found the strong evidence for mandatory traits in gay men to be intriguing. That was a poignant understanding given that Michael's boss, Bert Hardelean, was good-looking, well-dressed, charming, witty, and a good dancer; in short, he had gay stereotyped all over him.

One morning, then, a BMW landed in the Bert's Shirts & Skirts' parking lot.

"Hey, how are you?" the driver said to Bert.

"Phenomenal, yourself?"

"Good—I need a dress shirt I can change into."

The man removed his suit jacket, revealing a toned white shirt marked by a smudged red stain on the abdominal area of the garment.

"Cut myself shaving," he said, "no clue how I got it on my shirt."

"Yeah, shaving cuts are prolific little characters," Bert said as he looked through his stock before reaching a shirt to the injured man. "This one should fit. Changeroom's over there."

After the visitor paid for his shirt, Michael's gaze shadowed him to his car. But, as Michael turned his attention back upon the store, he tells my ghostwriter he found Bert's eyes studying him.

Bert smiled at his employee.

'I see that you're gay,' Bert's smile seemed to be saying, 'but it's okay with me if it's okay with you.'

And, if Michael's testimony is true, he realized at that moment that he was going to have trouble not falling into a deep crush on Bert of Bert's Shirts & Skirts.

Five more years later, a woman named Susan Smith—along with her nephew John Smith—entered Bert's Shirts & Skirts.

"*Welcome*," the proprietor said.

"Thank you," Aunty Susan said, smiling as she looked at our

crisply manicured host. "Um, my nephew and I are looking for a special tie to go with his graduation outfit, which—*sorry*—we already bought."

Bert grinned. "It's okay: even I don't *only* shop at my store."

Aunty Susan laughed. "Right, sorry, yeah, of course."

Bert chuckled back. "So what type of outfit do I need to match the tie with?"

"Oh, sorry, it's for a suit."

"Fair enough, one never knows these days—and what colour is the suit?"

"Oh, I think I have a picture..." my aunt said, her hand now investigating the inside of her purse. "Shoot, no I don't...wait, yes I do!"

"Okay, great," Bert said as he received the image. "That looks sharp," he added, looking at me. "Now, just for the purpose of assisting me in assisting you, is there a reason you're purchasing the tie separately from the suit? Does the tie have a special meaning?"

"No," Aunty Susan said, "well, yes, I wanted to help him choose his tie since I missed out on picking out his suit."

"Ah, very nice," Bert said, "then I shall put my best man on the task—*Michael?*"

"Yes, boss?"

"You have the helm. I'm going to help this young man find an important tie."

"Oh..." Aunt Susan said, chuckling. "*You're* your best man?"

"Yeah, who'd you *think* I meant?"

Aunty Susan laughed again. "No, no, that makes sense. Just double-checking," she said, giving me a faux-sheepish look that made me laugh out loud.

Bert grinned and took us to the tie section of his operation.

"So," he said, looking at me, "what are your goals with this tie? Are you wanting it to make a statement, or do you want it to be aesthetically pleasing?"

"Oh, um, I guess—"

"Can't we have both?" my aunt said.

"Well," Bert said, "you can have an aesthetically pleasing tie that makes a statement on the side, or you can have a statement tie that looks okay, but, in either case, you need to pick a priority."

"I see," Aunty Susan said, a smile toying with her face.

"You're unsatisfied with the choices?" Bert said, matching the lip curl.

"Well," Aunty Susan said, "I just thought—"

"That because I have my best man on the job that you'd wouldn't have to decide."

Aunty Susan shrugged with a grin. "Well, I didn't want to say it, but *Yes*."

Bert chuckled. "I don't think you *minded* saying that at all."

Aunty Susan gave me another pretend-sheepish smile which again made caused me to laugh out loud.

"Actually," I said, "um, I don't really want to make a statement with my tie, so—"

"No, no, no," Bert said, walking towards his backroom, "let me see what I can do."

"He's funny, eh?" I whispered to my aunt when Bert was out of view.

"Oh, really, you think so?" my aunt replied.

That stunned me. "Yeah, I thought you were—weren't you joking with him?"

"Oh, yeah, I guess I was … But, yeah, I guess he's funny. So whaddya think of the ties so far?"

I smiled internally at that. If it weren't for my aunt's attempt to cover something up, I wouldn't have realized there was something to look for.

Twenty minutes later, we'd settled on a tie, and I felt sad for my aunt that her conversation with Bert was nearly done.

"I'll ring it up," Bert said to his assistant as he approached the till.

"Of course you will," Michael replied with a sarcasm that was palpable even to my unskilled sensors.

Bert loaded up his good-looking smile. "Oh, hey, by the way," he said, looking back at me, "you said you'd be interested if we had one of these in a slightly darker shade—"

"Oh, no, that's okay," I started to say before realizing I was getting in the way of a helpful possibility, "actually, yeah, that would be great."

Bert chuckled. "Okay, well, if you leave me your number, I'll see if I can track one down. If I do, I can let you—or your *benefactor*—know."

Aunty Susan laughed.

"Great," I said, my heart revving its engines. "Um, except, um, our answering machine is broken, so, maybe, yeah, could you call *her* if it comes in?" I said so with such awkwardness that I was sure Bert and my aunt would tease my obvious lie.

"Sure," Aunty Susan said instead, "my number's fine."

"Of course," Bert said, "I can adapt to that—I don't call me my *best man* for nothing."

I gave another full laugh at that one, as much to expunge my adrenalin as to indicate my amusement.

SOCIO-TEMPORAL NOTE: In case you weren't around during that time, futuristic reader, an answering machine was the analog precursor to the digital voice mail. By virtue of its moveable parts, it was a reasonable (although unconvincing, in this case) claim that it was out of order.

Spotlighting Up a Room

A couple months later, Per and I graduated from high school; a pair of weeks into our reprieve, Aunty Susan announced that she would be delivering a new man to the family for our inspection. Per and I were both pleased and intrigued to attend the gathering; it had been a long time since our favourite relative had modeled a new boyfriend. Indeed, all four Smiths—plus Per's shy-seeming new girlfriend, Nicolette—waited with a high level of anticipation for the new arrival in our life.

"Hello, Smith family!" Aunty Susan called as she let herself and her companion in.

"Hello, Smith aunty!" Per replied.

Around the corner, came the voice of my graduation tie salesman.

"Oh, *hi*," I said, suddenly nervous. *Would it be a betrayal of the couple's origin story if I admitted that I'd witnessed it?*

"Hey, bud," Bert said, "how are your ties treating you?"

"Good!" I said as though the question were sincere. "Yeah, that tie was great."

"Oh, *right*," Aunty Susan said, grinning as richly as I'd ever seen, "I guess I don't need to introduce you two. Um, for everyone else, this is Bert. He runs the famous Bert's Shirts & Skirts."

"Hi, Bert," my father said, "I'm Susan's brother, Paul."

"Nice to meet you—I'm Bert," was the big-smiled reply.

"I'm Mary," Mom said, "we've all probably met you in your store a couple times over the years, but I'm sure—"

"Oh, yes, I remember *you*," the visitor said. "I was just maintaining Bert-client privilege when I said it was 'nice to meet you.'"

Per chuckled. "You don't have to pretend to remember us. We can take it."

Bert chuckled back and then studied my brother. "Now, *you*, sorry, I don't remember."

Per and my aunt laughed out loud at that.

"You may have finally met your match, Per," Aunty Susan said.

"Touché," Per said with a merry nod. "So I'm Per, and this is Nicolette."

"Great to meet you both," Bert said.

Per's nod turned inquisitive. "So, Bert, you remember John *specifically*, eh? Is there a story there?"

"Actually, yeah, it's a funny story," Bert said, "we met when your aunt and John were shopping for graduation ties at my store."

"*Really?*" Per said, looking at me. "So why didn't you say you'd met him already?"

"Oh, um, well, I didn't realize he was the person we were meeting today."

"Okay, fine, but did you realize that they were into each other when you saw them together?"

"Um, I don't know—*maybe*."

"So why didn't you say anything to us about *that?*"

"Um, well, it seemed private."

My brother looked at my aunt with his best incredulous face.

"John," she said, shaking her head, "what's the point of being a witness to gossip-worthy material if you're not going to gossip about it?"

Bert laughed. "I'm a little hurt, John: was I not *a little* worthy of gossip?"

Per laughed too. I fake laughed. And we all sat down.

"So I hear you're in accounting, Paul?" Bert said.

"Yeah, I work at Krueger & Chen."

"Good business?"

"Yeah, they do pretty well. There's not a lot of room for growth in this town, but they're doing well enough that I'm not too worried about it."

"An interesting take. Remind my über-capitalist father never to hire you. He's all about infinite growth or perish."

"Fair enough," Dad said, "yeah, I suppose Mary and I are doing well enough that I don't know that I'd be willing to give up our family-friendly work schedules for greater growth."

"So, if the books balance in your life, what more do you want?"

"Groan," Per said.

"I aim to please," Bert replied with a grin at my brother. "No, I agree with you," he said, returning his high-powered attention to my father, "*infinite growth* is a specious system in the long run."

"Yeah, I don't know what the right answer is on that one," Dad said. "I've heard arguments on both sides."

"Well," Bert said with a chuckle. "I don't actually know what I'm talking about. I don't even understand my *own* bookkeeping."

"So who do you get to do your books?" Mom said.

"Oh, well, I had to teach myself."

"So you *do* understand your own bookkeeping," Aunty Susan said with a laugh

"Oh," Bert said, stumbling in his elocution for the first time in my observation, "well, I'm sure I make a plethora of errors."

"Are we really going to talk about accounting all night?" Per said. "Because, if we *are*, I think I might have to go put my head in a vice until my brain pops."

"Per!" Aunty Susan said, shaking her head with a grin. "That's awful."

"*Awful*, yes," Bert said, "but impressively so. What a vivid description. Have you considered being a writer?"

"I don't know, maybe," Per said, suddenly beaming. (I would have thought his self-delight would have been tempered by the fact that he had borrowed his line from his former friend/devil spawn, Jake).

"Per's always had a gift for expressing himself," his mom joined in.

"How about you, Bert?" Dad strangely interrupted the gush. "Um, how's your business doing?"

"We've always enjoyed your displays," Mom added.

"Thanks," Bert said, hesitating for a moment in case—it seemed to me—anyone else wanted to comment.

"Yeah, aren't those great?" Aunty Susan obliged. "Although," she said, "when I first saw your ...what should I call them?"

"Proprietary presentations," Bert supplied with a wink in his voice.

"Yeah, *that's* it," Aunty Susan said, giggling, "so, when I first saw your *proprietary presentations*, I thought they might be a bit much for this town."

"I don't think that's true," Mom said.

Aunty Susan waved her hand. "No, but, when I went in there, I realized that the proprietor *himself* was a bit much for this town, so it was actually very honest advertising."

"Well!" Bert said, grinning. "This is a startling revelation."

The hand waved again. "No, no, it's just that you *are* a big personality—and I think it's very honest that you don't hide that in your advertising."

"Hmm," Bert said, "I'm not sure yet whether I'm offended. In the meantime, go on."

A few of us laughed out loud. I was the leader of the laugh track. I was pleased that both Aunty Susan and Bert still seemed to appreciate her teasing him.

"So I hear you work in the library industry, Mary?" was Bert's next exploration.

"Yes," my mom said as Per made a show for Nicolette of putting his head in his imaginary vice.

"Wow," Bert said after interviewing Mom for a few minutes about her work, "I never realized how much goes into keeping those libraries afloat."

"Was it worth finding out?" Per said with his playful voice.

"*Peter*," Dad said, looking calmly at his son, "if you don't have anything nice to say—"

"Then I'll have nothing to say," Per said.

"Per likes things of a little faster pace," his mother helped out, "so working in a library all day sounds pretty stuffy to him."

Bert looked over at Per. "What sorts of high-pace things are you into?"

"Well," Per replied, suddenly serious, "I like skiing, dirt-bike riding—and I totally wanna try waterskiing."

"And I hope you join him on these adventures?" Aunty Susan said, looking at Nicolette.

"Um," Nicolette replied, "if he asks me to."

That made me smile. Despite her shyness, Nicolette could sometimes say a lot with very few words.

Aunty Susan tilted her head in response. "So *do* you ask her, Peter?"

"I bring her to lots of crap," he replied. "But some things are just guy things."

Aunty Susan raised her forehead at my brother.

"You know what I mean," he said, "it's just, like, they're not really Nicolette's thing. She's not gonna be into, like, dirt biking, but we meet up with the girls afterwards."

"Is that true?" Aunty Susan redirected to Nicolette.

"Yeah, um, we usually meet up with them afterwards."

That one made me laugh.

"But," Aunty Susan said, shaking her head with a smile, "what I meant was: is it true that you wouldn't be into dirt-biking?"

"Um, yeah, I guess not."

"A ringing endorsement for your conclusion, Peter," Bert said.

"Those boys go pretty fast," Mom noted. "It's very impressive to watch, actually, but I don't think a lot of girls would be interested in signing up."

"Exactly," Per said.

I looked at Nicolette who had a blank expression available in return.

"Maybe," Aunty Susan said. "But Nicolette and I aren't *most* girls, so we expect to be taken on one of these excursions, Per."

Per laughed. "Fine."

It was soon time for my turn in the focus of Bert's questioning.

"So, John, I hear you work at a bakery?"

"Yes," I said, having already prepared my answer, "it's a cool place to work. My boss is great, and I have cool co-workers."

"Ah, try *hot*," Per helped me out.

Bert turned to me for confirmation of the Per-say.

"Yeah, I'm the only guy there, so—"

"Not just *the only guy*," Per returned. "The only guy who isn't a smoking hot girl."

Aunty Susan laughed. "We're all very proud of John for being the first not-a-smoking-hot girl to work at the bakery."

I forced out a laugh in reply, hoping my time in the heat was nearly done.

But, before he would let me off his hook, Bert segued his interrogation to my impending college plans. I hadn't anticipated that line of questioning, so my answers were too short to assist Bert in generating conversation.

"How about you, Per?" he redirected. "Is there a university or college campus in your future?"

"Yeah," Per replied, "I'll go next year. I'm going to have some fun first, though."

"Speaking of which," Dad said, looking at Bert, "Susan tells me you spent a gap year traveling the world. How was that?"

"Well," Bert said, smiling, "it was everything I hoped for plus so many things I never expected. It was—"

"What was your favourite place to visit?" Mom asked.

"Gotta be Africa—" Bert started.

"Yeah," Aunty Susan took over, "Bert has an amazing talent for immersing himself in different cultures."

And, for the first time in their interaction, it occurred to me that something about the new couple's relationship was off balance.

That evening, Bert and Aunty Susan walked through the sort of temperate summer evening and star-flickering sky that sometimes makes people say romantic things they shouldn't.

A day later, my Aunty Susan announced to the Smith family that she was going to be living happily ever after with Bert. The intensity of my aunt's smiles made me glad for her, but I now understood the basis for my speculation that there was imbalance within the couple: it seemed to me that Aunty Susan *idolized* Bert, which struck me as a dicey way to start a marriage.

In contrast, my mother clearly saw no such room for doubt; instead, she chirped excitement with a level of enthusiasm that I'd thought was reserved only for Per's accomplishments. My father and my brother, meanwhile, were cheerful in their celebrations, but neither seemed to me be as excited as their congratulations implied.

Regardless, there wouldn't be much time for any of us to get used to the introduction of Bert into our guardianship. Within only four weeks, Bert had harnessed all of his entrepreneurial skills to produce one of the shiniest weddings our town had ever seen.

Chapter 16
Dullard vs. Charmer

Saying Uncle

The wedding of Bert Hardelean and Aunty Susan Smith was to be one of the biggest events in our town's recent history. It was held at our fresh-faced local park, which was bordered by a forest on one side and light roads on the other three. Five minutes before wedding time, all were quiet. Neither Bert nor his co-star had yet arrived. There was a chipper curiosity zipping around the crowd: it knew that Bert would be making a grand entrance. And that merry enthusiasm was supported by Annette the DJ (of Sound Thinking: DJ Services) who supplied emotionally invigorating music.

With three minutes to go before scheduled wedding time, Annette slowly turned the music down to nothing; the audience knew that its anticipation would soon be over. Three perfectly timed seconds after the silence had begun, a horse-drawn carriage trotted around a corner in the near distance. That was Annette the DJ's cue: she slowly reunited music with the crowd's ears. The artistic sounds were simple but poignant as they articulated Wagner's familiar *Wedding March* tune.

The crowd instantly knew that the steadily approaching vehicle contained their bride to be. *But, if the bride was in the carriage, where was the groom?*

Aunty Susan's vehicle slowed to a stop just in front of the park. The driver stepped down, opened the carriage door, and allowed Aunt Susan—wearing an elegant white dress—to step out. There was a murmuring of approval from the audience. Aunty Susan looked around her. *Where was Bert?* For a moment, she seemed worried, and so the crowd was worried that she was worried. The carriage driver stared into the distance and tipped his hat towards a large collection of trees. The audience swiveled its head.

One of the trees ruffled its branches in response. A grey horse poked its head out and soon revealed its passenger to be Bert, who was wearing a black suit and a white cowboy hat. The audience gasped, then laughed, then applauded.

When the curtain closed on the ceremonies, the audience was invited to travel fifty steps across the park to enjoy a buffet lunch in a spacious, circus-style tent. As the guests enjoyed mouthfuls of conversation about our star couple, Bert and his wife stayed outside and had choreographed photos taken with their families.

"All right," Hari the photographer said, "Mom and Dad stand next to Bert."

LINGUISTIC NOTE: In wedding photographer lingo, 'Mom and Dad' refer not to the photographer's *own* parents, but instead to the parents of the bride or groom.

"Bride's Family," was soon called up to the flash, and I felt like a puppet as Hari told me where to put my limbs. "Okay, nephew number one—no, the *other* one—can you move in a little closer to your brother? Good, now put your arms by your side. Tilt your head up."

If you don't mind me switching metaphors mid-description, patient reader, my muscles and I soon felt as if we were playing a game of standing *Twister.*

"All right, I think we got it," Hari announced to my relief. "Now just the bride and groom, please."

"Groovy," Bert said before kissing his bride on the cheek.

"*Interesting,*" she said, "I think I liked it better when I had the privacy of kissing you with your hat on."

"Good point, my dear," he said, looking around. "*Where did I leave it?*"

"You left it back at the signing table," I announced heroically. "I'll get it."

"Oh, thanks, John."

"*Aww*," Per said with a chuckle from his lounging spot on the grass next to Nicolette, "but *I* wanted to get it."

"You can get the next one, Peter," Bert replied with a wink.

When I found the hat, I put it on and started to jog it back to its owner; consequently, the wind grabbed onto the prize on its way by and knocked it off. I picked it up and carried it from there.

"Thanks, John," Bert said, offering me a handshake upon my return, "you have performed your first official duty as my new nephew."

"Oh, you're welcome, um, Bert," I said, not sure whether I was supposed to call him by his new title.

"I'm your *uncle* now," he replied. "You can call me that, if you want."

"Oh, okay."

"Try it on for size," he said, with his irresistible grin.

"Oh, okay, thanks, um, *Uncle Bert*."

Per laughed heartily at that. "John, you're such a pushover. Honestly," he said, looking at Nicolette (who half-smiled back), "he's such a pushover."

"Why do you say that?" I said, knowing that Per was right in general but not sure how I'd been pushed over in this case.

"You just *are*—if Bert told you to call him, I don't know, *Eddie Murphy*, you totally would."

Uncle Bert looked at Per with a sophisticated smile. "John is simply a considerate nephew who is respectful of his elders."

Per laughed again. "He's a pushover."

"I highly doubt that," Uncle Bert said, shaking his head in a way that made me suspicious of his sincerity. While he didn't *sound* sarcastic, the arc in his eyebrow and lip provoked me to surmise that he was amused by the accuracy of Per's assessment.

Famous First Words

Several hours after the wedding of Uncle Bert and Aunty Susan, the great tent was a flow with conversation as we awaited the return of our bridal stars.

The tent lights faded, leaving us in a cozy darkness.

"Ladies and gentlemen," Annette the DJ announced, "please

welcome, for the first time, Mr. and Mrs. Bert and Susan Hardelean!"

The wedding duo entered the fabric room and followed a neon-lit path through the heart of the applauding crowd to their head table.

As the couple arrived at their important seats, the audience began its ritual glass clinking. The bride and groom did as they were told and kissed festively. The lights then returned to full as the smooching stars sat down. Simultaneously, nineteen-year-old Annette the DJ stepped up to her microphone.

SHALLOW NOTE: Annette the DJ—if you must know, shallow reader—was kind on people's eyes. Her microphone—if you must also know—was adjacent to the head table.

"Good evening, everyone. My name is Annette Leung—I'll be your master of ceremonies this evening." She paused there to consider her audience. "How did I get the job, you're wondering? Well, one day, I'm passing through your sweet little town, and I spot a place called Bert's Shirts & Skirts—so I figure, 'What the heck?—*I'm low on skirts*,' so I decide to pop in to get one." Annette the MC paused again, allowing her audience to giggle with anticipation. "Well, I left Bert's Shirts & Skirts with five skirts, three shirts, two pairs of shoes, and an umbrella."

The audience laughed.

Bert grinned and whisper-shouted something to Annette.

She laughed. "Bert has just reminded me that the outfit I'm wearing *right now* is, in fact, a Bert's Shirts & Skirts' original."

The audience chuckled again.

Bert grinned and yelled, "Doesn't she look great?"

The audience cheered.

Annette laughed and curtseyed back. "So, anyways, I'm at Bert's Shirts & Skirts, and I pull out my wallet to see if I can afford my new wardrobe, and—as I do so—Bert spots my business card for Sound Thinking: DJ Services, and he hires me right then and there to be your MC for today."

The crowd nodded at Bert's familiar tendency towards in-the-moment decisions.

Annette smiled. "So, if it turns out that I'm not any good at this MC stuff, then you all know which impulsive groom is to blame."

The crowd giggled.

Per pointed out Bert for those who were confused.

Annette laughed generously at my brother's contribution. "Anyways, I'm like, 'Bert, do you always make important decisions this quickly?' And do you know what he said to me?"

The audience shook its head.

"Bert gives me one of his *Careful now* smiles, and he says to me, 'I knew the very moment I met my fiancé that she was going to be the person I was going to spend the rest of my life with.'"

Some in the crowd made "Aww" noises which led the majority to begin clinking glasses again.

Uncle Bert and Aunty Susan stood up to perform their duty.

"By the way," Annette said as the wedding lips unlocked, "Bert asked me to mention that all of tonight's kisses are sponsored by Bert's Shirts & Skirts."

The audience laughed.

"Anyways, without further ado, I would like to introduce you to the head table. Starting from my immediate right, we have the bride's nephew, John Smith."

The audience politely applauded while I tried to cover my nerves with a smile.

"Next to him is another of the bride's nephews, Peter Sm—"

"That's *Per* to you," my brother called out with a grin.

"What's that?"

"I go by *Per*, not Peter."

"I see," Annette said with a smile at my brother before sneaking a *What's with him?* glance at the rest of us.

The audience giggled.

"Anyways, so that's Per *'Don't call me Peter'* Smith."

Per stood up and blew kisses to the crowd.

The audience seemed amused by that, and they applauded much more approvingly than they had for me.

Annette continued on to introduce Per's nervous girlfriend, Per's parents, the bride & groom, the groom's parents, and finally a pair of our town's most recognizable celebrities.

As some enthusiastic applause for Fire Chief Marco died down, Annette retook the spotlight.

"The head table introductions," she said with a wink in her voice, "have also been brought to you by Bert's Shirts & Skirts."

The audience laughed politely again.

"Actually," Annette said, taking the microphone from its stand as she walked out from behind the podium. "Looking through the program here, I see that I'm going to have to use the slogan, 'Brought to you by Bert's Shirts & Skirts,' quite a few times. We've got the wedding dress, the cake cutting, the *bride*—all sponsored by Bert's Shirts & Skirts."

Bert led the audience giggles on that one.

"So, to keep me from getting exhausted, I'm going to need an assistant to help me with acknowledging our sponsor."

Annette then walked behind the head tablers, her eyes flickering. She travelled the length of the table and then all the way back, teasing the audience's anticipation until she finally stopped at the person closest to the podium. She stopped, that is, at me! *What the dullard did she think she was doing?* She was going to give a dullard a heart attack.

"Hello there, Mr. John Smith," she said, looking down at me.

"Hi," I squeaked into the microphone that she held in front of me.

"Would you mind helping me out?" she said, using a fraudulent question mark.

"No, I wouldn't mind," I replied, preparing myself for a social catastrophe.

"Thank you. So what I need from you is a fancy-dancy announcer voice so that I can call on you to say, 'Bert's Shirts & Skirts,' every time I mention our sponsor. Do you happen to have a fancy-dancy announcer voice?"

"Um—"

"Excellent! So can you give me a, 'Bert's Shirts & Skirts,' please?"

She slowly moved the microphone back to my face.

I gulped and decided that, since I didn't have a fancy announcer voice, my best option for faking it was to simply go for my deepest voice.

"**Bert's Shirts & Skirts,**" I said slowly to make sure I didn't trip over any of the words.

And, to my enormous surprise, the audience laughed.

"You weren't lying about that fancy announcer voice," Annette said.

Only a few people in the audience seemed to appreciate the humorous fact that I hadn't actually made such a claim, but most of them laughed anyway.

"Ladies and gentlemen," Annette returned, "how about a round of applause for our announcer, Mr. John Smith!"

The audience clapped merrily, and—although I realized that they were really just appreciating Annette—I couldn't stop myself from feeling a certain joy of temporary stardom.

"John, himself," Annette continued, "is brought to you by ..." And again she put the mic to my face.

"Bert's Shirts & Skirts," I repeated, and the audience was once again gigglingly pleased with the results. In fact, to my dismay, I even spotted my mom laughing. (She later told me that my fake announcer voice was remarkably announcer-like.)

"All right," Annette said, "who here is hungry?"

There was a lighthearted cheering war between the tables.

Annette giggled as she again took her microphone away from its stand. She walked into the eye of the tables, pretending to size them up so that she could determine the order of operations for food consumption.

"Hmm, you all seem so hungry. *How do I choose between you? Do you think it'd be unethical to accept bribes?"*

After Annette finished giving out the order of operations for meal gathering, she paused once more.

"I've been asked to mention that today's meal has been brought to you by ..." She tossed her cordless microphone a metre to me.

I caught it, took a moment to feel relieved that I hadn't bobbled it, and then I delivered my line.

The audience chuckled lightly one last time as it prepared to gather food.

Immediately after that interaction, I was again surprised to conclude that I felt good about my role in Annette's performance. Despite my near heart failure, being Annette's assistant had been fun: I only had the one line to remember, and—every time I delivered it—I got a laugh. But, with every second past that first self-satisfaction, I began to worry that I'd used a stupid voice that was more annoying than funny.

That noble contemplation distracted my food-collecting efforts, so I returned to the head table with a meagre meal in front of me.

"You should have gotten more, bro," Per informed me. "It'll be a while before the lineup dies down again."

"I'm fine," I said, confident that my nervous stomach couldn't handle too many contributions anyway. "So did you guys think I sounded silly with that 'Sponsored by Bert' thing?"

"A little," Per said, "but it was pretty funny."

"It was great!" Nicolette erupted. "Don't listen to him."

I liked Nicolette. Normally, her alleged shyness limited her conversation, but I noticed that she often rallied her voice if someone else's emotions were on the line.

"It was definitely funny," Per said, "but, bro, you should've gone full out. People want to drink and party and laugh at a wedding."

"I thought it was great," Nicolette intervened again. "And people laughed, so don't worry about it."

"Okay, I'll try not to," I said, but—before I could decide whether I was telling the truth—my eyes were assaulted by the sudden re-approach of Annette the MC to our station.

"Hey," she said with a gallant smile.

"Hey," Per replied for the group, allowing me to relax into my position as a neutral bystander.

"Thanks for playing along," the pretty MC said, looking at me.

"Oh, you're welcome. Thanks for inviting me."

"No worries," she said with another smile.

That made me nervous, so I was about to seek out a random thought to fill the empty air, but, just in time, Per jumped in.

"If you need any more help, I'm your man."

Annette nod-smiled her *thanks*, patted both of us on a shoulder, and left to visit Uncle Bert & Aunty Susan.

Following the mealtime, Annette retook the microphone. She began by introducing some speakers who were designed to toast the bride and groom. The toasters—my father for Aunty Susan, and the mayor for Uncle Bert—were not gifted in the ways of public speaking, but that didn't really matter: it just made Annette funnier by comparison.

After her concluding remarks about the dull speeches, Annette had the lights turned out, and she put on a slide show which featured the childhoods of Uncle Bert and Aunty Susan but starred the voice of Annette as she quipped funniness at every image.

"So, in this picture," she said for one popular instance, "Bert has just learned to ride a bike—and you can see he's pretty pleased with himself. He's already calculating how this will improve the profit margin on his paper route and upgrade delivery services for his lemonade stand."

Bert laughed proudly at every joke.

Soon, it was time for Uncle Bert and Aunty Susan to stand at the microphone.

"First of all," Bert said, "I'd like to thank Ms. Annette Leung here for doing such a wonderful job as our MC."

The audience applauded its starlit.

"*Annette*," Uncle Bert returned as the clapping faded, "has been brought to you by..." he put the microphone in front of my face.

"**Bert's Shirts & Skirts**," I reported to the audience's continued amusement.

Uncle Bert's subsequent speech was predictably charming. He spoke of great admiration for his bride as well as his parents and his new in-laws with words that were poetic, insightful, and good-looking.

Uncle Bert concluded with a tip of his glass to the audience.

"To all of you."

"To all of us," we replied with chuckles as we tapped our glasses together.

Glancing the Night Away

After the speeches, a live retro band was called to the stage to perform their wares, and so many in the great tent decided to try their feet at some dancing. Others wandered around so as to visit with each other. But neither dancing nor mingling seemed to me like the appropriate behaviour of a dullard, so I stayed put, by myself, at the head table.

It's funny how a space can transform in moments from the centre of attention to the centre of solitude. But I didn't mind sitting alone at the table: it held great memories for me. It was there—not long earlier—that I had entertained an entire audience with my instructed wit. I smiled as I remembered the audience's laughter at the humour I'd borrowed from Annette the MC.

She was quite a girl, that Annette the MC. In fact, if I'd thought there were any way in reverse hell that she might be interested in me, I would have happily started up a crush on her. But, since the possibility of an Annette-to-dullard inclination was not plausible, I decided not to torment myself with a dullard-to-Annette contemplation. Instead, I watched my sweetheart chat with strangers, and I imagined what I'd say to her if it were me she was visiting.

Perhaps I would tell her how much I appreciated her willingness to lend me her funny words. I could then flash some modesty and tell her that she really should have chosen someone more extroverted to be her assistant—my brother, Per, for instance.

I smiled as I allowed myself to imagine the charismatic MC swooning in the presence of my humility. While my mind was busy creating that epic conversation between Annette and dullard, I accidentally let my eyes fix on Annette the person. That meant—to any observer who wasn't me—that my smile at the *imagined* Annette looked just like an *actual* smile at the real Annette. That wouldn't have been so bad if it weren't for the fact that, just as I was smiling in her direction, Real Annette looked my way, and—without any thought of my welfare—she smiled right back!

Quite rightly, I panicked in reply and immediately looked away, but the emotional damage had already been done. I was having enough trouble not building a crush on Annette when I knew that she'd never be interested in me. *How was I supposed to maintain my non-crush if she was going to respond to my blank stares with sweet smiles?*

Seconds later, I allowed myself to glance back at Annette just in case she was still looking my way. Nope. She was chatting with another guest. Fair enough. Now that I thought about it, I'd probably misunderstood her smile. Surely it was meant for someone else or intended to mock me. Yes, that sounded about right. So I returned to my prudent non-crush on her. But, just then, she looked my way again, and—*holy ghostwriter*—she smiled again! Okay, this time, I was sure the message was meant for me. I let the corners of my mouth rise up to impersonate a smile back. She chuckled cheerfully and then looked away.

Okay, that made more sense: her smile was not *mocking* me; it was empathizing with me. She was using her plentiful charm to placate my solo status. Yes, yes, that made sense. And this time I'd learned my lesson: I was not going to peek back at her again; after all, if I received one more smile from her, I could no longer promise not to fall straight into a maximum crush on her.

But, as I debated the reasonableness of that no-looking-back decision, my peripheral vision caught the image of someone walking towards my solo head table.

'Who could that be?' my reflexes wondered, and I inadvertently peeked up to see that—oh my ghostwriter—it was Annette. I forced a smile, and she smiled back for a third time! I looked away. *What was she doing walking towards the head table?* I was the only one *at* the head table. Nevertheless, I could hear Annette the MC's footsteps coming closer. *Was it possible that she was intending to talk to me?*

I stared at my empty wine glass as if it were the most fascinating beverage furniture I'd ever seen. The footstep sounds kept coming closer, but I just stayed focused on that empty wine container.

"How are you?" the sudden voice of Annette seemed to arrive out of nowhere.

'BANG!' my knee replied, hitting itself against the wedding table.

"Ouch—I'm good, thanks," I said, smiling as best I could.

Annette grinned at me. "Thanks again for being a good sport earlier."

Wow, apparently I was being invited into a real conversation with the person with whom I'd been having an imaginary chat—which actually was convenient because it meant that I had a lot of pre-tested material with which to work.

"Oh, you're welcome. It was kind of fun—but, actually, you probably would've been better off picking my brother. He's really funny."

"*Actually*," Annette said, strangely serious, "I picked you on purpose because you seemed like the kind of guy who could play along without trying to show off."

"Oh, um—"

"I needed someone who would do *exactly* what I told them—otherwise, it wouldn't've worked."

"Oh," I said again, dumbfounded by the notion that there could be a positive aspect to my dullness.

Annette shrugged with a smile. "*Anyways*," she said, and—without warning—she grabbed a chair and sat herself next to me. "So what're you up to this summer?"

I tried to hide my gulp as I replied. "Um, I work at a bakery, but I think I'm going to college in the fall."

"Awesome, what're you gonna study?"

Oh. I hadn't really thought about what I was going to investigate. I figured they'd let me know when I got there.

"Um," I said, searching for a cliché to help clarify, "I guess I'll just play it by ear."

"*Ear's to that*," Annette said, raising her beverage.

"*Ears*," I said with a giggle as we tapped glasses.

Annette's face turned sheepish. "Sorry, I grew up in a family of punners, so ..."

"I like puns."

"Really?" Annette said, raising her glass again. "Well, in that case, long live puns!"

I laughed. But, with no humour to add, I ventured to change the subject. "Um, by the way, you're a very good MC."

Annette nodded. "I know—it's because I'm really talented."

"Um, right, yeah," I said, trying not to look startled by the sudden boastfulness, "yeah, that makes sense."

Annette laughed. "It's not that I'm arrogant. It's just that emceeing is in my genes—my mom's a doctor, you know."

"Right, yeah, of course—wait, what's that got to do with being an MC?"

"Ah, *MC* ... *MD* ... they're only one letter apart."

I laughed out loud. "Oh, I see. Fair enough."

Annette smiled. "So how long've you known Bert?"

"Not long, actually. My aunt only introduced him to us like a month ago."

"Wow, that must've been weird going from stranger to relative in only a few weeks."

"Yeah, exactly, that's what I was thinking yesterday at the rehearsal dinner."

Annette furrowed her brow. "Don't you think that's a weird concept? I mean we've been having dinners all our lives. Who really needs to *practice* having dinner? I mean, I know it's a wedding, but really."

I laughed again at Annette's brilliance, but—since there was no way in dull heck that I was going to match her wit—I endeavoured instead to be the perfect straight man to her comedy stylings.

"Actually," I said with a smile on my voice, "I think 'rehearsal dinner' is supposed to mean the dinner *after* the rehearsal."

"Ohhh," she said with elite comedic timing that made me chuckle, "I guess that makes more sense."

There was then a tiny but powerful pause in the conversation. Annette smiled at me. I smiled back. How strange. I now felt comfortable smiling at Annette. In fact, you probably won't believe this, skeptical reader, but I think I even felt comfortable talking to her. She'd somehow tricked me into putting my nerves away for the conversation.

"Anyways," she said, "whaddya think of your aunt's wedding dress?"

"I like it."

"Me too, but, you know, I don't know about wearing *white* to a wedding. I mean, with all this food and wine around, somebody's bound to spill something on that nice white dress—and then she can never wear it again."

"I guess you're right," I said, giggling some more.

Annette smiled. "So how long have you known Susan?"

"Oh, um, all my life."

"Oh, right, she's your actual aunt. You usually get those at birth, don't you?"

"Yeah, I think so."

"Fair enough, so how long have you known your parents?"

I almost answered the question before I spotted that it was a follow-up joke.

As I laughed, I realized why I was so relaxed chatting with Annette: she wasn't visiting with me because she was intrigued by what I had to say; instead, she was using me as a practice audience for her comedy. Therefore, since my particular content didn't matter, the pressure was off me to say interesting things: Annette was only looking for key words from which to direct segues to her cleverness.

In fact, an hour into our conversation at the secluded head table, it seemed to me that, against all plausible expectations, Annette's uninterested conversation might have actually turned into uninterested attraction. She appeared, that is, to be so impressed with my ability to be her comedic punch-lining bag that she seemed to have concluded that I'd be a handy guy to have around. That was an ego-shaking discovery: even though I sensed that Annette liked me more for what she said when she was around me than for what I contributed, I couldn't stop myself from feeling significantly complimented by her alleged approval.

By the ninetieth minute of our conversation, Annette the MC and I were sitting closer together. She was now seen touching my arm every second or third time she approached a punch line.

Not long later, Uncle Bert invaded our sanctuary. "Hey, you two," he said. "You seem to be having quite the conversation over here."

"Not really," Annette said. "I'm bored outta my mind here. John's far too sweet," she added, touching my foot with hers, "to hold a girl's attention."

I blushed.

Uncle Bert smiled. "Well, John, my new nephew, I have a less daunting proposition for you: Annette here has agreed to housesit for me while I'm on my honeymoon. But Annette's a big-city girl, and I need someone to help her with the lawn mowing and yard work."

"What's *lawn mowing*?" Annette said with a big-city girl accent. "Is that, like, a type of cow noise?"

Uncle Bert and new nephew laughed.

"Actually," Annette said, now touching my ankle with her foot, "it would be nice to have someone around to keep me company while I'm babysitting Bert's ex-bachelor pad."

Uncle Bert smiled again. "So, John, whaddya say?"

Annette touched my leg once more to help me with my decision.

"Um, okay, I'll help."

Chapter 17
Dullard vs. Crush

The Confidential Confidence

As anyone who's not used to being flirted with can tell you, attractive reader, the day after believing you've received special attention is usually one of second-guessing whether it really happened. Surely, that is, Annette the MC had been simply bored or clumsy when she crossed our touch barrier.

Nevertheless, as I finished lawn mowing for the first time a few days later at Uncle Bert's, Annette approached me in well-tailored shorts and t-shirt and asked if I wanted to hang out.

So there I was, for the second time in only two months, sitting on a couch next to a beautiful girl. But this was no Stacy. Annette's prettiness was free to roam happily through my mind without any concerns that I couldn't stand her. In fact, Annette's high level sense of humour was not, as far as I could remember, completely out of the great Ashley's range.

"So what kind of girls do you like to date?" she asked.

I didn't want to startle Annette with my previously empty dance card, so I decided it wouldn't be a lie if I claimed my co-worker Stacy as a previous date since I had, in theory, been on a date with her.

"Well, the last girl I dated was, um..." Suddenly I felt embarrassed about my choice of previous date.

"She was what? A spy?"

I laughed. "No, um—"

"Then why all the secrecy?"

"Well, it's just...I shouldn't really have gone out with her."

"Why?"

"Um, because I didn't really like her."

"I see," Anette said with a grin. "So why *did* you, then?"

"Because she asked me to."

Annette laughed, which was unusual for her when I was the one talking. "So—*what?*—are you saying you could never turn a girl down?"

"Well, I *would have*, but I didn't know for sure that it was going to be a date, and she told me her friends were gonna be there, so—"

"Were they?"

"Not really."

"Not *really?*"

"Not at all, I guess."

Annette giggled again. "So her friends weren't really there, and she corners you, and what happens?"

"Um, not a lot."

"Did you kiss her?"

"Not really."

Annette laughed. "John! There are some things that 'Not really' doesn't apply to. If someone asks you if you like dancing or, I don't know, sports, you can say, 'Not really.' But I'm afraid it doesn't work with whether you kissed someone or not. It also doesn't work for questions like, 'Are you pregnant?', um, 'Do you wear a toupée?', and, 'Have you ever killed someone with an axe?'"

I giggled at the monologue. "I see your point."

"So," Anette said, slowing her cadence, "I ask the question again: did you or did you not lock lips with the girl you did not like?"

"I did not."

"Then, if you never even kissed her, you didn't date her."

"But I'm pretty sure we were *on* a date."

"How many dates?"

"Just one."

"Then you went on a date with her; you didn't *date* her."

"Oh."

"I'm just telling you this so you don't feel bad—you looked guilty about going out with a girl you didn't like, but I don't think you need to worry about it."

I nodded. "Oh, okay, sounds good to me."

"So how'd it end?" Annette said.

"Um, I sort of—"

"Now hold that 'sort of'—make sure it applies this time before you use it."

I laughed. "Good point. I told her that I didn't think we were a good match."

"Very bold. How'd she take it?"

"Um, she sort of…sorry, she *fully* got kind of angry at me, and she told me she was just trying to give me a thrill."

Annette let out a snort. "What a bitch. What, was she totally gorgeous?"

"I don't know."

Annette giggled. "You're honestly going with, 'You don't know'?"

"Well, um, she was very physically good-looking but not attractive—you know what I mean?"

"Oh, she had an ugly face?"

"No," I said, laughing, "she just wasn't a very nice person."

"Oh, right, that inner beauty stuff. I forgot about that."

There was then a brief pause between us—long enough for me to notice that my heart was thumping.

"You know, John," Annette said, "that story doesn't give a girl much confidence."

"Why?" I said, offended on her behalf.

"Because, apparently, your willingness to hang out with me tonight is no guarantee that you *like* me."

"Oh."

I paused there to consider the math of Annette's statement. If my calculations were correct, Annette was implying that she wanted me to prove that I liked her in a way that I hadn't connected with Stacy. My math seemed irrefutable. *But did I have the courage to initiate such evidence?* For a cruel moment, I recalled my many lost opportunities with Ashley. Enough of regret, I thought.

Annette smiled at me.

I smiled back, shrugged, and—with another thump in my chest—I went in for a kiss.

Don't worry, pessimistic reader, my math was right: Annette the MC was not averse to returning the gesture.

CURIOUS NOTE: My ghostwriter wonders if you're wondering, curious reader, whether the kiss took us any further into affection—*how many bases might have been reached*, as they say. Well, first of all, my ghostwriter and I are both Canadian, and so we use only hockey metaphors, not baseball-flavoured revelations, in this autobiography. Second, what kind of a book do you take this for, indelicate reader? My ghostwriter and I both believe in the book characters' bill of rights (BCBR) to keep such details private, and, therefore, we are not going to tell you if the referee called any penalties during the game. However, if you think such details matter to your readerly understanding, literary reader, we trust you to make your best inference.

A little while later, I felt Annette's face relaxing on my shoulder as we watched TV. I could see no way to improve upon life.

That elite feeling was matched, amazingly, the next evening by the look on Annette's lips when I arrived at Uncle Bert's.

"Hey, you," she said, smiling perfectly.

That put a fuzzy feeling on my cheeks. I'd always wanted to be *Hey-You-ed* by a girl.

"Hi," I replied, soaking in the success for a moment before sneaking in for a kiss.

Strangely, being an Annette-approved suitor of Annette the MC had more sway with my confidence than any previous achievement. Neither learning to speak nor to ride a bike nor graduating from high school had had such an influence on my spirits. For you see, intrigued reader, it seemed to me that, if a girl as smart and funny as Annette was not outraged by thoughts of romance with me, then perhaps I couldn't be all boring.

Meanwhile, I decided that it would be best if I waited a while to tell my uninterested Sweet On You colleagues and my equally non-inquiring family about the romance that I'd found at Uncle Bert's place. You'd think that my family might have noticed that I went to cut Bert's grass more often than the timid green space would seem to need. Or, better yet, they might have spotted the fact that the yard work frequently took me into the evening long past prime yard working hours.

I decided, though, that my family's lack of interest in me was probably for the best: if Per had discovered that I was seeing someone, he would surely have felt a need to investigate such an oddity. As comfortable as I was with Annette the MC, I didn't feel ready yet for Per to come over and tease me in front of her.

Now, worry not, concerned reader: even though Per wasn't able to poke at me for a relationship he didn't know existed, my apparent lack of girlfriend did give him the comedic material he needed for ongoing mocking of me around his own girlfriend.

One evening, I was surprised when I got home to find my parents visiting with Per and Nicolette in the kitchen.

"Oh, hi, Nicolette," I said. "How are you?"

"Pretty good, thanks," she said in her usual sweet but subdued voice.

Nicolette was Per's most shy girlfriend so far, which made me feel less timid when I was around her because I felt I should avoid increasing her anxiety with my own.

"How are you liking your new job?" I said.

"Oh, it's good, thanks."

"Are the customers driving you crazy yet?"

"A little, yeah."

"Like how?" Per said.

"Well, sometimes they get mad at me for like policy stuff, but I don't have any say in the setup of those policies."

Per nodded. "Yeah, people are idiots. So are you, like, ever tempted to like yell at a customer?"

"Um, no, not really."

Per chuckled. "You're too nice."

"I don't think that's true," Nicolette said, anxiety crossing her face.

"What? I'm just saying: if you let people walk all over you, they will."

"If you say so."

"So how about you, John?" my dad said. "What have your customers been up to lately?"

I was glad to be given an opportunity to babble over Nicolette's discomfort.

"Actually, there's this one woman. She's always annoyed no

matter what I say to her. Like, yesterday, when I asked if she wanted a bag, she said sarcastically, 'No thanks, I think I can carry *one* item.' But then today she was just as sarcastic when I *didn't* offer her a bag."

At that moment, I was pleased to notice that Nicolette seemed to be wearing a smile of recognition.

"Good story," Per interrupted with a laugh. "You have too much time on your hands, bro."

"Why?"

"Um, I don't know, I'm thinking maybe you need to get a girlfriend so you can tell better stories."

"*Be nice*, Peter," our mom said.

Per giggled to Nicolette. "My brother's never had a girlfriend."

"Oh ...how do you know that?"

"Um, I think he'd've told me if he had a girlfriend."

"But ...maybe it's a secret."

"Trust me, there's no girl. I'd know. Am I right, John?"

"Well," Dad said, "if it's a secret, then maybe he doesn't *want* to tell us."

"Exactly," Mom said; although I sensed her credulity was being tested by the wild speculation.

Per laughed. "See what you started, Nic? Next time, just take my word for it."

For a moment, I thought Nicolette was about to finally have a rant at Per; but, instead, she smiled and retreated to shyness.

Meanwhile, Nicolette's insight—or lucky speculation—about my romance had gained her my admiration. In spite of the fact that Nicolette's inability to voice more than a few words at a time sometimes made her challenging to be around (in the same way that I imagined myself to be a difficult companion), her thoughtfulness made me like her.

Don't Bring a Band-Aid to a Knife Fight

Despite the secretive nature of our romance, Annette the MC and I quickly became similar to a couple. In the evening, we would both return home (i.e. Uncle Bert's place) from our jobs (Sweet On You for me and a DJ shop at a nearby town for her) as if we were two halves of a marriage coming home to rub each other's feet—although, admittedly, her feet were generally more sore than mine, so they got most of our attention.

RATIONALIZING NOTE: Not to worry, protective reader, I was not at all concerned that my girlfriend might be a wee bit self-focused. She had the responsibility of being the sole provider of personality in our relationship: the least I could do was take on the non-skilled labour.

So, as I would contentedly try to press the day's tension out of Annette's feet and neck, we'd listen, riveted, to her day's experiences; we'd agree with her amusing indictments of the behaviours of her co-workers; and we'd generally feel good about herself.

One post-workday, though, Annette broke our pattern.

"Hey, John-John," she said, grinning at the weed whacker and me as she got out of her car.

"Hi," I said, turning off the grass cutting machine before suddenly turning off my smile. "What happened?" I said, staring at a professional-looking bandage on her hand.

Annette shrug-grinned. "Good question. Some people say the earth started with a big bang, but I think it was more of a little whimper."

"But what happened to your hand?"

"Oh *that*. Funny story, that. We got some new equipment in, and I'm opening the boxes with a knife—and I'm doing pretty well until Malcolm comes in and starts talking to me. *What am I supposed to do?* He's my boss, so I focus my attention on him instead of what Mr. Knife is doing."

I grimaced.

Annette tilted her head and eyebrows. "Why the sour face?"

"Oh, because—"

"You're assuming I *cut* myself with the knife?"

"Yeah, sorry."

"You shouldn't assume. Although, in this case, you're totally right. The tape gets caught on the knife, so I yank it, and—whoopsie—the box seems like it's bleeding."

I grimaced again.

Annette giggled. "Yeah, I'm with you on *that* sour face. It hurt like hell—although, it was a pretty good anatomy lesson. I got to see the inside of my hand!"

"Oh my God. Did you go to the hospital?"

"Yeah, Malcolm took me to emergency, which he wasn't too happy about."

"What'd he say?" I said with a fully crinkled forehead.

"Oh, you know, he kept muttering something about me needing to pay better attention to what I was doing and that he didn't have time for this. I don't remember. I wasn't really paying attention. I was more interested in my sliced-up hand."

"Yeah, *I should say so*. Are you okay? Does it hurt still?"

"Yeah, but it's good practice for the next time I cut myself."

"Why would you cut yourself again?"

Annette rolled her eyes at me. "Did we forget our sense of humour at home today?"

"Oh, sorry, it's just, you know, I don't like seeing you in pain."

"I'm a big girl, John … God, what's the big deal? Oops, I cut myself. Why's everyone making such a big deal? If a guy cuts himself, it's like, 'Oh well, *boys'll be boys*.' But, when I do it, it's like, 'Oh, no, she's so fragile. We must protect her from herself.'"

"Sorry, I just—it looks like it hurts—is there anything I can do? Do you need more bandages or painkillers or something?"

"No, I don't like taking drugs."

"Okay, but is there anything I can get you? I'm happy to go to the store."

"*No*," Annette said, suddenly staring at me. "Is there another word that would make things more clear for you?"

That one hit me in the stomach. "Sorry, yeah, you're right—sorry."

Annette sighed and her voice softened. "Thank you anyway, John-John. But, just for future reference, if I say I don't want something, you can trust me that I know my mind better than you do. I've been living in this brain all my life."

"Okay, yeah," I said, trying to hide my gulping throat, "that makes sense—sorry."

Twenty minutes later, I peered my sheepish face into the house. Annette was watching TV.

"Hey," I said when a commercial landed on screen, "I've gotta go to the store to pick up a couple things. Any chance you'd like me to get you some ice cream? That's what my mom used to get us when we were injured."

Annette looked up and manufactured a smile. "No, that's all right, thanks," she said with her flattest tone.

"Okay," I said, my chest fluttering with sorrow.

When I returned from the store with my trip-justifying purchases, Annette seemed to have fully recovered from my earlier drug-pushiness.

"*Hey*," she said, "where's my ice cream?"

"Oh, I thought you didn't want any."

"John, John, John...these words you speak never apply to ice cream."

I could tell Annette was being funny, but her earlier annoyance had me feeling too serious to laugh.

"But I thought you said I should trust you if you said—"

Annette shook her head with a smile. "Okay, I'm gonna let you in on a little secret. Girls have two types off communication. There's direct verbal communication—you've got the hang of that one. But, when it comes to ice cream, we don't wanna have to admit *out loud* that we want some. So, when I said, 'No, thanks,' I clearly meant, '*No* to me having to *ask* for ice cream, but *thanks* for getting it for me anyway.'"

Finally I laughed.

Annette grinned back. "Ahah, you brought your sense of humour back with you. Welcome back, John's sense of humour."

Oddly, I felt there was a tiny tone of condescension in that remark, but I decided to ignore the feeling.

"Well," I said, "I'm just gonna finish up the weed whacking, and then I'll see you inside."

When I returned again, Annette looked up at me curiously.

"How's the silent weed whacking going?"

I shrugged and handed her a small tub of ice cream. "I went shopping again instead."

"Very cute," she replied with a partial smile. "I'm impressed that you did it without me having to ask this time, but I still had to directly hint for it, so I don't know if I can give you credit for being fluent in girl yet."

I shrugged. "I wasn't really looking for credit. I just wanted to cheer you up."

"Okay," Annette said, full smirk, "whatever you say."

I again felt irritated by that line of humour, considering that I really did just want to improve my girlfriend's spirits, but I decided that both her self-inflicted physical wound and her boss-inflicted mental wound were enough to justify her condescending discourse.

The next day, my work ethic at the bakery was distracted by thoughts of Annette's romance ethic. Her behaviours hadn't been so harsh that her injured mood couldn't account for them, but a paranoid quiver in the back of my mind warned me that they represented something more significant.

"Hey, John," Amy interrupted my speculation, "guess what J.P. said to me?"

"I don't know," I said, tempted to guess something snarky about her latest obnoxious boyfriend, but, luckily, I didn't have the talent to fulfill my inclination.

Amy shook her head. "He's all like, 'Amy, you talk too much.'"

"Ouch, why would he say that?"

Amy sighed. "I don't know. I was trying to get him to agree to meet my friends, but he didn't wanna talk about it because he was 'watching the game,' but I was totally waiting till between the plays like my step-dad always says."

"Hmm," I said, "yeah, that's strange. I would think—if I was someone's boyfriend—I'd, I don't know, I think I'd want to hear what my girlfriend wanted to say."

Amy's face turned extra serious. "So you don't think he's into me?"

"Um, well, I don't know, but, if he *is*, I don't think he's showing it very well."

"You're right: if he's into me, he should be interested in what I have to say. I'm gonna tell him that."

That sounded to me like the catalyst for a breakup conversation, so I shrugged and said nothing to dissuade my semi-friend.

As we worked on our own for the next half hour, I smiled at the superiority of my Annette relationship to any of Amy's couple-ups.

I then smirked at my arrogance and decided I'd better double-check it for justification. It was an unfortunate contemplation: the quiver in the back of my mind suddenly broke free, and I realized that, if *I* had injured myself at work and had taken some criticism from my boss for it, the one person who could have reinvigorated my mood would have been Annette. In contrast, her displeasure with my attempts to sway *her* spirits demonstrated that I had little such influence on her.

Paperclipped Apart

I arrived at Bert's home that late-afternoon to find Annette neither in her work clothes nor her post-work relaxation clothes; instead, she looked casually decorated for visiting.

"How are you, John-John?" she said with a smile. "I'm going out with friends tonight."

"Oh, okay," I said, wondering why I wasn't invited. Perhaps Annette was trying to avoid putting early-girlfriend pressure on me (in impressive contrast with Amy's immediate demands on her boyfriends). "Um," I said, "I guess I'll stay here and watch the place, then."

Annette shrugged. "You don't have to. I'll be back later to check on it. I'm sure it can spend an evening by itself."

Hmm, I felt that I had made it clear—with my offer of house-watching—that I had little better to do than house-watching that evening and, therefore, could join Annette and friends without feeling burdened. But perhaps Annette was looking for more evidence that I wouldn't be offended by such an invite.

"You okay going by yourself?" I offered.

"Of course. I've been going to things by myself since I was in Girl Guides."

"How long ago was that?" I said, smiling in anticipation of comedy.

"Last year," she obliged.

I laughed on cue. Indeed, it seemed to me that we'd made a humorous breakthrough in negotiations. But Annette declined to finalize our deal.

"So," she said instead, "do you want me to drop you off at your house on the way?"

As we drove, there was a loud silence between Annette and me.

"Um," I said, "so which friends are these?"

My alleged girlfriend launched into a series of biographies that, for the most part, I'd already heard, which was convenient because the familiarity allowed me to keep up while simultaneously pondering why Annette didn't want to introduce me to her friends.

But the flow of my decadent negativity was interrupted by a clever remark from Annette, which, in turn, provided me with an epiphany. Perhaps Annette's friends were brilliant like her, in which case, maybe she hadn't invited me to meet them because she thought I might be intimidated by such a collection of elite people. Yes, I could live with that explanation.

As it would turn out, Annette was to spare me such a daunting scenario two more times over the next few days; each protection reinfected my confidence. I started to wonder if the only reason she'd acquired me was so that she wouldn't be by herself while she was house sitting in an unfamiliar town.

That hypothesis was supported on a Thursday evening when I arrived at Uncle Bert's to find an odd bit of circumstance. Annette was dressed in the fanciest outfit I'd seen her in since she'd starred in Bert's wedding (that wasn't the odd part—wait for it, impatient reader).

"Hey, John-John," my sweetie said, "I'm going to the city. I'm meeting my friend Malinda for dinner."

"Oh, okay," I said, referring my mind to Annette's high school stories. "*Malinda*—she's the girl who won that big academic award, right?"

Annette nodded with a big smile. "Yeah, good memory."

"Yeah, it's funny," I said. "The people in your stories start to seem—"

Annette's mobile phone rang just then; she grabbed it without delay.

"Hello . . .? Hey you, I'm just about out the door ..." My eavesdropping ears then detected a change in the mood of the conversation. "Well, can't you just help her with it later?" Annette said, sounding strangely whiny. And she continued in that voice for another minute before finally accepting the bad news that she'd just have to hang out with her boyfriend for the evening. She hung up and looked at me with a scowl. "Damn," she said, "I was really looking forward to this. I never go to nice restaurants."

I, meanwhile, was too disappointed (by Annette's inability to grasp the obvious replacement) to feel much sympathy.

"Yeah, that's too bad," I tried.

"Hey, do *you* want to go?" Anette said.

"Oh," I said, suddenly wishing I'd been more compassionate, "um, yeah—if you want me to?"

"Yeah, let's go."

It was a delightful moment: I was finally invited to an event reserved for Annette's clever friends, and yet I wouldn't have to go to the trouble of being intimidated by them since they wouldn't be there.

Sadly, though, twenty minutes into our drive to the city, Annette received another call from Malinda who announced that the something that had come up had come down and that she could make it for dinner, after all.

"Awesome!" Annette told the phone with more enthusiasm in her voice than on her face. "But, um, the guy I'm seeing's with me now, so it'll be three of us."

In that voice tone of Annette's, I reminded me of an annoying kid brother being included by parental force into his older sibling's important teenager gathering.

Annette ended the call and looked at me with an eye roll. "So Malinda can come, after all."

"Yeah," I said, "she can't make up her mind, can she?"

"Nope."

"Well, it'll be cool to meet her after hearing your stories."

Annette nodded coldly. "Malinda's very smart. She's just finished her first year at university, and she made the dean's list every semester."

"Good for her," I said.

But my ghostwriter informs me that I was missing Annette's point. *We weren't praising Malinda; we were preparing for her.*

We arrived at the appointed restaurant to find Malinda already waiting for us at a table. (If you must know, ever shallow reader, Malinda's appearance was somewhere between plain and attractive.) She looked up from a book and gave Annette a warm, "Hello, Beautiful."

"Hi, Brilliant," Annette retorted.

Malinda's face turned serious curious. "What happened to your hand?"

"Oh, just cut myself shaving," Annette said.

"How?" Malinda said.

"You know how it is—the razor has trouble getting around the knuckles."

"You really shave your hands?"

"No, sorry," Annette said. "Just trying to be funny. Anyway, this is John."

"Hey, John," a crisp but friendly voice replied. "So nice to meet you."

"You too," I said as we sat down.

"What are you reading?" Annette asked her friend.

"*Gulliver's Travels*," Malinda said. "Jonathan Swift—he's so funny."

I looked at Annette; I was anticipating her making a pun-ly play on the author's name, but, instead, she went with a flat, "Why, how's he funny?"

"He's so dry. He can say the strangest things with a straight face. For instance, have you read his *Modest Proposal*?"

"No, I'd like to, though."

"Have *you*, John?" Malinda said looking at me.

"No, I haven't read it either," I replied, pleased to be asked.

"Here, I'll read a bit of it for you," Malinda said, flipping through her book.

I smiled at Annette. She stared back.

"Okay," Malinda said, sitting up in her chair. "Here we go. He says:

> *I have been assured by a very knowing American of my acquaintance in London, that a young healthy child well nursed, is, at a year old, a most delicious nourishing and wholesome food, whether stewed, roasted, baked, or boiled; and I make no doubt that it will equally serve in a fricasee, or a ragoust.*

Annette laughed when Malinda finished. "That's hysterical," she said with a wide-brimmed smile.

I, however, was unable to find any such hysterics in the writing. I wasn't sure what was so funny about having a *boiled baby* for dinner.

"You don't think it's funny?" Malinda said, looking at me with apparent interest.

"Um, I don't quite understand it."

Annette swung a look at me. "It's funny, John."

Malinda offered a smiley grimace. "It seems I should've given you some historical background. You see, Swift begins the piece by characterizing the poverty in Ireland. His era had small children begging for food on the streets. But it's a satire, so what he does is he writes in a very casual manner about the terrible nuisance of having so many abandoned and malnourished children bothering the good citizens of Ireland. And he proposes that, by eating the poor children, the upper class would rid themselves of a nuisance while simultaneously providing themselves with some very nice meals."

I nodded sincerely. "Okay, I think I get it now."

"Basically," Malinda said, "I'd characterize *A Modest Proposal* as an exaggerated depiction of how the upper class treated their poor."

Malinda then read another portion of the proposal, and, that time, the talk of boiled babies—*serving equally well in fricasees and ragousts*—left me giggling.

With me amused, the literature lesson was complete, so Malinda suggested that we take to our menus. I expected Annette to look at hers and mutter something like, 'The entrées look good. They have boiled baby ragoust for only twenty quid.'

But, once again, Annette the MC scorned her duties as the comedienne.

"So, John," Malinda said after we ordered, "what do you like to do with your time?"

"Oh, I'm working at a bakery right now."

"He's going to college in the fall," Annette added.

"What do you plan to study?"

"I'm going to play it by ear," I said, remembering Annette's pun to the same comment on our first meeting. But there was no encore.

Malinda smiled. "That's what I did too. I didn't want to restrict myself to just one discipline. So I decided to take everything: English lit., philosophy, psychology, sociology, anthropology—"

For the next several minutes, Malinda itemized her list of favourite academic stars.

"So, Annette," she finally concluded, "how goes the DJ life?"

"I'm not really a DJ. I'm more of a host for events—and I play music at them."

"And how's that going?"

"It's going well."

"Yes, but in what *way* is it going well?"

"I don't know. I guess the more I do it, the more comfortable I am being creative with it."

"It's interesting that you say that," Malinda said, "because a *venturesome personality* is considered to be one of the five ingredients of creativity. It's likely that you've taken countless risks in front of lots of people. And I would characterize that as courageous—*and* venturesome, for that matter. And so it seems now that your courage is paying off, and you're feeling more comfortable being creative in front of an audience."

"That's so interesting," Annette said, using the most earnest-sounding voice I'd ever heard from her. "Um, what are the other four ingredients of creativity?"

"Well, first," Malinda said, pausing to scan her memory, "the first is *expertise*. One needs to have a lot of information upon which they can create new ideas."

At that point, Annette ought to have begun entertaining Malinda and me by trying to portray herself as the ultra-creative person that her friend was describing.

'Well, it just so happens,' she might have said excitedly, 'that I know everything there is to know about, um, *paperclips!*'

I would have been pleased to laugh at such an addition to the conversation.

"And then the second ingredient," Malinda continued instead, "is *imaginative thinking skills*. A creative person seems to be able to take an ordinary object—"

'*Like a paperclip!*' Annette could then have said.

"—and," Malinda persisted, "they seem to have an ability to take that ordinary object and create something new from it."

'I might take my paperclip,' Annette could then have said, 'and I might make some nice paperclip earrings.'

"So then the third category," Malinda continued, "is …right… the *venturesome personality* that I was describing."

'I will sell my paperclip earrings to the entire world!' Annette might then have announced.

"And then the fourth category," Malinda said, "is what's called *intrinsic motivation*. It seems that people who are intrinsically motivated are creative because they *enjoy* being creative—they don't seem to be doing it for reward or praise."

'I would make my paperclip earrings even if no one would buy them,' Annette could then have stated dramatically.

"And the final ingredient," Malinda concluded, "is what's characterized as *a creative environment*. The most successful and imminent scientists and writers are those who have had creative colleagues to motivate them."

'*Oh*,' Annette could then have said, glancing at Malinda and me with a frown to indicate that we were *far short* of being creative colleagues. 'Well,' she would then have said, 'I guess four out of five creative ingredients isn't bad.'

Oh how I would have laughed at Annette's brilliant punch line.

But no such crescendo arrived. Instead, Annette quizzed Malinda for elaboration on her five categories of creativity. As she did so, it occurred to me that Malinda was to Annette what Annette was to me. Everything Annette said, Malinda turned into a segue to her intellectual thoughts. Annette's role, then, was not to be interesting, herself, but to give Malinda topics on which *she* could be interesting.

It was a disconcerting discovery. My role as mere fodder for Annette the MC's humour had been appropriate because, after all, I was a dullard with nothing interesting to say anyway. But it was unsettling to watch Annette—a distinguished non-dullard—acting solely as a springboard for someone else's non-dullness.

The longer the conversation with Malinda went on, the more I became frustrated with Annette's lack of genuine participation. *Who did she think she wasn't kidding?* And, since negative thoughts breed negative thoughts, I soon found myself feeling disturbed that Annette was clearly embarrassed by what *I* had to say. Nearly every time Malinda asked me a question, Annette intervened and answered for me. I was soon, therefore, convinced that, when Annette had excluded me from her nights on the town, she wasn't protecting me from her intimidating friends: she was protecting *them* from her boring boyfriend.

As Annette and I left the restaurant an hour later, my mind began discussing with itself whether I should complain to Annette that she seemed to be embarrassed by me.

"What'd you think of Malinda?" Annette spoke first when we got in her car.

"She seemed smart."

"She *is* smart—she's brilliant."

"Maybe," I said, "but she's not funny like you."

"You think I'm *funny?*" Annette replied as she pulled the car out of the parking lot.

"Of course, I think you're funny. Don't *you* think you're funny?"

"Sometimes, I guess. Like when I'm in front of an audience, or when I'm around you, John-John. But, when I'm around Malinda, I think I'm totally not funny."

"But maybe that's because you don't make any jokes when you're around her."

"I used to, but Malinda never thought my jokes were funny."

I shook my head at that one. "Okay, well, if Malinda doesn't think you're funny, then maybe she isn't so smart, after all."

Annette smiled and stopped the car.

"You're adorable," she said, before leaning over and giving me a kiss on the cheek.

That was an insensitive thing for Annette to have done. I was mad at her, and it's difficult to stay angry with someone when they give you a kiss on the cheek and tell you that you're 'adorable.' (I dare you to try it out for yourself if you don't believe me, skeptical reader.)

So, as Annette returned to driving us home, I decided to discard my negative thoughts for the evening; instead, I quizzed Annette on her high school existence and collected a bounty of new anecdotes starring her.

Happy Birthdate

I woke up so refreshed the next day that I decided to risk everything and invite Annette to my father's birthday party, which was scheduled for that weekend.

CLARIFYING NOTE: By party, I, of course, mean the dullard equivalent, which is a quiet dinner at a restaurant.

"Hey," I said, "would you be in to coming to my dad's birthday party?"

"Oh, I'd love to, but I'll be DJ-ing."

"Oh okay," I said, relieved that I could postpone introducing her to my family.

But then Annette realized something, and she paused.

Well, a pause, it turns out, is worth a thousand words, and I realized what Annette had realized: *I hadn't told her yet what day my father's birthday was.*

"Um..." we both commented.

I decided to yield to Annette's stammer because I hoped that she would be the one to point out her mistake.

Instead, her hand burrowed into her purse. "I've got something for you...Whaddya think of this?" she said, handing me a photo.

A picture—like a pause, they say—is worth a thousand words. And they aren't lying. The image Annette provided spoke eloquently about Annette and me sitting alone together at Bert & Susan's wedding reception. The picture went onto describe how Annette and I were laughing at something that Annette was saying.

"Wow, who took this?" I said.

"Hari, the photographer. I picked up the pictures today."

"Wow, I didn't realize anyone took a picture of us."

"Neither did I—I guess we were so into each other that we didn't notice."

And, holy ghostwriter, Annette had done it again! I couldn't very well complain that she'd snubbed my dad's birthday right after she made such an affectionate statement.

So what was a dullard to do? Obviously, I'd be dimmer than I thought if I were to break up with the best and only girl who had ever been willing to date me. Yet it also seemed silly to stay with someone who claimed to be *into me* but clearly did not respect me. I could think of only one way to navigate between those two ridiculous options and that was to procrastinate deciding what to do.

On the evening of my dad's birthday, I sat in my room and stared with blurry eyes at the picture of my girlfriend and me. A loud knock bumped my door open.

"John!" my brother blared. "We're leaving in two minutes."

"Right," I said, pulling myself up, intending to leave my somber mood behind so as to show appropriate deference to my dad's birthday.

I thought I was doing a good job of faking chipperness on the ride to the birthday restaurant, but I noticed I was frustrated that Aunty Susan hadn't been able to come. The scheduled end of her and Bert's honeymoon missed the birth date by only one day, which had prompted her to suggest to her groom that they come home a day early, but Uncle Bert had insisted that my dad would not want the newlyweds to rush home just for him. Initially, I had supported Uncle Bert's right to an unabridged celebration of his nuptials, but, as my dad quietly drove us—and Per and my mom nattered away about where we should go for dinner—I felt resentful of Bert's honeymoon greed.

SILLY NOTE (Unnecessary Reading): My smug ghostwriter claims to wonder why we didn't just delay the birthday celebration to the later date of Aunty Susan's return, which, in turn, makes me wonder if my ghostwriter has ever met dullards before: if a birthday isn't celebrated on its assigned date, then—by definition—it's *not* a birthday!

Next, I noticed at dinner that my brother's girlfriend's unrelenting shyness was irritating.

"So, Nicolette," Mom said to her, "are you eagerly counting down the days to your trip?"

"Um," Nicolette replied as though she'd never been asked a question before, "yeah, I guess."

There was then an awkward pause as we waited for her to elaborate.

She didn't.

"So ..." I said, "you guys go somewhere every year?"

"Um, not really—well, yeah, pretty much every year."

Per yawned performatively at that. "Happy birthday, Dad. We sure know how to a throw a party, don't we?"

Nicolette blushed.

I grimaced on her behalf, and my displeasure with Per's girl-friend was transferred to Per, himself.

At the end of the dinner, my meal—plus tip, plus my portion of my father's meal, plus tip—came to $35, but, only possessing two twenties—and not possessing the courage to ask for change—I emptied my wallet with a smile as if I'd put in the perfect amount.

"I think someone put in too much for tip," Mom said.

"It was probably me," Per said with a chuckle.

"No, it was John," Nicolette said.

"Fine, *you* take it," Per said, handing me the surplus. "I could've used the money, you know," he added with a smirk at Nicolette.

"But it's not yours," she said.

"*Thanks*," Per replied, "yeah, I was really gonna to try and rip off my brother for some change."

"Oh, sorry," Nicolette said, returning to her mute state.

I would have empathized with Per's frustration with Nico-lette's occasionally literal reception of his jokes, but his harshness in pointing it out—combined with the sincerity of her intention on my behalf—satisfied me that he deserved whatever he got.

Upon arriving home, I realized it was time to return my atten-tion to Annette the MC. I was hoping everyone would go to bed so that I could sneak out to visit her, but, tragically, both Per and our dad were still in social moods, so I was forced to undergo a game of cards.

Two hours later, I was finally free to surprise Annette. I rode my bike through a chilly summer evening that made me question the hospitality of my destination. I arrived to find Uncle Bert's curtains flashing with the lights of an active TV, so—with slightly lessened nerves—I knocked on the door.

I heard footsteps and then a pause. I was pleased to think the delay was the result of my sweetie checking her peephole. The door opened to a grinning Annette.

"Hello," she said, going in for a chipper kiss. "I thought you'd still be out dancing the night away with birthday dads."

I laughed. "Nope, we just played cards."

"With alcohol-inspired consequences, I hope," Annette said as she led me to the couch. "I was just starting a bad movie. Care to make fun of it with me?"

I did, indeed, and I was treated to a wonderfully terrible movie that contained brilliantly entertaining narration from Annette throughout. It was the most romantic night of my life so far as we fell asleep in front of the TV with interlocked ankles.

I woke up early the next morning with my back kinked by the couch, and my nerves similarly disturbed by a worry that my parents might be worried and wondering where I was. But then I realized my family would assume I either had morning bakery work or lawn mowing to do, so I settled into cooking breakfast for my girlfriend. The subsequent meal was serenaded by giggled reminiscing between us about the movie we'd mocked the night before.

When the breakfast was vanquished, Annette took in a great sigh. "John-John, how are you doing?"

"I'm fine," I replied, suddenly nervous.

"I'm *not*," she said, "I'm really upset. Actually, I feel like I'm gonna cry."

"Why, what's the matter?" I blurted, ready to take on the culprit.

"I don't think we should see each other anymore."

"Oh. How come?"

"Because, now that Bert's coming back, I'm moving back home. And I just can't do a long-distance relationship. You know what I mean?"

"Um, I guess."

Annette shrugged. "It's like: there's certain things that shouldn't be done long distance—lifeguarding, surgery, and ... *relationships*. I'd miss you too much." Annette smiled more than I would have thought, considering her earlier claim that she was on the precipice of tears.

Still, I didn't want to upset her, so I didn't question her.

"Okay," I said, ignoring my own emotional inclinations, "you sure?"

Annette smiled and gave me a kiss on the cheek. "No, I'm *not* sure. The way you're so sweet about this makes me want to change my mind. But I can't do it. If I changed my mind on this, you'd never trust me again."

Chapter 18
Dullard vs. Charmer II

The Break Up Break Down

Now, I must say, having Annette break up with me wasn't as much fun for me as you might hope, optimistic reader. The bike ride home drenched me with contempt for my boyfriend failings. It was an addictive feeling as I critically examined the boring things I'd said in response to Annette's many noble attempts to entertain us during our weeks-long relationship.

But my anger at myself could not hold off my sadness forever. As I neared home, I felt some especially despondent thoughts building from a distance. When they landed aggressively in my stomach, I wanted to get off my bike and lie down.

Nevertheless, I arrived home a minute later. My parents, Per, and Nicolette were setting up a barbecue in the backyard. Again, I subdued my emotions as I walked into the scene.

USEFUL NOTE: Since the romance of Annette and me had been kept secret, it seemed logical that the breakup should remain confidential as well.

"Hey, John," my mom said. "You were gone early this morning."

"Yeah," I said, touched that she'd noticed, "couldn't sleep, so I went to Uncle Bert's to do yard work."

"That's a lot of yard work," Per replied with a laugh.

"Were you there by yourself?" Nicolette said, looking at me with such sweet concern that I couldn't evade it.

"Um, no, Annette was there—the MC from the wedding—she's doing the actual house-sitting, I'm just—"

"Out of your league," Per said with a chuckle. "Did you try to chat her up?"

"No."

"Why not?" Nicolette said.

"Well, Per's probably right—"

"Per's just joking," Mom interrupted. "Nobody's *out of your league*, John."

"Thanks," I said, shocked by both the sentiment and the warmth with which it was expressed.

Unfortunately, there are few things more dangerous to one's composure than a loved one expressing care when they don't know you've been hurt. I felt my emotions rise up through my cheeks and into my eyes. Uh oh, I could lose emotional control at any moment. Something had to be done!

"So, John," Mom continued, "if you *are* interested in this girl, you just have to find a way to show her that there's something interesting about you that she'd like to get to know."

"Like what?" I said, trying to smirk over the feelings rushing around my face (only a criticism from my mother could keep the tears away now).

"Well, you have to figure that out for yourself," she said. "First, you have to figure out what sort of traits she might be interested in, and then you have to decide whether in some way you might match what she's looking for. And, if you *do*, then ask yourself how you can accentuate those parts of your personality that may not yet be so readily apparent to her."

"Okay," I said, still touched by my mother's sincerity of concern; but I was protected from my emotions by the fact that she apparently couldn't come up with a specific trait that I could call charming.

"So do you like her, bro?" Per said with a strange, non-mocking tone.

"Um, yeah," I said, wondering what he was getting at.

"So why don't you ask her out? It's amazing how many girls'll say 'Yes' just because you ask 'em—that's what happened with Nicolette."

Our mother nodded. "Asking a girl out takes confidence. And girls like confidence."

"Okay, maybe I will."

In saying so, I glanced over at my dad who was, it turned out, watching me with a curious face that convinced me he suspected there was more to my story than met my testimony.

That made me smile. I felt unusually cared for by each member of my family (and their girlfriend). It seemed that, when my chips were down, they were there for me. I was tempted, therefore, to admit that my crush on Annette was actually post-relationship, but I wasn't *quite* confident enough in their concern to risk it.

Instead, I listened contentedly as they switched to chatting about what Per was up to. When it seemed safe to do so, I snuck my mind off on reminiscences of Annette the MC, which at first made me smile; but at second—as I considered their impeding stoppage in production—had my insides churning again with disapproval for myself.

"Hello, Smith family!" Aunty Susan's voice interrupted those ponderings.

I looked up to see my returning aunt and uncle looking relaxed and cheerful. I tried to join their happy mood as they entertained us with tales of honeymoon adventures, but my mind couldn't resist taking occasional breaks to compare my failed relationship to their successful one.

At the bakery the next day, the phone rang in the middle of a busy moment; as was her custom, Amy rushed to respond to it.

"John, it's for you," she said, clearly disappointed in the result.

My heart knew its job and started pounding with full anticipation. *Perhaps Annette had called to announce a change in priorities.*

"Hello?"

"John, it's your Uncle Bert."

"Oh, hi," I said, feeling my heart trotting to a stop and my mind realizing a customer had arrived in my area. "Sorry, I'll be right with you."

"Okay, I'll wait," Bert said.

"No, I meant, um, I can answer a quick question."

There was no answer from Bert.

"Uncle Bert?" I said, wishing I hadn't included his uncle title which could only prove to my customer that the delay was not even business-related.

My uncle laughed. "Oh, sorry, I thought you were still talking to the customer."

"Nope," I said, faking a laugh to hide my irritation. "So what can I do for you?"

"Doughnuts! Can you bring over a half dozen or whatever you call it, a half baker's dozen, to my place tonight? Susan and I want to make you dinner as thanks for you watching the place."

"Okay," I said, too impatient to explain that I already had plans to wallow for the night.

"Hello, new nephew," Bert said when I arrived a few hours later. "Your aunt is still dinner shopping. But I'm glad because I wanted to talk to you."

"Oh, was there a problem with the yard work?"

Uncle Bert laughed. "No, your lawn mowing was a *cut* above."

I forced a smirk

Uncle Bert looked me over with his sophisticated smile. "It's just that you seem a little down."

"What makes you think that?"

Uncle Bert smiled again. "You miss Annette, don't you?"

"Why would I miss Annette?" I demanded.

Once more, Uncle Bert's face slid into a knowing look. "I saw you two at the wedding: you guys were pretty into each other."

"Oh," I said, feeling a cool flood of anxiety rush to my belly, "well, it turns out that I was into her, but she wasn't into me."

"Well," Bert said, "she missed out on something great then, eh?"

My uncle was so charismatic in his delivery of that wild notion that I nearly believed him.

"So, John," Bert said as he, Aunty Susan, and I sat down to burgers on his back porch, "pretty soon you'll be a college boy. Tell us how you feel."

"Nervous."

Uncle Bert's forehead crinkled as though I'd just said that I was afraid of apples.

"There's nothing to be nervous about, John. College is a great time. You'll meet more people at college than any other time in your life."

"Honey!" Aunty Susan replied with a chuckle. "Don't be daft. I think that's exactly what makes him nervous. Correct me if I'm wrong, John."

"What's he got to be nervous about?" Uncle Bert said, sounding startled. "John's a great conversationalist. And not a lot of kids can say that these days."

I couldn't help adoring Uncle Bert for making such a claim even though I knew it was preposterous.

"John," he continued, "you're going to have a blast at college: the parties, the drinking... the *women*." Uncle Bert raised his eyebrows at that last intriguing part.

Aunty Susan half-rolled her eyes. "I don't think John is really into partying, honey. Not that you shouldn't go to parties, John, but it's never really been your thing, has it?"

Bert's crinkled forehead returned. "Of course, he's into partying! If you're not into partying, then what's the point of going to college?"

"Um," Aunty Susan said with a laugh, "maybe he wants to *learn* something."

"*No*," Uncle Bert said. "College isn't about the books. It's about the people. I learned more about business in the first year of running BS&S than I did in four years of training at the top business school on the continent."

"Really?" I said. "You don't learn anything at college?"

"Well, you learn *some*. But you can't learn anything important by putting your nose in a book. If you worked for me, John, I could teach you more in a month about the world than any sociology textbook ever could."

"Honey!" Aunty Susan said, shaking her head. "I don't think John wants to come and work for you."

"Of course he doesn't. I'm just saying college isn't about the books. It's about the people. And, let me tell you, John, you'll meet some people. Pretty soon you'll forget that what's-her-name ever existed."

And that was the clincher. The allusion to Anette immediately and instructively reminded me of my inability to interact properly with people.

"Um," I said, "you'd *want* me to come and work for you?"

"Well, *yeah*, you're a hard worker; you have great integrity; you'd be my dream assistant."

"What about the assistant you already have?"

"Well, unfortunately, Michael finally quit—and I'm glad for him—but he didn't give me much notice. Actually, he gave me his notice as a wedding gift."

Aunty Susan laughed. "Um, honey, I think Michael didn't give you *much notice* because he was heartbroken."

"Why?"

"Because, I don't know, *you* got married."

"No," Bert said, now at maximum crinkle, "he's watched me, you know, get to know ladies before."

"And how many of them did you marry?"

"True," Bert said, nodding with a sheepish face. "I guess you're one of the first to lock me down."

Aunty Susan laughed again.

"Um," I said, "are you sure you'd want me to work for you?"

"Of course, he *would*, John," my aunt replied. "But that isn't the question. The question is whether you want to disrupt all your plans just to help out your aunt's new husband."

I pretended to ponder the question, but my answer was set.

Chapter 19
Dullard at Work II

Feigned Farewell

I was nervous when I told my parents about my plan to postpone college to instead hang out with my brand new uncle for a year, but my mother seemed to believe that Bert would be an excellent role model, so she persuaded my father not to object.

Meanwhile, when I announced to my Sweet On You co-workers my intention to retire from Sweet On You, there was talk of sadness among my colleagues. Several people declared that they would miss me; in fact, they said they wished they'd been able to get to know me better. Oddly, though, during my subsequent last two weeks at Sweet On You, those same nostalgic co-workers seemed to make no new effort to investigate me. The possible exception was Amy who insisted that she disapproved of my departure.

"Why are you leaving me?" she said, with a whiny child voice. "What am I going to do without you?"

"You'll come and visit me at Bert's," I said.

"Okay, yeah, yeah!" she cheered. "Let's hang out—and you have to come back here and visit me."

Amy confirmed that intention on my last day at Sweet On You when she provided me with a going-away card that claimed we would be 'FF,' which I understood to mean 'Friends Forever.' Nevertheless, we both lapsed in our responsibilities to gather our forever friendship. We did bump into each other occasionally around town, at which point we reminded each other of our duties to our alleged alliance, but, strangely, neither of us took any action to execute our agreement.

I was not hurt by Amy's lack of friendship follow-through, especially considering that I wasn't pursuing the meetings, myself, but I was surprised by it since she had seemed so determined to continue our camaraderie. Of course, with my ghostwriter's help, I now understand that I wasn't really a destination friend for Amy: I was more of an impulse friend such that—if she was around me— she was pleased to chat; but, once we weren't regularly in each other's vicinity, there were no reminders for her to think of me.

But don't cry for me, sensitive reader: I must confess, once Amy wasn't around to tell me the details of her inept love life, I didn't think much of her either.

The Importance of Being Ernie

I was cautiously confident as I walked to my first day at Bert's Shirts & Skirts. After all, my previous first day on a job had put me in the company of a plethora of beautiful female strangers. By comparison, a first day of working for a lone honorary uncle seemed like nothing to be nervous about.

The BS&S CLOSED sign was up when I came upon the store; I peered through the windowed door and saw no Bert, so I knocked for his attention. He did not appear, so I pulled on the door, just in case, and was rewarded.

"Hello?" I called.

"Hello!" a backroom-Bert voice approached. "Welcome, Ernie," he said grinning as he landed in the main store area.

"Hi?" I said, wondering for an embarrassing moment if some-one named Ernie was actually supposed to be having his first day of work. "I'm John," I clarified with no hint of humour on my face.

"And I'm Bert," my uncle said, handing me a nametag, "which would make us Bert & *John*—I prefer the sound of *Bert & Ernie*, don't you?"

SOCIO-TEMPORAL NOTE: Bert & Ernie were a pair of fictional roomates on a well-recognized American children's show at the time of Uncle Bert's joke.

"Oh I see," I said, laughing nervously as I looked at my new identification, which read:

ERNIE:

Bert's Assistant

And, actually, I was pleased with the title; I'd long wanted a nickname to match the one my brother had gotten when he was six.

INTRIGUING NOTE: Looking back with the aid of my ghostwriter's hindsight, I realize now that Bert may have only intended 'Ernie' to be a first-day-on-the-job bit of fun, but I took to the nickname so earnestly that he may have been inspired to keep it around.

"All right," my uncle said, "now that we've settled on our names, shall I take you on a tour of the work we'll be doing?"

"Sounds good."

"Okay, well, preliminarily," Bert said as he walked us around his company, "you just have to remember that Ernie is the *anti-Bert*—i.e., you should always be doing whatever I'm *not*. So, if I'm servicing customers at the till, get to the floor and fold the trail of rejected clothes that they've decided not to buy. But, if I'm on the floor helping customers match their tastes to our clothes, get to the till and greet anyone else coming in. I may then send my customers to you for service, or I might service them myself, in which case…?"

"Get to the floor and fold their clothes?"

"Quite right…" Bert said with his powerful grin. "All right," he continued, "so, obviously, the two mediums you'll be working with are the clothes and the till. With your bakery experience, Ernie, the till will be the easier of the two, so let's start there."

Bert talked through the till's buttons gently but swiftly. "Sorry," he interrupted himself, "am I explaining this too slowly for an experienced till-man, like yourself? I don't mean to condescend."

"No, no, it's good," I said, wishing he wouldn't interrupt himself in the middle of an explanation.

"Okay, just be aware," Bert said, "I'm never patronizing about the same thing twice, so enjoy it while it lasts."

Within half an hour, Bert decided that the store and I were ready, so he opened us up for the day's business.

"It'll probably be a while," he said. "In the meantime, we sort and rack the new merchandise."

That task I immediately took to like an eager child to a Christmas morning toy. I had always enjoyed folding my own clothes; in doing so, I'd often sought out new and more precise methods of compaction that wouldn't leave me wrinkled; I had rarely been successful in those endeavours, but I'd tried enough of them to instantly be able to appreciate—and, therefore, reproduce—the genius within the BS&S systems of folding and hanging.

A few minutes into my enjoyment, the door rang with our first customer.

"Hello, Mrs. McKegney," Bert said, beaming at an eighty-year-old-looking woman.

"Hello, Bert," she said as her eyes examined my presence.

"That's my new assistant, *Ernie*," Bert helped out.

"Really?" Mrs. McKegney said, still watching me.

I locked my face into a smile.

"Yes, of course," Bert said with a chuckle in his tone while I held my bland cheerful face. "All of my assistants are named Ernie. That's how I choose them."

"That's not true," the lady said, finally turning to my boss, allowing my facial muscles to relax, "*Michael* wasn't named Ernie."

Bert giggled. "Well, why do you think he's not my assistant anymore?"

The lady smirk-frowned. "So how *is* Michael?"

"He's left for college just this morning, actually."

"Good," the customer said, before turning back to me. "Are *you* not going to school?" She had a teacher-like voice that immediately made me not want to disappoint her.

"No, not yet," I offered. "But I plan to eventually."

The lady sighed with her eyes. "Don't wait too long."

"Okay."

"Now, Bert," she said, "what have you got in the way of scarves and winter gloves? My granddaughter's birthday is coming up, and winter won't be long behind, so I'd like her to be prepared."

"Good plan," Bert said, walking towards his backroom. "Preparation, after all," he added, pausing at the border to his destination, "is one of the most important ingredients of being, well, prepared."

"There are *other* ingredients to being prepared other than preparation?" Mrs. McKegney replied.

"Of course," Bert said before disappearing into his backroom.

Mrs. McKegney looked at me as if I were to blame for Bert's strange claim.

I smiled back in an attempt to indicate that I was as confused as she was.

She smirked and shook her head.

"The most important factor in being prepared," Bert returned with an armful of scarves, "is knowing *what* to prepare for."

His customer rolled her eyes in reply but then shifted her face to me and flashed me a smile before returning to Bert.

"Let's have a look, then," she said.

Bert charmed Mrs. McKegney and me for several more minutes before she was ready to select her granddaughter's new fall and winter protection. I moved to the till to receive her.

"Ernie, will you help Mrs. McKegney with her purchases?" my boss said. "And give her the ten percent pre-winter discount."

"Oh, okay," I said, impersonating confidence in my ability to perform the second part of the task. My old bakery till had required me to hit the discount button first and then the size of the reduction second, but, at Bert's place, I pondered, *was it the other way around?*

"Is something the matter?" the customer asked.

"No, no," I said, typing in the old bakery method.

My till beeped accusingly at me.

"Perhaps you should get Bert to help you."

"No, sorry, I've got it now. Sorry, I was just confused because the last till I used was similar but different."

Mrs. McKegney raised her eyebrows at me. "I see. Well, I trust next time you'll remember which job you're at."

"Yeah, for sure," I said with a smile.

"Excellent," Mrs. McKegney said as if we had just made a breakthrough. "I look forward to it, then."

"She's a character, isn't she?" Bert said as we watched Mrs. McKegney carefully place her granddaughter's gifts in the passenger side of her car. "She's impressed only by competence—or, at least, the appearance of it. You'll get her next time."

As it turned out, most of the customers who came into the store that day were entertaining either by their own personalities or, more commonly, by Bert's as he provided excellent biographies of their customering histories after each transaction.

I walked home that evening feeling interacted with in a new way and thus somehow less wounded by the loss of my girlfriend.

My parents appeared intrigued and perhaps even amused to hear about Bert's charming ways, and I enjoyed the rare position of narrator in our family discussion (Per wasn't home yet). We soon took up a movie for viewing, and I decided to get some ice cream to complete the mood.

Just as I'd filled my bowl, I heard outside Per talking to a girl who sounded much louder than the Nicolette for whom I'd become used to having to strain my ears.

The loud-voiced girl and Per were laughing when he opened the kitchen door.

"Hey, bro—this is Dellia."

"Hi, nice to meet you," I said, trying to hide my surprise at her not being Nicolette. I'd had a lot of practice witnessing Per trading in his girlfriends but never so suddenly before, especially considering Nicolette's record-breaking stay in the role.

"How's the ice cream?" Dellia said with a bit of a smirk.

"Good, you want some?"

"Ah, no thanks. You know how much fat's in that stuff?"

"I assume *a lot*?"

"Ah, yeah."

Per laughed. "What do you think, bro? It comes from a cow."

"Right," I said, trying to appear amused.

Dellia nodded and then scanned the room. "What's with the wallpaper?" she concluded.

As my brother joined in on the mocking of our mother's taste in décor, I noticed myself feeling uncomfortable in the presence of the newborn couple. Dellia's large volume of voice, combined with her instant opinions on anything in her presence, had me nervous that there would be other things on my person that might be worthy of scolding.

In short, I missed Nicolette.

The next time I saw Per without Dellia, I asked what had happened to Dellia's predecessor.

"Yeah," he said, "I don't know. She was too quiet—it annoyed me."

"Right," I said, "I guess that won't be a problem with Dellia." That was my attempt to discredit Dellia on behalf of Nicolette.

"Yeah," he said, chuckling, "she's a talker. It's awesome, though. I'm not bored outta my mind anymore."

That comment bothered me on behalf of Nicolette, but there was nothing I could think to say to save her from Per's implied characterization.

Back at BS&S the next day, Bert continued to charm me as he charmed his customers.

"You've made a nice choice," he said, smiling at a ninety-some-thing-year-old woman, who had giggled at anything resembling humour in Bert's comments throughout her shop.

"Do you have a seniors' discount?" she asked as an excessively attractive woman entered the store.

"We certainly do," Bert said. "Why do you ask?"

"Because I'm a senior."

"You are *not*."

"I am *too*," the lady replied, laughing again as her beautiful rival approached my folding area of the store with a hefty smile that was clearly meant for the conversation going on behind her.

"I think I'm going to need to see some I.D.," Uncle Bert stated.

The giggly lady shrugged her giggling shoulders, pulled out her identification, and handed it to Uncle Bert with wide, amused eyes, awaiting his next move.

Uncle Bert squinted back and held the I.D. up to the light, glancing back at the giggly lady to make sure he was looking at her in the photo and not her older sister.

"All right," Bert said, handing the card back to his customer, "I'm giving you the ten percent seniors' discount plus an extra five percent to help out your forgery business. I always like to support entrepreneurialism in young people."

As the lady giggled her way out the door, I felt my spine tingling with appreciation for my uncle.

So, apparently, did the overly attractive woman: she sent me an amused, Bert-approving smile.

I smiled back but had little else to say on the matter.

"Is there somewhere I can try this on?" she said.

As I directed her to the changeroom, I noticed—in glancing—that my boss/uncle was watching the exchange.

Once the pretty lady was hidden away, Bert lofted gracefully my way and joined me in my menial task. When our customer came out of the changeroom, wearing an outfit that clung descriptively to her smooth form, she seemed content and then pleased as she spotted Bert's hind quarters looking back at her. I tried to smile pleasantly at her without, I hoped, appearing too enthusiastic about the skills of her gripping dress.

"What do you think?" she said, aiming her eyes at me even though her voice was clearly meant for Bert, who was still looking in another direction.

My boss swiveled around and nodded scientifically at the dress.

"*Depends*—if you're trying for the dowdy librarian look, then I'm afraid this won't do. But, if you're hoping for stunning, then you've done well."

The pretty woman laughed harder than she needed to. "You're quite the salesman, aren't you?"

Bert's forehead crinkled. "Not at all," he said. "I own the place, so I care much more about inspiring repeat customers than making particular sales."

"I see," the woman said, apparently pondering her retort.

"So what look *are* you trying for?" Bert helped out.

"Actually, you weren't that far off. As of September, I'll be a teacher."

"Really? And will that be your debut in the role?"

"Yes—well, I've worked in the classroom for my practicum—but this will be my first time with a class all to myself. I moved here for the job."

"Welcome," Bert said, half-bowing. "Is it high school or elementary?"

"High school."

"Then we should look for a middle ground between this stunning outfit and the aforementioned dowdy librarian look."

"What's wrong with a *librarian look?*" the teacher replied with an anticipatory smirk.

"Nothing, but the librarians are kind of possessive of it."

The woman chuckled. "Well, I'm not afraid of librarians."

Bert's forehead went full crinkle. "You *should* be. Those librarians know a lot about revenge from their constant reading of books. You don't want to risk their wrath."

The teacher laughed. "I never thought of it that way."

"But you don't want to look too stunning either," Bert said. "You'll distract the boys, and the girls'll either be jealous or become infatuated with you."

"That's a very thorough assessment."

"Yes, well, I was once a high school boy, myself, and most of my girlfriends were girls, so ..."

"I see your point," the woman said.

"Why don't you try this on for size and comfort?" Bert said, reaching into two separate racks and producing two hands full of a single outfit.

"Okay," the woman said with a soft voice as though she were shy.

The next half hour produced a thoroughly cheerful interaction between Bert and customer as they built her new wardrobe, which—although professional-looking in its designs—tended, in its complimentary relationship to its wearer, to be closer to the stunning side of Bert's spectrum than the dowdy side.

When they finally reached the till, I realized—by the continuing pitter-patter of their conversation—that it wasn't one of those times that I was to handle the transaction.

"I'll go and fold the rest of them," I said.

Bert nodded. "Thanks, Ernie ... So," he said to the beautiful customer, his hand beginning to play the till like an instrument, "you will, of course, get the ten percent new teachers' discount."

"Wow, thanks," she said, "if I'd known, I would've gotten that last shirt."

"It's in there," Bert said with raised eyebrows as he lifted another of the garments to reveal the item she hadn't been able to decide on. "I figured I'd throw it in to complete the outfit, *on the house.*"

"Oh, thank you," the teacher said, beaming.

That moment struck me as enough already. My uncle's rapport with my beautiful customer had been forgivable on the grounds that he was known to charm most of his patrons—beautiful or dowdy—but this new level of friendliness seemed *personal* to me.

As I walked home that afternoon, I felt a great reduction in excitement about my life with Uncle Bert as boss and mentor. His charm had lost some of its charm. *Why was he so comfortable flirting so conspicuously in front of his own wife's nephew?* I guess he figured that I'd be too timid to say anything. He was right about that: I wasn't sure if flirting was a crime punishable by informing the flirter's wife—and, even if it were, the thought of starting such a conversation with my aunt was too embarrassing for consideration.

Instead, then, I focused on lamenting my cowardice; said shame segued nicely back to other thoughts of self-disappointment: that is to say, I resumed feeling bad about my breakup with Annette the MC.

A week into that depression, I stared at the clothes I was folding while Bert amused another pretty customer.

"What's on your mind, Ernie?" he said, after the prettiness left.

"Nothing much," I said, feigning a smile.

"Thinking of Annette, perchance?"

"I guess."

Bert sighed. "It's time we got you over her."

"Thanks, but I don't think I'm ready for that yet."

To my annoyance, I *did* appreciate my uncle's genuine-seeming sentiment; nevertheless, *resentment* remained my lead emotion when I contemplated my boss. In our negotiations for me to give up school, he had implied that working at Bert's Shirts & Skirts would be better for my emotional health than going to college where there would have been numerous interesting girls to remind me of Annette. In reality, though, my dull life at home—by being so uneventful—was reminding me daily, by contrast, of the brief romance I'd had.

Unfortunately, as you can imagine, imaginative reader, stargazing about a life with a former rejecter tends to make it even more difficult to recover from their absence. Instead of learning to live without your ex-darling, you may start to see them as your only chance at happiness—a chance that you squandered with your dullness, unattractiveness, or whatever your faults happen to have been.

And, of course, the only two means of curing such angst are (A) the discovery of new romance, and/or (B) the passage of that pesky stuff named Time. Since there was no hope in my telescope of discovering the former, I decided to let Option Time be my guide to recovery.

Chapter 20
Dullard vs. Charmer III

Bert Flirts with Skirts

By the time I'd worked three months at BS&S, I had become comfortable in the role of Bert's underling. Certainly, by vice of his continued flirting with non-Aunty-Susans, I still found him to be less charming than he seemed, but his ability to get along with any stranger was worthy of my dullardly admiration.

"All right, Ernie," he said on a late fall afternoon, "tell me what you think of this for my annual Christmas display. I propose that, this year, the surprise will be in the delay. I'm going to wait five days longer than usual so that everyone'll be wondering if I've forgotten." Uncle Bert chuckled at that. "And then, in the middle of the night—if you're willing—we're going to put it all up in one go so it'll look like it was there all along. Whaddya think?"

"Sounds good to me," I said, pretending cheerfully that my influence was indeed relevant. "Yeah, I think people'll like that."

Bert apparently couldn't agree more, and I was able to enjoy myself in his especially upbeat company for the next several hours. But then a beautiful customer naïvely invited herself into the store. Bert quickly wrapped his charm around her and helped her pick out a quality item.

"That'll be forty-six fifty-two," he said.

"Oh?" the beautiful customer replied. "I thought it was already fifty dollars before tax?"

"Oh my," Bert said. "I'm sorry. The till gets a little biased when it thinks a customer's made a particularly good choice. *Till!*" he said, looking down at the machine. *"You know you're not supposed to do that."*

"Oh," the lady said, "um ..."

"Okay, let's try this again, shall we?" Uncle Bert said, tapping away on his till. "So that'll be thirty-nine fifty, please."

The beautiful target chuckled. "Um, that's still less than fifty dollars."

"Oops, sorry—*Till, I told you not to do that.* Sorry, I don't think the till's gonna budge on this one. Is that okay?"

As always, said flirting had a significant impact on my ability to enjoy my time around both my uncle and myself. I tried to comfort my conscience on the grounds that I still wasn't sure that my uncle's wrongfully directed flirting was a sufficient enough crime against marriage for my aunt to want to know about it, but I quickly ruined that excuse by noting that I still could have complained to Bert about his open-ended flirting.

The next afternoon, a boy named Jordan Zaluski came into the store. For the most part, Uncle Bert still liked to serve the customers as I organized the clothes, but I'd come to surmise that, if my boss suspected a customer was going to bore him, he'd assign them to me. Jordan, who was fourteen years old physically, but about six years old mentally, was one such patron.

"John, would you help this handsome young gentleman, please?"

"Sure," I said, and I tried to copy Uncle Bert's technique for making people feel significant. "Hello, sir, can I help you?"

"Um," Jordan said with a serious face, "I got all this ..." he pulled a couple crumbled balls of money out from his pocket. "I saved it from my allowance. And I want to get Mom a present."

"Okay, what kind of thing do you think she'd like?"

"I dunno. It's Mom's birthday."

"That's nice. So what kind of clothing do you think she'd *like* for her birthday?"

Jordan wasn't able to provide details of what his mom would like, so we spent several minutes seeking out something nice. Jordan settled on a high-end peach-coloured scarf.

"But, you *know*," I said, "these red scarves here are on sale. I bet your mom would like one of these just as much, and they're only *fifteen* dollars."

Said downsell strategy was a Bert-approved technique. He often aimed to build customer trust by offering the sale items first. In this case, though, I was downselling because I was worried that Jordan's wrinkly money might not add up to much more than $20.

Jordan did not approve of my helpfulness. "No," he said to the red scarves. "I want peach!"

"Are you sure?" I said, scouring my brain for another Bert strategy to apply. But nothing came to dull mind, so I restated my initial argument. "These red scarves are pretty nice too."

"No! Mom likes peach!"

"You don't think she'd like red too?"

"No. She likes peach the most."

"Okay," I said, suddenly touched that Jordan was so insistent on picking the colour that he was convinced his mom would prefer. "I guess you know your mom better than I do."

"She likes peach," Jordan repeated, frowning at me.

I frowned at me too. "All right, let's take your mom's new scarf to the front so you can pay for it."

Jordan squinted up at me.

I reached over to take the scarf so that I could fold it en route.

My customer quickly pulled it away from me, and he kept the item pressed to his body. He was eyeing me. He seemed convinced that, if he let me carry the scarf to the register, I'd somehow switch it for the red one.

As such, I felt insurmountably stupid for having managed to provoke Jordan to think that I was against him. And yet a cascade of goose bumps on the back of my neck couldn't resist standing up and cheering Jordan and the sincerity with which he wanted to pick out the perfect gift for his parent.

As we arrived at the till, I prayed to the providers of Jordan's allowance that they had given him enough funds to cover his purchase. I wasn't sure what I was going to do if they hadn't.

Jordan again pulled the crumpled bills out of his pocket and put them on the counter. He looked up at me as I unraveled his money. He was around $15 short.

"Do you have any more?"

Jordan reached deep into his pockets, and he poured about $4 of change onto the counter.

"That's all of your money?"

"Uhuh," Jordan said, looking up at me with concern. "I saved it from my allowance."

"That's fine," I said, and I gave Jordan a bag for his scarf since he wouldn't let me put the item in the bag.

As Jordan left my view, I sent my hands to my own pockets to pick up the rest of his tab.

"What are you doing, Ernie?" Uncle Bert said with crinkled brow as he came out of the backroom.

"Oh, um, the kid—he didn't have enough. So I'm just putting in the rest."

"Fair enough, but why didn't you just ask me to mark it down?"

"Oh, I didn't think—"

"John, I give discounts all the time."

"But that's only when ..." I stopped myself from pointing out that, lately, Uncle Bert's discounts most often applied to beautiful women.

"When *what?*"

"Um ..."

My uncle stared at me. "John, put your money away."

"Okay."

Uncle Bert sighed. "Do you really think you did that kid a favour? He's going to have to learn some time that he can't get everything he wants just by making people feel sorry for him."

"But I don't *feel sorry for him*. I admire him."

"Oh, spare me. I'm not in the mood today."

"Oh, sorry."

"You lock up," my boss said, handing me his keys. "I'm done for the day."

Now, ordinarily, being in charge of locking up the store by myself (and thus getting to count the till and run the till's end-of-day reports using my own preferred order of operations) would have been an enjoyable adventure; but, considering that I'd provoked the opportunity by angering my uncle, I wasn't able to appreciate the twists and turns of the mission as much as I should have.

I arrived home to find my parents, along with Per and loud Dellia, watching one of my mom's favourite movies (which had been an annual sighting in our childhood). My brother's new girlfriend was nevertheless unrestrained as she mocked the legitimacy of every scene.

"That's so stupid—why doesn't he just *give* her the money?"

Per laughed. "Because he's a moron."

My mom looked displeased by the commentary, but she didn't object, so the free-flowing critique continued.

Meanwhile, being in an already faltering mood, I spent the first half of the movie fantasizing about the words 'Shut up!' and how they would sound on my lips if I sent them in Dellia's direction. However, by the second half of the show, I remembered that I had some worrying to do.

What was going to be the consequence of my quarrel with my boss? The possibilities could be represented by two basic clichés: (A) the disagreement would turn out to be a bump along the road of a happy connection, or (B) the incident would, in fact, be a molehill out of which a mountain would be made.

Since I'd never argued with Bert before, I had no way of knowing whether he was a bump-in-the-road or a molehill quarreler, so I had every reason to be terrified that the next day I would be discovering the commencement of a forever-strained interaction with my boss/uncle.

As such, that next morning, I approached BS&S with the sort of aggressive butterflies in my stomach that one should only have to endure during first dates, interviews, and playoff games of one's favourite hockey team. I was glad to see Bert at the till when I got to the door. I wanted to get our painful first interaction dealt with as soon as possible so that we could settle into however Bert intended our relationship to be thereafter.

"Hi," I blurted as I came through the doorway.

Bert looked up and smiled as if we had nothing to dread about.

"Sorry about yesterday," he said, "I must've gotten too much sun on the weekend."

"Oh, okay, thanks, yeah, sorry if I said anything—"

"Nope," my uncle said. "Nothing for you to apologize for."

"Oh, okay," I said, embarrassed to be involved in a one-sided apology.

For the rest of the morning, Uncle Bert was especially complimentary of my work. But, of course, since I was aware of the conciliatory inspiration for the kudos, I knew not to ingest the content without plenty of skeptical seasoning. Nevertheless, I was touched by Bert's efforts to fix any possible damage to our relationship. I hadn't realized that a non-dullard could be so concerned about a dullard's good opinion.

"Hey John," my uncle interrupted these contemplations from the other side of the store, "may I borrow your services for a moment?"

"Sure," I called back, looking up to see that Bert had an attractive young female customer in his midst. It was an odd time for my uncle to be accessing my services. "How can I help?" I said when I arrived on the scene.

"Would you mind helping this young woman, please? She's looking for some shoes for a party tonight."

"Oh, okay, um ..." I pointed the pretty lass in the direction of the BS&S shoe department. "If you don't mind following me?"

We walked without conversation as I tried to understand what the Bert my uncle was doing transferring a perfectly pretty customer to me. Perhaps he wasn't feeling well.

"Great, thanks," the pretty lady said when we arrived at the shoes.

As she looked over a pair of heels, I turned my eyes towards Bert to see if he could give me a hint as to what was going on.

He winked in reply.

A shudder of realization rippled through my body. *After I found the shoes for the attractive lady's feet, I was clearly expected to sweep her off of them.*

It was a shocking and scary task, which was further complicated by the fact that, in reality, I wasn't feeling specifically attracted to the attractive lady. Sure, she was pretty, but I saw no Annette-level brilliance peeking from behind her lovely smile. Yet, with Bert's expectations lurking nearby, my nerves grabbed onto me anyway.

"What do you think of these?" I said, handing a cheerful choice to my customer. Tragically, my nerves shook my delivery, and I dropped one of the shoes en route. "Oh sorry," I mustered.

"*That's okay*," the pretty lady said with serious emphasis as if I'd actually committed a crime worthy of an apology. "These are great," she added with a patronizing, sympathy smile. "My *boyfriend*'ll love me in these."

Oh my mortification. She'd convicted me of a crush that I hadn't committed.

So, as you can imagine, empathetic reader, I was relieved several minutes later when the pretty customer finally settled on her footwear and left the store.

Uncle Bert was not daunted by the customer's escape.

"You know, Ernie, I think you might be onto something with that shy-guy routine."

That made me laugh. In fact, to my surprise, I was suddenly giddy. Not because I agreed with my uncle's assessment that *shy* was the way to a woman's date book, but because I now realized that Bert had donated the pretty customer to me as a gesture of goodwill towards his wife. Indeed, by trading me into the role of beautiful-women flirter, it occurred to me that my uncle might have redeemed us both.

But perhaps that was just a one-time contrition, so I waited—with nervous optimism—for the next beauty to be caught by Bert's Shirts & Skirts. Two heart-murmuring hours later, she landed in the parking lot, and Bert raised his eyebrows at me as she approached us.

I grinned back, hoping with full stomach flutter that we were tilting our eyebrows to the same plan.

"Good afternoon," Bert said, smiling pleasantly at the arriving customer.

"Hi," she said, half-smiling back.

"What can we do for you?"

"Do you guys have any Christmas ties? I wanna get one for my dad."

"Certainly. Ernie, can help you with that?"

I felt euphoria soak my insides as I rushed over to Bert and beautiful customer. In fact, I was so pleased that I was barely nervous to interact with the attractive client.

"Impressive," Bert said when she left. "Your confidence has improved."

"Oh, I don't know about that," I said. "I'm just in a good mood."

Bert replied with crinkled eyebrows that made me laugh.

The next day, Bert was true to his eyebrows. Every attractive and/or young female customer who came upon the store was sent my way. And, after each transaction, Uncle Bert surrounded me to check on my progress.

"Did you get a phone number?"

"No, not this time," I said, shrugging contentedly since, in reality, I had no intention of trying to collect contact info. (Not that I would have turned down a lovely lady's number if she had offered it to me, but I could not fathom a circumstance in which I would break the customer barrier and ask for such a prize.)

In retort, Bert spent much time jovially shaking his head at me for not putting in more effort; in turn, I was jovially sheepish about it. I loved that mock and take: it seemed to me to be the way an uncle and his nephew were supposed to work together (i.e. his flirting was to be done at home, while mine was prodded for by him as he tried to inspire me to become a ladies' man in his own image). Indeed, he was now the good uncle that I'd hoped for when Aunty Susan had picked him out for me.

Two weeks into that delightful time of being happy with Bert, I spotted a pretty customer arriving by athletic foot in the parking lot. She wore a ponytail that poked cutely through the back of her baseball cap, along with athletic pants and shirt that illuminated her sharp physique. I liked her sporty attractiveness right away, and so, for a moment, I considered genuinely trying to flirt with her. Obviously, she wouldn't go for me, but it would be a nice treat for Bert.

"Hi," she said as she came into the store.

"Hey there," Bert said, approaching gently.

"I've often jogged by here," the girl said, glancing around, "and I've always wondered what it was like."

"I hope I don't disappoint," Bert said

"No, I like it," the girl said. "You own the place?"

"As far as I know."

"*As far as you know?*"

"Well, my assistant there may be smarter than he looks—who knows what he might be doing with the accounting books on his lunch breaks."

I laughed at that as I approached the till for my beautiful-customer instructions from Bert.

"Hey," the beauty, herself, said, looking at me, "you must be the new owner of this place?"

Bert and I laughed. "Not *yet*," I said, pleased with myself for keeping up.

"Yeah, *not yet*," Bert said, "he still needs to learn to forge my signature before I'll even think about selling the place to him."

"Fair enough," the girl said with a smirk.

And then there was a moment of friendly eye contact between Bert and beauty.

"So?" I said. "Um…was there something you were particularly interested in today?"

"Yeah, I guess I could use a dress for the fast-approaching Christmas party season."

"We've got dresses," Bert replied. "Ernie, can you watch the till? I think I've got the perfect option for our new friend here."

"Oh, okay," I said, waiting for the revelation of how Bert would segue the manoeuvre into an opportunity for me to flirt with the curious customer. For a moment, I latched onto the possibility that he really did think that he had a particular dress that would work for her (we were a clothing store, after all). But, as I watched my uncle caress the woman with his best charm, I knew that Bert the flirt was back.

It was a terrifically painful feeling to realize that the new leaf that my uncle had turned over was now going to decay. To be flawed, as he was, had been forgivable, it seemed to me, on the grounds that he'd given up his misdirected flirting the moment we officially noticed it. Indeed, once he'd seen his behaviours through my eyes, he seemed to have realized what they were. But his return now to his flirty ways—with our epiphany still fresh and available to him at all times—was a harsher insult to Aunty Susan than any individual flirt had ever been.

For a few more weeks, Bert continued to donate most of the beautiful customers to me, but I was so uninterested now in even faking a flirt with them that Bert surely got bored of watching me waste his opportunities, and he gradually reclaimed all of the attractive clientele.

Two Sides of a Different Coin

A few months after rejecting Bert's attempts to set me up with his prey, I settled back into my role of watching Bert flirt with the pretty female customers and charm the rest. But, whereas previously I had at least been able to admire his charismatic way with his clientele when he wasn't hitting on them, I now watched all of his performances with scientific eyes.

And, one afternoon, I spotted a tiny but shocking hole in Bert's way with customers. A sixty-ish-year-old woman came to BS&S to buy a wallet for her husband, and—after Uncle Bert gave her the change from her purchase—the lady looked briefly at a grizzly bear design on the back of her new $2 coin. With curiosity on her face, she then flipped the coin over to the portrait of Queen Elizabeth side of the money.

"This coin is indecent," she remarked with slyness on her voice.

"I *know*," Uncle Bert replied. "The Queen has a *bear* behind."

The lady chuckled. "You've heard that one, eh?"

"Well, I work with cash all day, so ..."

"Fair enough," the woman said with a half-smile.

It was a strange moment. As the lady headed for our exit, Bert made no attempt to redeem her joke effort.

Now, it should be noted that Uncle Bert had not *ruined* the lady's fun by predicting her punch line; her mood was surely going to live to tell the joke another day. But it would have been so easy for my boss to have allowed the friendly customer to finish the humour and thus leave the store feeling good about her comedy. Even *I* could have done that.

And so my scientific eyes began watching Bert even more closely, and I was soon troubled to find out that coin-humoured customers weren't the only ones to occasionally receive only a half dose of Bert's charm. He was never ungentlemanly with anyone, but—given his power to improve moods with a single smile—mere politeness from him seemed to me to be the most contemptuous treatment available.

But why were those few customers being treated differently? It was clearly not an attraction distinction because the non-pretty customers—although not flirted with—often received my uncle's maximum platonic charm. *Hmm, perhaps they were only given such an honour when pretty women were in the vicinity.*

That turned out to be an excellent hypothesis: once I considered it, I noticed several occasions in which Uncle Bert turned up his charm on a not-so-beautiful customer just after a beautiful one had entered the store.

However, while the notion was certainly worthy of further research, it clearly did not tell Bert's entire story because there were many instances in which Bert charmed the non-beauties even when there was no beauty lurking nearby.

Nevertheless, in spite of lacking a clear flirtful explanation to justify every instance of Bert's charm, I was thereafter sternly skeptical of it all.

Eventually, Uncle Bert's unimpressive usage of his impressive collection of charm had me pondering an arrogant question. *If I had Bert's talent, would I make better use of it?* I couldn't see why not. Unlike Bert, I would try to be a benefit to those around me without the requirement of reward; and, unlike me, I would be able to pull it off.

For instance, as far as I could tell, Bert did not enjoy talking to customers of *thick*, English-as-an-additional-language accents.

CLARIFICATION NOTE: In contrast, it's clear to me that Uncle Bert appreciated customers of thin accents (because he liked comparing stories of world travel with them), but I'm confident that he found thick accents to be too tedious and unaware of his wit to be worthy of his time.

As such, Bert always directed the heaviest brogues (and language limitations) to me. Ordinarily, that would lead to a mundane interaction as I tried with few words and too many gestures to figure out the customer's needs; but, in my new fantasy existence—where Bert's talents were my own—the inherited conversations gained new eventfulness.

First, I was able to ponder myself copying Bert's investigative genius and thus asking far-from-home consumers where their accents were from and, in turn, what had brought them to our neck of the world. Those turned out to be excellent openers for imagined dialogue: the foreign customers replied, in my mind, with a flurry of rich tales of their journeys. Indeed, their imaginary approval soon supplemented even my most dull interactions.

Back in reality, one afternoon, a seventy-something-year-old gentleman started up the following conversation with me:

"How much is this?" he said.

"Um, that's twenty-nine ninety-five."

"So over *thirty-four* when you add the tax?"

"Oh, yeah, around there," I said. "Let me check." As I typed the numbers on my calculator, I imagined myself making a brilliantly whimsical joke about calculators taking over the world.

The customer shut down both my actual calculator assistance and my imagined calculator comedy with a wave of his hand. He then plunked down his money, one bill at a time. Halfway through the task, he noted:

"This business of charging five dollars of tax for a thirty-dollar item is ridiculous."

"How so?" I said, imagining that I had instead offered a comically intriguing argument for why taxes weren't so irritating.

The man did not notice my imaginary musings, but I still enjoyed having them.

That pattern repeated itself the next day as I helped an under-confident seventeen-year-old girl pick out an outfit: she came out of the BS&S changeroom with a shrug of self-disdain, but I—in my imagination—caught her attention with an excellent compliment that surely would have provoked a tiny smile to visit her face if I'd said it aloud.

Unfortunately, those dutiful daydreams were sabotaged by reality. While Bert was in the backroom on a quiet Tuesday morning, my first ever BS&S customer came into the store with sad contemplation gripping her eyes.

"Excuse me, John ..."

"Yes, hello, Mrs. McKegney."

"Hello, can you show me what you have in black skirts and blouses?"

"Sure, of course," I said as calmly as I could. As I walked her to the formal area, I searched my mind for something soothing to say. I found nothing useful to offer, so, instead, I looked at Mrs.

McKegney as gently as I knew how. "Um, would any of these be of interest?"

The customer observed the skirts I'd presented and began feeling their fabric.

I stood watch.

Mrs. McKegney took in a full sigh and gazed up at me.

"Um..." I said, but I caught myself as I realized that she was examining my face; clearly, she was preparing to say something that mattered.

She looked down to the blackness of the skirts again and then back at me.

I gulped out a smile.

Mrs. McKegney sighed again. "My husband just passed away."

"Oh, I'm sorry," was all I could think to say. "I'm so sorry."

She nodded. "It was very sudden."

"I'm so sorry," I said again, my heart thumping.

Mrs. McKegney stared at me. *Was that really the best I could do?*

My temple began to perspire. This was the moment. Here stood a grieving woman looking to me for some tiny utterance of comfort. But nothing arrived in my mind. *What was the point of fantasizing about how great I would be if I were more like Bert if I could never do anything worthwhile in the real world?*

"I'm so sorry," I said, "I guess, at least...maybe it's easier than watching someone die slowly." I paused, hoping for a twinge of comfort to find expression on Mrs. McKegney's face. But no such relief arrived.

"I would have liked," she said, "to have had some warning. I would have liked to have had an opportunity to say, 'Good bye.'" Then she looked down with the full weight of her disappointment, and she stared vaguely at another skirt.

My thoughts were overpowered by remorse. My improvised words weren't going to cheer up an acquaintance who had just lost her husband. She wasn't looking to hear that his death wasn't so bad, after all. She was just hoping for a little compassion.

So I made a pact with myself: I was never again going to try to be more than I was. That consoled me a little, and for a moment I second-guessed my daydream about what I could have done with Uncle Bert's talent; instead, perhaps I should have been imagining what he could have done with my heart.

Chapter 21
Dullard vs. Dullard

The Old College Try

It was in the next month that I decided that I had learned what I needed to from Uncle Bert, and so I determined that I should think about reuniting myself with my postsecondary education plans. But, for some deluded, subconscious reason, I asked Uncle Bert what *he* thought of the idea. Why my subconscious would tell me to do something so stupid, I cannot fathom. I'd worked at Bert's Shirts & Skirts for nine months by then, and I had certainly come to know Bert well enough to recognize that when he said, "John, why would you want to go to college?" he meant, 'Ernie, why would *I* want you to go?'

"Oh," I replied, "well, it just seems that I should go to school *some*time—if I wanna have a career or anything."

"If it's a *career* that you seek," Bert said, "then look no further than your uncle."

That comment put me in an awkward tone of voice. "Um, I really like working here, but I don't know if—"

"No, no," Bert said, "I wasn't meaning that you'd wanna stay working here forever—although it's not *that* horrible a fate, John," he added with a laugh.

"Sorry."

"No need to apologize, my young apprentice. I guess Ernie means more to Bert than Bert means to Ernie."

"No, no, it's not that. It's just—"

"You'd like a career of your own," my uncle finally let me off his hook. "Yes, I figured you would. You've got too much going for you to work for your uncle your whole life."

My eyebrows instinctively raised themselves in accusation toward the overinflated compliment.

"I'm serious, John. I've been around enough success in my life to know what it takes to get there."

"Right. Well, anyway, wouldn't going to school help me get there?"

"That's hard to say," Bert said, crinkling his forehead in thought. "School probably won't hurt you—you may eventually even get some decent contacts via that route—but, as to content, you'll just be studying a bunch of theory instead of actually learning."

"But," I said, trying to evade a sarcastic impulse, "I have to start somewhere, don't I?"

"True, but you have to know where you're going first. So what exactly do you wanna study?"

"Oh, I'm not sure. That's why I wanna go to school."

"So you're just gonna randomly pick courses from the catalogue and hope that one of them fits?"

"Yeah, sort of."

"Well, if it's profession identification that you're looking for ..." Bert paused and looked as if he was having a good think about a great unorthodox possibility. "I tell you what—why don't you stick with me a little while longer? Next vacation, I'll take you on a tour of my old stomping grounds in the city, and I'll introduce you to some real players in a smorgasbord of professions, and then we'll get you a *job* instead of just theoretical training for one."

"Um, well, I think I should just go to school. That way, I can have classmates and professors."

"*Professors?*" Bert said, chuckling. "These are the people who spend their hours writing books about each other! Honestly, John, the only ones who read their books are their rivals, their families— *if they're lucky*—and their poor students. I still remember Professor Leiderman—he had us reading his *own* book and expected us to write an essay on it. Let's see: *shall I disagree with a book by Leiderman in a course by Leiderman? Tough call. Maybe I'll go ask Leiderman for advice.*"

"Right," I said, chuckling politely back. "But, um ...I guess I *do* want to learn from the professors, so—"

"So *learn* from them! Learn from their mistakes. Don't drown yourself in books that only apply to an imaginary theoretical world. I'll introduce you to some characters who do the stuff that the professors only write and dream about."

My instincts told me not to trust Bert, but my curiosity was activated, and my cowardliness broke the tie, so I decided to let the college application deadline pass me by.

I was nervous to tell my parents about my renewal of Bert services for another semester. Strangely, though—when I did unveil my news—they seemed to think that I now had a greater right to make my own decisions than I had the previous year when I was only a few weeks out of high school.

"Are you sure that's what you want to do?" Dad said.

"No, but it just seems like, I don't know, a good opportunity."

"It probably is," Mom said. "But maybe you'd meet more people at school?"

"Maybe, but Bert says he'll introduce me to people I can learn from."

"John," my mother said, "I think Bert's an excellent teacher for you in theory, but, so far, in practice, I haven't noticed much of an effect."

"So you want me to be more like him?"

"Of course not, but it wouldn't kill you to learn from his best qualities."

"Like what?"

"Well, his confidence, his sense of adventure."

"Right, okay then," I said, suddenly feeling empty of both traits and thus certain that I wasn't ready for college. "Then I'm sure: I want to work a while longer with Bert to get some connections."

"Are you sure, John?" Dad said. "School is very much doable for you. I see no reason why you wouldn't excel there."

"Thanks," I said, almost tempted to prove him right, but more interested in proving my mom right.

A few evenings later, Per had his own news to present while he, my parents, and I were watching TV.

"This is dumb," he said in the middle of a show I was interested in.

"You don't have to like it," Mom said calmly.

"I know," Per said with a confused glance at his mother, "I'm just saying."

I suspected, though, that our mom's shocking display of defiance was directed more at Dellia—and her influence over Per's TV opinions—than Per, himself.

Nevertheless, Per kept sullen for a few minutes until, just before the commercial-break cliff-hanger, he inquired:

"Who writes this crap?"

"Per," Dad said. "Do you really need to—"

But Mom overruled her husband with a laugh. "I guess it's not the best, is it?"

"It's crap," Per said with a shake-of-the-head chuckle.

The above non-TV dialogue continued past the TV break, and so I decided that—if I was going to miss the rest of the show anyway—I may as well join the conversation.

"Hey," I said, trying to camouflage my dislike for Dellia, "how's Dellia doing? She hasn't been around as much lately."

"Broke up with her yesterday, bro."

"Oh, how come?"

"Because she wouldn't stop yammering in my ear all the time. She had to have an opinion on everything. I couldn't put my socks on without her telling me they were the wrong ones."

"Oh, I hadn't noticed that," I said. And, in defence of that lie, I thought it might be insensitive to kick Per's failed relationship while it was down.

"She just liked you a lot," Mom said, smiling a little too merrily. "She just wanted you to know what she was thinking."

"Well," Per said, "I would've been fine not knowing every single detail, thanks. You know, I actually miss Nicolette. She didn't say enough, but at least she was *nice*."

This time it was I who smiled a little too cheerfully as I enjoyed Nicolette's poetic revenge.

A month later—two weeks after my college application deadline had expired for the season)—my uncle wore the strangest disposition I'd seen on him since he'd tried to get me to do his flirting for him.

"Hey, John, do you mind handling the customers today? I'm not in the mood today."

"Sure. Everything okay?"

"Of course. Everything's always in order. I just feel like giving the customers a break."

Neither of those notions were supported an hour later when I stood at the customer counter typing a pretty woman's more-complicated-than-usual transaction into the till.

"You seem calm in the face of complexity," she said with a smile.

"Oh," I said, surprised by both her interest and her intellectual-sounding tone, "um, thanks, but the till does the work."

"Yes, but—correct me if I'm wrong—but you have to tell the machine the order of operations, or it won't work."

"Um, yeah, I guess you're right, but I guess that's what I like about machines like this. It'll always do, like, the exact same thing every time according to a few simple rules. So, if you just follow those simple rules, the till will never make a mistake."

The customer nodded. "I like that."

"Thanks," I said handing the woman back her card.

At that moment, I spotted Bert floating towards the conversation. He took a healthy look at the form of the woman standing finely before me, and then he looked at me and raised some impressed-with-me eyebrows as if I'd had something to do with the attractive woman's arrival in our store.

"So do you work in retail too?" I stammered at her.

"No, no," she said, "but I like to shop in it."

"Don't we all?" Bert arrived.

The woman turned to look at my uncle.

"Yeah, I guess so," she said, sounding confused by why he was there.

"I hope so," Bert said. "Otherwise, I'm in the wrong business."

"Well, it looks like you're doing okay."

"Only because I've got good help," Bert said more seriously than I was used to during his flirting. "Ernie, here, makes everything run smoothly."

"That's a good endorsement," the customer said, looking at me. "Get him to write that down for your future references."

"Are you trying to tempt him to leave me if I don't give him a raise?" Bert said with a grin.

"Well, I doubt you'll be able to keep him here forever," the customer said, winking at me in a mentorly way.

"Um—" I gulped.

"Well, you're quite right, of course," Bert said, smiling knowingly at the customer, "he's a talented fellow, but I'm curious as to how you figured it out so quickly?"

"Oh, um, well, you just told me that he makes everything run smoothly around here, so I figured from that. Plus," she added, glancing at me, "he's obviously got a good head on his shoulders, so—"

"*Indeed*," Bert said, "a good head on his shoulders *and* a good heart in his chest: he's a great catch for a boss as well as for the right young woman of sufficient dowry."

That comment hit me as though it were a puddle launched from a passing truck.

But the woman chuckled and then turned to me with the same mentorly smile that had accompanied her wink.

"I'm sure he is," she said. "Well, boys—it's been great. I must be off. See you again."

"Cheers," Bert replied.

The moment the door closed behind the customer, I turned to glare at Bert.

"That was odd," he said with crinkled brow and scrunched lips. "I guess you were doing better before I got here."

"I wasn't doing *anything*," I shot back.

"Well, regardless, it worked."

"No, it didn't!"

"Come on, she *liked* you. She winked at you."

"That wasn't a *wink*. It was—"

"Um, John, I think you may want to double-check your dictionary—"

"But it wasn't a *seductive* wink."

"Of course, it was."

"No, it was more like how *you* wink."

"What do you mean by that?"

"Like, when you wink at me. Like, I assume *you're* not trying to flirt with me."

"Oh, I see," my uncle said. "Well, I'll take your word for it. Anyway, sorry I interrupted."

"No, that's okay," I said, embarrassed once again to have

provoked a one-way apology, especially since Bert was apparently just trying to help me with my alleged flirting.

My uncle smiled back and then returned to his backroom.

He came out twenty minutes later. "Hey, Ernie, whaddya say we close up the shop at noon, and I take you for lunch?"

Bert and I didn't have much to say to each other on the short walk to our unusual assignment, but, once inside the restaurant, Bert's charm rose up to regular levels; he had the hostess smiling, the waitress laughing, and soon even my nerves were cheerful.

"All right, John, my boy," he said after we'd ordered, "I suppose you're wondering what's up?"

"I suppose I am."

"Well, I've been thinking…maybe you were right: maybe it's time for you to get out there and be among your own kind."

"*My own kind?*"

"Yeah, people your own age. I think maybe you should follow your heart and go to college."

"Oh," I said. Indeed, my brain scrambled, trying to figure out what would provoke Bert to go against his own judgment. There was only one reasonable possibility. "Uncle Bert, are you firing me?"

Bert laughed. "No, of course not—if it were up to me, I'd keep you on as my assistant forever. But I'm starting to think it may be in your best interest to learn among your contemporaries."

Uncle Bert was not making any sense. *How could he want me to do what was in my best interest if it conflicted with his own much-cherished interest?*

"But I thought you said that college was—that I couldn't learn anything from college."

"Well, you don't necessarily have to go to college. All I'm saying is that someone with a great personality like yours shouldn't be stuck in a small town working for his uncle."

"Wow, okay," I mumbled—and rightly so: Bert must have been desperate if he was willing to stoop to complimenting my personality.

"Look, John, I know a guy who's got some clout with a good company in the city, and he tells me he's got a job opportunity open that doesn't require a lot of experience. If I get you an interview, will you go and talk to him—*as a favour to me*—just to see what you think?"

I knew that Bert was trying to manipulate me, but I couldn't fathom for what purpose, so I had no valid reason to turn down his puppeteering. Besides, I was curious as to what he had in crafty mind.

Chapter 22
Dullard vs. Charmer IV

The Tangentleman

To my surprise, I wasn't as nervous as I'd planned on being when I arrived at the enormous building in the big city in which I was to have my interview. I suppose the fact that I had no particular desire to get the job may have subdued my anxiety.

As I entered the oversized structure, I noticed that—despite its square exterior—it was confusing to navigate on the inside. After taking several wrong turns and receiving some contradictory directions from suited strangers, I finally tracked my way to Chet Williams' office where I found a handsome man in his near forties.

"Mr. John Smith, I presume?" he said with a hefty smile. "I'm Chet Williams."

"Nice to meet you," I replied, my nerves now arriving without permission.

"How was your journey in?" Chet said, taking my hand for a good shake.

"It was good, thank you."

"That's what I like to hear," Chet said, still squeezing my palm. "I try to avoid travelling, myself. I've always thought that traveling was overrated. I mean they call it 'home sweet home' for a reason, don't you think?"

I'd never thought of the *home sweet home* expression as a slogan for the anti-traveling coalition before, but Chet had made a good point, so I agreed to it, hoping he might reward me with the return of my fingers.

"Have a seat," Chet said, finally letting go.

I sat down, now fully nervous.

"So," Chet said, "let's have a look-see at your resumee …Interesting, I see that your first job was at a bakery. How'd that go?"

"It was pretty good, actually. I liked it because I got to work with lots of different people, so I learned how to adapt to people."

"Nice," Chet said. "Did they let you sample the doughnuts?"

"Sometimes, yeah."

"Lucky you. You gotta love doughnuts."

"Yeah," I said, trying to smile, "that was a bonus."

"All right, very good," Chet said. "How about your job with Bert's little clothing hut. How'd that go?"

"Good, I've learned a lot from Bert about dealing with customers and, you know, adapting to their needs."

"Right on," Chet said. "Bert's an old buddy-a-mine from his daddy's company, you know?"

"Yes, he told me that."

"How is the old sod?"

"Good, I think."

"Ah, good ol' Dirty Berty," Chet said with a sigh.

I smiled my appreciation of the rhyme.

"I used to call him *Dirty Berty*," Chet explained. "He tell you about that?"

"Ah, no, it hasn't come up yet."

"That's Dirty Berty for you. He was always trying to make people think he was all sophisticated. What a guy. He was something with the ladies, though. He could charm the cross off a nun."

"Yeah, I guess," I said.

"I've got an apartment near here," Chet replied.

"Do you like it?" I said instinctively.

"Sure do. Home sweet home—couldn't be happier with it." Chet then proceeded to tell me about an adventure that he and his sweet home had been on together. "So that's why," he concluded a minute later, "I decided it would be smarter to buy the wood finish."

"Sounds like a good choice."

"You betcha," Chet said, full grin. "You know, I never did understand Mozart. Do you like Mozart, Johnny?"

"Um …" I said, so startled by the seemingly unprovoked topic change that, for a moment, I assumed that Mozart's day job must have been wood finishing. "I don't know much about him."

"That's okay," Chet said. "But did you know that Mozart's dad was a pretty decent composer in his own right?"

"No, I didn't know that."

Chet was apparently pleased to hear it. "Well, you learn something new every day, don't you, Johnny?"

"Yeah, for sure."

Chet smiled. "Very good. So what other qualifications do you bring to us?"

"Well, I work hard."

"Very good."

"I'm punctual."

"Good. That's what I like to hear. They say it's better to be late than never, but I say it's even better to be on time."

"Fair enough," I said with an appreciative smirk.

Chet seemed to ponder that. "*You know what*," he said with a smile, "I wonder if anyone ever advertises a Mozart concert and then plays Mozart Senior just as a joke."

"I don't know," I said, genuinely amused by the thought.

"Well, *think about it*," Chet said. "Mozart Senior's music is probably way simpler and easier to practice—so they advertise Mozart, and people are gonna assume it's Mozart Junior when really it's Mozart Senior. So they'll get the same crowds, but they won't have to learn such challenging music."

"That's funny," I said, still amused but too nervous to laugh.

"And I'm sure they'd save money on royalties too," Chet continued, "because Mozart Senior's music probably costs less." Chet then chuckled some more and looked at me to join in.

I did my best, and Chet seemed pleased with my effort.

"Well," my interviewer concluded with a chuckle, "I like a good laugh in the morning, don't you, Johnny?"

"Yeah, definitely."

"*Very good.*"

And so went the interview. Chet would ask normal interview questions which I would start to answer until, it seemed, he got bored and changed the subject apparently to whatever most recently had popped by his brain. I would then respond by displaying interest in his musings, which, in turn, seemed to impress him.

After forty-five minutes, Chet smiled at me. "You're a pretty neat guy, aren't you, Johnny?"

I couldn't think how Chet could have deduced that since I'd said so little during our conversation, but I wasn't going to argue.

"Um—" I said instead.

"Well," Chet concluded, "you're my man. You've got the job!"

"Oh, okay, thanks," I said, too stunned to be more gracious. "Um, would it be okay if I took a day or two to think it over?"

"Sure," Chet said, "take as long as you need—you've got two days."

I traveled home with a job in hand and a confusion in head. As pleased with myself as I was to have been offered a job with a big-city company, I still couldn't fathom what possible motivation Uncle Bert could have had for obtaining me the new livelihood.

The Loyalty Royalty

It was late in the evening when I got off the bus from the big city. I walked home through a refreshing breeze. As I approached the Smith house, I spotted an extra car in the driveway. I didn't recognize it, but it had a new-car shine to it. *Could my parents have upgraded?* As I came to the front door, I could hear conversation beyond it. My nerves were suddenly awake as I opened the unlocked door. I stepped inside, and I found my mom, my dad, and my *Aunty Susan* sitting in the living room. Aunty Susan's face was stained by tears.

"What's wrong?"

"Bert's leaving town," Dad said.

"*Leaving?*"

Aunty Susan took in an elongated sigh. "He says a small town is—*what did he say?*—too much of a *cage* for a character like him. He needs *wide open city spaces.*"

"Wow ... and, um, you didn't wanna go with him?"

"He didn't invite me."

"*He didn't invite you?* You're his wife!"

My aunt shrugged and stretched the side of her mouth with her teeth.

I stared at her, searching for something helpful to say, but I still wasn't sure I understood what was going on.

Aunty Susan sighed. "It's got nothing to do with *wide open space*s," she said, "well, not literally anyway. In reality, he's looking for…Mrs. Hogart saw him leaving the store with a woman on his arm."

Oh my ghostwriter. Uncle Bert had run off with one of his flirtings.

"Aunty Susan," I said, holding my eyes as hard as I could, "I'm so sorry."

My aunt seemed to take my word for it.

Per arrived home from work twenty minutes later.

"Holy Hell," he said, upon learning the news. "What's wrong with that guy?"

"It was so strange the way he did it," Aunty Susan said. "Well, not strange for him—it was *so Bert*. But it was like it was a surprise party—the way he snuck everything into the house while I was at work."

"He snuck stuff *in*?"

"Well, first, he did all the things he gets in trouble for *not* doing. Not that I'm a nag, but he always forgets. And then there's all these presents—things that I'd mentioned in passing—and a new car out front."

"He bought you a car?"

Aunty Susan nodded with a smirk. "You may have seen it on your way in. I brought it over to show you guys the results of my marriage."

My mother shook her head. "Like you're going to care about a car when your husband's just left."

"I know," Aunty Susan said. "But it's as if he thinks he's in a movie, and he's making his big heroic exit. I think—in his… *deranged* mind—he equates memorable with heroic. Even when he's being awful, he wants people to think how unique he is."

"What a spazz," Per said.

By 5 a.m., we were starting to giggle at Bert's follies.

"I guess *now*," Aunty Susan said, looking at me, "we know why Bert sent you for that job interview."

"I guess *so*," I said. But, really, it only explained why Bert had nothing to *lose* by getting me the job; it still wasn't clear what he had to gain.

"He genuinely liked you, John."

"What? *Seriously?*"

"He admired you. He said you were the most down-to-earth guy he'd ever met."

Bert actually liked me? That seemed implausible, but why else would he have gotten me a new job? How strange. Bert had deserted his wife, and yet he seemed to have imposed on himself some sort of duty to provide me with work after he'd gone. For a moment, I felt honoured that Bert might have cared about me. But the moment didn't last long. I soon smacked myself with some shame for letting myself care what a scoundrel like Bert Hardelean thought of me.

"So did you get the job?" Aunty Susan interrupted those speculations.

"Yeah. But obviously I'm not going to take it."

"You got the job?" my mom said, sitting up in her chair.

"*Apparently*," my dad said.

It was the strangest thing that I'd ever heard my father say; it was clearly meant to be a sarcastic jab at my mother. Wow. Five in the morning can produce some surprising results. Lucky for my dad, my mom was clearly too tired to care enough to notice.

"John," Aunty Susan said, staring at me, "why aren't you going to take the job?"

"Because, I don't know, it's like dirty money."

"No, no, no, John, *please* take the job. I mean, *don't* if you don't want it, but you have to separate what Bert did to me from him helping you get that job. You deserve it: you've worked hard for it, John." My aunt sighed and put her hand on mine. "Please don't take that away from me…well, unless you really don't want the job."

I, myself, could not separate Bert from his cruelty to my aunt. But I could see that, if I accepted the job, Aunty Susan would feel a smidge better.

"If you really want me to, Aunty Susan, I'll take it."

Aunty Susan nodded with a smile.

So, seeing no higher consideration than my aunt's momentary comfort, I signed up with the big company in the big city.

Chapter 23
Dullard In Transit

Oysters vs. Butterflies

My dad drove me the hour and a half trip to the big city on a Saturday night. With an assembly line in our hearts, he unloaded our vehicle while I delivered the boxes to the apartment that my parents and I had scouted out a week before. En route, I enjoyed the then uncommon-for-me experience of riding an elevator.

As I watched the passing floor numbers light up above the elevator doors, I chuckled in recollection of my week-earlier trip on the same conveyance. I had noted then that the elevator designers had made a mistake and forgotten to include Floor 13 on their display. My mother had laughed and explained that apartments often excluded that particular floor number because of rampant rumours that the number 13 was unlucky; the explanation had made me chuckle at my superiority to superstitious simpletons.

Outside of my reminiscing a few minutes later, some more boxes and I approached the elevator for another ride, but we slowed down as I noticed that the doors were headed to close before I could get there.

Oddly, though, while I was still a few strides away, a twenty-something-year-old woman already on board stuck her arm into the path of the elevator doors, which—after assaulting their interrupter—retreated to their open-door position.

"Going up?" the woman said with a smile—and a remarkably nice smile it was!

"Yes, I think so," I said, hopping aboard. "Thank you."

"Do you know which floor?"

"Oh, right, thanks," I said, making my selection as I balanced two boxes in one arm.

And get ready to be impressed, usually not-so-much reader, because—spurred on by the significance of immigrating to the big city—I felt oddly unafraid of the friendly woman. All I needed was a topic of conversation, and I'd be happy to chat with her. Now, you might think I would have noted my boxes and talked about moving into the building. 'Did she know the good restaurants in the area?' Or 'How did she like the city?' Or any number of newcomer questions. But, cruelly, I was too dull to think of the obvious.

"Um," I said instead, "ever notice the way they don't have the number 13 for these elevators?"

"Yeah," she said, "it's funny how superstitious people are, isn't it?"

Oh. She already knew about that—perhaps an editorial comment then. "Yeah, don't they realize that they're still *on* the 13th floor? Just because it's *called* 14 doesn't mean it's not the 13th floor."

She nodded without enthusiasm. "Yeah, people are weird, eh?" She then turned back to facing forward as if we weren't having the most exciting conversation I'd had in months.

I decided to take her lack of looking at me as a cue that she preferred to stare ahead than to chat, so I let her be.

When her floor arrived, she smiled at me again. "See you," she said with a tone that was more polite than sincere.

"See you," I replied, wondering why we were making such bold predictions.

During the next few moments—in which retroactive analysis ran supreme in my brain—I felt ashamed of the interaction with my elevator friend. Unfortunately, that prevented me, a few minutes later, from sharing the details with my dad, which probably would have benefitted me, considering that he might have persuaded me to be pleased with myself for at least making an effort. Instead, as it was, I left me alone with my mean-spirited self-critique. That did not do much for my mood.

An hour later, my father, my boxes, and I sat in my apartment, and we munched away on take-out food, which I had proudly purchased for both of us.

It was strange not having my mother or brother there to star in the conversation. My dad and I were so used to being supporting actors in our family dynamic that it was hard to know how to carry the show ourselves. For a moment, the walls of my abode could only hear the percussive rhythms of our chewing.

I looked hopefully at my dad, willing a thought worthy of conversation to land in my mind.

"Well, John," he said, "you've made it."

"I don't know about that," I said. Indeed, my earlier excitement regarding my brand new life in the big city had now flipped over to its other side and become a collection of nerves.

"What's the matter?" he said.

"Oh, nothing big. I'm just a little nervous."

Dad nodded. "Understandable. But you know what, John, you've always succeeded at anything you've set your mind to."

"Really, you think?"

My father looked at me carefully. "I don't think I've ever seen you give anything but your best."

"Maybe," I said, letting out a light chuckle, "but effort and success aren't really the same thing, are they?"

"Well," Dad said, "when I look back, I regret more the times I didn't put in a full effort than the times I didn't succeed."

"Fair enough," I said with a mild smirk. I considered pointing out that that still didn't justify his claim that I was *likely* to succeed. But, as I looked at my father's earnest eyes, I realized I did not want to defeat his hope for me. "Yeah, fair enough," I repeated instead.

"Good," Dad said. "I know you don't really believe it right now—but try to keep it mind, okay?"

"Okay," I said, letting a smile sneak onto my face.

"Oh, hey," Dad said, "speaking of great efforts, your mom and I got you a house-warming gift."

He ruffled through a bag and produced a DVD of Charlie Chaplin's *City Lights*. As I took the item in my hand, I felt a punch of nostalgia. It was my favourite of Chaplin's films, but I required some protection from my emotions, so I played hard-to-get with my appreciation.

"Wow, this is the boxing one, right?"

"The very one."

"Awesome, thanks. *I love that one*—I think it's my favourite."

"Yeah, that's what we thought."

"Yeah, Charlie Chaplin's great, isn't he?"

My emotions were still banging around my chest, so I repeated my banal approval a couple of times, and then I changed the topic to less controversial matters, such as where I should do my grocery shopping and whether I should buy a table for mealtime.

An hour later, my dad left my new home, and I stepped alone onto my eighth floor balcony. It was a cool night, and my hair enjoyed the feeling of the wind.

I looked out at the world.

'I'm your oyster,' it seemed to whisper back.

But, with my stomach already full of butterflies, there wasn't room for oysters.

Party of Wonder

Sitting in my apartment on Sunday morning, I decided to begin my first official day in the city by testing the bus route to my new workplace. As I came along the hallway from my apartment in search of elevator services, there was a lady—who looked to be a veteran of about seventy years—who was just getting off the elevator with some morning groceries.

I smiled at her as I walked towards the vertical carriage that she was vacating.

Now, you'll want to note, watchful reader, that there was, with my pace of approach, easily enough time for me to catch the elevator before its electric doors closed, but the lady—like her younger counterpart had the day before—stuck her arm out and blocked the doors open for me.

"There you go, dear."

"Thank you so much," I said, rushing to the doors so that she wouldn't need to hold them anymore.

"You're welcome, dear," she said; but, as she released the gate, she tilted out of its way and, in doing so, caused a can of soup to tumble out of her paper grocery bag. "Oh dear," she said.

So I took a couple quick strides to retrieve the renegade grocery item.

"Thank you, dear," the woman said, "what a clumsy blunderer I am."

"No, not at all," I said, pretending not to notice the elevator doors closing again. "Um ..." I added, not sure where to go from there.

"Are you new to the building, dear?" the woman said.

"Yeah, I just moved in yesterday."

"Well, welcome then," the woman said, clicking the elevator retrieval button.

"Thanks, you too," I said.

Thankfully, the elevator reopened to rescue me from that moronic comment.

"Well, nice to meet you," I said.

The woman smiled quietly. "You too, dear."

As I walked to the street in search of my bus stop, I reminisced over my conversation with my new neighbour. In spite of my various errors during the discussion, I felt that somehow our mini-meeting had been a highlight of her day—and perhaps mine. That contemplation left me feeling guilty that I hadn't made more effort to continue the discussion, but I pardoned myself when I considered our large distinction in ages: surely the woman and I didn't have enough common ground for sustained conversation.

During my subsequent bus ride, I passed a section of the city in which I noticed some women dressed somewhat like the prostitutes from action movies. They were sticking themselves out at the world with clothing that was much grungier and faces that were far less pretty than the movie prostitutes. The sickly sexualizing produced a sadness in me that had never occurred during my action movie viewing.

I wished I could do something to help the ragged creatures. *Perhaps I could buy them a night free from their work?* I quickly realized that that was a stupid thought to have had, considering they would surely just accept the money and then go right back on duty. And so it seemed to me that there was nothing a concerned spectator could do for the pained strangers. One of the women then caught my examining eye and sneered at me through my passing bus window. Quite rightly, therefore, sorrow overloaded my chest.

Strangely, I felt worse for the women on the streets than their drug and insanity-stained male colleagues. I don't know if that was evidence that I was sexist against women or against men. Either way, I was surprised and further saddened by it.

Soon, the bus was finished its tour of the dark ages and returned to civilization where it dropped me off at a bus stop that was three-minutes brisk walk from my new workplace. As I came around a city corner and into the view of the beautiful, monster-sized building, I was amazed and somewhat inspired by the fact that I had been invited to spend a quarter of my time there.

The next day, I travelled in an excellent mood to my first day of work. James Brown was singing 'I feeeel good' in my earbuds, and I felt in concert with him as I watched the world through my bus window portal.

A few minutes into the ride, my Walkman batteries died. Luckily, the bus provided its own entertainment.

SOCIO-TEMPORAL NOTE: The Walkman was the the most famous portable-music player of my then time.

Near my seat, a pair of skillfully dressed teenaged girls were standing and chatting.

"So," the shorter of the two said to her friend, "Mr. Leeky or Mr. Kan teaching you math?"

The taller friend pondered that for a moment. "I think I'd take Mr. Leeky—he's more boring, but I find him easier to understand."

"Yeah," the short one replied, "I know what you mean, but he puts me to sleep, so I'm not paying attention anyway."

"True enough," the tall one said. "Okay, who would you rather get a ride home from after school—Mr. Saxton or Ms. Freidleman?"

"Saxton," the short girl replied, "or, I don't know, he can get weird when he's trying to be all inspiring."

Her friend laughed. "Yeah, but at least he's not always talking about *Girl Power*. If Ms. Freidleman says 'You go girl' to me one more time—"

Shorty laughed. "Next time, just tell her, 'Actually, Ms. Freidle-man, I'm not eleven anymore.'"

"I know, right? Okay, how about this? Your dad picking you up from a party or your mom?"

"Definitely my dad. Unless it was like a baby shower or something like that—like after my cousin's—'cause my dad hates that stuff, but after a *party* party…the one time my dad picked me up, he said nothing judgy to me at all—we actually just listened to sports radio the whole way home. It was so awesome."

"I'd take my mom," the taller friend said. "Neither of my parents have picked me up from a proper party, but I think she'd be pretty okay with whatever if I called her to pick me up."

"Yeah, your mom's awesome," the short one said. "Okay, so how about this: being attracted to a *friend's* boyfriend versus being into, like, the son of one of your *mom's* friends?"

As the short girl mulled that over, I pondered the casual tone with which the pair had referred to their parties. For them, it seemed that such gatherings were an obvious portion of their existence that went along with school supplies and teachers. For me, teenager parties were a faraway imagining; in fact, I had yet to be invited to one during all of my years in the demographic. I wasn't troubled by that result because I imagined that I lacked the skills for successful participation in teenager parties anyway. But, now that I was less than a year from graduating from my teenager years, I wondered if I might make a friend at my new job who might invite me to a post-teen party.

Twenty minutes of pondering later, I entered the intimidating, super-sized foyer of my new workplace, where I found people moving in many different directions. It was not unlike an ant farm: all participants seemed to have a purpose without ever reaching a destination. And it was clear that my momentous first day on the job was not something any of them gave much thought. Indeed, it seemed that no one would have noticed if I had reversed my stride and returned to where I belonged.

AMBIGUOUS NOTE: You may have noticed, observant reader, that I haven't identified what sort of workplace I was joining. My ghostwriter claims, 'The breed of the workplace has nothing to do with the story of our book,' and so he's not going to waste his 'ghostwriting energy' on it. Instead, he says, my new workplace will simply be identified as 'Ambiguity,' and he'll leave it to you, wise reader, to imagine the genre. Sorry about that, disappointed reader, but I am merely a pawn in my ghostwriter's controlling games.

Chapter 24
Dullard at Work III

Pro & Conversations

"Mr. John Smith," Chet Williams said, holding out his hand. "Welcome to our fine company. Are you excited?"

"Yes, definitely."

"I bet you're nervous too," Chet said, his hand now locked onto mine.

"I guess a little, yeah."

"Nervous is good," Chet said. "Did I ever tell you about my mom's garden?"

"No," I said, wondering with interest how Chet was going to relate a garden to nervousness.

"Well," he said, finally letting my hand be on its own again, "you're in for a treat. My mom has all the colours of the rainbow in that garden of hers. I'm talking red and blue, green and blue, yellow and ..."

As Chet listed each colour within the spectrum, I found myself feeling frustrated with how long he was taking to relate them to our established topic of nervousness. It wasn't until Chet started telling me the best way to take on weeds that I realized that he had no intention of relating his garden-variety lecture to nervousness. Instead, he had once again changed the topic of conversation without telling anyone.

Chet grinned when he concluded his monologue. "All righty, let's get you to work. Follow your leader," he said, walking us out of his office and into an adjacent room. "Welcome to your office. Pull up a chair next to your computer and start 'er up."

Chet wasn't giving me much time to take in the fact that I now possessed an office. In the moment I had to peek at my sparse but square surroundings, I noted that I had a window overlooking one of the Ambiguous parking lots.

I turned my computer on.

"Perfecto!" Chet said. "Now, do you know how to X-ate a Y?"

"No, sorry."

"No problemo. Take your Y from your W—"

"What's a W?"

"Good question," Chet said, preparing not to make any sense on the matter, "that's the thing that keeps the L and the M from getting lost."

"Okay, and what are the L and the M?"

"They're important. You don't want to lose them, trust me."

"I see. But ...what *are* they?"

"They're basically identical to each other."

"Oh, okay, so ...what do they do?"

Evidently, Chet found my confusion to be confusing. But Chet was patient with me. He tried his explanation again, but this time he used extra emphasis so that his teaching would stick somewhere in my brain.

"Basically," he said, "the L and the M have the *same* function. They do the same thing. And the W helps to keep them from getting lost. Got it?"

"I guess so."

"You betcha! You'll do fine. So I want you to take your Y and X-ate it."

"Right—sorry, what's the Y again?"

"It's basically the thing that holds everything together. Have you ever ridden a roller coaster?"

"Yes," I said with interest, for I had always found metaphors to be excellent clarifiers. But, unfortunately, three minutes into the metaphor, I realized that it was only a metaphor for itself. In fact, to be completely accurate, it should not really have been called a metaphor at all. 'Tangent' would have been a better word for it, 'Irrelevant tangent!'

And so went Chet's teaching. After half an hour of it, I realized that I wasn't going to learn much from it and that it would be best if I simulated comprehension so that Chet wouldn't feel any obligation to elaborate. (The sooner he finished impersonating a teacher, the quicker I could try to figure out what he'd been showing me.)

Thirty apparent—but only fifteen *actual*—minutes later, Chet finally left my work area. As I'd hoped, without Chet there to distract me, I was able to unpeel his instructions. In fact, by lunchtime, I had a basic grasp of what it was that I was supposed to be doing. However, because I'd spent the entirety of my morning trying to *figure out* what I was supposed to be doing, I had not yet been able to get much of it done—which is to say that I became nervous when Chet came by to check on my progress.

"So how're you doing, Sir John A. Macdonald?"

"Um, I didn't get that much done. I've just been trying to get used to the system."

"No problemo. How much *did* you get done?"

"Um, I just entered the one Q into the N-database."

"Perfecto," Chet said. "That's great."

That one confused me: from Chet's perspective, he had explained my tasks to me perfectly. *So why wasn't he disappointed in my paltry progress?* But this was no time to be solving such riddles; Chet had a more challenging brainteaser in mind for me.

"So, Johnny Appleseed, your boss is ready for lunch. You wanna join me?"

Oh. I was hoping to spend my lunch hour taking a break from work—or at least from Chet—but, as far as I could desperately determine, there was no solution to the conundrum of how to turn him down without offending him.

"Sure," I said instead.

"Excellentio. Follow your leader…I'd invite Erik," Chet added as we walked, "but he's not here today."

"Right," I said, about to ask who Erik was.

"And, besides," Chet said with a chuckle, "it's not like he'd come anyway."

"Right," I said, pretending that I knew Erik's antisocial antics well. I was again then about to ask who exactly Erik was, but Chet had already moved onto other topics.

Chet's meandering stream of narration stopped when we entered the Ambiguous cafeteria. Whatever topic he was on vanished from the conversational landscape as he scanned the faces already in the large food room.

"Let's see," he said, "is little Tally here today?"

The question was asked with such a firm lilt at the end of it that I thought that he wanted me to answer.

"Um," I said.

"*Ahah*," Chet took over, "there she is—let's go say 'Hi' to Tally."

"Tally-ho!" Chet said, beaming at an early-to-medium-aged woman.

"I beg your pardon?" she replied with a smile. "*What* did you call me?"

Chet laughed. "No, no, I meant, *Tally-ho*—as in the greeting."

"Oh, I see, I thought you were insulting me."

Chet laughed again. "If I was going to insult you, I wouldn't do it to your face."

"Thank you," Tally replied, "I'd appreciate that."

I laughed.

"I'm Tally," Chet's friend said, smiling at me.

"This is John," Chet answered, "he works for me. You guys can't have him."

"Well," Tally said, "Elsje'll see about that."

"How come Elsje's not here?" Chet replied.

"You know Elsje: she thinks lunch breaks are for the weekend."

Chet laughed. "Yeah, I was discussing workplace effectiveness with her the other day."

Chet seemed pleased by his empty anecdote: apparently, just the fact of having spoken to Elsje was meant to be impressive.

"*Well*," Chet said, looking at the cafeteria line up, "maybe we'll join you."

"Sure," Tally said with a voice that reminded me ever so slightly of the one I'd used to agree to Chet lunch. "Bernice is coming too so don't be put off if I've multiplied by the time you get back."

"Not a problem," Chet said. "You coming, Johnson & Johnson?"

"Oh," I said, glancing at the bag lunch in my hand. "Sure," I said, deciding that I didn't want to impose on Tally until Chet was ready.

"Are you getting something?" Tally said.

"Oh, um, no."

"Then grab a chair. It'll give me a chance to start negotiations for stealing you for Head Office."

I laughed. "Okay, thanks."

"Elsje won't let you steal him from me," Chet said. "She's too loyal to me for that."

Tally shrugged with a smile. "That may be, but I know where the transfer forms are, *and* I have a copy of Elsje's digital signature."

Chet laughed. "Elsje wouldn't do that to me."

Said comment seemed to me to have missed the point of Tally's humour, but—since Chet had used the remark as his parting quip—I decided not to point it out.

"So, John," Tally said as I sat down, "is today your first day here?"

"Yeah, how could you tell?"

"You have a bit of a getting-to-know-your-surroundings look on your face."

"Yeah, that makes sense," I said, pleased that she was watching me closely enough to make such an observation. "What about you? How long have you worked here?"

"A lot longer than I expected when I started."

"Why's that?" I said, surprised that she was being so interesting so quickly.

"Well, my boss is far too good to me to motivate me to look for a job that's in my field. And my husband and I could use the money, so—"

"Right," I said, and—even though Tally was about a decade older than me—I felt a tiny smidge disappointed by the news of Mr. Tally.

"*Hey,*" Tally said, suddenly looking up.

"Who's this?" a younger-than-Tally woman said with bored intonation.

"This is John—he works with Chet. It's his first day today. John, this is Bernice—she works in Head Office as well."

"Hi," I said.

"How are you?" Bernice replied flatly as she slumped in her chair. "The lineup's as slow as fricken' molasses today."

"That's unusual," Tally said.

"Nope," Bernice said with a look of surprise at Tally's ignorance, "just like every other day."

There was then a bit of a strained pause, which—lucky for Bernice—she didn't seem to notice since she was now concentrating on her food.

"So, John," Tally said, "how's your first day going?"

"Oh, it's pretty good," I said, scrambling for an interesting thing to say. "Um, yeah, it's a bit confusing trying to figure out how everything works, but—"

Bernice smirked as she took a bite of her food. "Try working in Head Office for a day. Your head'll be spinning. We have to be on top of, like, *so many things* at once."

"Yeah, I'm sure. I wasn't meaning to complain. It's just… because it's my first day—"

"You should've seen me on *my* first day," Bernice replied with a full mouth. "I felt like I had to be a fricken' brain surgeon to understand all the stuff they were throwing at me. But I was like, 'I got through high school even though I was like strung up in bed with chronic bronchitis for half the year, so I think I can get through this.' But it was fricken' hard. You have no idea."

"Yeah, that sounds awful."

"You know it," Bernice said, returning to her food.

"So," I said, looking at Tally, "how was *your* first day here?"

"Oh, mine was pretty easy, actually. My boss was amazing. Actually, I think it's the boss that determines—"

"Yeah," another mouthful of Bernice arrived, "my last boss was like that. He, like, made everything simple, but sometimes that made it harder because it meant I had to be all organized all the time and keep everything in their assigned spots. That was annoying."

"Yeah, that makes sense," I said, irritated on Tally's behalf by the interruption, "is that how it is for you, Tally?"

"No, not really. My boss is pretty easy to work for. So long as you're getting the job done, she doesn't care where you put everything."

"That's what I'm like with clients," Bernice took over. "If you wanna see Steven, I don't care about the details so long as it fits in my little schedule."

"That makes sense," I said trying extra hard to keep my face from showing the growing annoyance I was feeling in Bernice's direction.

"You know it," Bernice said.

After Tally and I started a couple more topics, which Bernice subsequently finished with her superior experiences, Chet returned.

"Hey, Bernice," he said. "How's life treating ya?"

"Same as always," Bernice replied, returning her focus to her food.

Chet nodded and turned to Tally. "So what've you got against cafeteria food?" he said with a smile.

"Oh, nothing: I just don't like paying for it."

"Tell me about it," Bernice returned. "But it's like, I have to feed the dog and the boyfriend when I get home—I don't feel like fixing lunch too."

That comment from Bernice had no opportunity to linger into awkwardness because Chet segued off of it before anyone couldn't respond. Indeed, Chet and Bernice quickly engaged themselves in a fast-paced bout of competitive conversing. Whereas Chet could tangent away before Bernice's points were finished, Bernice always had something more important to say about Chet's digression. Yet, amazingly, neither competitor seemed at all annoyed with the conversational greed of the other.

Meanwhile, I was startled to realize that Tally had faded out of the conversation. That was disappointing to me, considering that she was clearly the most interesting of the four of us.

After lunch, I returned to trying to decipher Chet's instructions for what work I was supposed to be doing. It was not an entirely dissatisfying process as my assignments continued to illuminate themselves as I progressed through them.

A few short-seeming hours later, Chet smiled at me from my office doorway.

"All righty, John Dillinger, you've done your time for today. I'll walk you out."

"Oh, okay."

"Erik probably called in sick today," Chet said, chuckling as we walked down the exit hallway.

"Who's Erik?"

"Your office neighbour—great guy, very smart. But Elsje wouldn't be happy, obviously."

"Right, who's Elsje?"

"*Elsje Anders*—our leader. Great gal."

"How so?" I said, surprised to be suddenly interested in what Chet had to say.

"Well, for one thing, she's smart as a whip. I love talking to Elsje. She's so serious about our work. You'll love Elsje. I used to drive a convertible."

And, with that, Chet had changed the topic to that of a car he'd noticed outside of a window we were passing. I was too interested in the previous topic to endure a new one, so—spotting a stairwell—I faked an exit route.

"Oh," I said, "this is me here, so—"

"So, unless you run off to the circus tonight, we'll see you tomorrow, John Ringling."

The bus ride home that evening was fatigue-filled. Not because my work had been difficult, but because my nerves had had a long day. I was therefore content to spend the evening relaxing in front of sitcoms on TV. I didn't even feel lonely about the fact that there was no one to tell about my day. I was too tired to discuss it anyway.

On my way to work the next day, I continued pondering the possibility that I might make a friend at Ambiguity. After all, the place seemed to have the population of a small town: surely that gave me a high probability of compatibility with at least one Ambiguous colleague. Admittedly, I had previously lived in an actual small town with the population of a small town without having made any friends, but perhaps now having the fellow citizens as co-workers would give me a free introduction.

It was a flawed hope. You see, it turns out that the greater the number of co-workers one has, the less likely one is to interact with them. Moreover, Chet's two-person department had not much reason to hang out in person with the rest of Ambiguity, and—when it did—Chet did the talking. Nevertheless, proximity of office did force one other co-worker to meet me.

I arrived in my work hallway to find the office next to mine filled by someone I hadn't met yet. Having not been introduced, I walked on by and into the path of Chet coming out of his office.

"Johnny DiMaggio! How's life?"

"Good, thanks. You?"

"Surviving. I'm still thinking about the game on Friday. What a contest. And the cheerleaders weren't too bad, themselves—do you know many gay people?"

"Um, not that I know of."

Chet laughed. "Good answer. They say one in ten of us glides that way. But I only know a few gay people, and I definitely know more than ten times those few people, so you do the math: somebody's in the closet."

"That's possible," a voice came around the corner featuring a nearly handsome, early-thirties-looking fellow. "But it's also plausible, Chet, that the mainstream society in which *you* subside is so homophobic that some of the LGBT folks go elsewhere."

"Touché," Chet said, grinning. "Didn't I tell you he was smart, J.S.?"

"Yeah," I said, not sure what to add.

"Erik," Chet said, "this is my new deputy, John Smith."

"My condolences," Erik replied with a smile at me. "Don't misunderstand me, Chet, there are closeted homosexuals in every aspect of life; however, there are some regions that are less homophobic than others, and so it's reasonable to expect that there's going to be a higher concentration of us where we're more accepted."

Oh. So Erik, himself, was gay. I'd never officially met a gay man before. And—although I didn't have any objection to Erik's style of attraction—I did suddenly feel nervous about saying something wrong.

"Um," I said, "I'm from a small town. I think you're probably right—it's probably harder to be gay there than—"

"*Absolutely,*" Erik said, almost tripping over his words as he spilled them out. "It's conceivable that rural areas have a lower population of gays and lesbians than urban areas. Obviously, they'll have the same number of gay kids, but I think it's entirely conceivable that more gays and lesbians emigrate from rural regions to urban regions than the reverse." Erik then nodded at me with what seemed like approval.

Chet laughed. "Good stuff. I like a little sociology to start my day. Did you watch the game on Friday, Erik?"

"Unless you're referring to the xenophobic immigration debate they had on CNN, then no."

"You missed out. The players weren't xenophobic, but they were—"

"This is football we're talking about, I presume?"

"Right you are."

"Yeah, well, exchange xenophobic for sexist, and you're all set—what's with the all the half-naked cheerleaders?"

"Don't get him started on the cheerleaders, Johnny Bright," Chet said as if I'd had anything to do with it.

"Not to mention *racist*," Erik added. "I understand they don't allow black quarterbacks because the quarterback leads the team, and they don't think African Americans are clever enough to run the team."

Chet smiled at that. "Actually, both quarterbacks on Friday were black. They used to be racist a long time ago up there in the NFL, but the CFL's been pretty good as long as I've been bringing my binoculars to check out the cheerleaders. Did you ever see Warren Moon play, Johnny Unitas?"

"Yeah, I've seen footage."

"Who's Warren Moon?" Erik said, irritation biting into his voice. "Wait, isn't he from the NFL?"

"Yes sir," Chet said. "He came to play up here first, though, back when they didn't like blacks calling the plays in the NFL. He broke every CFL record they could come up with, and that's when the Houston Oilers decided they wanted to win more than they wanted to be racist."

"Not so fast," Erik said. "Just because they're willing to profit off the backs of African Americans doesn't mean they weren't racist."

"Touché," Chet said with a laugh. "So, Johnny Howard, you ready to get to work?"

Talking to Erik was the most intriguing aspect of my second day at Ambiguity. He was more coherent and far more interesting than Chet but no less exhausting a person with whom to share a conversation. I guess his parents had taught him that, if he didn't have something socio-political to say, he shouldn't say anything at all. And so I found myself nervous about every sentence I put in the air when Erik was around because I never knew what would turn out to have sexist, racist, and/or heterosexist implications.

At lunch hour, Chet invited me to join him at the cafeteria

again, and so—since I didn't have a viable excuse ready—I agreed. As we traveled there, I hoped we would encounter Tally and even Bernice so that I could again take a break from being the focus of Chet's lack of concentration. But my accidental rescuers were not there this time. Instead, Chet lectured me on one of his favourite subjects—his boss's boss, Elsje.

"She's such a smart cookie," Chet boasted. "She's like a genius, but sometimes she outthinks herself, and her instructions contradict what she's told me about a previous project. But she'll never admit when she's wrong. She's always got a rationalization to explain away her mistakes. Elsje's so funny."

I couldn't help internally defending Elsje's reputation on the basis that Chet did not strike me as the best person to be determining whether genius-level thinkers were contradicting themselves.

Nevertheless, I nodded at Chet's wisdom—not because he couldn't handle disagreement, but because I worried that any sense of disapproval might distract him into a spontaneous segue. My plan paid off: before Chet's eventual natural segue, I was able take in enough information to allow me to come to an interesting suspicion. Chet's pride in Elsje, I noticed, was similar in strength to Tally's pride in *her* unnamed direct superior, and—since both lauded managers worked in Head Office—I wondered if they might be the *same* cherished boss.

That evening at home, I was subject to slightly more noticeable loneliness than I had experienced the previous night; I was increasingly aware of the fact that I had no one with whom to swap work and Chet stories.

The next day at lunch hour, I was relieved to find that Chet wouldn't have to worry about being strangely interesting for a second day in a row. Tally was again sitting at a table waiting for Bernice. After a brief chat, Chet dispatched himself to join the cafeteria lineup, and so—just as in our first meeting and in every cafeteria caucus to come—Tally and I were allowed a few minutes to ourselves with some enjoyable conversation (for me anyway) before the conversational pirates returned.

"So," she said, "how's it going now? Still trying to get a handle on what you're supposed to be doing?"

"Actually, it's starting to fit together now—I think it kinda makes sense now. How about you?"

"Does my job make sense?"

"No, I meant—"

"No, it's a good question," Tally said. "When you've been doing it as long as I have, it actually stops making sense after a while—or, at least, it goes in cycles. Right now everything's kind of a blur to me."

"How come?"

"Well, I guess it's not so much that the job doesn't make sense: it's more that it doesn't make much sense to me why I'm doing it anymore."

"Oh, that's too bad. How come?"

Tally shook her face with a smile. "Look at me giving up all these details. I bet everyone comes to you with their problems."

"No, not really."

Tally smirked at me with raised eyebrows. "Well, I'd appreciate if you'd just say that they *do* because otherwise it looks like I'll just tell *anyone* my problems."

I laughed. "Okay, everyone comes to me with their problems."

Before Tally could take advantage of that requested lie, Bernice arrived to take over the conversation.

"The line's as slow as fricken' molasses today," she said so earnestly that I thought she must have been making fun of herself by copying exactly what she'd said the first time I'd met her.

Thankfully, just in case she wasn't kidding, I held in my giggles.

As we waited for Chet to return, Tally and I continued to construct the conversation since Bernice was not one to start topics.

"So," Tally said, "John was just telling me about how he's starting to get a handle on his job."

"You just gotta do it to learn it," Bernice said as she chomped into her food.

"Yeah, you're probably right. I've been trying to—"

"When I first started here," Bernice said, mouth now full, "nobody taught me anything—I had to figure everything out myself, so—"

"Yeah, I've had it easier than that," I said.

Bernice shrugged.

And we had ourselves a long pause.

"Um," I said, "so, Tally, did you find you had a lot of help when you first started here?"

"Actually, yeah, my boss was awesome, so I didn't get the pleasure of struggling."

"You were fricken' lucky," Bernice said. "Nobody taught me anything."

I felt that we'd already been on that loop, so I endeavoured to change the subject.

"So how far do you guys live from here?"

"Not too far," Tally said, "I'm only twenty minutes by car—five minutes by helicopter."

I laughed.

Bernice rolled her eyes. "You don't have access to a helicopter. But you *are* lucky. I'm at least half an hour away—*both* ways."

Oddly, it was a relief when Chet returned to supply some random subject matter for Bernice to outdo. Chet's tangential offerings meant that neither Tally nor I had to submit our lowly experiences as conversational sacrifices to Bernice's impressive comparisons. And I doubted that Chet even noticed when his topics lost their focus and became about Bernice. Sure, he quickly segued from her experiences to whatever next arrived in his mind, but it wasn't really any extra work for him to tangent from Bernice instead of from himself.

Meanwhile, in spite of the fact that Tally had a valid reason to subdue her personality once Bernice and Chet were both there to compete for the conversation, I still wished she would resist. I could accept my own lack of participation—I didn't have anything more interesting to say than Bernice or Chet anyway—but Tally's continued exile from a conversation of which she was clearly the most interesting member was saddening.

As such, I decided in the middle of one of Bernice's improvements to one of Chet's stories that, when she was done, I would again try to segue the topic onto Tally.

"Until you've had chronic bronchitis," Bernice soon said, "for your entire Grade Twelve year, you don't know what it's like."

"That's rough," I said. "How about you, Tally? Have you ever had to take time off?"

"Legitimate time off?" Tally replied. "Or—"

"Yes, *legitimate*," I said with a giggle.

"Then *no*."

I laughed. "Then how about *illegitimate*?"

"Well," Bernice said, "at my last job, they wouldn't let me take time off for my nephew's birthday party, so I totally had to call in sick."

As Chet segued from that, there was, as far as I could tell, a smile on Tally's face that seemed to indicate that she was amused by—and maybe even appreciative of—my futile effort to reverse her Bernice-induced shyness. Said speculation put a grin in my chest.

In fact, I can tell you, anticipating reader, that—in future cafeteria gatherings of our foursome—I would try at least once per meeting to artificially re-invite Tally into the discussion. On every occasion I would fail, but, almost every time, I received the same sneaky smile as reward from Tally.

Now, even though I only had two conversations with Tally in my first week at Ambiguity, just the potential for talking to her on the other three days made my overall work time more enjoyable. As I pondered that strange result late Friday afternoon, it occurred to me that my mini-time with Tally was the closest I had come to having a friendship-inspiring conversation with anyone during my first week in the big city. Talking to Chet, of course, was too frustrating to qualify, and interacting with my office neighbour, Erik, continued to be so socio-political that I felt too nervous that I was going to say the wrong thing to enjoy it.

"I'm making my exit," Erik startled me in the middle of that thought. "Have a good weekend, John."

"Oh, okay, thanks—you too," I said. But, before I could turn back to my work, I realized that Erik had leaned into my doorway. Our conversation was clearly not finished. "Um," I said, "so what're you up to this weekend?"

"To be announced," he replied. "Joshua and I might go see that new documentary I was telling you about."

"Oh, is Joshua your boyfriend?"

"*Partner*," Erik said with a smile.

"Oh, is it bad to say *boyfriend*?"

"No, it's fine, but it's another way that we get outed."

"Oh, okay, sorry. So what's the documentary about again?"

"Y'off, Erik?" Chet arrived.

"That's the plan."

"So is it subtitles or politics tonight at the movies?"

"I imagine a little of both. And is it formulaic cookie-cutter comedy or formulaic paint-by-numbers action for you?"

Chet laughed. "A little bit of neither. I'm going to take our boy here out for drinks to celebrate his first week on the job."

That news, quite rightly, put my stomach in need of some antacid.

Erik looked back at me. "You don't have to go if you don't want to, John: he doesn't own your weekend."

"Of course I *don't*," Chet replied. "But the kid's new in town. You don't have plans, do you, Johnny?"

The offer of inventing an excuse was tantalizing, but the fear of being questioned for details scared me off in the split second I had to decide whether to go for it.

"Um, no," I said.

"It's irrelevant anyway," Erik snapped at Chet. "He doesn't *have to* have plans. He has ownership of his weekend. You don't have the right to force him to go anywhere."

Chet laughed again. "Of course not. J.S., would *like* to go for drinks?"

"Um, sure, although I'm not really into alcohol, so—"

"That's okay. You don't have to drink to go for drinks."

"Oh, okay."

"You don't have to go with him," Erik said.

"It's okay. I'd like to."

Erik shook his head at me as if I had betrayed him. "Whatever," he said, removing himself from my doorway. "Just make sure you bill him for the hours."

"Not a bad idea," Chet said. "And I'll bill the company for the drinks."

So, an hour later, I could be found sitting next to Chet in a pub, and I was feeling exhausted about it.

SOCIO-GEOGRAPHICAL NOTE: In case you're confused, non-Canadian reader, by the notion of a not-yet-twenty-year-old fellow taking part in a pub-based chat, please be aware that at that time and location, nineteen-year-olds were permitted to enter—and partake in the commodities supplied by—saloons and other alcohol-sharing establishments.

My boss, by then, had already broken the world record for most unprovoked tangents in one conversation. Although, in Chet's defence, his uncoordinated, non-stop talking did give me an opportunity to scan what it was like to be in a bar. According to movies, it was a good place to meet women. But, upon my real-world inspection, I found no data to support the claim. Most of the women present were residing in co-ed groups of individuals who seemed to already know each other. I saw no evidence that they were looking for new friends.

"Well, Johnny B. Goode, it's been a pleasure," Chet finally concluded the evening with a chuckle. "But, next time, don't talk so much."

I found that to be an irritating sarcastic accusation. While it was true that I wasn't known for supplying an abundance of conversation, Chet had no way of knowing so given that he always segued off what I had to say before he could find out how short-winded I was.

The next evening, I discovered that the loneliness I'd experienced during the week prior was just a rehearsal for the stomach-churning solitude of a Saturday night in which I didn't even have the fatigue of a full work day to dull the feeling.

I was relieved, then, to arrive at Sunday evening when the anticipation of another work week—and the possibility of some more Tally time—defanged my loneliness.

Open Door Politics

In my second week at Ambiguity, I once again collected two interactions with Tally; I used the second opportunity wisely and investigated my suspicion that Elsje—Chet's favourite name to drop—was her boss.

"Very perceptive," Tally replied. "Yeah, Elsje's the boss for me. I wish she *wasn't*—if she was even a drop more intolerable, I'd have gotten out of this job by now."

"What would you do instead?"

"If you'll agree not to laugh, I'll answer your probing question."

"Okay, I agree."

"All right, I want to train parrots to sing the national anthem."

"Really?"

"No," Tally said, chuckling, "I just wanted to make sure you wouldn't laugh."

"Oh, okay," I said, giggling.

The subsequent conversation about Tally's hopes for her and her husband's future was the highlight of my second week at Ambiguity.

But it was not necessarily the most exciting moment that week. After lunch on Wednesday, I heard a chipper male voice entering the office of my neighbour, Erik.

"How are you, mate?" the visitor said, without the Australian or English accent that I was used to finding attached to the expression.

"Surprisingly well," Erik reported back with a friendlier-seeming voice than I was used to hearing from him. "How's the other side?"

There was then a silence that I guessed was a sigh from the visitor before he said, "We're chugging along, but—as you know—red tape sometimes gets caught in our wheels. I'm doing what I can, but it's tough sledding."

"Gotta love the bureaucracy," Erik replied.

The visitor laughed. "You're not far off. I don't know what I'd do without it now. I've been caught in it for so long that I'm not sure if I could keep up with the pace of *unimpeded* progress."

"Yeah," Erik said, seeming to laugh, "don't you hate it when employee rights stall the glory of progress?"

"*Easy now,*" the visitor said, still sounding cheerful, "I'm on your side. There's no one in management who cares more about your rights than yours truly. We've just gotta make sure we maintain a dialogue and work together, and we'll keep Ambiguity on her leash."

"Fair enough," Erik said. "It's good to hear that you're still standing up for us."

I'd never heard Erik sound conciliatory before—and I still wasn't sure that I had. For the next few minutes, the visitor continued boasting about his role in protecting employees; Erik gave him hollow-sounding agreement throughout.

"Well," the visitor concluded, "I must check in on old Chet. You let me know if you need anything, Erik. You know my number."

The visitor's footsteps were now engaged and soon the perfectly suited figure of an aggressively good-looking man in his early forties passed by my office. His face was serious for a moment, but then he looked into my office and a grin grew onto his expression.

"Hey there," he said, changing his direction like a human-seeking missile. "You must be Chet's new associate?"

"Yes," I said, standing up to defend myself against his rapid approach.

"I'm Glenroy Garrison," he said, looking me in the eyes as his hand assertively hugged mine.

"Nice to meet you, I'm John Smith."

Glenroy's vivid eyes seemed to be decoding my soul. "I've heard excellent things about you, John. You're doing a marvelous job."

"Thanks," I said, skeptical that he knew what he was talking about but unable to stop myself from feeling flattered.

"I've got a meeting with your associate right now, but—if you've got the time—I'd greatly appreciate a conversation with you afterwards."

"Sure, that'd be great."

"Excellent," Glenroy said, before lobbing a full grin my way and then sauntering off to Chet's office.

I kept both ears open for the impending conversation, but, oddly, it was quiet and hard to distinguish and then shut in by the closing of Chet's office door; that was disappointing, but I figured Chet would share the contents of the discussion later, so I merrily returned to my work. Ten minutes later, though, the Chet-Glenroy meeting increased its volume and so started to seep beyond its closed door and into the hallway.

"That's not really my concern, is it?" I think I heard from Glenroy.

"Well, maybe it'll be of concern to Elsje!" Chet seemed to reply.

"*Elsje?*" Glenroy barked back. "What's she got to do with this?"

"Well, *mate*, she is your boss, isn't she?"

"My, my, Chet," I now heard clearly from Glenroy as Chet's office door reopened. "For someone who's on as thin ice as you are, I wouldn't be worried about someone *else's* boss."

Chet forced a laugh. "That's great advice coming from *you*."

"Yeah, it *is*, actually," Glenroy retorted, suddenly calmer, "it's the last advice I'm going to give you. Don't waste it."

"What *else* am I going to do with it?" Chet heckled back. "You know what Oscar Wilde said about advice, don't you, *mate*?"

"Nope, and I don't care," Glenroy replied as he started up his footsteps again.

"He says to always *pass it on*," Chet hollered just before Glenroy came back into my view.

Chet's rival was staring ahead violently, which made me feel safe from any awkward eye contact between us, but then, inexplicably, a smile jumped on Glenroy's face, and he turned and looked at me.

"I promised you a meeting, didn't I?"

"Oh, um—"

"I *did*," he said, cheerily wandering into my office. He then closed the door and sat down.

My hands were still attached to my keyboard as I faked a smile at my guest.

"So, John," he said, "my job is to support you in your work by ensuring that you have all the tools and leadership that you need to succeed."

"Okay. Thanks."

"So is there anything that you need right now that you're not getting?"

"No, but, um …*thanks*."

Glenroy smiled. "I see that you want to be the sort of employee who just gets his work done, keeps his head down, and doesn't ask for anything, but the truth is, John, you'll be a better employee if you let me know anything you might need to help you get your work done more effectively."

"Oh, okay, thanks. Um, yeah—no, there's really nothing that I need at this point. I'm still pretty new."

Glenroy smirked. "It's actually *because* you're new that you're probably the most likely person to teach us something. Chet and I have been at this for so long that we're not always going to see the problems that are right in front of our face."

I nodded as seriously as I could. "Yeah, I guess that makes sense, but I haven't noticed anything yet. Maybe I'm still too new."

Glenroy gave me a crisp nod back and reached into his pocket. "All right, mate. This is my card—give me a call when you *do* start seeing things. We'll go for lunch."

"Okay," I said, staring at the card. *Would it be treasonous to take it?*

Glenroy was already standing and reaching out to me with a confident, card-filled hand.

I felt a cringe in my conscience as I accepted the controversial item.

I expected Chet to come around the corner within seconds of Glenroy's departure so that he could question me about my conversation with his apparent enemy. I should have gone to him first, but, of course, I was too cowardly to bring the discussion to Chet. Instead, I waited for my disgruntled boss to land in my office and demand that I empty my pockets and confess my sedition. Strangely, he did not. Instead, he stayed in his own quarters for an hour; when he finally let himself out, he said nothing to me about Glenroy. In turn, I wished that he would accuse me so that I could explain that I hadn't betrayed him (at least not intentionally).

Chapter 25
Dullard vs. Loneliness

Chet for Chat

On my bus ride home that afternoon, I was in the middle of a good think about Chet and Glenroy when a woman of mid age, and questioning eyes, got on the bus; she had a lot to say to the driver of our vehicle.

In the middle of their dialogue, the driver started us moving suddenly but not as abruptly as you would have thought given the woman's subsequent voluptuousness of stumble and then lunge for a bus pole. Her eyes turned vengeful: she now had a lot more to say to our driver.

At the next stop, the aggrieved passenger yapped a final jab at our pilot and then travelled down the aisle, scanning each of her fellow travellers as she passed us.

When it was my turn to be looked over, I smiled.

She squinted back and sat down next to me.

"Do you know the time?" she said.

"Yeah, it's 5:25."

"How do you *know?*"

"Um," I said, glancing at my timepiece, "it's on my watch."

"I never trust watches," the woman said, "—how do you know it's *right?*"

"Um, well, I guess it matches my clock at work."

The woman chuckled. "Right. How do you know *that's* right?"

"Um," I said, spotting a big decorative clock outside, "it seems to match *that* clock too."

"I never trust clocks," she replied, shaking her head at me.

"Oh…"

"Next stop, First Street," the driver announced.

My neighbour shook her head once again. "I never trust the drivers to tell me what stop I'm at."

"Oh, how come?"

"How do I know they're telling the truth?"

As it turned out, there were several other factions (pedestrian walk signals, horses, men wearing hats) that my new friend didn't trust.

At the risk of sounding a wee bit condescending, easily offended reader, the woman's earnest paranoia was endearing to the point of being amusing. Indeed, as I walked from the bus to home, I smiled as I reminisced over our conversation. I was rather pleased with my bus life. However lonely I might have been at home, on the bus, I was always captivated by my fellow passengers and my own ponderings about them.

On the Friday a couple days later, Chet asked me out for drinks to celebrate my second week on the job. I couldn't see why not (especially on such short notice), so I was again forced to endure the conversation of someone who couldn't follow his own train of thought. That was especially frustrating on the rare moments that Chet accidentally said something interesting. He talked, for instance, of his hero—our boss's boss, Elsje—but, before I could acquire any useful details about her, Chet segued to whether he would consider naming his own child, 'Elsje.'

I decided the following week that I was going to come to work on Friday with a claim of *other plans* for the evening. I was in the middle of constructing said pre-alibi on Thursday afternoon when Chet arrived at my office to visit.

"Hey, Johnny Cochrane, how're the ARGs coming along?"

"Oh, um, I just read this memo from Head Office that said they don't want the ARGs until next week. Do you still want me to do them?"

"Yeah, may as well. That way, we've got 'em all set to go."

"But…won't the numbers change by next week, and then I'll have to do them again?"

Chet shrugged. "Let's cross that bridge when we come to it."

"Oh, okay," I said, pondering whether to point out that—since we knew the data was going to change—we could be *certain* that tallying the numbers in advance would cause us to cross the same bridge twice.

"So, Johnny Cash," Chet interrupted my annoyed introspection, "I'm outta town tomorrow night."

"Oh, where're you off to?" I said, smiling a little too hard at the fact that I wouldn't have to finalize my Friday night excuse, after all.

"Going to see Mother Goose—so maybe we should go for drinks *tonight* instead, eh?"

Oh. "Um ..."

And so the usual conversational delinquency was soon underway.

The next week, I arrived every day with my drinks-avoidance excuse prepped and ready to go. But this time I didn't need it until Friday.

"Johnny Mathis, you up for drinks tonight?"

"Let him have his weekend," Erik said, arriving behind my boss. "John's probably got a hot date tonight."

"*Do* you, JohnFK?"

"Well ...*no*," I said. (Indeed, it would never have occurred to me come up with such a far-fetched excuse.)

"Then we're on for drinks?"

"That's a red herring," Erik said. "Chet, you're blackmailing him. You're his boss, so there's a tacit obligation here that, if he doesn't consent, he'll suffer consequences down the line."

Chet laughed. "There's nothing *tacit* about it! John doesn't have to come if he doesn't want to, but—if he *wants to*—who am *I* to stop him? If Elsje asked me to go for drinks, I'd feel no tacitness. So, John, you're under no tacitness—do you want to come?"

"Sure," I said, feeling it was too late now to try my own—not nearly as flashy—excuse.

The next Friday, I decided to try a preemptive strike.

"Hey, John T. Kirk, what's up?" Chet said first thing in the morning.

"Oh, um," I said, my nerves at full throttle, "I'm going to see my parents this weekend."

"Neato! Good for you—it's funny the way people park, isn't it?"

Wow, he'd tangented off the excuse before details were required—perhaps I'd finally found a benefit to Chet's attention deficiency.

Seven hours later, Chet stopped by my office.

"So you up for drinks tonight, Johnny Mac?"

"Oh, um, no—like I said, I'm going to see my parents."

"Right, that's tonight. Well, have fun."

And, with that, I was finally free to be by myself on a Friday night.

The freedom, while lonely, was so refreshing that I decided to take friends-based plans to work the following two weeks as well. Consequently, Chet was soon forced to determine that I was popular enough to have friends. Unfortunately, the more my popularity rose in his eyes, the more sheepish I felt in my own. *Why couldn't I take a few hours out of my boring life to make someone else's existence a little less lonely?*

Every few weeks, therefore, my guilt would overpower me, and I'd agree to another night of tangents with Chet, which, in turn, would serve nicely as a reminder of why I'd been avoiding Chet's invitations in the first place.

Gathering of Loneliness

By three months in the big city, I was enjoying life at Ambiguity in spite of Chet's faux conversation. I had come to a decent level of proficiency with the work I was confusingly assigned, and I was starting to feel like an important—albeit insignificant—cog in Ambiguity's wheels. Plus, about two lunchtimes per week, I was able to hang out with Tally at the cafeteria for a few minutes to discuss our matters before Chet and Bernice arrived to break things up. Those little dialogues with Tally were unfailingly rejuvenating to the energy stores that Chet had always depleted in me in the days since my previous Tally talk. And, since I never knew when I would get to converse with her, each lunch hour provided a mini-rejuvenation as I planned out what I would say to her if she was there.

In contrast, life after Ambiguity wasn't going so well. Neither the city nor my neighbours had yet noticed that I existed. And, even though I was a regular at the nearby grocery store, the familiar cashiers never ventured more than an uninterested smile and 'Hello' my way. In short, I continued to be lonely.

The solitude was a surprise to me because I had moved to the big city expecting that the crowds of citizens found within might make me feel less solo than I had been in my small hometown. But it turns out that living in a city overflowing with humans that one doesn't interact with can actually make a lonely person feel *more* segregated from the world.

Sometimes I forced myself to get out of my apartment to wander around the city. One evening, I randomly travelled into the seriously poor area, which featured the strained faces of prostitutes, addicts, and mental health patients who had lost their doctors.

As I passed by that sad neighbourhood, my mind replayed for me a debate between Chet and Erik regarding whether such people deserved more government assistance. Erik had argued that the street folks were "marginalized" by socio-economic forces out of their control, which had prompted Chet to laugh and argue that—if they were marginalized, they were "self-marginalized" by their own bad decisions. That, in turn, had caused Erik to seethe about "the apathy of white, middle-class males."

I remembered feeling, at that moment, a little marginalized, myself, and wondering if I was compelled by Chet's request for people to share some of the responsibility for their fates. But now, as I glanced into the weary eyes of those sitting with their hats pleading in front of them, I noticed that—regardless of whether I believed that they owed themselves more determination to get out of their struggles—I still wished for them a better life. And so I wondered what I could do to help.

The first thing I did was make a donation to a charitable organization that seemed on point. Initially, I found such passive action to be unsatisfying, but—as I'd proven many months before—I was no Bert Hardelean: I did not have any skills to inspire anyone, let alone those who required high-level, outside-the-dullard thinking to resist their marginalization.

So I placated my concern by sending money towards the problem. I'm not trying to fish for compliments, generous reader: I certainly wasn't giving a lot of money, and I didn't even send my subsequent funds to those whose plights I passed by every day. Instead, I switched the direction of my donations to charities whose victims' credibility could not be questioned even by Chet. I justified the distinction by the fact that, even though I was sad for the people setting up homes on the local streets, I felt worse for those in not-so-rich countries where turning down marginalization seemed to not even be an option in theory. Thus, every time a frail prostitute on the street wounded my heart with her feeble attempts to be sexy, the money she provoked me to donate to her relief was sent to a land far away from her.

The suffering societies to which I sent my miniature funds reminded me of my childhood love, Ashley, who had started her life surrounded by extreme misfortune. *How many of Ashley's first friends*, I wondered, *were forever imprisoned by poverty and malnutrition?* Quite rightly, those contemplations left me shaking my head with disdain at myself for ever lamenting my own, insignificant, loneliness.

Unfortunately, my rejection of my self-pity (for the sake of other-people-pity) could only compete with my loneliness for so long. Even though I realized my personal melancholy was self-indulgent, I could not stop myself from fantasizing about an upgrade to my social situation.

One evening, then, I decided to seek out a place where talking to strangers was expected. My first instinct would have been to go to a bar, but—with the help of my after-work Chet-versations—I had come to realize that pubs were not as good at connecting strangers as had been advertised on movies and TV. Instead, then, I nervously approached a dance club (having no idea what the heck I was doing).

Oddly, there was a long lineup just to get into the building. Apparently, I'd come on a busy night, so I left and returned a few days later. But, once again, I had to stand in an unmoving lineup. There was a gaggle of firmly dressed females in front of me, but I saw no evidence that I was allowed to start a conversation with them *before* we entered the club—not that I would have had the courage to do so anyway.

Once my part of the lineup finally got to the entrance, I encountered a large man who expected me to *pay* to go through the doors he was guarding. As I handed him my cash, I wondered why the attractive girls in front of me had escaped the same payment. I found that apparent prettiness favouritism to be disconcerting but soon forgot about it as I entered the club to discover an attack on my ears. There was a continuous banging sound coming from the direction of the club's music speakers. And, strangely, several people were attempting to dance to it. I looked around for a conversation booth in which I could discuss the unnecessary volume of the music with a receptive female stranger, but I quickly noticed that all the women seemed to have arrived in animated bundles of four or more. That wouldn't do. I had enough fear of initiating a meeting with *one* person, let alone a group. Indeed, the thought of attempting to infiltrate one of those excited cohorts left my heart beating at the pace of the alleged music.

I spent a few minutes suffering under that contemplation and watching an impressive crowd of dancers before I realized that, even if there were an individual interested in conversation with me, the size of the music would overrule any attempt to hear each other making fun of it. So I left the club twenty minutes after I'd paid my way into it, and I cursed movies for once again having lied to me about a means of meeting women.

Chapter 26
Dullard in the Ring III

The Juke Boxer

On my subsequent Monday morning bus ride, there was on board an angrily dressed young-ish man listening to equally argumentative music. He had his music dialed up so loudly on his head phones that they acted like shared speakers for everyone near the back of the bus. Indeed, I could hear most of the grandiose lyrics from several seats away. That sort of bus-based obnoxiousness happens sometimes, non-transit reader, and the rest of us generally just try our best to ignore the musical chalkboard-scratching that results.

But the twenty-something woman sitting next to our human juke box was apparently in a combative mood.

"Excuse me," she said, curling her neck to face him, "can you turn that down?"

"What?"

"Can you turn your music down? We can all hear it."

At that point, our gentlemanly broadcaster shifted his face to his accuser and told her—in not so gentlemanly terms—to go and mate with herself.

On hearing the suggestion, the objector took in a hefty breath. "Why are you so rude? I've got a huge headache. Can't you just turn your music down, so we can all ride the bus in peace?"

Our rage-music aficionado glared back at her. "Who the hell are you to tell me to turn my music down? Get the hell out of my face, bitch."

"Why should I?" his critic replied. "You're the one playing music in *my* face."

The implication of hypocrisy seemed to ignite something in our DJ, and he began a louder and faster rant which critiqued the woman's fitness for social interaction. The anger presented on his forehead provoked me to worry that he wasn't going to limit himself to a verbal altercation.

And so, just as they had many years before when Jocelyn was abused by Gator, my nervous legs activated without my authorization. I stood up, but I held my three-feet-away position to avoid provoking the Gator-like figure.

I had no idea what to say, so I just impersonated a character on TV.

"Okay, buddy, I think that's enough," I said with a gulp in my chest.

"Who the hell are you?" the musical fellow replied, shooting to his own feet and taking a swift step into my area.

"I'm just a person on the bus, like you," I said, stiffening my arms.

The man nodded, his forehead growing smaller as his eyes grew bigger. And then—like his Gator ancestor had before him—he released his fist from its holster and swung his knuckles square into my chin. I stumbled backwards and saw sparkling dust in my vision. I was suddenly terrified as I realized that Per wouldn't be there to help me this time. I rushed my hands up to receive the next attack while I contemplated where I should aim my counter strike.

"Hey!" I vaguely heard someone say.

And then I sensed two men were moving towards us.

"I'm leaving," the musical pugilist announced, body checking his way through the bus doors.

"You all right?" one of the arriving men said to me.

"Yeah, thanks, I didn't see it coming."

"Yeah, he got you with a sucker punch. It happens to the best of us."

"You okay?" the woman who'd initiated the venture said. "Sorry, I just didn't want to listen to his garbage."

"Yeah, that's okay," I said.

"You okay, buddy?" the other of my rescuers said. "You took quite a shot."

"What happened?" the now-arriving bus driver said.

All was explained, and the police were called. They said they'd do their best to track down Gator the Second. In the meantime, they complimented me for trying to help but suggested I call them first if ever I spotted danger in the future.

My chin was sore, but it didn't seem damaged enough to go to the hospital, so I continued onto work as though nothing had happened. But, while I offered the world my neutral expression, my mind was a whirlwind. I was glad that I'd had the courage to step in again, but I was ashamed of losing the physical encounter. The bystanders and the police had all been nice, but their voices were condescending when they tried to cheer me up.

"Hey, good for you for trying," one man had said. "Don't feel bad. He was a big dude."

The 'Don't feel bad' of it had me feeling bad. Apparently, the observers were a little embarrassed for me, and so—suddenly—so was I.

When I arrived at work, I did not plan to discuss my morning violence, but I realized—as Chet landed in my office—that I wanted to talk about it.

"Hey, Johnny-Come-Lately, bus trouble this morning?"

"No, sorry, there was an incident on the bus."

Chet's eyes powered up as he grabbed for a seat. "What happened?"

I told the story without even an interruption from Chet.

"Holy cow," he said when I finished the tale. "You all right, bud?"

"Yeah, I'm okay—just a little shaken up."

"I should say so. That's scary stuff. Great job standing up for the girl."

"Thanks," I said; indeed, for the first time, I felt appreciated for my effort to help.

"Hey, *Erik!*" Chet called. "Come in here. John's got a story to tell."

Upon completion of my second rendering of the tale, Erik looked at me with seeming compassion.

"That's traumatic," he said. "You okay?"

"Yeah, I'll be fine. I'm just a little shaken up."

"I should say so," Chet said again.

"Yeah, that's traumatic," Erik replied. "It's a tough one because I wonder if it would've been better if you'd stayed out of it."

"Will wonders never cease," Chet replied for me. "Johnny Stallone did something heroic, Erik. Let's not—"

"No, no," Erik said, "I appreciate you were trying to help. And I admire you for it. At the same time, I wonder if we sometimes underestimate women to be able to handle situations for themselves."

Chet waved off the analysis. "Bah humbug. Who knows what would have happened if Johnny Macchio hadn't stepped in. Maybe the thug would have hit the girl. Would you rather *that*, Mr. Feminist?"

Erik pondered that. "Yeah, it's a conundrum. As men, we should be doing our part to fight against male violence against women, but—at the same time—we don't want to take away women's agency to speak their own truths."

Chet looked at me with a face that clearly said, *What the hell is he babbling about?*

I accidentally laughed.

"This is serious stuff," Erik corrected.

"True," I said, "but, when someone's literally shouting, like, ragefully at another person on the bus, I don't know that I'm thinking about all that stuff. I was just trying to help."

"Fair enough," Erik said. "This stuff is complicated. I think you did the best you could given the situation."

By Erik's tone of teach, he still seemed to me to be implying that I had lots more to learn. Nevertheless, I appreciated Chet's defence so much that I was satisfied with the sum of the conversation.

By lunchtime, I decided not to take my tale to Tally—not that I wouldn't have loved to have had her thoughts on it, but I didn't want to seem like I was boasting in the direction Chet was claiming for me. Besides, if I knew Chet, he would bring it up for me.

"Hey," she said as I sat down. "What's new?"

Her tone of cheerful curiosity made me realize that I wanted to tell her about my wild morning. Plus, given my usual boring conversational fare, I had no right to keep from Tally this most exciting of incidents.

"Well," I said with a chuckle, "I was punched on the bus this morning."

"What? How? Why?"

I told the tale for a third time.

"Oh my Lord," Tally said. "You okay? Does it hurt?"

I shrugged. "It's sore."

"But not much of a bruise," Tally said, scanning my face, "after *all that*, it'd be nice to have a battle scar to show off."

"Yeah," I said, laughing.

Tally grimaced. "Sorry, I shouldn't be joking about something like this."

"No, you *should*. It makes me feel better."

"So awful. God, I feel sorry for you *guys*."

"Why?"

"Well, there's just all this pressure on you to stick up for women, but—in a situation like that—it's not the woman who's gonna get punched in the face."

"You think?"

"Yeah…hold on…let me search my brain to make sure I have this right. Yes, search complete: guys who punch women do it behind closed doors, rarely out in public. But there's much less stigma against punching a *man* in the face."

"Yeah, I guess."

"So it's like there's these campaigns that tell men to defend women against harassment. Easy for the campaign to say. It's the guy that jumps in who's gonna get punched in the face."

"I guess. But—"

"I see what you're saying," Tally said. "You weren't thinking about any pressure from those campaigns when you jumped in to help that woman, am I right?"

"Exactly."

"But—"

"What are you guys talking about?" suddenly arriving Bernice said.

"One sec, Bernie," Tally said. "Okay, John, answer me this: if that goon were yelling at another *man* like that, would you have been as likely to step in?"

"I guess not. So you're saying the only reason I stepped in was because I was pressured by society to do so."

"No, no, no, I wasn't saying that. I just mean—what *am* I saying? You stepped in because you're an awesome guy who wanted to help a person who seemed to be in trouble. But also ...well, there's so much pressure on men to put yourselves at risk when a woman's involved. Or am I way off?"

"Yeah, I guess you're right."

"Oh my God, I hope you don't think I'm saying that you didn't do something awesome. I just mean that I think it's unfair that guys have this pressure to put themselves in that kind of situation. Or just ignore me."

"Okay," I said, forcing a chuckle so as to appear cheerful about her analysis.

In my mind, though, I felt a little like a lab rat in both Tally's and Erik's musings. Nevertheless, they expressed their concern with such kindness that I was confident that they were at least rooting for me as I ran through their mazes.

Overall, shockingly, Chet received my emotions' top score for his flattering response to the incident. In last place, of course, was Bernice who—upon learning about my transit troubles—quickly segued to her own most recent commute-based conflict.

Chapter 27
Dullard vs. Brother III

Per Noelle

A few weeks later, on a Saturday afternoon approaching Christmas, I was in the middle of recovering from my monthly Chet hangover when my home phone made an unusual ringing noise.

"Hello?"

"John, it's your mother. We're thinking of driving down to see you. How would you like a visit?"

"Oh," I said, oddly nervous, "yeah, of course, come on over."

My unusual nervousness was followed by unusual pleasure at the thought of having visitors.

Soon my apartment buzzer buzzed, and my heart rate quickened as my family arrived for their second official visit to my city life. I was greeted by the familiar faces of my mother, my father—who patted me on the shoulder—and my brother, along with a semi-familiar face.

"John, this is Noelle," my mom said on Per's behalf.

"Hello, I'm John," I said, trying to figure out where I knew her from.

"Hey," she said, going in for a hug, "it's so nice to finally meet you."

"Yeah, you too," I said. And, during the hug, I pondered the fact that it had only been a couple months since the breakup of Per's last romance, which meant that Noelle's 'finally' couldn't have had to wait *that* long. Holy ghostwriter! *That* was where I knew Noelle from: Noelle looked remarkably similar to Per's *ex* ex, Nicolette.

"How are you?" she said, post hug. "This is such a great place."

"Thanks," I said, reaching for a convenient cliché, "it pays the bills."

"*Pays the bills?*" Per said, giggling.

"Sorry—brain cramp—I meant it keeps a roof over my head."

"You're funny," Noelle said.

"He *wasn't* joking," Per corrected.

"Yes, he *was*. He's your brother—give him the benefit of the doubt."

Per laughed. "What for?"

Noelle rolled her eyes with a giggle.

"Because he's your brother," my dad said with his serious voice.

"Yeah, I *know* he's my brother," Per said, "which is why he knows me well enough to know that *I'm* just joking too."

My dad looked at me.

I nodded with a smile.

"Okay, sorry, then," Dad said.

Soon we were squished into the sparse seating of my living room.

"How are you, son?" my dad asked.

"Well, work's gotten better," I said. "Chet's changed the system up, so now I have to get used to that, but—"

"John works near the bottom of the food chain at Ambiguity," Per explained to Noelle.

"Good for you, John," Noelle said, smiling so cheerfully that I was almost certain she was sincere; and yet there was something vacant in her expression that caused me to wonder if she had any basis for her approval.

"We have news," Mom said. "Per has started a new job too."

"Oh, where at?"

"It's that new, very posh restaurant they opened up."

"Do you like it?" I said, looking at Per.

"It's good coin," he replied.

"They were very particular in the interview process," Mom said. "As a waiter for these places, you have to be able to make the patrons feel welcomed and comfortable, and, of course, Per does all of that wonderfully."

"Well," Per said as if he were about to be modest, "since the customers like me, I get pretty good tips. Like, I do better than Stacy, who's hot and flirty, but she sometimes gets pissy—so I get, like, two percent more than her even *with* her flirting."

"Poor Stacy," Noelle said with a giggle.

"She's lucky she's hot," Per said. "Otherwise she'd do even worse."

"Yeah, she *is* beautiful, isn't she?" Noelle said

"Wait a minute," I said, "*Stacy* as in Stacy from Sweet On You?"

"Oh, right, yeah," Per said. "She did work it there. *Why?*—Did you have the hots for her?"

"No," I said a little too abruptly.

"I think you're lying," Per said.

"There's nothing wrong with being attracted to a beautiful girl," Noelle added.

"Sorry to break it to you, bro," Per said, "but she's got a boyfriend now—not that she was in your league anyway," he added with a giggle.

Admittedly, I was tempted to point out that Stacy had actually invited me to join her league once, but I overruled that thought on the grounds that (A) even though I loathed Stacy, it seemed to me that it would somehow be tacky to turn-down-kiss and tell, and (B) I didn't think Per would believe me anyway.

Later on, when Noelle stepped away to visit the washroom, there was bit of an adjusting-to-the-new-dynamic silence produced by her absence. As such, more from feeling a need for something to say than from an intensity of curiosity, I inquired as to whether Per had noticed the similarity of appearance between his current girlfriend and her predecessor's predecessor, Nicolette.

"Ah, yeah," he said. "They're *sisters*, bro."

"You're dating Nicolette's sister?"

"Yeah, so?"

"Isn't that kind of awkward?"

"Not for me. I never met Nicolette's parents—thank God—so they just know me as Noelle's boyfriend. As far as I'm concerned, it's between the sisters to have a cat fight if they want. Nothing to do with me."

"And," my mother whispered, "Per had been broken up with

Nicolette for over a month before he even met Noelle. So it's a coincidence but certainly not untoward."

There was an awkward pause just then as those of us who weren't convinced that Per was fully toward tried not to show it.

"Oh, by the way, John," my mom interrupted, "I ran into one of the girls from the bakery."

"Oh, who?"

"Was it Stacy?" Per asked with another giggle.

"No, it wasn't Stacy," Mom said. "Sorry, I don't remember her name, John. Do you remember, Paul?"

I looked hopefully at my dad.

"Oh, shoot," he said, "no, I don't remember—sorry, John. I know it wasn't Stacy, though."

"Yes, Dad," Per said, cycling through a full eye roll, "*I'm aware it wasn't Stacy.* You don't have to take everything literally."

"Maybe it was *Amy*?" I tried.

"Who's Amy?" Noelle said with a grin as she returned to the room.

"Oh, just a friend from the bakery I used to work at."

"*Really?*" Noelle said.

"She has a boyfriend," I replied almost curtly to keep Noelle from pursuing her grin.

"I don't remember her name," Mom said, "but she was very pretty—"

Per laughed. "Well, that narrows it down. Given we're talking about Hotties R Us Bakery."

My mother laughed back and shook her head at Per's brilliance. "Well, let's see," she said, "she had dark features ..."

My mom went on to itemize my anonymous co-worker using zoomed-in descriptors which I'm sure were accurate but, nevertheless, weren't informative to me since I didn't think of peoples' faces in terms of their individual zones.

"Oh, okay," I said, trying to end the futile discussion, "I think I might know who that is."

My mom nodded. "Well, anyway, she said that she and her boyfriend might be moving out here, so I gave her your number."

"Thanks."

"I thought it wouldn't hurt for you to have a friend out here."

"Yeah, thanks," I said, both touched and excited.

"So," Noelle said, "are you seeing anyone special, John?"

"Um, no, not really."

"Not *at all*," Per said with a laugh.

"How come?" Noelle said, looking at me seriously as if it were my option to be dating or not.

"Well, actually, I've found it really hard to meet anyone in this city."

"She's out there," Noelle said. "As soon as you stop looking, you'll find her."

"Thanks, that's a nice thought."

"You just have to make sure that you make it clear that you're open to meeting someone so that girls can see that you're available."

"Oh, okay," I said, wondering if that was consistent with her suggestion that I *stop looking*.

"Um," Per said, "if he does that, then won't he be *looking* for someone—didn't you just tell him *not* to do that?"

"You're so funny," Noelle replied with a laugh.

There was then a group silence as it became clear that Noelle genuinely believed that Per was merely kidding and that he, of course, knew that her two suggestions could easily coexist.

My mother was forced to end the pause. "Well, John, I think you should listen to Noelle. I think she's right."

"On which of the two opposite points?" Per said.

I couldn't help smirking at that one.

But my mom just frowned. "The *second* one. You have to let girls know that you're available."

"I agree," Noelle said. "You never know if you don't try."

I found that suggestion to be both presumptuous and unhelpful. Noelle seemed to be implying that I could flip an internal switch to improve my personality, but she gave no specific information about how I could provoke such a change—other than being 'open' to meeting women, which I'd *thought* I was.

Nevertheless, I enjoyed the company of my family with Noelle included more than I had without her; consequently, I was pleased with Per's choice of Noelle for new girlfriend.

After my family's visit to my compound, I spent much thought on my mom's news that she had given my number to one of my former Sweet On You co-workers. If only my mother had remembered the girl's name, I would have had a better idea of how excited I should be. As it was, the mystery of the person's identity left me more intrigued than I would have been by the maximum anticipatory enjoyment I would have received had I known for certain that it was Tabitha, my bakery favourite.

Chapter 28
Dullard vs. Loneliness II

The Light at the End of the Fridge

Six weeks later, having not received a call from the mystery co-worker, I was well on my way to forgetting about my mother's plan for me to have a friend. Instead, my loneliness had doubled its efforts.

As I sought a glass of milk before going to bed, one evening, I noticed the light inside the fridge. It reminded me of the occasional moment in childhood when I fell awake in the sparsely populated wee hours of the night. I remembered wandering around the dark and strangely quiet home hallways and seeking out the fridge for some juice. At that time, the fridge light that had greeted me was soothing, for it had seemed to be a representative of the bright lights of the day time: it was willing to hang out with me anytime I opened the fridge until the rest of the family was ready to rejoin me.

That feeling that had once comforted me was now in perfect cruel contrast with the fact that the current light on my face was keeping me company on behalf of no one.

The Social Butterflight: Episode I

Now, let us look in on a Thursday evening around eight months into my Ambiguous career. By then, Thursday was locked in as my favourite evening of the week because it meant that the work week was just about done, but I didn't yet have to endure Friday night by myself.

In this Thursday case, a sitcom was in the middle of keeping me company when, without warning, my phone rang. *What was my phone doing ringing on a Thursday night?* Maybe there was a girl at work who had a crush on me. I giggled at the ridiculousness of such an idea. It was obviously just a telemarketer. Oh well, at least someone wanted to talk to me.

"Hello?"

"John!"

"Yes," I said, surprised at the telemarketer's familiarity.

"It's *Amy*."

"Oh," I said, trying to recognize her voice, "hi, Amy."

"From Sweet On You."

"Right, *Amy*, of course. Sorry, I'm just surprised to hear from you."

"Yeah, I hope it's okay. Your mom gave me your number. I ran into her, and I told her I was moving here, so ..."

"Yeah, that's great. So what brings you out?"

"You'll never guess what happened!"

Amy's many long ago attempts to get me to anticipate what she was about to tell me flew back into my irritation.

"Um, I don't know—what happened?"

"So, like, my boyfriend was moving here, so I decided to apply for school here—and I got in!"

"That's great—congratulations."

"And my boyfriend's awesome! I can't wait for you to meet him."

"Yeah, that'd be great," I said, skeptical of both of our claims.

"So," Amy said after half an hour of discussion regarding her new life, "I'm going to a party tomorrow night. You wanna come?"

"Um, I don't know: parties aren't really my thing."

"But Ryan's not going, and I hate going by myself. *Please*."

Even though it was the sort of invite for which I'd been hoping, I realized, as I received it, that such a party event was likely going to be too loud and crowded to be something that I would enjoy. But, simultaneously, I understood that the regret from turning down my first non-Chet-or-family-based social opportunity of the year would be worse, so I agreed to go.

As I walked in the direction of my pre-party meeting with my long lost co-worker, I was nervous about what details I might be able to provide if she asked questions about me. That, of course, was an irrational anxiety, considering that Amy had never asked about me before. Nevertheless, I decided to plan ahead, just in case. It seemed to me that my work life at Ambiguity was probably my nearest-to-interesting detail, so I rehearsed telling Amy about how it was a strange place to work because there were so many people there and yet so few to talk to.

I took a deep breath as I arrived at Amy's apartment building to pick her up for the short walk to the party. She came down immediately upon my buzzing, and—after an Amy-scream-based hug was undertaken—she grinned at me with apparent curiosity.

"It's awesome to see you," she said, starting us walking in party direction. "What've you been up to?"

"Well," I said, pleased with myself for having prepared, "it's actually kind of interesting because I'm working in this huge organization, but I only know a few people—"

"*Totally*," Amy said. "That's what it's like at college. There's so many people that, I don't know—it's not like high school where I knew everybody's business. It's weird. I'm so glad I have a boyfriend already. It's so much harder to meet people here."

"Right," I said, amused by how quickly the focus of our conversation had rotated.

"I know what you're thinking," Amy said

"Really?" I said, suddenly panicked that she'd caught me teasing her in my thoughts. "Um, what do you think I'm thinking?"

"You're thinking that, like, if Ryan's such a great guy, why isn't he going to the party with me? But the thing this is: he doesn't really *like* college students—he thinks they look down on him. I still wanna go, though, because it's the first party I've been invited to, but I don't wanna go by myself, so ..."

"Sounds good to me," I said. Indeed, I was not offended that I was being used as a security-blanket-style friend. Instead, as ever, I felt complimented that I was considered worthy of the role.

Unfortunately, though, when we got closer to the apartment gathering, my nerves became obnoxious. As Amy rang a loud apartment buzzer, I asked myself if it was too late to turn and run the other way.

"Come on up," a crackly voice heckled me.

As it turned out, the party wasn't nearly as scary as I'd always assumed the parties during high school would have been if I'd been invited. For the most part, people stood or sat around drinking or smoking or toking. Amy and I were scanned from many directions when we entered, but no one seemed offended by our presence, and the stares quickly dissolved.

"Amy!" the formerly crackly voice screamed. "You came! How are you?"

"Good!"

"Is this him?" Crackly Voice said, looking at me.

"No, Ryan couldn't come. This is my friend, John. He's from my hometown."

"How are you?" Crackly said, grinning at me with such force that I had no choice but to consider the crazy possibility that she'd developed insta-friendship feelings for me.

"Good, thanks—thanks for having me. How are you?"

"Great, there's so much food here. How could I be unhappy with that? So why didn't he come?" Crackly said, returning to Amy so suddenly that I was forced to second-guess my hypothesis that she was interested in my company.

"He's a *guy*," Amy said, laughing. "He's doesn't know anybody, so he wanted go out with his friends instead."

"Neo-Neanderthal," Crackly said. "Well, we'll have fun without him—you guys should help yourself to food."

On our way out of the food zone, another girl launched her way into my friend.

"Come with me," the newcomer said. "Sorry," she added to me, "emergency girl-talk meeting."

"Oh, okay," I said as Amy and the girl talker retreated into a bedroom.

I was left in a room infested by strangers. I searched their faces for a smile, and I found one on Crackly's lips—it wasn't directed at me, but wallflowers can't be choosers.

"Hey, John," she said in the middle of a laugh as I invaded her area, "this is Amed."

"Hey," Amed said, before turning back to Crackly. "So are you going to tell me why you needed to put curtains on a window that's opaque?"

"Because it looks pretty, *silly*," Crackly said, giggling as she pushed on Amed's shoulder in a way that made me realize that I had interrupted a high-level flirtation.

So I backed away (with no objection from the flirters), and I was soon collecting various 'Hey's from around the room. In the near hour it would take for Amy to come out of girl-talk chambers, I completed three rounds of the apartment. My favourite room was the kitchen, where I could make it look like I was there for the food. The time alone had me wondering why 'girl talk' was taking precedence over protecting me from social pain, but I supposed the 'emergency' must have been serious, and so I diagnosed myself as greedy for worrying about my petty comforts, and I took another turn about the room.

"Hey," a guy in a baseball hat said, looking up at me before surprising me with additional syllables. "You checking out the talent too?"

Oh. "What do you mean by *talent*?" I said, having a good idea of the answer, but not sure how else to respond.

"Well, I guess that depends if you like guys or girls," he said. "Don't worry, buddy: I'm cool either way."

"Oh, thanks—no, yeah, I prefer women in terms of dating ... Um, how about you?"

"Same," he said. "There's a couple of gorgeous ladies here tonight, eh? But it sucks 'cause nowadays guys and girls can be friends. It's hard to tell who's going out and who's just friends. In my dad's day, it was totally obvious who was fair game."

"Yeah, that's interesting," I said sincerely. "I never thought of it that way."

"I just don't get it," the hatted fellow replied. "I mean I *love* women, but I've got enough friends."

"Oh," I said, "but, um—you don't like talking to women, just because?"

My hatted friend laughed. "Of course, I like *talking* to women, but, seriously, if you knew you could never get with a chick, would you hang out with her instead of your guy-friends?"

"Yeah, why not?"

"Oh *please*. No guy would actually rather hang out with his chick-friends than his guy-friends."

"Why?"

"Because girls think differently than we do. Like, girls are more high-maintenance. It's like I can go out with friends, meet a girl, and just *leave* with without saying a word, and my buddies won't care. You try that with a chick-friend and she'll be all, 'Oh my God, I was worried. Where'd you go?'"

Hmm, it was difficult to respond to Hat-man given that he seemed to be conversing under the protected assumption that all males—including myself—were the same guy, and all females were the same girl.

"Well," I tried, "I think I'd be worried if we were hanging out, and you just disappeared without saying anything."

"Oh *please*, you'd just assume I hooked up. C'mon, guys aren't like that—we don't get all emotional about shit like that."

As Hat-man performed that rant, it occurred to me that Hat-man's belief in the universality of male and female personality was present in everything he said, and, therefore—if I wanted to argue for variability among the sexes—I would need to do so constantly. That sounded so exhausting to me that I wished for the solitude that Hat-man had interrupted.

"But," he continued with a laugh, "girls are always policing behavior: a chick'll be like, 'You shouldn't've said that—that person's very sensitive about that. You need to go and apologize.' And it's like, 'Thanks, Mom.'"

"That's interesting," I said. "But I guess I would rather someone tell me—"

"Oh *please*," Hat-man said again before telling me something else that all of us guys thought.

Thankfully, in the middle of his next diatribe, Amy finally returned.

"Hey," she said, "sorry about that."

"That's all right," I said. "Everything okay?"

"Yeah," she said, smiling, "I'll tell you later."

I glanced at Hat-guy, who was clearly trying to assess Amy and me to see if I had taken her out of romantic circulation. I searched my dull brain for a way to confirm that she was unavailable, but I could not conceive of a means of doing so without awkwardly drawing attention to his attraction.

"So," I said instead, "Amy, this is—sorry, I didn't catch your name?"

"James," he said, smiling at Amy, laying the ground work, I supposed, for a flirtation if she was available.

"Nice to meet you. I'm Amy," she said, smiling back with more sweetness than was necessary.

An awkward pause followed; and it occurred to me that James, himself, would probably prefer to find out right away—however awkwardly—that Amy was already partnered up, instead of wasting his time talking to an ineligible bachelorette. So I went straight for blunt.

"Amy invited me because her boyfriend couldn't come."

"Right on," James said. "I'm gonna get another drink," he added with a wink of appreciation in my direction.

As James retreated, Amy turned to me with a scrunched forehead. "Why'd you say that? Makes it sound like I can't come to a party by myself."

"Um," I said, trying to decide how much secrecy I owed James, "well, I just thought he kind of liked you, so I was letting him know that you had a boyfriend so that—"

"He was just being *friendly*," Amy interrupted with a laugh. "You sound like Ryan—he thinks every guy's after me too."

"Fair enough," I said, not wanting to disagree with a criticism of Ryan. "Maybe you're right. So what's the matter with your friend?"

"Oh, right," Amy said, switching to a whisper. "She just found out her crush broke up with his girlfriend, so, like, obviously, we had to have an emergency girl-talk session."

"Right, of course."

Amy's return to the position of justifying my presence at the party made it bearable. And, while the rest of the evening was boring, I'm happy to report that I was so relieved to get home that night that I did not feel at all lonely as I fell asleep to the waning TV hours.

Chapter 29
Dullard vs. Cupid

Hopes & Schemes

The best aspect of Amy's party was telling Tally about it the next week at Ambiguity while we were waiting for Bernice and Chet at lunch. Tally smiled and even laughed at my description. Once she'd heard my full report, she informed me that Amy was "an immature little thing" and that she hoped I would maintain my lack of romantic feelings for her even if she were eventually freed from the shackles of her awful boyfriend.

"You're the type of guy," she said, "who girls like her always end up with, but she doesn't deserve you."

"Oh," I said, surprised and honoured to hear it.

"When she finally starts flirting with you—and she will, *trust me*—promise me you'll turn her down."

I immediately consented to the anti-proposition; as I did so, I felt embarrassed that the contract was indeed required to ensure that I could resist Amy were she ever dullard-inclined.

Now, in spite of Tally's compliment that I was entitled to be so discriminating when it came to romantic matches, there was still the problem of not having any applicants against whom to discriminate. Sure, I'd be delighted to meet a closer-to-my-age Tally-alike who wasn't already coupled up and was willing to be interested in a dullard—and I wouldn't have minded winning a lottery or two while I was at it—but, in the meantime, it seemed prudent to have a backup plan.

Tally smiled. "I guess I shouldn't burn all your bridges, though, eh?"

"Right, I guess not."

Tally chuckled. "So has anyone piqued your interest lately?"

"Well," I said, trying to be funny, "I guess there's always women who I find interesting, but they're usually either already partnered up or they're not interested back."

Tally nodded. "That's a good start."

"Oh...why?"

"Well, you know, it's good to have crushes even if nothing can come out of them because then you get to know what kind of women you like."

"Didn't I already know that before?"

"Maybe, but maybe you were *wrong*. Like, maybe you think you're into talkative girls, but, in person—when you have an actual crush on a chatter bug—maybe you realize that you find her constant yapping to be really annoying. A crush lets you view a person through the intense lens of a romance without having to go through all that annoying dating."

"But—"

"Yeah, I see what you mean," Tally said. "Even if it's painful, dating's kinda part of the fun, isn't it?"

I laughed. "Exactly, you read my mind."

"Is that *okay*? Some people don't like it when I read their mind."

I laughed again. "No, it's okay. I don't mind."

"I had a feeling," Tally said, shrugging with pretend arrogance that made me chuckle in my belly.

Bernice arrived soon after to break up the entertainment.

"Hey, Bernice," Tally said. "How's the lineup today?"

"Slow as molasses," Bernice replied.

"So," Tally said as Bernice sat down, "we were just talking about determining one's type. Did you know that Jeff was your type right away, Bernie?"

I smiled at Tally's attempt to give Bernice a free takeover of the conversation. But the odd thing about Bernice was that she preferred to intercept conversations when they were already freely flowing—it was not her style to take part in the construction of such dialogues.

"I don't know," she said, followed by a shoulder shrug and a large bite of food.

I smiled at Tally.

She almost giggled back.

"Um," I said, taking my turn, "how did you meet Jeff?"

"At a party. Why do you wanna know?"

"Oh, we're just interested," Tally said.

"Yeah, I'm sure," Bernice said. "But, if you need to live vicariously, maybe just buy a romance novel instead of interrogating me."

I couldn't resist a wee chuckle at that. "Fair enough," I said. Indeed, it was presumptuous of us to invite Bernice directly into the conversation instead of waiting for her to dominate it when she was good and ready.

"Oh, hey, by the way, Tally," I said, "I know you like people watching—well, there was this guy preaching on the bus today, and it was really weird because—"

"You think *that's* weird," Bernice finally arrived. "Try having a freak outside a club on Friday night while you're waiting in line. He was all like, 'This life of promiscuity is a sin, and you must give yourself to the Lord,' and it's like ..."

Helpfully, said sermon finally gave Bernice her rightful spot at the head of our conversation.

I decided the next mini-time I was able to converse with Tally (a few days later) that—since she had investigated my lack of love life—I should probe deeper into her aspirations, so I checked in on her intention to find a new career.

"It's not an easy decision," she replied with a sigh. "Even if it goes perfectly, I probably won't make much more than I do right now—they so overpay me here."

"But—"

"Yeah, I see what you mean: money isn't everything."

I laughed. "Right—good mind reading again."

Tally gave me a shallow shrug-and-smile. "Thanks, but, seriously, you don't think it's a bit stupid to give up a good job for, I don't know, something that's not even always been my dream? It just happens to be something that sounds like more fun than this, but it could just be, you know, grass-is-greener syndrome."

"No, I don't think it's stupid."

Tally laughed. "*Well, that solves that.* Do you have any reasoning behind your outrageous claim?"

"Um, well, if it didn't work out, you could get another job like this one again pretty easily, couldn't you?"

"Not like this one—not with the same overinflated wage and a boss like Elsje."

"Oh, right. I guess it is a good job, isn't? But, I don't know, I still don't think it would be *stupid* to leave."

"A justification is still required," Tally said.

"Well, it's not like you don't *know* there's a risk. You would just be doing something that you think could make you happy. I don't see how that could be stupid."

"Serial killing makes serial killers happy," Tally said, raising her eyebrow, "—aren't *they* stupid?"

I giggled. "Um—"

"I see what you mean," my mentor said. "Serial killers are a nasty lot, but not necessarily *stupid*."

I laughed out loud. "Exactly!"

"So you think I should do it?"

"No, not at all."

"But I thought you said I wouldn't be stupid to go for it?"

"You *wouldn't*. But, if you *do* go, I'll have no one to talk to around here."

Tally chuckled. "I see. That's very sweet. But you can always talk to Bernie or Chet."

I smirked at that, but—given that Tally and I had never officially discussed the failings of our conversation companions—I dared not laugh.

"That's true," I said instead with my best straight face.

Tally grinned back and changed the topic for us.

Thereafter, during my turns to ask Tally questions, I decided to check in regularly on her plans to leave Ambiguity. She seemed each time progressively more intrigued by her hopes and dreams, but she continued to question the intelligence of pursuing them.

I, in turn, repeated my insistence that her intellect could not be cross-examined if she was aware of the risks and was making an informed decision to overrule them; that claim of mine may have artificially made it seem that I thought the perils of her plan would be defeated. In reality, of course, I had no evidence—other than my belief in Tally's talent—that her daunting pursuits would be successful.

Meanwhile, during her turns to ask me questions, Tally often checked in to see if I'd found someone to date yet.

"You know," she said, one afternoon, "I wonder if you'd like my younger cousin. I think your personalities might be a good match."

"Um," I said, surprised, intrigued, and scared of the possibility, "well, the bigger question is whether she'd like me, isn't it?"

Tally laughed. "No, of course not. No, I'm sure she'd like you. She's had trouble meeting nice guys who aren't intimidated by her—she's very bright, just like her cousin."

"Right, well," I said, trying to match Tally's humour, "I'm not *at all* intimidated by you, so I guess I wouldn't be intimidated by your cousin."

"Yes," Tally said. "Methinks this could be a good match—although, be warned: I'm not sure if she's looking for something right now."

"Of course," I said, appreciating Tally for setting a soft groundwork for my ego to land on in case Cousin Tally wasn't impressed by Tally's description of me.

"Okay," Tally said, "so you're a go? I have your permission to set something up?"

The directness of the question obviously increased my nervousness, but the promise of hatred from myself—if I turned down the romantic opportunity of a dull life time—destroyed any possibility of delay in my answer.

"Yes," I said, "I am definitely up for it."

The only thing missing that night on my gleeful bus ride home was someone with whom to celebrate the bright possible future that now awaited me. But my dissatisfaction in that regard was quelled by the bright future, itself. I could any day be meeting a person with whom to share all topics of conversation. *Who might she be?* Her status as both a cousin of Tally and someone who intimidated people with her intellect surely put her at a near Ashley level. That, in turn, was concerning, considering that Ashley-level women were outside of my attractiveness catchment area, but perhaps Tally's recommendation of me would temporarily blind her to that fact.

Gratitude Adjustment

The next evening, my calendar notified me that it was my brother's birthday. That meant—since I'd copied Per by being born on the same day as him—that it was my birthday as well. Now, the tricky thing about sharing a birth date with someone is that—when you call them on that date to wish them a happy one—your call comes necessarily equipped with the simultaneous circumstance that you are calling someone on *your* birthday, which means that you appear to be grasping for birthday acknowledgment. I didn't want to look like I was craving attention, so I delayed calling Per, hoping that he would be the one to make the problematic call. An hour into the standoff, my phone rang.

"Hello?"

"Hey, bro," Per's voice said, "you gonna be there in ninety minutes?"

"Um, yeah."

"Okay, don't move."

Ninety minutes later, my family arrived at my apartment. Now, I must confess: when my parents and brother and Noelle landed unscheduled in my home to celebrate the weekday birthday of Per and me, I couldn't resist feeling touched by the sentiment. It was almost like a surprise party. And you probably won't believe this, pessimistic reader, but we even spent some time during the gathering talking about me.

"So, John," my dad said, "how are you finding it now at Ambiguity? Are you adapted to the new system yet?"

"It's going good," I said. "I'm actually starting to like the system. I understand how everything works now, and I do the same things over and over, so it's actually kind of cool because—"

Per laughed. "Only John would be excited about doing the *same thing over and over.*"

"Per!" Noelle said with a playfully scolding voice. "Don't be mean."

"I'm not being mean. I'm saying that John's unique."

"You're so funny," Noelle said, shaking her head. "Well, it didn't come across that way."

Noelle's generosity of compassion made me smile: I had always enjoyed Noelle's sister's kindness, and I appreciated seeing it in Noelle too.

"Per," my mom joined in with a look of amused disapproval, "Noelle's right—not all of us can be as creative as you are."

"True enough," Per said. "All right, John, go ahead: what else do you like about doing the same thing all the time?"

"Um, okay, well—"

"No, wait," Per said, grinning. "Let me see if I can guess: when you get to work, you set up, like, *John's Epic Battle Station*, so, like, you've got your computer, your mouse, your coffee mug, and, like, your calculator all set up, and you're like—"

"Okay, Per," Dad said. "That'll do."

Mom smiled. "Per, where did you get this flair for making things up? Your dad and I certainly didn't give it to you."

Per shrugged. "You *know* I've always been good at making stuff up."

"I know, but I think maybe you should be a writer—or something of that ilk—instead of picking on your brother with your wit all the time."

My brother frowned at his girlfriend. "Did you tell them?"

"I didn't say anything. I knew you'd tell them in your own way."

"Tell us what?"

"I *am* writing—I'm writing this awesome movie."

"You're kidding! What's it about?"

"Well, all I know so far is it's going to be like an action thriller—but it's going to have this totally cool twist at the end."

"I'm impressed," Mom said.

With the discussion of my work life complete, it was soon time for presents.

My dad gave me a framed picture of Aunty Susan standing in front of the old Bert's Shirts & Skirts. Aunty Susan had decorated the store with a crisp new design starring a grand new sign which read, SUSAN'S BETTER THAN BEFORE STORE.

I felt a cool breeze tickle my chest as I looked it over. "That's so great," I said, trying to keep my voice from breaking. "That's awesome—*thank you*."

"Can I see?" Noelle said. "Oh, cool—a picture of your aunt. I like her."

Per rolled his yes. "It's not just a picture of our aunt; it's a picture of her with the new sign."

"Oh, I see, *neat* ..." Noelle said with the same empty cheerfulness.

Per rolled his eyes. "*You know*, after she got dumped by her philanderer of a husband, and she took over his business—well, *this* is, like, the final result."

"She's done very well with it," Dad said. "I'd estimate her profits will be on par with Bert's by the end of the year."

Mom nodded. "She sends her love, by the way, John. She's got the flu, so she didn't want to get the rest of us sick."

"Right, right, that's awesome," Noelle said (referring, I assumed, to the gift now in her hand, rather than the flu).

Next, after Per received a less interesting but more useful gift from our dad, I was pleased by a present from my mother. She gave me, as she often did, a nice hardcover novel. I wasn't necessarily an enchanted fan of the books she chose for me, but I always kept and often read them because they were gifts from my mom.

After Noelle gushed about my mother's "wonderful" selection, she grinned and announced that it was her turn to give a gift. That was a happy moment for me as I was pleased to have completed my role as gift receiver—a cringe-provoking role in which I had to watch myself *performing* reactions.

"Thanks, babe," Per said, smiling at the fancy shirt he received from his girlfriend.

"It's for your work," she said.

"Very nice," Mom replied. "You'll look very smart in that, Per."

Per smirked at his mother's choice of adjective.

"And this is for *you*," Noelle said, smiling at me.

"Oh ... thank you."

"You're welcome. Happy birthday."

"Thanks," I said, and I unwrapped another book.

"Your mom told me that you're a great reader."

"That's so nice of you," I said, scanning the book jacket. "Thank you. This looks really good," I claimed, before babbling aimlessly for another minute about why it would be the great read of my life.

As Per then unraveled his gift from our mother, I discovered myself to be feeling a cheerful affection for his girlfriend. Indeed,

I hoped that he would not botch this relationship by going after another member of her family.

Hopes & Schemes Continued

The visit from my family distracted me from what should have been a second evening in a row of nervous introspection regarding my hoped-for date with Cousin Tally. But, worry not, concerned reader: the next day—upon seeing Tally at lunch again—my anxiety fired right back up again.

"So," she said, "I talked to my cousin—"

"Oh, okay," I said, trying to keep my excitement from spilling onto my voice. "What did …ah, what did she say?"

"Well, she's actually had a lot going on over the last year, and it turns out she's not really ready to date right now."

"Right, that makes sense."

"It's nothing personal, John. She said you sounded great. It's just—"

"Oh, yeah, yeah, it's fine. She's not looking to go on a date right now. I understand that." As I said so, I felt my cheeks getting emotional. Somehow the rejection from a stranger felt more personal than any in-my-face dismissal could have been.

Just between you and me, confidential reader, I felt like walking away from the conversation at that point—not because I was mad at Tally, of course, but because the disappointment had taken away my energy to talk about it. But I didn't want Tally to feel bad for having tried to do something nice, so I forced a smile and searched my brain for something else to discuss. The first thing that landed in my mind was Tally's plot to leave Ambiguity.

"Oh," she answered, more cautiously than I was used to, "um—"

"What, has something happened?"

"Actually, yeah, I just got accepted. So, shock and disbelief, I'm leaving."

"Wow, when?"

"In three weeks."

That new news piled onto the unavailable-cousin news to stomp on my emotions. In five minutes, I had lost both my potential for a grand romance and my favourite person to talk to. But, with a hearty sigh, I gripped my face muscles and held onto composure.

During the last days of Tally at Ambiguity, Chet and I saw her and Bernice more often than usual in the cafeteria. Several times in the course of our private discussions, Tally tried to inquire about how I was feeling regarding my lack of romantic future, but, on such occasions, I redirected the conversation back to procedural questions regarding how she was going to be running her new life.

With two days to go before her defection, I felt left out of what mattered to Tally. It seemed that, whereas I was losing my favourite person to talk to, she was gaining a new life of excitement that did not require a dullard lunchtime companion to supplement it.

Just then, however, I received on my desktop a first-ever email from Tally. I eagerly clicked it open.

'Hey John,' she wrote. 'Can you do me a favour?'

As I nodded dumbly that I would, Tally's message went on to request that I create an excuse for missing my usual Chet-based lunch that day so that I could instead go to a nearby café where she and I could have an entire 'uninterrupted' hour—i.e. sixty minutes without Chet's and Bernice's debilitating contributions— to discuss our farewell. The email yanked me out of my greedy melancholy. I was so honoured to be worthy of a private meeting with my conversational mentor that I arrived at our secret gathering ready to make peace with any discussion she had in mind.

"I'm glad you came," she said, once I'd settled into my seat. "I didn't want to miss the chance to say thanks for being such a great person to talk to."

"Thank you," I said, "but you're the one who's good at—"

"Yeah, yeah, yeah," Tally said. "Quit copying me. This is *my* meeting."

"Okay," I said, giggling.

"You know," she said, "you've influenced me more than you know."

"Really? How?"

"Well, you've got this attitude that—I don't know—it somehow makes me feel confident. And it isn't just your insistence that my plans aren't stupid; it's also that you act like it's because it's *me* who's thinking of doing them that you don't think they're stupid. If people are supportive people, in general, they're usually supportive of *everyone* going after their dreams—since, of course, dreams are always considered noble things to pursue. But you seem to actually be in favour of me doing my thing because—correct me if I'm wrong—but it's like you actually believe that *I, specifically,* can do it."

I nodded aggressively. "Yeah, *exactly.* I really do think that you've got something that most people don't that makes you—"

"Good enough," Tally said, raising her hand to quash my babble. "I said you should correct me if I was wrong, not if I was right. So the point of this is that it's my turn to influence you. So whaddya want help with? New career, new apartment, new girlfriend?"

"Oh, okay, well," I said, too bewildered to turn down the kindness, "I like my job, and I like my apartment, so—"

"A new girlfriend, it is," Tally said. "Okay, first of all, it's not too late to set you up with my cousin."

"I thought she wasn't interested in a blind date?"

"Well, she was being—she's had a rough year, and she's being lazy about fixing things. But I'm pretty sure I could still talk her into it."

"No, it's okay. She already gave her answer. I don't want to push her into something she doesn't want."

Tally sighed. "I figured you'd say that. So I think what we need to do is assess your current portfolio for meeting women. What have you tried so far?"

"Not much. I went to a dance club once—which I hated. Also …I've gone to bars with Chet, and that's about it."

"Okay, I see your problem," Tally said. "You're a soft-spoken guy, and yet you're trying to meet women in places that are too loud and crowded for them to get to know you. You need to go somewhere that you don't have to hit on a girl to talk to her."

Tally was soon telling me the standard advice that I should try to meet women at events, such as co-ed sports or classes, wherein activities other than hitting on people were part of the attraction. I had heard that sort of recommendation before, and I'd generally ignored it as too much time spent being uncomfortable in large groups of people for too unlikely a payoff, but—in the voice of Tally—the myth of the activity-based meeting grounds seemed more plausible.

After I was sufficiently inspired by dating advice, Tally instructed me to call her or—"better yet"—come visit her in the faraway city for which she was deserting me. I doubted I would take advantage of said generosity, but the offer provided me with further evidence that my admiration for Tally did reflect back at least a whisper.

I would see Tally one more time at the usual Bernice-and-Chet-sabotaged lunch, but the secret meeting I had with her sits much more assertively in my memory, so, from it, I derive her unofficial last Ambiguous words to me.

"I'm going to miss you," she said.

"Me too," I said, trying to keep my words short so that they didn't get choked up.

Tally then gave me a hug and pretended not to notice that I was once again just barely winning the argument with my tear ducts.

"All the best, you deserve it," she said.

"You too," I copied once more, which—oddly—made her laugh.

Chapter 30
A Boring Samaritan

The Guiding Slight

With Tally's departure, I was obligated to keep alive her legacy—of trying to increase my romantic chances—by seeking out activities where other humans might be. As I looked through notice boards for my options, I had trouble spotting something that wouldn't feel fake to me. If, for instance, I joined a painting class, without ever having had any previous interest or talent in the subject, then I would surely feel a bit creepy as I tried to get to know the female painters in the room. The same went for ballroom dance, badminton, and yoga.

So, with procrastination as my guide, I maintained my standard non-romantic life, but I scanned for possibility wherever I went. One day, then, as I stood in the elevator on the way out of my building, I spotted a framed advertisement for a fitness class. While I read, the white-haired apartment neighbour with whom I had spoken on my first day in the city was standing next to me and was apparently watching me. I learned so as I glanced at her.

Upon getting caught in the act of watching me, my neighbour did not suddenly look away as one might expect; instead, she smiled at me. Perhaps she was amused by my perusal of the fitness class poster. I blushed to the thought.

Ten minutes later, as I arrived at my grocery store destination, I was confronted by a trio of tweenaged girls in uniform.

"Excuse me, do you want to buy some cookies?" one of them chirped.

"Oh, okay, sure."

"They're three dollars a box," the chirper announced.

As I pulled out my money, Chirper-girl gave a curt nod to the girl holding the cookies.

"How many boxes would you like?" the cookie holder said.

"I guess *two*, please."

"Okay, thank you," she said with a full grin as she handed me the merchandise.

"Kendra!" Chirper snapped. "You have to let him pay me first."

I handed the critic my money, and—as I did so—I watched the continued gleefulness of Kendra. She seemed genuinely excited by my two-box purchase. Don't worry, judgmental reader, I was not under the ego-caressing impression that buying cookies was some great act of philanthropy. To the contrary, it occurred to me in that moment that—if I really wanted to be helpful to the world—I ought to spend my energies working for a virtuous cause.

That thought, in turn, led me to remember my arrogant aspiration, two years earlier, to acquire something like Bert Hardelean's talents with people so that I could use them to improve unhappy moods. Luckily, I'd realized then that I lacked the charisma to plagiarize Bert's skills. The memory refreshed me now as I was pleased to be reminded that my charitable energies were best spent writing cheques to those with the aptitude to do the work.

Strangely, though, as Chirper-girl handed me my change, it seemed to me that she was not particularly skillful in her appreciation of my generosity. Instead, from the moment I'd agreed to the transaction, she was so caught up in the details of the exchange of my money for her goods that she forgot to acknowledge me for it. In short, she struck me as an inelegant spokesperson for her cookie-selling organization. *Well then: if she could be on the front lines of a semi-charitable cookie company, why couldn't my unskillful energies be useful too?* A quiver travelled around my insides: *I was going to volunteer for a charity.*

As I thanked the cookie squad, I noticed—over the short shoulder of Chirper-girl—that there was a woman smiling at me. Don't get excited, easily excited reader; it wasn't a romantic smile, but it did get me thinking that it would be neat to meet a woman over charity work.

That daydream, in turn, had me second-guessing myself. *Had my search for a date made me want to do something charitable, or was it the other way around?* After a quick pondering, I confirmed with myself that charity work was something I wanted to do, regardless, and that finding a date was to be an accidental but appreciated by-product. I hope that's okay with you, critical reader, but I think the order of operations of my thoughts will back me up. (Please feel free to check the transcript if you're skeptical.)

Now, to both my ghostwriter's and my shock, I did not put a lot of procrastination into my plan to join a charity. Instead, I spent only a few days researching suitable candidates, and—within only a couple more days—I selected what seemed to be the best option (that is to say, I picked the one with an office close to Ambiguity so that I could visit it on my Ambiguous lunch hour). Then, on a warm but rainy workday afternoon, I told Chet that I had some errands to do, and I traveled to the offices of what I'll refer to as the Green Cross.

A Blank Canvass

Walking from a rainy afternoon through the surprisingly inconspicuous doors of the Green Cross in search of a cause provoked a momentous feeling in my stomach. I was surprised, therefore, when I arrived at the organization's front desk to find not, as I'd imagined, an eager reception for my offer of services, but instead the top of a receptionist's head as she typed away on her work. The casual manner in which she moved her fingers and mouse made me suspicious that she hadn't heard me arrive, so I contemplated whether I should announce myself or just wait for a lucky glance. The latter, of course, was my selection. But, after a few moments of waiting, the awkwardness of my position overpowered me, so I shuffled my feet to supplement my chances. That did not help as the woman continued to consider each keystroke.

"Um," I finally squeaked out, "I was wondering—"

I was stopped mid-squeak as the woman looked up at me with a weak smile. She had a kind but not necessarily friendly face, which appeared to be three or four years more experienced than mine.

"Sorry, I'll just be a second," she said.

"Oh, yeah, of course," I squeaked again. "Take your time."

The receptionist didn't acknowledge that remark, which left me wondering if I'd been too squeaky for hearing. I put some intense contemplation into that question until finally my muse looked up at me again.

"Okay, how can I help you?"

"Well," I said, now much more nervous than I had intended on being, "I was wondering about volunteering with you guys—is that ...*possible?*"

"Let's see," the woman said, opening up a drawer and pulling out some paperwork. "Fill this out, and I'll see if Lesley's available to talk to you."

I felt as if I were in a doctor's office complaining of a sniffle. I took the form to a nearby chair as I heard the receptionist dialing and then informing someone of my presence.

"What's your name?" she called to me in the middle of the conversation.

"John."

"*John...?*"

"Smith."

"John *Smith*," she told the phone. "Yeah, no appointment—I think he just showed up."

I felt a shudder roll through my innards.

"Okay, I'll tell him fifteen minutes—Lesley says fifteen minutes," the receptionist said as she hung up the phone, "but bet on twenty minutes to half an hour. Lesley is notoriously distracted."

"Okay, thanks," I said, touched to be given such insider-timing. "Sorry about *just showing up*—I guess I should've called to set up an appointment."

"No problem," the woman said, suddenly looking right at me. "We need volunteers, so we can't really afford to be picky about when you come in."

"Thanks," I said, honoured by her kindness, especially considering that she did not seem to be a naturally gentle person. Indeed, as we both then returned to our tasks, I felt an urge to somehow become better acquainted with the variably mooded woman.

The form I was assigned asked me several personal questions:

What was my motivation for wanting to volunteer at the Green Cross?

Did I have any experience with the type of folks they serviced?

How might I deal with certain Green Cross situations?

I focused my pen on the first question and began blithering a truth-originating lie about having been inspired by Bert and his [theoretical] efforts to do right by his community.

"What made you decide to come here?" the receptionist interrupted.

"Oh," I said, looking up, "well, I'm putting here that my, um, uncle inspired me, which is partly true, but really I just got tired of…I don't know…I guess I thought maybe I could be of some small help."

"Good enough," the woman said. "Just put *that*, then."

"Really? It's not too short?"

"Nah, they're not going to turn you away unless you say something really obnoxious."

"Oh, okay, thanks," I said, happy to extrapolate the recommendation to all of the form's queries. The adaptation went well until I reached the backside of the form where a demand for references was made. I was startled that such testimony would be required for me to do something for free, and I was even more concerned as I considered that I didn't have many people to recommend me. In the professional reference column, I was able to nervously mark down *Mr. Chet Williams*, but, in the friendship category, I wasn't convinced that I had any options. I wished Tally were there to direct me, which, in turn, had me deciding to write *Tally* down.

I brought the form to my advisor when I was done. As I handed it to her, a flurry of spontaneity overtook me.

"Whaddya think?" I said.

"I'm sure it's fine," she mumbled with a bored shrug before sending her eyes genuinely into the document. "It looks good to me," she concluded. "But I like these things short, so don't take my word for it. You could always mention that you saw one of our bus ads in the 'How'd you hear of us?' section—Lesley'd love that."

"Okay, thanks," I said, embarrassed to be adding an unambiguous lie to my first correspondence with my cause (but not willing to decline my hoped-for friend's advice).

After scribbling in the suggestion, I handed the lie-filled form back to the receptionist.

"Great, now you can just relax and wait for Lesley."

"Okay, thanks…I'm John, by the way."

"I saw that. I'm Rayann."

"Nice to meet you."

"You as well," the receptionist said, smiling blandly back.

As I waited for Lesley, Rayann and I didn't converse much, but she did narrate some of her work for me.

"Why do people do that?" she muttered.

"What'd they do?" I said, looking up eagerly.

"Oh, you know, why don't people write their *names* on the notes they put in my inbox?"

"Yeah, that's weird. You can't be expected to know everyone's handwriting."

"Yeah, it's like they think I'm their personal assistant, and no one else gives me things to do."

"Yeah, that's so annoying."

"Yup," Rayann said.

The conversation faded away from there.

"Why the hell?" Rayann remarked a few minutes later.

"What?" I said, grinning.

"Oh, people love to request these *Thank you* letters, but they never tell me which format they want. Should I *guess*? Should I phone him *again* to ask him which one?"

"Yeah, maybe just guess," I said, nostalgically grabbing onto the wisdom that my PE teacher, Mr. Boyko, had once given me. "And then—if you get it wrong—maybe he won't forget to put it in next time?"

"Not a bad idea," Rayann said as she picked up the phone and dialed. "Hi, Henry…I got your letter…which format do you want…? I don't care—*it's up to you*…okay…bye." She hung up the phone and rolled her eyes at me. "He's like, 'Oh, which do *you* think?', and I'm like, 'I don't care,' but there's like no acknowledgment that he forgot. It's as if it's my job to phone him and ask which format every time. Why can't he just pick the thing, himself? There's a box right there on the form for him to pick. The guy's got fifteen degrees but no common sense."

"That's funny," I said, fascinated but not sure which part I should comment on. "Um, yeah, it's weird how people will just do the bare minimum sometimes, isn't it?"

"You said it," Rayann said.

The conversation then dissolved again, only to return with Rayann's next narrative outburst.

Eventually, a woman in her middle forties arrived right on Rayann's cue (i.e. fifteen minutes later than the interviewer had promised), and she appeared pleased to see me.

"You must be John Smith," she said, smiling grandly.

"I *am*," I said, standing up.

"Nice to meet you, I'm Lesley. Why don't we go to my office for a dialogue? Thank you, Rayann," she said, glancing back as we walked.

I also looked back, and I spotted—on my new crush's face—a squinting, eyebrow-raised acknowledgment that seemed to say to her superior, *Why are you talking to me?*

"Thanks for waiting," Lesley said with another smile as we walked.

"No problem," I said, impressed by her ability to acknowledge her delay without actually having to go through the nuisance of officially apologizing.

"So," she said with a fully rounded smile as we sat down in her office, "I'm really glad that you've come in today. Tell me a little about yourself."

"Okay," I said, and I took to explaining—with as much enthusiasm as my personality could manage—my work at Ambiguity.

"Sounds like very interesting work."

"Yeah, it's—"

"I'm wondering *also*," Lesley interjected, "what you do in your leisure time?"

My mind was blank on that one, so I randomly grabbed for a cliché pastime.

"I guess I like talking to people."

"Sounds like you're very social," Lesley said.

"Right," I said, panicking that I'd falsely advertised my social skills, "I mean, it's not like I'm an extrovert, but I like people."

"So do *we*," Lesley said with another smile. "That's a very important part of the work we do. We care about the people we serve."

"Okay," Lesley said a few questions later, "for what area of the organization would you most like to volunteer?"

"Oh, um, well, where do you have the most need?"

"Good question. Actually, we're soon to be starting our annual fundraising drive. With your social skills, I think canvassing might be a good fit for you."

"Okay," I said, "but, um, can I canvass *with* someone at the start?"

"That should be fine. Take along anyone you'd like so long as you're always present, with your nametag on, during the transactions. Your friends should neither handle the money nor talk with the donors without *you* being present. They can carry the receipt book for you if you'd like, but you should always be the one to fill it in for the donor."

"Okay, sure," I said. I didn't have the courage to say that I'd meant that I wanted Lesley to provide me a partner with whom to canvass while I learned the rules of the road.

"So have you ever canvassed before?" she said.

"No, sorry."

"No need to apologize. The trick is you want to smile, make eye contact, and—most importantly—you want to avoid giving people an opportunity to say, 'No.' Start by asking them if they know much about the Green Cross—if they *do*, wonderful! They know how important our cause is. *Would they like to make a monetary* investment *in our efforts?* But, invariably, they won't know much about us, so your job is to *tell* them. Don't ask them if they have time to chat—that's an opportunity for them to say that they *don't* have time. Instead, if you go straight into your presentation, invariably, they'll listen."

I nodded politely at Lesley's tutelage, but—between you and me, confidant reader—I was wary of imposing on people presentations that they would have declined if they'd had the opportunity.

"And," Lesley continued, "maintain eye contact with them throughout your presentation and keep an eye out for any indication that they're persuaded. If you see a moment in which they look particularly impressed, grab onto it! Ask them right then if they'd like to make an investment in our efforts. And give them a suggested dollar figure. People tend to give less to door-to-door canvassers than they do over the phone, so start as low as fifty dollars. If they decline, then you can suggest twenty-five dollars—if they decline that too, then you can simply ask them how much they'd be comfortable donating."

"Okay," I said, now worried about becoming the star of someone's anecdote about why they don't like charity canvassers.

Lesley, however, seemed pleased with my official agreement, and—after giving me an explanation regarding how to process the proceeds of my canvassing—she directed us back to Rayann's desk.

"Rayann, John is going to be joining us as a canvasser, so he'll need a nametag printed up and a book of tax receipts. And, actually, we'll send those out to you, John, so that I can check your references first."

"Oh, okay," I said, reminded to be nervous about that.

"*And*," Rayann said, handing me a form while directing a condescending voice towards her boss, "he needs to drop off this criminal record check to the police—right, Lesley?"

Lesley nodded confidently as if she had implied the instruction. "*Exactly*—and," she said, smiling grandly at me one more time, "if you have any questions, call me here any time."

"Thanks—you too," I said, gulping as I spotted the incoherence of my reply.

After stopping off at the nearby police station to submit my ID and criminal record check form for inspection, I returned to Ambiguity a few minutes late. Upon belated arrival, I discovered a suggestive grin from Chet. I wasn't too worried about being late since I had never known Chet to be a temporal bean counter, but the victorious bemusement on his face provoked me to assume he was teasing me for my rare case of failed punctuality.

"Sorry I'm late," I said, "I was—"

"No problemo," he said, his grin growing, "I understand you've got a hankering to be a Green-Crossing guard?"

"Oh," I said, stunned by his omniscience, "how'd you know?"

"Lesley just gave me a call."

"Oh, right, sorry—I should've asked if that was okay."

"Not to worry," Chet said, "Les and I had a good chat."

"You know Lesley?"

"I do *now*. We go recently back. Delightful gal—she kept wanting to talk about *you*, though."

"Oh—"

"Don't worry, I was singing and dancing your praises."

"Oh, okay, thanks."

"No worries," Chet said, filling up another big smile. "Happy to do it."

Chet left my office watching me with that same grin. At the risk of sounding ungrateful, magnanimous reader, it seemed to me that—in that expression—Chet was charging too much appreciation for the easy service he'd provided.

On the bus ride home that evening, I contemplated dinner. Thankfully, for you, reading along reader, that dull thought was distracted by the conversation of a tripod of teenagers. They began with a commentary about why one of their absent colleagues was apparently a bit of "a bitch," but then—to my surprise—they discussed how they might assist in feeding poor people in less successful lands.

"Maybe we should try to bring in, like, that all-day-famine thing to raise money?" one of the two girls commented. "I'm sure Ms. Gil-Teakins would help us."

"Yeah, yeah, I'm *so* there," the second female said.

"It's a possibility," the male replied with a sigh. "But I resent how gimmicky those self-imposed famines are. Shouldn't people donate because it's the right thing to do? Us being hungry for a day has no bearing on whether people in Africa need food or not."

"I totally agree," the first female said, "but people need the gimmick."

"Why?"

"Because it's like, don't you think that adults sometimes donate to our stuff more because they're supporting *us* than our cause? So, if we just ask them for money without *doing* anything, they'll be like, 'But you didn't *work* for it.'"

The male smirked. "True enough, but—"

"I *so* know what you mean," the second girl said. "It's like my little brother: people'll donate to any cause he's at all involved in.

Not because they really care whether he sells enough raffle tickets for new baseball uniforms or whatever, but just because they want *him* to feel good when they buy a ticket from him."

"So," the male teenager said, "perhaps there's a way for us to capitalize on people's illogical need to support youth initiatives just because we're younger than they are—but, like, without us having to have a big famine about it."

"I guess so," the first girl said.

"You're just trying to get out of having to be hungry for a day," the second girl said, laughing.

"You know me well," her friend replied with a smirk.

At that point, my thoughts naturally segued to my own pending fundraising efforts. *Would I be willing to use Lesley's pressure-canvassing approach?*

Conveniently, I avoided my question by reminding myself that I was still a Tally recommendation away from having to make such a decision.

The next day at work, Chet stopped by my office for the first of his mid-morning visits.

"John R. Tolkien! How are we?"

"Good, I think. Although," I said, hoping to dissuade my boss from a long visit, "it feels like I have more work to do than when I left last night."

Chet laughed. "Ahh, yes, the law of the multiplying inbox. So have you started yet?"

"On my work?" I said, aware that Chet had actually just segued to something else, but I couldn't think to what.

"That *too*," he said, "but, no, I meant with the Green Cross— has Lesley got you working on anything yet?"

"Oh, no, not yet—they're still checking my references."

"You put down more than just me?"

"Oh, sorry—no, it's just that they asked for more than one, so …"

Chet laughed again. "Yeah, no worries, Prince Johnny. I know how it works: you just *used* me for my reference."

I found that line of Chet's humour to be more difficult than usual to respond to, so I was pleased at that moment to hear the ringing of my phone.

Oddly, it was an outside line. "Sorry, I should take this ..."

Chet nodded his forehead at the phone and stayed to listen in.

"Hello, this is John Smith in the RQB department?"

"Hi, is John there, please?" a bland female voice asked.

"Yes, speaking."

"Hey, John. It's Rayann from the Green Cross."

"Oh, hi, Rayann. How are you?"

Chet looked pleased. '*Rayann?*' he mouthed.

I shook my eyes to indicate that she was nothing for me to get excited about, but Chet's eyebrows stayed raised, and he sat down to get a better listen.

"Good, thanks," the cause of Chet's curiosity replied, "so Lesley just asked me to call to say that your references look good—and I'm sure the Criminal Record Check's just a formality—so I'll be sending out your Green Cross canvassing kit today."

"Great ...or I can just pick it up at lunch today if you like?"

"Sure, whatever," the bland voice replied.

For a moment, I was disillusioned by Rayann's lack of enthusiasm for my meet-up plan, but the second I was off the phone, Chet supplied all the excitement I was hoping for.

"So, Johnny Cusack, you've been holding out on me—who's this *Rayann?*"

"Oh, she's just from the Green Cross. She was just phoning to let me know that my references checked out."

"Of course they *did*," Chet said, full grin. "I told you I'd get you in. I had that Lesley wrapped around both of my little fingers."

"Right," I said, putting on my best smile, "um, thanks for doing that."

Chet shrugged faux-modestly. "You know how you could make it up to me?"

"How?"

"Find out if there's a *Mr.* Lesley."

"Really? But you only talked to her on the phone."

"Yeah, but we had a real connection—we were definitely riding the same wavelength."

"Oh, okay. Well, I don't know when I'll see her—"

"You're going there at lunch, right?"

"Maybe, but I don't know if I'll see her today."

"Well, John Henry White," Chet said, standing up, "*today* is my favourite day of the week to get things done. Just see what you can find out, okay?"

I now resented my short trip to see Rayann and the Green Cross. *How was I supposed to subtly investigate Lesley's marital status?* The right thing to do, of course, was to not inquire at all and then to tell Chet that I *had* and that I'd discovered her to be already encumbered with a spouse. Surely what Chet didn't know couldn't hurt me. But fate, it seemed to me, should not be toyed with. *What if Chet and Lesley had the makings of an excellent pairing, and I cost them his pursuit by giving him fraudulent information?*

Once again, I was received by the top of Rayann's head upon my arrival at the Green Cross, but, this time, I was content to wait.

"Hey, John," she said when she finally looked up.

"Hi, how's it going?"

She sighed. "I'm exhausted. I don't get why my bosses keep asking me for the *same* information: why do they never remember what I tell them?"

"Yeah, that's weird," I said, delighted, once again, to be included in the tirade.

Rayann smirked. "Can you imagine if—I don't know—*I* forgot what they'd told me about stuff they wanted *me* to do? And I kept asking them the *same* questions? I'd be labeled incompetent."

I shook my head in vehement (although unearned) agreement. "Yeah, I guess, when superiors make those kind of mistakes, they're considered—"

"Exactly," Rayann said, "it's beneath them to worry about those petty little details."

"Yeah, exactly," I said.

There was then a pause between us.

"So ..." I said, figuring I could kill the awkwardness and my duty to Chet in one foul segue, "is Lesley one of those people who forgets what you've told her?"

"Sometimes. She's better than most, though."

"Right, so, um, is she married?"

Quite rightly, Rayann stopped her work to stare at my question and me.

"What's that got to do with anything?"

"Oh, um, well, it's just that I'd heard that people who are

married with kids are better at picking up details faster because, um—"

"Yeah, I guess that makes sense," Rayann said.

"Right," I said, still hoping for an answer to Chet's question, but Rayann was back tapping on her keyboard. Ordinarily, I would have left embarrassing enough alone, but I'd already put my reputation in a precarious position: I *at least* wanted the payoff of not having Chet pester me to do further research. "So, um, *is* she?"

"Is she what?"

"Married with, you know, kids."

"Oh, yeah, she's got three kids. She's got that scent of a mom on her, don't you think?"

"Yeah, I guess so—well, how do you mean?"

"She's just got that *Everything's under control so long as I'm around* attitude, don't you think?"

"Yeah, I guess you're right," I said.

Rayann shrugged her lips and went back to work.

Inspired by my increased interaction with Rayann, I walked in a cheerful mood through a light rain back to work. As my Walkman serenaded me along, I pondered my appreciation for the receptionist at the Green Cross. *Was it a well-founded crush, based on specific appreciations, or was I enthralled with her simply because she was a female within an appropriate age radius who had interacted with me for longer than a grocery purchase?*

I decided that both answers were well-represented in my inspiration. In spite of her mild grumpiness, I felt a sincere camaraderie with Rayann. The fact that she'd proven herself willing to be grouchy around me made the moments when she *wasn't* seem extra sincere. Yet, if I were to be honest with myself, I would have preferred that the surliness be reduced a wee bit during our interactions. *But who said I had to be honest with myself?* It was a crush, not a relationship—it wasn't as if I had the courage required to ask Rayann out; instead, as Tally had recommended, I was just trying out our compatibility from afar.

With my crush officially approved, I returned to work and was greeted by a high-eyebrowed smile from Chet.

"*So?*" he said.

"Oh, right, yeah, sorry—she's married."

"Damn—you sure?"

"Yeah, she's got three kids."

"Tough break," Chet said, sighing to my relief. "*Although* ..." he quickly took it away, "is the dad still around?"

"Yeah, I think so."

"You *think* so?" Chet said, eyebrows cruelly rising back up. "How do we know we're not dealing with a single-mom situation?"

"Um," I said, scanning my memory desperately for conclusive results, "well, I asked Rayann if she was married with kids, and she said, 'Yes—she has three kids.'"

Chet nodded. "I see what you're saying. It looks bad, but it's still not conclusive. I don't think we should call off the search just yet."

"Oh—"

"So, next time you're in there, probe a little further, will you, Johnny Carson?"

I lamented my updated obligation for much of the afternoon, but, by the time I reached the end of the work day, I was ready to move onto considering how and when I was going to apply my bag of canvassing goodies, which turned out to be an endearing collection. I had received a nametag (which featured my own name already typed on it), a map of my canvassing territory, a pamphlet regarding the Green Cross's good work, and a Lesley-written memo reminding me how to talk to impending benefactors.

During my bus ride home after work, two ladies in front of me eagerly compared stories of their university-attending daughters.

"Kelly's doing very well," one of the moms said. "Her French professor was very impressed with her interpretation of the novel they're reading."

"That's wonderful," the second mom said. "Parvinder's doing really well also—she's actually taking one extra course this semester, and she's still maintaining her first class grades."

Those upbeat sounds of gushing put me in the mood to canvass an area where such complimentary parents would reside. So I decided that on Saturday I would aim for a nice family-looking neighbourhood in my territory.

A few minutes later, the bus dropped me off; as I walked home,

I contemplated Lesley's canvassing instructions. My brain and I wondered if I could muster the assertiveness she'd told me to display while in the doorway of an innocent stranger.

That evening, as I was watching TV, my phone started ringing. I entertained myself by imagining that Rayann had decided to throw grumpiness to the wind and call me for a visit.

"Hello?"

"Hello," an empty female voice said, "is Mr. John Smith there?"

"*Speaking.*"

"Mr. Smith," the voice replied without improving its spirits, "this is Yvonne from [Newspaper Press]." The telemarketer did not stop to hear my disappointed acknowledgment of her identity; instead, with the same empty tone, she inquired as to which of her company's two daily newspapers I enjoyed reading most frequently.

"*The Sun*, I guess," I said, immediately regretting that I'd given her information on which she could attach her telemarketing suction cups.

"That's excellent," Yvonne said, her voice lilting as much as it seemed capable, "because we have a special gift opportunity for you right now that will allow you to receive *The Sun* for one month for free. What address would you like me to send that to?"

"Oh, actually—thanks anyway—but I don't think I'd read it that much."

"That's okay—it's free so just read the ones you want. It's no cost to you. So, in order to send it to you, I need to know: are you living in an apartment or a home?"

It took me another couple minutes to pry myself loose from Yvonne. When I finally succeeded, I resolved that I would not be utilizing Lesley's assertive system during my donation-gathering on Saturday.

As canvassing day approached, I decided that I should launch my first canvass in the late afternoon so that I could line up with people preparing for their impending dinner gatherings without disturbing their actual mealtimes. That seemed like a good plan until Saturday morning arrived full to the brim with time to wait through until the late afternoon; so I paced around my apartment, completing household chores that could have waited another week.

Once my living quarters sparkled as if I had friends to visit me, I still had hours to go until departure time. So I went for a jog and then a shower, both of which seemed like they would be lengthy efforts until I realized how little meaningful movement they had inspired on my clock. Reading was my next attempted distraction, but I repeatedly forgot to pay attention, so I closed up the book and grabbed my remote to see if the television could help me out. It did, indeed, as I came across an easy sitcom and then a charismatic old movie.

Two fun movie hours later, it was time to go—and I was now actually leaving a little later than I'd intended, which was probably fortunate because I was able to rush through my anxiety. I arrived outside to find a rainy city, so I called upon my umbrella for assistance. As I walked with splashing foot prints, I considered postponing the endeavour to another day. But, before I could humour such cowardliness, a *Don't you love the rain* smile from an umbrella-less female stranger instructed me forward. Perhaps the residents of my canvass would appreciate my rain-braving attitude and would reward the Green Cross for it.

I soon found a house-based neighbourhood and headed in to the middle class community as if I were going into a storybook forest with countless charming and unexpected characters awaiting me. I made my way several blocks in so that there would be no clear escape route. And you'll be proud to read, usually disappointed-in-me reader, that—once I'd settled on a first house to visit—I did not hesitate. I took my now damp feet down its path and prepared to surprise myself with what I had to say.

I rang a cold door bell and was immediately greeted by the sounds of a yappy four-legged resident within; that gave me confidence that I'd selected a family home. The stairs near the doorway were soon sounding with the weight of an occupant, so I forced a smile onto my chilled lips, and I tried to pull some air through my nose and into my lungs.

SOCIO-TEMPORAL NOTE: Before we meet my canvassing fate, I should grant that door-to-door charity collectors may seem to you, modern reader, to be an unsafe group for citizens to open their doors to, given that the vulnerable home-dwellers can't guarantee the seemingly random visitors' positive intentions. But I can report that, in the time and location in which I was taking on this adventure, we neighbourhood fundraisers were a common feature, and so our antics—while perhaps annoying to some—were not officially diagnosed as a safety faux pas.

The door opened to a squinting female senior citizen face, along with an angry little dog face that continued to bark insults in my direction; in their background, I heard distinguished-sounding music that seemed to be part opera and part comedy.

"Hi," I said, "sorry to interrupt, but my name is John Smith. I'm a volunteer for the Green Cross." I held out my nametag for the lady and her companion to see.

"You've picked quite the day for it," the lady said with a smile before swatting her protector quiet.

"Yeah, I know—I just … this is actually my first day doing it, so I was a bit nervous …" I stopped myself at that inappropriate word, but the lady leaned her ear forward as if she was wondering what the delay was about. "Um," I continued, "so, yeah, I was a bit nervous, so I just kind of wanted to go for it while I had the nerve."

"That's an excellent way to deal with your nerves," the lady said. "So how has it gone so far?"

"Actually, you're the first, so—"

"So *quite* well then, as far as you know," the lady said with a dry smirk.

I laughed. "Yes, I guess so."

"Well," the lady said, "congratulations seem to be in order for you *going for it*."

"Thanks," I said, as the opera singers in the lady's background stopped singing and started talking to each other. "Sorry to interrupt your show."

"Pshaw," the lady replied. "The magic of recorded music—I can have them begin again any time I desire."

"Oh, okay," I said

"So I imagine you're collecting donations for the Green Cross?"

"Yes, actually—are you interested in hearing about the work they're doing?"

"That's all right. I'm pretty confident you're doing good work. I would like to make a donation, however."

"Oh, okay, thanks," I said, having trouble containing my grin.

The lady smiled back. "Will you excuse me while I retrieve my chequebook?"

She returned two minutes later with a contribution of $25.

"Thank you. You're very generous," I said, hoping she would understand that I felt her kindness on behalf of more than just the Green Cross.

"You're very welcome," she said.

That, I'm sure you can appreciate, appreciative reader, was as good a possible canvassing debut as I could have conceived, and so—with a confidence-filled stride—I travelled to the next house.

A man answered my call with an expression-free face. "Yes?"

"Hi, I'm John Smith with—"

"I'm not buying anything," he cut to my chase.

"Oh, okay, well, this is actually for a charity, so I don't know if—"

"Does it *cost* me anything?"

"Um, I guess, yes."

"Then you have my answer," he said, his forehead lifting up in a teacherly expression of disappointment.

As the cranky man closed his cranky door, I decided that my confidence was not going to be swayed by one person who had been born on the wrong side of the bed, so I jumped across a puddle and headed for another possible donor.

I was soon face to squinting eyes with another senior female citizen; my success with her predecessor had me stereotyping her as likely to be kindhearted as well, so I cheerfully launched in.

"Hi, I'm John Smith with the Canadian—"

"Thank you anyway," she said, smiling as she closed her door.

"Oh, okay—"

"Good luck," she added quickly before her door closed as if she weren't the one shutting it.

The next home I came upon was impressively endowed in size and in the number of its attending vehicles, so I pulled my stereotyper out once again and guessed that such a wealthy household was more likely to have funds available for donation to a charitable organization.

That turned out not to be the case as the woman who answered the door told me that she couldn't afford to help. Now, I don't mean to be critical, compassionate reader, but I found myself skeptical of the woman's reasoning. Had she denied me access to her wallet on the grounds that she already had other causes that she believed in more or even because, on principle, she didn't support charities or door-to-door canvassers, I would have been content, but—given the quality of her home and surrounding vehicles—I found the poverty excuse to be difficult to comprehend.

Of course, it was possible that the woman had spent so much on her living and driving quarters that she had nothing left to offer, but my snarky thoughts to the contrary slowed my pace as I continued on to the next house. Not to worry, concerned reader, my canvassing mood was still in reasonably good shape, but the rain was starting to feel colder than when I'd started.

The next door that I knocked upon revealed the amused face of a male forty-something-year-old.

"Hi. My name is John Smith ..." I began.

The man smirked but did not reply.

"Um," I continued, "I'm volunteering for the Green Cross, and I'm wondering if you'd like to make a donation to help—"

"I don't think so," he interrupted with his smirk still imprinted on his face.

"Okay," I said, and I turned around before he shut his door. The man's reaction irritated me more severely than the grumpy man's from earlier. Smirking-man seemed to be treating me as though I were a door-to-door salesman trying to trick him into buying something for which he had no use.

At that point, my canvassing energy was done for the day, but I decided to see about ending on a not-so-low note. I was declined by the next two door-answerers, but they were both polite about it, which had me resenting the prior smirker even more. The politeness of his two followers hadn't required much energy on their part—nor had I made them work for my resulting departure.

I was pleased and relieved to receive a $10 donation from the next doorway-occupant, and so—noticing that I was emotionally exhausted—I thanked myself for my good work and picked up a cheerful video on my way home.

SOCIO-TEMPORAL NOTE: Videos were the entertainment streaming service of the time—except you had to go to an out-in-the-world store to pick up your viewing preferences, and you could only take home as many movies or episodes as you and/or your team could carry.

On Sunday morning, a renewed enthusiasm for canvassing burrowed through my mind, so I decided to go again and to treat any canvassee-rudeness as though it were the result of the irrelevant-to-me grumpiness of people whose opinion I had no reason to take personally.

When, for instance, a woman twenty years my senior told me gruffly that she was too busy to talk, I smiled back (perhaps wondering if it would have taken her any longer to redirect me with a polite voice). And, when another person of that same generation told me that he did not buy from door-to-door salesmen, I was—I'm proud to say—amused by the continuing collective confusion regarding the distinction between salespeople and volunteer charity canvassers. And, when a gentleman of about my age replied to my request with a, "Sure, man—how's ten bucks sound?", I was pleased with both him and his rude predecessors who seemed all the more comical when compared to the graciousness of someone half their age.

That was nice, but I couldn't trick my mood forever: after two hours of receiving rudeness from one third of my canvasees, I was once again emotionally tuckered. As I walked home, though, I realized that I could reduce my exhaustion in future canvassing attempts by monitoring my rudeness-threshold and then stopping just before I reached it. That was an inadvertently brilliant plan because it turned out that counting rude people made them more entertaining to come across and so increased my capacity for receiving them.

Chapter 31
Dullard vs. Power Boss

The Sap In Power

On Monday morning, I rode the bus to work feeling a strange inclination to be more annoyed with Chet than usual. My lunch hour discussions with him and sometimes Bernice were more painful than ever now that they were contrasted with the Tally era.

I arrived at my workstation and found a standard moronic email from Chet; the discovery provoked me to decide that—while I had to put up with him as boss—I could no longer compel myself to endure his and Bernice's non-conversation during lunch. It wasn't as though they would notice any conversational difference if I weren't there. Consequently, I plotted to start the removal of myself from our unofficial trio by missing an occasional lunch so that I could gradually work my way up to permanent exile.

On that first day of my desertion scheme, I travelled to Chet's office around the time he would normally be going for food. I intended to justify my visit with a work-related question, but my hope was that the lunchly time of my arrival would cause a tangent in his mind to thoughts of hunger, which, in turn, would provoke him to announce that it was time to go. I could then say that, sadly, I still had work to do before mealtime. Even my ghostwriter admits that that was a smart plan—although, he also notes that its success would depend on some delicate manoeuvring.

As I came upon Chet's doorway, I heard a sturdy sixty-something-year-old female voice coming from within his office.

"Mr. Williams," she said, "I cannot make this any clearer: you can utilize whatever tools you need. All that I ask is that you are attentive to the fact that these supplies do not come from a bottomless pile—they cost the company money, so please do not use them frivolously."

"Oh, yeah, of course," Chet's voice responded with such a chipper tone that I wondered if the female voice had been as harsh as I had perceived.

Unfortunately, even though I was riveted to find out what the woman was going to say next, the risk of being caught in the act of eavesdropping was too great for me to linger outside Chet's office any longer.

Half an hour later, Chet arrived at my office with a smile.

"That was Elsje."

"*Elsje? Really?*" I said, surprised to attach her famous name to the harsh voice that I'd just overheard. "Like Tally's former boss, right?"

"Right," Chet said, "but she's our boss too."

"Right, sorry, so what'd she say?"

Chet grinned. "Come to lunch, Curious John, and I'll tell you all about it."

Chet was right, of course: the promise of Elsje-talk was too intriguing to let my lunchtime escape plans get in the way, so I postponed for another day.

As foreshadowed by Chet's lack of acknowledgment at the time, the derision I'd heard in Elsje's voice during my eavesdropping was not a part of Chet's lunchtime report; instead, he gleefully told me about a new initiative that he and his mentor had "discussed."

By the time our next lunch hour approached twenty-three hours later, the Elsje topic was exhausted, so I decided to use my nearly $100-worth of canvassing proceeds as my excuse to miss our next conversation.

"Hey, Chet," I said, leaning into his office, "I'm going to use my lunch hour to drop off some money at the Green Cross."

"Great!" he said. "Is Lesley gonna be there?"

"Oh, right," I said, now seeing the error in my misdirection. "Okay, sure, if I see her, I'll look for a wedding ring."

"That's what I like to hear, Johnny Lennon. Get 'er done."

I arrived at the Green Cross with increased optimism for my crush on Rayann. Now that I was bringing money in for the organization, perhaps she would see us as colleagues instead of acquaintances.

"Hi?" she said after the usual delay.

"Hey, I just wanted to drop off my first canvassing results. It's not a lot, but I figured I may as well get it out of my wallet."

"Great," she said, reaching for my submission and then placing it on her desk for examination. "How was it?"

"It was good," I said, revving up a critical essay, "some people were really nice, but—"

"That's good—how long'd you go for?"

"Oh," I said, grieving the loss of my rant, "I don't know, a few hours."

"Good for you," Rayann said as she finished counting my efforts. She seemed disappointed in my results.

"Um," I said, "is that not a lot for the amount of time I canvassed?"

Rayann shrugged her face and eyebrows, and then—to my delight—she looked right at me.

"Nah, I'd say that's about normal. But don't worry about bringing the money in after *every* canvass—you can wait till you've got a little more built up."

That comment, I don't mind confessing to you, priestly reader, scrubbed some of the luster off my crush. I had, by then, come to find Rayann's grumpiness to be endearing, but—if she wanted to maintain my interest—she would need to be less indifferent to our opportunities to see each other. Of course, I wasn't going to let go of the crush just yet—since I didn't currently have any other options available—but I now officially recognized that Rayann was a temporary crush to tide me over until I encountered a more plausible alternative.

I returned to Ambiguity expecting another inquisition from Chet on the status of Lesley, but I was intrigued instead to hear Elsje back and surly in my boss's office. I perked up my ears, but, once again, the content of their conversation was muffled by a closed door.

So I let myself stand on the border between Chet's and my

office as though I were having a good think about my workload for the afternoon. That stationary eavesdropping may have been a worthy risk had I been able to decipher the murmuring of Chet and Elsje, but—as it was—I had put my reputation in peril for no possible benefit.

To prove that point, my neighbour, Erik, came out of his office just then, which provoked me to startle back into movement. If I had held my position, I might have persuaded him that I really was just caught in a moment of motionless meditation. Alas, my obvious embarrassment provoked him to justify it with his favourite *Tsk, Tsk* face. He held it for the entire long second in which we passed each other. Consequently, for the first time, I wished Erik would have enunciated his judgement with his usual dogmatic words: at least then we could have discussed my blunder and moved on. Instead, I sat in my office with a shudder through my core.

After a good twenty minutes immersed in that self-loathing, I finally heard the door to Chet's office open.

"Thank you, Mr. Williams," Elsje said.

"Any time, Boss Lady," was Chet's boisterous retort.

The moment *Boss Lady's* footsteps disappeared from the hallway, Chet journeyed to my office to tell me how pleased he was that he and his favourite Ambiguous leader were getting closer.

"She's such an über brainiac," he said, "so I must admit, Johnny Q. Public, it's pretty flattering that she's so interested in our lowly take on things."

Indeed, over the next few weeks, the alleged camaraderie between my boss and his boss's boss continued to grow. And, from what I could barely overhear, it sounded as though I was not the only person to find Chet to be the most annoying person ever to interrupt a train of thought.

To my delight, one Monday morning, Chet and Elsje stopped closing Chet's office door on their conversations.

"Good morning, Mr. Williams," Elsje said as she arrived in Chet's location.

"Morning, ma'am."

"Chet," his boss replied, "why do you think I instated the HG policy?"

"Refresh my long lost memory. Is that the one where we're supposed to use the HGs more often?"

"Yes, Chet. And why do you think I put that policy in effect?"

Chet laughed. "I don't write the policies, ma'am—I just follow 'em."

"The HG policy," Elsje replied, "was instituted to stop the production of MBs. And, therefore, the fact that you have been, as you put it, *following* my HG policy—while continuing to produce MBs manually—is missing the point of the HG policy."

"Oopsie daisy, I never thought of that."

"Why not?"

"Well, as far as I know, it wasn't mentioned in the HG memo."

"Yes it *was*, Chet. I sent you a memo. Carried within that memo was a rule. And carried within that rule was a spirit …" Elsje paused there for a moment. "Mr. Williams, there is a public garden, at the entrance of which, there is a sign. The sign reads, SEEING-EYE DOGS ONLY. What do you think that sign is meant to tell us?"

"That's pretty simple, Madame Boss. They're saying that, if you take your dog into the garden, you'd better be blind."

"Right, Chet—but please don't call me, 'Madame Boss.' Now, what you've just told me was *indeed* the spirit of the sign. However, if one looks at the letter of the sign, one might interpret it to mean that *people* aren't allowed in the public garden—after all, it's a SEEING-EYE DOGS ONLY garden."

Chet laughed. "I'm with you, Mrs. A. So those sign makers need to read their own signs before they—"

"No, Chet, the point is that *of course* people are allowed in. That's the spirit of the sign, and it's perfectly clear. And the same goes for the memo I sent you."

"Right, so you're saying that, when I read that memo of yours, I took the letter of it instead of the spirit of it—am I right?"

"Precisely—"

"And you're saying that sometimes taking the letter of things doesn't make much sense—like with that SEEING-EYE DOGS ONLY sign: it would be pretty stupid if I didn't let myself in the garden even though that's what the sign *says*." Chet laughed again at the humour as if he had invented it.

"Correct," Elsje replied, "the literal words in the law are sometimes different from the spirit of them. Please keep that in mind the next time I send you a memo."

"Yes, ma'am."

I missed out on the final salutations to that meeting because Erik walked by my office just then; this time, he sent me a distracting but unreadable smile.

Two weeks later, Elsje arrived in Chet's office once again. "Mr. Williams, did you receive the memo that said that no ANCs were to be used outside of the RY-department?"

"Yes ma'am—now *that* was a memo. It was well written, it was to the point—"

"Chet, if you received the memo, why have I been informed that you produce at least five ANCs every week?"

"Mrs. A., a wise woman once told me about a public garden that had a sign on it that said—"

"Yes, I remember, Chet. What is your point, please?"

"You taught me, Mrs. A., that there's a difference between the law and the spirit of the law."

"Chet, first of all, my name is *Anders*, not 'A.' And, second, the rule I gave you was that there was to be *no* ANC production. What spirit provoked you to ignore that?"

"Well, Mademoiselle Anders, your law was that you wanted us not to produce ANCs, right?"

"Correct."

"Well, for me, that law didn't make a lot of sense—ANCs make my job a lot easier. So I realized that the spirit of me having an easier job was more important. And I realized—"

"Thank you, Chet, I think I understand now. Let us make two new rules—both of which I want you to follow to the letter. First of all, my name is *Elsje* or *Mrs. Anders*, not *Mademoiselle Anders*: I am neither French nor unmarried. Second, from now on, if you want to break one of my rules, I want you to call my office and check with me first."

"*Okay*," Chet said, clearly delighted that his boss's boss wanted him to call her with his ideas. And call her he did: almost every day Chet thought of another rule that he'd like to break.

Poor Elsje: she couldn't compete with Chet. Sure, she had logic and a stern voice on her side, but Chet was immune to the former and intrigued by the latter. It must have been a strange experience for Elsje: she was surely accustomed to her employees fearing her (especially if she wanted them to), but Chet refused to be afraid of someone who was from the same generation as his mom.

Chapter 32
Dullard and the Neighbour

The Neighbores

In spite of Elsje's justified annoyance with Chet, I wondered if she was unnecessarily mean in the way that she demonstrated it. And so, with Tally no longer there to praise Elsje—and Chet still not to be trusted in his confused worship of her—I was forced to follow my new intuition that Mrs. Elsje Anders wasn't the nicest of bosses. I contemplated that notion during another Saturday afternoon of canvassing for The Green Cross.

By then, I had come to appreciate canvassing for its own sake, and I'd begun to forget that I'd taken it up with a bonus hope that it might help me meet people (i.e. female people). Occasionally, however, during canvassing, I'd imagine the door being answered by a girl in my age and attraction range who would be so impressed with my canvassing efforts that she'd invite me in for conversation. But then I'd interrupt my happy speculative fiction with remorse for having had impure thoughts about canvassing.

On one such occasion, my guilt motivated my canvassing, and I arrived home with a personal best in both total donations and encounters with rude canvassees. Consequently, as I entered my building's foyer, I was too fatigued to rush after the closing doors of the elevator. Yet, as I slowed my elevator-pursuing pace, an arm stuck out and stopped the shutting gate.

I hurried up and found inside the doors the friendly face of the senior apartment neighbour who—my first morning in the building—had once dropped a soup can in the process of trying to help me catch an elevator ride.

The déjà vu of the gesture returned me to a good mood. "Thanks," I said with my biggest smile.

"You're welcome, dear."

With neither of us possessing any further conversation on the matter, I began browsing my canvassing receipts to confirm my preliminary count.

"Who are you collecting for, dear?" my fellow traveller suddenly asked.

"Oh," I said, taking hold of my nametag, "for the Green Cross."

"That's wonderful."

"Thanks."

We paused at that.

"So," my neighbour filled in the gap, "why have you never come to me for a donation?"

"Oh, um, it's just that I felt like, I don't know, that neighbours are off limits."

"*Off limits* from *what*, dear?"

"Um," I said as we stepped off the elevator to our floor, "it's just that I was worried that neighbours would feel obligated to give me money."

"Don't you *want* us to give you money?"

"Well, yes," I said, stopping at her door to finish the chat, "it's just that it seems like bad form to go around my *own* building—"

"Well," my neighbour said, "I would like to make a donation."

"Really?" I said, a smile overtaking my face.

"I don't see why not," my elevator companion replied. "Would you like to come in for a moment while I get my chequebook, dear?"

So we entered my neighbour's apartment, and I was asked to have seat on a couch while the couch's owner went to gather her donation. She returned, a moment later, with a sharp $20 bill.

"Here you go, dear. I realized I had cash."

"Wow, that's wonderful," I said. Indeed, in the canvassing world, $20 is a coup. But an unsolicited $20 donation—that's the stuff that canvassing-legends are made of. "Who should I make the receipt out to?" I asked.

"Miss Elizabeth Braun," my neighbour replied as if she were introducing herself to me.

"Nice to meet you. I'm John—"

"John *Smith*," Miss Braun completed with a smile.

"How'd you know that?" I said, my mind speedily considering the possibility that I had some sort of neighbourly following.

"It's on your nametag, dear."

"Oh, right."

Miss Braun smiled again before changing the subject on my behalf. "Can I make you some tea?"

Did I want some tea? Well, *not really.* But tea implied sitting to drink it, which implied more conversation with Miss Elizabeth Braun, which sounded interesting. So I randomly asked for tea with sugar and milk.

Miss Braun and I then began what may have been the dullest interaction in conversation history. It turned out, you see, that Miss Braun—like her neighbour beside her—was a bit of a dullard. As such, we began our dullard dialogue by discussing the local weather for the day, which led to thoughts on the best rain gear to wear and a little about the quality of the recent weather forecasts. From boring beginnings, our conversation then took a dull turn as we next considered the city's traffic problems, or lack thereof, for the day.

Eventually, having completed my beverage, it seemed appropriate to take my leave of the dullard meeting.

"Thanks for the tea … and conversation," I said. "I enjoyed talking to you."

Miss Braun appeared to be more touched by that sentiment than a dullard would have thought, considering the blandness of my words.

"Thank you, dear. I enjoyed talking to you too," she said. "I hope you'll come by again sometime."

"Yes, that'd be great," I said. And I wasn't even exaggerating.

In fact, only a couple days later, I came home from work with a hankering to talk with Miss Braun some more.

She answered the call with a smile. "Hello, dear. I was just thinking about you."

"Oh, thanks," I said. "Um, I was wondering if I could return your hospitality and invite you over for some tea?"

"That would be lovely, dear," Miss Braun said, and—as seemed appropriate—she began to exit her apartment.

"Oh," I interrupted, "I just realized: I don't have any tea." (In fact, until the day previous, I had *never* had any tea. And, to be honest, I didn't really like it.)

"That's okay, dear—I'll bring the tea."

"Oh, okay..." I said, mortified that I was inviting my neighbour over to serve me. "But I've got juice...or milk...or *water*."

"It's okay, dear—I like to make tea."

Our second neighbourly discourse carried with it more flavour than the first one. Miss Braun and I now seemed to know each other well enough to talk on a less formal basis (in fact, she asked me to refer to her as *Elizabeth*), and slowly we were able to learn some details of each other's lives. Elizabeth, I discovered, was a retired nurse. And, if you ask me, she was a very good one. Although, if you asked her—which I *did*—she was just your average healthcare worker. Indeed, I discovered that she preferred to talk about her co-workers' exploits instead of her own.

"There was one doctor," she said, "—Dr. *Skinner*—he was a wonderful doctor. But he was also a wonderful man. Some of his patients, poor dears, they were old and dying. There was nothing that could be done to save them. But Dr. Skinner—he checked in on them so attentively every day during his rounds, just so they'd know that they were important to him."

The story had me feeling nostalgic on Elizabeth's behalf. "So do you think," I said trying to think of a comparison that she might enjoy, "that today's doctors have, you know, that same kind of compassion?"

Elizabeth smiled. "I don't think medicine has changed as much as people say. We used to have wonderful doctors like Dr. Skinner, and we have wonderful doctors today too. And we used to have some real stinkers who should have been quarantined from talking to the patients—and we have some of those today as well."

"I like that," I said. Indeed, Elizabeth's tidy categorizing of society motivated me to do better during my own participation.

Elizabeth smiled and asked me how my canvassing was going.

In response, I endeavoured to entertain my new friend by telling her about some of my best canvassing-rejection experiences.

"You know, dear," she responded, "people work hard for their money—sometimes they have their own things they want to do with it."

"Yeah, you're right," I said, embarrassed that my attempted humour had been mistaken for genuine whining.

An hour of dull conversation later, the visit ended for that evening too. But it continued again a few days later at Elizabeth's apartment. A couple days after that, it returned to my apartment—and round our little neighbourhood we went.

Within a few months, it came to be that I would come home from canvassing on a Saturday afternoon, and I would go directly to Elizabeth's apartment where she would mark down my totals in our official Canvassing Diary. On one day we would be joyous about a record individual donation, and on another we would excitedly determine that I had reached a career milestone in total collected money. Then we'd play Yahtzee.

Sometimes, as she rolled our Yahtzee dice, Elizabeth would say something like, "There's a new young lady in the building. She's quite lovely. Why don't you ask her out to a show?"

I would always laugh at the absurdity of such a suggestion, but—secretly—I loved it when Elizabeth talked so. She had quickly replaced Tally as the only person in my day-to-day inter-actions who actively promoted the notion that I was interesting enough for lovely young ladies.

It thus felt like a bit of overkill on fate's part, one evening, when my phone rang while I already had Elizabeth over for company. The juggling of hosting and answering was more than I was used to.

"Hello?"

"John!—It's Amy."

"Oh, hi, Amy, how are you?"

"Ryan's driving me crazy," she said. "He's still an awesome boyfriend, but he gets totally jealous. Like, I had this group project last weekend. It was two guys and one other girl, and Ryan's all, 'I don't want you studying with two other dudes—tell the prof you want a different group.' And it's like, 'Ryan, I can't trade groups just because you're jealous.' And he's all, 'I'm not jealous—you don't see *me* hanging out with other *girls*.'"

My back muscles tightened as I realized that I had managed to incite a full conversation with my long-babbled former Sweet On You co-worker while my neighbour was waiting. But Amy left no holes in her narration for interruption. I tried to use an about-to-interrupt tone in my auditory nods, but—if she noticed my intention to cut her off—it only caused her to rush through her pauses for air even faster.

"So," she continued, "I'm like, 'Ah, what about *Charmaine?*'—She's this hot new girl across the hall—and he's like," (Amy switched to a mocking deep voice), "'Uh, I was setting up her TV, and she was totally the one hitting on me.'" Amy snorted at that. "*As if*—so I'm like, 'Ah, so why the hell didn't you leave, then, if she was flirting with you?' And he's like, 'I didn't wanna be rude.' And I'm like, 'Oh, okay, so it's okay for *me* to be rude to my classmates and quit my group for no reason?'"

"Yeah," my voice boomed into the monologue, "that's pretty hypocritical of him, but, sorry, I can't talk for long—I've got a guest."

"Is it a girl?" Amy said with a smiley voice.

"Not really."

"Okay. You can tell me later. I was actually just calling because I was wondering if you wanted to come to another party. Ryan can't go, and I don't wanna go by myself."

"Um, sure," I said.

Elizabeth smiled when I told her about the invitation. "Well, that sounds exciting, dear."

I shrugged. "Yeah, I guess. It makes me nervous, though."

"Well, nerves come and go," my neighbour said.

"Fair enough," I said, pleased to receive a new platitude from my neighbour, "maybe you're right."

"Anyway," she said, "I'm looking forward to hearing all the details of the party."

"Thanks," I said, smiling to the thought; indeed, now that I had an audience for my results, I was more interested in them, myself.

Chapter 33
Dullard in the Ring IV

The Social Butterflight: Episode II

When Amy and I arrived at her party, she was quickly spotted by our old girl-talking friend from the last such event.

"Amy! I didn't know you were coming—how are you? You look cute."

"Thanks! So do you," Amy said in a way that made me suspect that the return compliment was more reflexive than genuine.

The Amy thief grinned. "I've gotta show you something—come with me."

"Okay, back in a sec, John," my companion replied with an allegedly sheepish face.

So, once again, I was alone at a party that Amy had invited me to. There were, in the living room I was inhabiting, several groups of people chatting—including a pair of female partiers on the floor, drawing on pieces of paper obscure images that resembled faces. That didn't seem too intimidating, so I travelled their way.

"Hello," I said.

One of them looked up. "Hi."

"What are you drawing?"

"We're doing portraits of each other."

"Can't you tell?" the other said, laughing.

"Oh, yeah, definitely."

Both artists laughed. But then they reengaged their focuses on their abstract pictures.

Apparently, it was my move, but I'd already used my best material with 'Hello,' so I wandered away as if I had other artists to check on.

During my escape, I noticed a girl holding an empty wine glass, looking out a window. But she seemed too pretty to be alone for long, so I waited for a less intimidating conversation partner.

Ten minutes later, the window-neighbouring woman was still standing by herself, so I wondered if it was too late to be spontaneous about an introduction.

The door to the apartment opened.

I glanced back and ...*oh* ...*my* ...*ghostwriter* ...I was staring into the face of evil.

"Per's brother!" he cheered.

"*Jake*," I said, surveying my brother's sociopathic, adolescent companion. "How are you?"

"Aroused," he said, looking at my window-visiting friend.

"Um," I said, feeling awkward about his confession.

"Hold this," he said, handing me a paper bag of juice boxes before setting a collision course for the window-woman.

Two minutes later, he returned with a laugh. "*Dyke*," he said as he retrieved his juice from my hands. "She's waiting for her girlfriend."

"Oh," I said, not sure if he was joking or not.

Jake rolled his eyes. "So, Per's brother, you'll never guess what happened to Ashley Anonti."

"Is she okay?"

"I guess that depends on whether you think getting married in your early twenties is a total hick thing to do or not."

My ghostwriter. Even though I hadn't seen Ashley since high school, Jake's claim was still a heart-gulper.

"Um," I said. "I don't think there's anything wrong with that."

Jake snorted a laugh. "You'll never guess who she married."

Oh my ghostwriter! "Dale Rostrovich?"

Jake boomed a Gator-like laugh. "Christ, you're still just as dumb—didn't you ever realize that I made that whole Dale-Ashley thing up? That's hilarious: I forgot all about Dale the Whale. As if she'd have gone for him, though. For all her holier than Jesus attitude, she knew she was hot and could have had any guy she wanted."

"So who'd she pick?"

"Mr. All Everything."

"Who's that?"

"Don't play dumber—you don't remember Andrei Vishnevski? As in, Andrei the giant *phony*-evski?"

Of course—*Andrei!* He was an emblem of decency in all my acquaintance with him. I sighed with something like relief. *At least Ashley hadn't picked a jerk.*

"So what're you doing here?" Jake said.

"My friend Amy invited me."

"I didn't know you had friends. Congrats."

"Right—what are you doing here?"

"Amy invited me too—we hooked up a while back. But I'm here because parties are a great place to meet women. Or to experiment—whichever happens first."

"What kind of experiment?"

"See that guy over there talking to the dyke?"

"Yeah?"

"Total homo. But he's still hiding in the closet. So I'm gonna pretend to hit on him and see if I can get him to come *out* for my amusement. In fact, I think I'll do that now. See you, Per's brother."

"Wait—do you have to do that?"

"I don't *have to* do anything, Per's brother, but I *want* to."

"But, if he really is gay, then let him come out when he wants to."

"Where's the fun in that?"

"I don't know—does everything have to be fun?"

Jake laughed. "I'm afraid so. I'm going now, Per's brother."

Now, even though my childhood nemesis would be free to have his sociopathic way with the world during the many past and future occasions in which we would not be near each other's company, this one conquest in his path still seemed to me to be worthy of my resistance.

"Don't do it," I said.

"Why the hell not?"

"Um ...because ...*I said so*," was all I think to say.

"Good answer, Per's brother. But, if I lived my life according to what you wanted me to do, then I would also be a loser who stands by himself instead of talking to hot women. Thanks anyway," he concluded before starting again towards his target.

And so I did what I should have done in Grade Seven, but which was no longer appropriate: I reached my leg out for Jake to trip over.

He did so nicely and landed loudly on the wood floor. The subsequent bang silenced the conversation of the room.

"What the hell are you doing?" Jake shouted, rushing to his feet.

"Stopping you from being an idiot, like always," I yelled back as Jake sped my way.

"Who the hell do you think you are?" he said, giving me a hearty push on the chest.

At that moment, Jake and Per's brother discovered something we should have anticipated. Jake was not a strong guy, which meant that my pectoral muscles easily absorbed his shove.

"Ah," party host Beth yelled, "if you guys wanna fight, take it outside."

"All right, let's go, Jake," I said, even though I wasn't sure how I would feel about beating up someone who wouldn't be able to do any return-damage.

"I don't wanna fight," Jake said. "He just tripped me for no reason—so maybe he should go outside and fight with himself."

"Fine," Beth said, staring at me. "Can you leave, please?"

I glanced around at the many faces watching me, but was relieved to see that Amy was still in another room and so hadn't witnessed my violent behaviour.

"Fine," I said. But, before I left, I looked at Per's intended victim. "Hey, don't trust this guy—*whatever he says*. He's always trying to mess with people to see how they react. Just ignore him and walk away."

The intended victim looked curiously at me.

"Oh," I added to Beth, "and do you mind telling Amy that I had to go?"

"Fine," she said.

But I suspected that she would instead be telling Amy about my hooligan antics.

I came out of the party building to see my best bus option driving past my stop; I didn't have the emotional firepower left to wait for its next iteration, so I decided to walk home. It was a lengthy endeavour that gave me time to think about the night's news and events: I began with the Ashley & Andrei revelation.

It made sense that she would go for him: he was, after all, a '9' on the Grade-Seven girl-authored handsomeness scale. That was suddenly proof to me that even Ashley—who purported to be into nice guys—was, in reality, more interested in a guy's attractiveness than his kindness quotient.

USELESS NOTE: To the above assessment, my ghostwriter asks why I've changed my mind about recognizing into evidence the fact that Andrei was, throughout elementary and high school, an indiscriminately friendly guy. But, if my ghostwriter has to ask that question, I can't help him!

So, from that annoyed consideration of my former love's husband choice, I moved on to a more painful analysis. The moment before I tripped Jake, aggressive action had seemed to me to be my only option for defending his intended victim, but—in the harshness of hindsight—my action now felt crude. That thought wounded my stride as I imagined the party-goers shaking their Jake-loving heads at my audacity. By the time I returned my chilly self to my apartment, I was so disgusted with myself that a fly on the wall of my emotions would have assumed that the incident had featured me charging at Jake from behind with nun-chucks.

My voicemail, meanwhile, was murmuring for attention. I was confident that a police constable was going to be sanctioning me for my party violence, but I was too tired to be especially nervous as I activated the message, which turned out to contain the excited voice of Amy.

"Oh my God, John, what happened? Beth's all like you were trying to beat up Jake? I was like, 'That's totally not John's style,' but Jake's like, 'Yeah, you were a total psycho,' and I'm like, 'I don't think so,' but Aaron says he saw it too, so I'm like 'What the hell?'—but I'm sure Jake must have done something to start it, so give me a call as soon as you get this."

I was, at first, touched by Amy's faith in my need for provocation before violence, but—as I re-listened to her message for nuance—I determined that the greater weight of her concern was focused on taming her curiosity. Nevertheless, I dialed her number.

"Hello?"

"Hey, it's John."

"John! What happened?"

I concisely described my conversation with Jake.

"Really? That's it—you wanted to beat him up for *that*?"

I gulped. "Well, I just wanted to stop him, but I guess it was an overreaction."

There was a pause as Amy apparently thought about that.

My faced heated up during the delay.

"I don't know," she finally returned, "I think that was pretty cool of you—to stand up for Aaron like that."

"Really?"

"Yeah, totally—you're such a nice guy."

Amy's approval had a positive effect on my mood.

Meanwhile, despite Amy's assistance in reducing my shame-levels, I was still terrified the next evening to tell Elizabeth that I'd been kicked out of a party for violence—especially considering that my aggressiveness had been caused in part by my hope to defend someone against an anti-gay sociopath. Not that I thought Elizabeth would be in favour of Jake's evil ways, but—in my small profiling experience—people of Elizabeth's generation had, in that era, a higher than average tendency towards heterosexism, so I wondered how she'd react to the lead victim of my story.

My stereotyped concern was lent credence in my nerves as Elizabeth wore a disapproving grimace during my narration.

"So," I said, "I didn't want Jake to mess with the guy, so I tripped him—"

"You tripped him?"

"Yeah, I couldn't think what else to do to stop him, so I just stuck my leg out, and he fell on the floor pretty hard."

"Oh my. Was he hurt?"

"No, I don't think so."

"How did he react, then?"

"Well, he jumped up and shoved me."

"Did you defend yourself?"

"I didn't need to. The host yelled at us, and Jake persuaded her that *I* was the problem, so she told me to leave."

Elizabeth took in a sigh that I could see was leading to judgment.

"And that was all of the dramatics?" she asked.

"No, yeah, that was it," I said, now holding my breath in anticipation.

Elizabeth shook her head. "I don't think it was right for you to trip that young man, no matter how awful he was."

"Yeah, I know—you're right."

"Still, it was very brave of you, dear. Not many people stick their neck out like that."

"Oh, thanks," I said, gulping out a smile.

Indeed, I was delighted to make it into Elizabeth's purgatory on that one.

Chapter 34
Dullard in the City

Lanes of Conversation

On a late Saturday afternoon a few months later, I decided to celebrate an arduous but uneventful day of canvassing by picking up some snacks at my nearby supermarket. As I made plans to pay for the groceries, I noticed that the bounty of my shopping was just few enough to qualify for a cashier express lane, so I hopped aboard. Thirty seconds into the wait, though, I realized that the cashier who was running my lineup was not particularly speedy in the ways of cashiering. She seemed either confused or impressed by many of the items she was handling and paused to comment on them. Moreover, she either didn't notice or offered no attention to the healthy line building from her station.

By the time I determined that the non-express lane next door would have been my faster option, I felt it was too late to switch horses. I'd committed to my lane, and I was going to (slowly) see it through. However, the lady in front of me was clearly not as loyal to her first instincts. Her eyes jumped around the competing lineups searching for a soft spot. The intensity of her pursuit was mesmerizing as she seemed to take every movement in the lineups personally. Indeed, she looked ready to jump lanes at any moment, so I casually moved my basket and me out of her get-away path. But, sadly, she never spotted an opportunity that was fast enough to pull her away.

Finally, when that intense lady was next up for meandering conversation with our cashier and was swiftly placing her items in the ready position on the grocery treadmill, another grocery-store employee popped around from the other side.

"Excuse me," she said, looking at me, "I can help you—*in order*—at the next till if you like?"

"I'm next!" Intense Lady chirped, tossing her purchases back into her basket, before bumping past me.

The new cashier gave me a startled look.

I shrugged back with a smile.

She smirked ever-so-slightly and then went to greet the anxious lady-in-waiting. I followed behind to join the new lineup, only to discover that the person behind me had also zipped ahead of me; so I'd officially lost ground in the transaction. But, worry not, concerned reader, I was too riveted by these events to be bothered.

"Sorry," the new cashier said to Intense Lady as she met her at the front of my new lineup, "I would've asked you if you wanted to switch also, but I thought you'd already started putting your purchases down."

"No, I was next," Intense Lady replied.

"Right, yeah, sorry," the cashier said, now working on the woman's items, "I just thought you were already settled in there."

"Well, *I'm here now*," Intense Lady retorted.

"Oh, yeah, of course, I just didn't want you to think I was ignoring you."

"Well," Intense Lady replied, "I *was* next."

"Right," the cashier conceded, "sorry about that."

Intense Lady shrugged in reply.

I'm embarrassed and proud to say that at that point I displayed on my face a look of startled amusement in retaliation to Intense Lady. I'm sheepish to say so because Intense Lady could have looked my way at any moment and discovered my silent, solo gossip. I'm contented, though, because, as it turned out, it was the cashier who, just then, glanced in my direction and responded to my expressive look with a wee smirk before transferring her eyes back to her customer.

That second connection between us—combined with the fact that she was well within my age and attraction range—had my heart beating with interest. So I aimed my concentration on her conversations with the two customers ahead of me, hoping for a point of commonality between us. Unfortunately, the remaining interactions were barren of meaningful communication.

So, when it finally came my turn to talk to her, I decided to revert back to what had connected us in the first place, our common surprise and apparent amusement regarding the behaviours of Intense Lady.

"Hello," she said. "Sorry about that."

"No, don't be *sorry*," I said. "What a strange lady, eh?"

"*Right?!*" the cashier said with a double nod as she scanned my selections.

"Yeah, she kept misunderstanding what you were saying."

"Yes, exactly! And the way she cut you off. I mean, I guess she was first, but, come on, you're all just trying to get home here."

"Exactly!" I said.

The cashier shook her head with a half-smile. "I guess she was in a rush, but I just don't think there's any excuse to be that rude."

That comment made me smile more enthusiastically than I should have; in fact, I felt an impulse to try to expand the conversation. Don't worry, cringing reader, I had no intention in that moment of asking the nice cashier out. However, it seemed to me that, if I could widen our discussion a morsel, I might be able to build enough rapport that she would remember me the next time we met in a grocery line.

"Okay," she interrupted my wild introspection, "that'll be twenty-six thirty-sven."

I paid for my purchase in silent consideration of my options for banter, but, as the charming cashier handed me my change, she smiled her "Have a nice day" with such friendly contentedness (regarding my departure) that I realized our romantic affinity was a one-way correspondence. So I wished her an equally high-quality day and got out of the store relieved that I hadn't embarrassed myself with unrequited flirting.

Elizabeth, of course, did not concur with my assessment when I told her about it. I, in turn, was delighted—as always—by her biased reaction; ultimately, though, I remained convinced of my conclusion.

A Saturday later, I rode the bus home from the farthest reaches of my Green Cross canvassing territory; I was pleased because I'd managed to complete one full cycle of my assigned region. A sad song on my Walkman, though, questioned my good mood. Perhaps Lesley would want me to take a break from canvassing now that I'd mined my entire area. That might mean that my already thinly sliced crush on Rayann would have no interactions to maintain it for a while. I would miss my crush on Rayann. She was so … on the bus! My ghostwriter—there she was, only two seats and an aisle away from me, reading. *What was she doing outside of the Green Cross?* I almost didn't recognize her without a desk attached to her waist.

Elizabeth's disappointed-in-me advice to always go for romance when I had the chance told me there was to be no stopping me this time. Indeed, there was no bus-ly reason that I shouldn't start up a conversation with a Green Cross colleague. I even had a decent conversation-starter topic available, given my recent canvassing achievement.

I stood up and walked towards the seat beside Rayann. One step, two steps, and …I inadvertently spotted her reading material over her shoulder. It was a magazine—one of those women-help magazines—and, by the headline of the article that she appeared to be reading, the publication seemed to be giving her advice on how couples could fare better during clothing-optional encounters.

It seemed to me that Rayann would not want to be interrupted by a colleague while she was engaged in such private reading, so I kept walking. Unfortunately, I could see nowhere to sit that wouldn't illuminate my face for Rayann's viewing, so I scampered off the bus at its next stop.

"But, John," Elizabeth said, an hour later, "if you'd just sat down in front of her, she might've realized you were there and closed her reading if she was shy about it."

NOTE OF DISCRETION: To protect Rayann's privacy, I had only told Elizabeth that my friend was reading a relationship advice column.

"Oh, I guess you're right," I said. "Why didn't *I* think of that? It's like I sabotage myself."

"That's very true, dear."

"Why do you put up with me?"

"Well," Elizabeth said, "I suppose, if Rayann was reading *relationship* advice, wouldn't that mean that she already has a young man in her life, dear?"

"True," I said. "Good point—so why are we picking on me?"

"Because you hadn't thought of that at the time, so—from your perspective—you should have talked to her."

"Right again," I said, chuckling as I rattled the Yahtzee shaker.

On the Monday lunch hour that followed, I felt less nervous than usual as I approached the Green Cross. I realized that—even though Elizabeth hadn't proven conclusively that Rayann was pre-attached—my already anemic crush on her couldn't sustain the weight of a suspected rival. So the fauxmance was officially over.

I came into the Green Cross office to see the usual top-of-the-head look from my former crush.

"Hey, Rayann," I said, without even waiting for permission.

"Oh, hi, John. How's it going?"

I made something up about being in a good mood, and then I asked her if Lesley might be available to discuss my next task now that I'd exhausted the first one. Rayann dialed up her boss and reported that Lesley would be available in fifteen minutes.

"Which means half an hour," she said with a smirk.

"At least she's consistent," I replied.

"True," Rayann said, almost chuckling. "Do want some coffee or tea or water or something while you wait?"

"Thanks—no, I'm good, thanks."

That was an exhilarating moment and provoked an interesting question. *Had my crush-free confidence made me more worthy of Rayann's consideration, or was her improved treatment just the coincidental result of a happy mood?* There was no way to determine the answer just yet, so I decided there would be no harm in reinstating my crush a little longer until I found out.

Meanwhile, Lesley had a meeting come up, so she was forced to accommodate me earlier than she'd planned.

"Hello again, John," she said, smiling as voraciously as in the past, but with rushed breaths as she walked us to her office.

"Hi, nice to see you again," I said, taking a Chet-placating glance at her wedding hand, but it darted away to shut her office door before my eyes could catch it.

"So..." she said as she sat down, putting her wedding hand underneath the other, "Rayann says you've canvassed your full territory. That's really wonderful to hear, John—we're lucky to have you."

"Thanks."

Lesley offered another large smile, held it for a moment, and then moved on.

"So Rayann said you were looking for a new assignment?"

"Yeah—"

"What do you have in mind?"

"Well, I don't necessarily need a new assignment—if you wanted to give me a new territory, that would be good too."

"Oh, I see," Lesley said, "so I'm gathering that you were just looking for more of the same?"

"Right," I said, suddenly embarrassed by my boring aspirations and, therefore, panicked to find another option. "Maybe also... maybe I could stand outside of malls and collect—"

"That's a very inventive idea. We've never done it before, but you're willing to do it?"

"Yeah, of course."

"Then I'll talk it over with my colleagues to see if it's feasible. Sound good?"

Lesley stood up, allowing me to catch her wedding hand alone for a moment. It was clearly marked by a wedding band—*poor Chet.*

"Yeah—sounds great," I said. "And, in the meantime, do you wanna give me another territory to work on?"

Lesley accepted my offer and escorted me back to my on-again, off-again crush.

"Rayann, can you set John up with territory C?—I don't think we've done that one for a while." Lesley then stopped and turned to me. "Thank you again, John. I'll let you know about your idea. We're very lucky to have you." Lesley smiled another big one upon receiving my thanks and went back to her office.

I turned to Rayann, who was focused on her task. Her attentive mood seemed to have already worn off.

"Well?" Chet said, upon my return to Ambiguity. "How went the reconnaissance mission? Did my Lesley reveal herself to you yet?"

"I'm afraid so. She has a wedding ring, so—"

"I had a feeling," Chet said. "Well, I can't win 'em all."

"I guess not. Sorry it didn't work out."

Chet chuckled. "It's not like I'd picked out our wedding china, John Juan—don't take it so hard."

"Oh, okay—"

"How about you, Johnny Glenn? Anyone of interest in your solar system right now?"

I was surprised by the question since it seemed to be about me. In fact, I was so honoured by Chet's apparent interest that I decided to try answering his inquiry.

"Well, actually, I was kind of interested in the receptionist at the Green Cross."

"Great, so why don't you go for her? At least one of us should benefit from you volunteering there."

"Thanks, but—"

"You know how I feel about *buts*!" Chet said. "They're best used for sitting on."

"Right," I said. "Okay, thanks for the advice. I guess I should get back to work if you want this report done by the end of the afternoon."

Chet laughed. "Avoiding the topic because we know I'm right, are we?"

"Yup," I said.

By Friday, I'd received full approval from Lesley to institute my 'inventive' idea to panhandle for donations like so many charities before us. Two Saturdays later, after Leslie had negotiated a deal with my local mall, I was standing behind a Green Cross display in the main entranceway of the shopping centre.

It was a strange experience as I came to feel like a fly on the mall's wall. So many people walked right at me—and then past me—without ever seeming to look at me. It was an impressive display of selective unawareness. Nevertheless, I was content in my people-watching position. A lot of parents and their pet children were out, and, on more than one occasion, a two-to-three-year-old got away from their pack and had to be chased down by their previously dignified elders. I was surprised to see how undisturbed the mini-people were when, mid-stumble-sprinting, they were plucked from their route and carried back to their group.

As I enjoyed that contemplation, a short man with a hat and a beard walked towards me and showed no sign of veering away.

"Hello," I said.

He did not look at me; instead, he focused his eyes on my Green Cross collection container. He looked at it carefully, read its instructions, and then continued on his path without any acknowledgement of my existence.

'*Have a nice day*,' I resisted saying for fear of it sounding as sarcastic as I was feeling.

To my—and hopefully *your*—surprise, polite reader, that reading-my-material-without-acknowledging-my-presence behaviour was not an isolated weirdness. At least twice more that day (and at least once more in every subsequent occasion), a person arrived at my display, disregarded my greeting, stared at what my charity had to offer, and then departed without a single pleasantry for me. (Although, on rare occasions, after investigating my cause, the ignoring mall-goer would contribute something to my donation container; consequently, I always felt compelled to thank them, which, in turn, would provoke a confused nod back from the loner donor.)

Eventually, I decided that I needed to increase my presence in the mall-patrons' pathways, so I smiled as cheerfully as I could at each passing shopper. That caused some to veer wider around my presentation, but some smiled back. It was a surprising experience to at last be seen after feeling like a hidden camera for so long. Finally, a fifty-something woman walked directly into my space, and she didn't even avoid my eyes.

"*Hey*," she said, as if we were old friends. And she reached into her pocket and dropped some change and a crumpled bill in my container.

"Thanks," I said.

"Yeah, no worries—you guys are great. Have a nice day."

"You too," I blurted back.

As the woman continued on, I wondered if she had any idea how much influence she'd had in promoting her suggestion. I was subsequently pleased, though, to discover that she was not the only one of her kind. A couple people an hour would shed their change into my container as they walked by, and, for the most part, they treated me as though I was an equal participant in the transaction.

A cheerful breeze refreshed me on my walk home that late afternoon. In that mood, I was intrigued as I spotted from a distance a cluster of people gathered around my apartment building. Upon closer inspection, I realized it was my family drinking coffee and eating doughnuts.

"Hey," I said as I arrived, pleased to see that Per's Noelle was still a member of the group.

"Where *were* you?" Per said, shaking his head with a grin. "You should always be expecting a surprise inspection."

"Sorry, John," my dad intercepted, "we should have called ahead."

"But that would've ruined the surprise," Per said. "How was I supposed to know this would be the one time John decided to have a life?"

"Yes, John," my father said, "it was rude of you not to be ready for us in case we wanted to surprise you."

Per rolled his eyes. "Yeah, Dad, I was being serious about that."

"What's the surprise?" I said, looking at my mother.

"We'll tell you inside," she said, smiling with such enthusiasm that I knew that it was Per-related.

"Okay," I said, opening the door to the building. "Hi, Noelle."

"Hey," she said, going in for a hug that was so merry in its grip that I figured she was involved as well. *So she and Per were either with child or marriage licence.* I put my guess on pregnancy and smiled at the thought of being an uncle.

Unfortunately, the elevator ride, itself, was not the most comfortable interaction in Smith-family history. It's a funny circumstance when your companions have told you that big news is coming soon but that you can't talk about it yet, so you have to supply an alternate, sacrificial topic to toy with until the timing is correct for the real conversation.

"So, John," my mom said, "how's Ambiguity?"

"Pretty good, actually. You know, I think I've gotten used to Chet now."

"Why'd you have to get used to Chet?" Per said.

"Well, I find him kind of irritating—"

I was cut off by the sound of the elevator grabbing onto our stop and opening its doors. Indeed, the silence returned as I led us down my hallway and unlooked my door; we all seemed to be preparing ourselves for our particular contribution to my upcoming surprise.

As it turned out, my prognostication missed by one: Per and Noelle were getting married.

Chapter 35
Dullard vs. Brother IV

Tackily Ever After

Now, Per and Noelle may seem to you, urban reader, to have been awfully young to be collecting nuptials, but—before you utter such judgmentalism out loud—you may want to consider the sociological phenomenon that small town citizens tend to tie their knots earlier than city folk.

I was pleased for both members of the couple—as well as for the rest of us since Noelle brought a warmth to Per's character that he had not previously provided on his own. I was also happy for my parents who appeared proud to have someone as nice as Noelle joining our team. But I was curious about how Noelle's team felt about Per. More specifically, I wondered what Noelle's sister, Nicolette, might be thinking about her ex-boyfriend transforming into a brother-in-law.

In my observation, Nicolette had always been shy and sweet, so I wondered if those temperaments would make her feel awkward around the unnatural couple instead of rightfully irritated with them.

The above contemplation kept me company on my long-distance bus trip home for the wedding weekend many weeks later. Halfway along, it occurred to me that I might be able to reduce Nicolette's possible pangs of awkwardness by being a friendly confidant during the festivities. The assignment made me less nervous about my own participation in the pending social obligations.

Fifty minutes later, as the bus hummed into town, I was infiltrated by the standard bittersweet feelings that come with returning home after time away.

NOTE OF FULL DISCLOSURE: I had previously been home for Christmas, but that was when the town was camouflaged by snow and decorations. This was different.

There was nothing to hide the fact that my hometown didn't seem to have missed me. Familiar sights reminded me that my old stomping grounds had survived without my presence, while a pair of new businesses told me that the place had progressed without me.

My first evening home was spent with a small but giddy gathering of wedding elite. Their enthusiasm—especially my mother's—tamped down my standard social anxiety. Meanwhile, Nicolette was on wedding assignment elsewhere, so I wasn't yet able to activate my plan to befriend her in order to protect her from her imagined-by-me discomfort. I did learn, however, that we had matching ranks on our respective sides of the wedding party, which meant that we were honouary dates for each other.

My inaugural chance to mingle with allegedly anxious Nicolette came the next day in the late afternoon at a large wedding eve barbecue. Twenty minutes in, Per and Noelle could be seen chatting with their Best Man and Maid while I was at the dessert table trying to be inconspicuous as I strategized how to approach Nicolette. She was, at that moment, talking to a boring-looking older relative but was managing an admirable display of listening.

"Hey, John," Noelle the bride called me from her nearby position, "come talk to us."

I was touched by the invite even though it was disruptive to my plans.

"Hey," I said as I approached the wedding couple.

Noelle beamed. "Have you met my best girl, Janet?"

"No, how are you?"

"Enchanté," Janet said as she examined Per and me. "Wow, you guys look alike."

"That hurt," Per said.

"Yeah, that was mean," I added with a giggle.

"Per—*be nice*," his fiancé said. "Now that you're getting married, you don't have to be the most handsome guy in the world."

My brother nodded cheerfully. "That's comforting, but I'd like to at least be better-looking than *this* guy."

The Best Man—a gregarious simpleton named Sean—and I laughed.

The bride shook her head in sympathy at me. "I think you're *very* handsome."

"Thanks," I said, faking a smile back.

Sean chuckled. "Noelle—you know what your problem is?"

"Careful," Per said.

"I didn't realize I had one," Noelle replied.

"You need more beer," the Best Man said.

"I don't drink beer, so—"

"Then *I* need more beer."

"Okay, but come right back—I want to go over tomorrow… Hey, hon," she then said, turning to Per, "can you go get Nicolette?"

"You know *I want to*," my brother replied, "but why can't *you* do it?"

"Because she's talking to Aunt Louise: I love Aunt Louise, but her stories don't really ever end—if I go over there, then both of us'll be caught."

"Good point, but I'm her niece's future husband—you don't think she'll want to talk to me too?"

"I'll do it," I said, "I'm nothing to Aunt Louise."

"Thanks, bro," Per said, patting me on the shoulder as I nervously set off on my task to save my brother's ex from not only her babbling aunt but also her presumed-by-me babbling anxiety.

As I travelled to Nicolette, my movement provoked her to glance my way, and she smiled at me. Before I could reply, she turned back to her aunt to confide something, and—upon receiving a nod—she walked towards my approach.

"Hi, John."

"Hey, Nicolette!" I over did it. "It's nice to see you. How are you?"

"Oh, you know. I'm… well, actually," she said, switching to a whisper, "I'm glad you're here. It's nice to see a friendly face."

Wow, my Nicolette-anxiety-reduction plan seemed to be going exactly as hoped, which, of course, made me suspicious that it was about to implode.

"Yeah, you too," I replied, ignoring the nerves in my own stomach that were suddenly clamouring for my attention, "we'll have to keep each other company this weekend."

"Yeah, yeah, that'd be great," Nicolette said, full smile. "So what're you up to these days?"

I'll spare you the boring content of our discussion regarding what each of us was up to, appreciative reader. The more significant communication between us was found in our soon-to-be relaxed demeanours with each other throughout the wedding weekend. Indeed, after we finished our bland updates and completed wedding rehearsal preparations with the rest of the wedding party entourage, we sat back and made observations to each other about the incidents going on around us. Mine were generally obvious, while hers were either obtuse—as she missed the point of something—or clever as she saw something unusual hidden beneath my standard sightings.

For instance of obtuseness, in reference to a joke that Aunty Susan made during a rehearsal dinner toast to the groom, Nicolette asked me why my aunt would lie about her age.

I shook my head assertively. "Oh, no, I think she was just joking about that."

"I don't think so. She seemed serious."

"But why did everyone laugh, then?"

"Well, they probably thought she was joking."

"But—" I stammered, horrified that my aunt's playfulness was being so abused.

"It's not like I think she's bad for lying about her age," Nicolette offered. "Why shouldn't she? It's nobody's business what her age is."

"But she didn't lie! Aunty Susan's always making jokes like that."

Eventually, Nicolette conceded the point, but her backing down seemed to be more the result of the issue mattering more to me than from a genuine alteration of mind. Consequently, I had no choice but to diagnose Nicolette as suffering from a mild intellectual deficiency.

But then, for instance of cleverness, she made a unabashedly profound observation as she pointed out that my mother seemed to have a propensity for auto-complimenting Per and Noelle regarding wedding arrangements even in cases that featured decisions the couple had neither initiated nor particularly cared about (such as the flavour of the cake that I'd set up through Sweet On You).

Overall, Nicolette and I agreed that the wedding ceremony and reception were lovely. Although, if you're looking for details of the big day's events, curious reader, I refer you to any bouquet-tossing wedding that you have attended. Nothing went wrong—beyond the occasional mishap with the placement of flowers (which only the bride and one of the mothers noticed)—and there were no Per-Noelle specific happenings that would help the guests to distinguish the proceedings from the last wedding they had witnessed.

The interesting part, for our purposes, then, occurred after the formal part of the wedding evening when a DJ arrived with music and talk of dancing. To start, Per and Noelle had their romantic first dance, and then various members of their parental crews got involved before finally the entire wedding party was asked to join the ritual. Nicolette and I were once again matched up; thankfully, neither of us were particularly rhythmic in the ways of dancing, so—instead of sharing the awkward conversation that would have been produced if there had been no distractions—we were able to focus our close-in chatting on determining how we might improve our movements.

Happily, our obligation to the dance floor was soon complete, and we returned to the vacant head table to continue to share observations about our surroundings. To my surprise, as I was sitting with Nicolette watching other people dance, I felt some painful nostalgia for my long ago private wedding-table conversation with Annette the MC. That memory of such a content time—combined with my enjoyment of Nicolette's company—had me unfortunately feeling a smidge intrigued by her. That would not do. She was both my brother's ex-girlfriend and his current sister-in-law, and both titles seemed to me to make any romantic collaboration between us a tacky one. Instead, then, I decided to focus on how she was feeling—specifically how she felt about her sister taking over a relationship that she had started. I hesitated for fear of provoking the discomfort I had tried to protect her from all weekend, but then I decided she was more likely to appreciate my friendly interest than resent it.

"So," I said, "how do you feel about Per marrying your sister? Does it bother you?"

"Good question," she said, a smile tickling her lips.

I felt my sweat break as she considered her answer.

"Actually," she said, "I got over him a long time ago, but it still bugs me that they never thought about me when they got together—they barely said anything to me about it."

I nodded more aggressively than I'd planned. "Yeah, they just seem so into their own thing and not worried about you."

Nicolette smirked. "Exactly. I don't know if I could do that—if a guy's my sister's ex, he's my sister's ex. It seems off limits to me. But I guess I shouldn't be putting restrictions on who people can fall for."

That was the longest speech I'd ever heard shy-Nicolette offer. "Yeah," I said, "if they fell for each other, fine, but it might've been nice if they'd put up some resistance."

"Totally!" Nicolette said. "That's what I think. I just don't think I could've done it—my sister's ex would feel like an ex...family member."

"Yeah, I know what you mean."

"What about you?" Nicolette said. "Could you go for one of your brother's exes?"

"No, I don't think so."

"Yeah, I don't think I could either," Nicolette said. But then she paused and smiled at me. "Unless, um, I don't know, unless, you know, they were just teenagers at the time and enough time had passed."

My face was suddenly warm. "Yeah, I guess that would change things."

Nicolette smirked. "Or," she said, lowering her voice as she examined my eyes, "if your brother dated *his* ex's sister, then maybe you wouldn't feel so bad about dating, um, the ex, herself?"

I blushed. "Yeah, maybe that wouldn't be so bad—what do you think?"

Nicolette smiled and took a deep breath. "I don't think it would be bad at all." And then she put her hand on my hand.

That, of course, caused a delightful racing of my heart, but, cruelly, I simultaneously experienced a large contingent of guilt overtaking my brain.

Nicolette either spotted an indication of those feelings on my face or she felt her own version because she suddenly seemed sad.

"I don't think it would be bad at all," she said. "Actually, I think it could be a cool match, but I still don't think I could do it—it still feels weird to me."

"I know what you mean," I said.

Nevertheless, Nicolette and I kept our hands together for the next hour as we watched the dancing. The fact that we both knew that our handholding was a symbol of what wasn't to be made it one of the most romantic moments in my history.

When the DJ announced that the evening's final song was approaching, Nicolette turned to me with a smile.

"So you still think we're making the right decision?"

I shrugged half-heartedly back. "Yeah, unfortunately, I do."

"Me too," she said. "But I was hoping you'd try to change my mind."

I laughed. "I was hoping you'd try to change *my* mind," I said, only half lying.

Nicolette sighed. "Well, John—if only we were as tacky as the people we're trying to protect from our own tackiness."

I smiled at that. Nicolette really was more interesting than she seemed when she wasn't getting Aunty Susan's jokes.

When I returned home to report to Elizabeth the details of the near romance I'd found at my brother's wedding, she scolded me once again for not taking chance up on its offerings. She made some bold statements about it being okay to court whomever I felt a connection with—brother's prior companion or not—but, unofficially, I think she suspected that she would have done the same as me if it had been her sibling's former dance partner.

Elizabeth's hidden approval was comforting. But even more pleasing to my heart was my subsequent realization that—even though Nicolette and I couldn't date each other—I now had a long-distance crush to finally supplant poor neglected Rayann.

Chapter 36
A Boring Samaritan II

Relationshipwrecks

A month after my brother's wedding, I began a Monday with my usual pattern of checking my email to see if there were any Chet-errands I could warm up with before I started on my more significant work. I discovered a message from Chet which mentioned politely but importantly that my recent work with a new database procedure was producing an annoying by-product on one of his files. The message irked me since it was *his* idea for me to switch protocols; in fact, I had asked him if the change would yield any side effects, and he had insisted that the new plan would "run like Bambi."

Nevertheless, the lack of accusation within Chet's request took the sting out of his lack of responsibility. So I immediately sent a conciliatory reply, complete with an apology for the difficulty and a promise to fix it.

Half an hour later, my desk phone rang out loud. It was right on Chet's cue. Whenever we had an email discussion, he couldn't resist phoning or attending my desk to confirm our findings. So I sighed and reached for the phone—at least he'd decided to phone instead of visit. But, oddly, just as I was about to pick up, I noticed that, in this case, Chet's call seemed to be coming from an outside line.

"Hello, this is John Smith in the RQB Department?"

"*Hi, John in the RQB Department*! It's your Aunty Susan!"

"Oh, hi!—I was wondering who'd be calling."

"Did you think it might be a girl?"

I laughed. "No, I'd thought it was gonna be my boss."

"Oh," my aunt said with a smiley voice, "office romance, then—I'd like to hear about that."

"Right," I said, laughing again.

"Actually," my aunt said, "the reason I'm calling is because I'm in town meeting with a supplier, so I thought I'd take you for lunch."

A couple hours later, Aunty Susan arrived at the parking lot under-looking my office. I would have preferred meeting her at the restaurant so that I wouldn't have to worry about making introductions to Chet or Erik, but Aunty Susan cruelly said she wanted to have a "peek" at where I worked.

So, of course, as I waited for my aunt—and contemplated my fear of awkward interactions—Chet arrived in my office.

"Johnny Hancock," he said, "I just got your email, so, yeah, that'd be great if you could help me out and be extra careful about your new QC protocols creating those DROs."

"Yeah, no problem," I said, glancing out the window, hoping Aunty Susan might have changed her mind and gone back to the parking lot. "Like I said in my email, it's easy to—"

"I don't mean to be a stickler," Chet said. "It's just those things put a needle in my paw, so it'd really help me out ... *if you don't mind?*"

"Right, of course, I just didn't realize it was doing that—it's no big deal to switch them off."

"Much appreciated. If you don't know how to do it, I can lend you my expertise, but I really need that changed ... *if it's okay with you?*"

"No, it's fine," I said, now officially panicking about the imminence of my aunt's arrival. "I've already changed it, but thanks for the offer."

"Great, if you can just make sure of that, my world would spin a little more easily."

"Of course, I'm really sorry about that," I said, hoping that a full-weighted apology might convince Chet that I had gotten the point.

"No worries, John Paul Two. No apology necessary. In future, if you could just be careful—"

"Yup, *got it,*" I said a little more sharply than I'd planned.

"Hi, I'm looking for John Smith," I suddenly heard from the hallway.

"Oh, there's my aunt—I'm meeting her for lunch."

"Then what're you talking to *me* for?" Chet said. "Get a move on."

"Thanks," I said, rushing into the hallway. "Oh, hi Aunty Susan."

"Oh, there he is," Aunty Susan said, smiling at Erik. "Thank you."

"No worries," Erik said, sliding back into his office.

"My my, John," Aunty Susan said, grinning at me, "this is quite the building."

"We like it," Chet answered. "Work sweet work."

"It's like a labyrinth," Aunty Susan replied with a smile, "you guys must get lost just looking for the restroom."

"Exactly," Chet said, "I stopped looking years ago."

Aunty Susan laughed (a gesture that I could only assume was forced).

"Anyway," I said, "we should go."

"Always in a rush," Chet said, smiling at Aunty Susan. "I'm Chet—John's boss—you must be Aunty Susan."

"That I am," Aunty Susan said. "At least that's what my nephews call me."

Chet laughed.

I took the laughter pause as an opportunity to re-invoke exit time.

"Nice to meet you, Chet," Aunty Susan said again as I took a step towards leaving.

"Likewise—where are you taking my number one employee?"

"Hadn't decided yet—anywhere you'd recommend? I'm not from here."

"None of us are," Chet said. "But I do know the area, and I'd recommend the little bistro around the corner. I go there so often I can't remember what it's called, but they've got the best sandwiches."

"Sounds good. What do you think, John?"

"Yeah, perfect."

"Nice to meet you, Chet," Aunty Susan tried again.

"Likewise. Enjoy your lunch."

As we got into the exit stairwell, Aunty Susan smiled at me.

"We don't have to go there unless you want to—I was just being polite."

I was relieved to hear it. For, as I'd told Chet many times, I didn't like the food at the bistro.

During lunch, Aunty Susan told me about her business in town. "The wholesaler," she said with a mysterious smile, "was very funny. We had a good conversation."

"That's nice," I said, wondering whether she would want an investigation of her strange facial expression.

"What?" she said, smiling again.

The new smile seemed to be even more communicative than the first. "It's just ..." I hesitated, "are you *interested* in the wholesaler?"

"Sure," she said, "why not? Now he just has to ask me out—but I don't see that happening any time soon."

And so Aunty Susan and I spent the rest of our lunch commiserating with each other's lack of relationship. I realized, along the way, that my dad's younger sister was not nearly as elderly as I imagined my favourite aunt would be by that time.

Before we were finished divulging all of our details, my watch beeped to let us know that my lunch hour was over, so we walked back to the Ambiguous parking lot.

"I might have to come back in again on Friday, John. I'll call you again if I do—if you're up for it?"

"Yeah, sounds great," I said, pleased that we might have a sequel discussion of our dating incompetencies.

On Friday morning, I was nervous about my aunt's possible call for a reunion of our gossip. That is to say, I was concerned that, if she returned, Chet might impose *his* conversation on her again, so I decided to preempt the possibility. If she called, I would assertively suggest that we meet at the restaurant instead of Ambiguity.

Aunty Susan did indeed call, and—as I was explaining my *meet there* plan to her—I heard annoying footsteps approaching my office.

"Johnny Bucyk ..." came Chet's loud voice, "oops, you're on the phone."

I smiled my *Sorry* face.

Chet grinned, sat down across my desk, and spent his wait time watching me like a puppy does a family member eating dinner.

That made it difficult for me to concentrate on selecting a restaurant.

"Um, maybe we should just meet at the same place as last time?"

Chet smiled when I hung up. "Lunch with Aunty Susan again?"

"Yeah, how'd you know?"

Chet chuckled. "All the time you've been here, John, she's the only one other than me that I've seen you go for lunch with."

"Right, of course, *smart.*"

Chet nodded his approval of my assessment. "You know, you can take a longer lunch if you want. I'm sure you and Aunty Susan have a lot to talk about—I don't mind."

"Really? Thanks. That'd be great, actually."

"No problemo."

"Thanks," I said again, feeling rather pleased with Chet.

Ten minutes before lunchtime, Chet returned to my office.

"John-Claude Van Diner, I don't have any plans for lunch—do you mind if I join you and Aunty Susan?"

"Oh ...um," I said, hoping a perfectly phrased diplomatic rejection would arrive on my lips. "Sure," I said, "that'd be great."

"Excellentio!" Chet said. "Should I dress for business or casual?"

As we walked, my mind was drenched with anxiety about the moment that Aunty Susan would see me arriving at the restaurant with Chet on my arm. In that morsel of time, Aunty Susan would have no choice but to assume that I had invited the interloper without caring whether to check with her first. And I would have no way to indicate to her that it was Chet, alone, who had hijacked our plans.

SOCIO-TEMPORAL NOTE: As discusseed previously, modern reader, we were still existing in the early time of cell phones—an era in which neither Aunty Susan nor I were yet participants, so I'm afraid I had neither texting nor Twittering options to alert her to our plight.

My above fear of Aunty Susan's reaction to Chet's sudden appearance in our private lunch was such an intense player in my thoughts as Chet and I travelled to our destination that I could barely spare any room in my brain to be annoyed with whatever he was babbling about.

As we arrived at the restaurant, itself, though, a bonus worry busied my nerves: it occurred to me that Chet might object to our choice of eatery; after all, he'd overheard me telling Aunty Susan that we were going to the 'same place as last time,' and 'last time' we'd allegedly gone to the bistro that he'd recommended. *Would Chet be wounded by our anti-bistro choice?*

"So …" I said, "we decided to go here."

Chet scanned the building.

My chest tightened.

"Looks dandio to me," he said.

Chet then opened the door for us with such merriness of pull that I was confident that he was unaware of his right to feel wounded by our rejection of his recommendation. But that was only a small victory: the greater agony for my nerves still awaited me at the moment of revelation to Aunty Susan that I had delivered an annoying sidekick to our private conversation. I could only hope for an early washroom break from Chet so that I could explain to my aunt what had happened.

Chet smiled as we walked towards our table. "Nice place they got here."

"Yeah," I said, nauseated as we rounded the corner to my aunt.

"Hey, Aunty Susan," I said, "Chet, um—"

"I invited myself along," Chet said. "I hope you don't mind—I won't stay the whole time. I was hungry, and I didn't have the energy to pick out a place, so I just followed John."

"Um," I replied, shocked and impressed with Chet's blame taking.

"Well, glad you could you join us," Aunty Susan said.

"So, Aunty Susan," Chet said once we'd settled into our strange situation. "To what does your nephew owe the honour of a second visit in a week?"

"Supplier problems for my business," my aunt replied, "—I own a clothing store. Well, not really supplier problems—supplier *challenges*, as they say."

At that point, Chet did something very odd. Instead of tangenting, he asked a follow-up to his own question.

"What's the challenge, if you don't mind my asking?" he said.

"It's a bit weird, actually..." Aunty Susan replied, and—with no sign of interruption—she began telling a detailed story, clearly unaware of the strangeness of Chet's behaviour.

As my Aunt talked, my mind scrambled to understand the circumstance that had provoked her tale. Surely Chet must have asked his supplementary question by mistake: perhaps he was confused by two competing tangents in his mind.

But, just as I was about to compliment myself on that assessment, Chet asked another question that was completely on point! And so Aunty Susan—oblivious to *The Twilight Zone* happening around her—went ahead and answered that one too.

That unfathomable pattern endured throughout lunch as Chet continued to spend his time asking Aunty Susan open-ended questions and then listening to her answers without making any attempts whatsoever to interrupt. *Was it possible that the most annoying conversationalist I'd ever known wasn't so annoying, after all?*

"So," Aunty Susan said, half an hour into the weirdness, "how's my nephew doing at Ambiguity?"

"Just dandy. He works hard, and he's great to work with."

Aunty Susan smiled. "He gets that from his aunty."

Chet and I chuckled.

"I'm sure he does," Chet said with a bonus laugh, only to segue the subject in my aunt's favour. "Did you get to see a lot of our Johnny growing up?"

"Yeah, I only lived a town away—well, until a few years ago when I moved to the same town—so John got to see extra lots of his Aunty Susan at that point."

"Wait a New York minute," Chet said. "When Bert called me about getting you a job, John, he said that you were his nephew-in-law." Chet looked at Aunty Susan. "You're not Bert Hardelean's wife, are you?"

"No," Aunty Susan said quickly. "Well, I *was*—but not anymore."

And then there was an eerie pause. Oh...my...ghostwriter. Aunty Susan and not-so-annoying Chet seemed to be interested in each other!

As I considered that abominable possibility, it occurred to me that it was quite natural that my boss and my aunt might appreciate each other. They were of the same approximate age and cheerfulness level, and—when Chet wasn't being himself—he actually gave off a charismatic first impression.

But, while I was pondering that epiphany, Chet was interrupting the eerie pause.

"Berty, Berty, Berty," he said, "he never did know a good thing when he had it."

Aunty Susan smiled a little.

And then there was another pause.

"Excuse me for a moment," Aunty Susan said.

Chet stood up for her as she left to visit the ladies' room.

"Johnny," Chet said the moment she was out of range, "I like your aunt."

"So do I," I said, trying to avoid the issue.

"But I mean I *really* like her. You know, in the way that Cary Grant likes Grace Kelly."

"Oh, I see. Well, it wasn't that long ago that she and Bert broke up. I don't know if she'd want anything else right now."

Chet nodded. "Well, do you think you could give her my number, just in case?"

"Maybe, I don't know."

Chet grinned at that. "Maybes are better than rabies."

But I wasn't so sure about that.

"Well," Chet said when Aunty Susan returned to the table, "I must get back to the grind. Take your time, Johnny Depth," he added, as he stood up to leave, "I won't need you for a while." He then looked at Aunty Susan. "It was very nice to meet you," he said, offering her his hand.

"Nice to meet you too, Chet."

The eyes of my boss and my aunt seemed to interact as their hands shook.

After Chet left, my aunt loaded up a question. "Chet seems nice. Is he a good boss?"

What a loaded question! If I told Aunty Susan how annoying Chet was, then she would surely feel an aunt's obligation to dislike him too, which would ruin Chet's chances of charming her. *Did I really want to ruin Chet's chances?*

Well, considering that Aunty Susan was my favourite relative, it did seem reasonable to block the most annoying person in earth history from infiltrating her world. *And yet isn't it written somewhere in the social constitution that one should let one's friends and favourites decide for themselves whom they find to be irritating?*

But, then again, Chet wasn't playing fair. He hadn't disclosed his annoying personality during his encounter with my aunt. *Who's to say whether Chet would let my aunt in on the secret of his hidden annoying identity if and when they started dating?* My poor aunt could spend months falling for non-annoying Chet only to have him suddenly reveal his true personality.

There were just too many issues on the line in that one 'Is he a good boss?' question, and so I couldn't decide whether I should tell my aunt the truth. But a microsecond into that mental stalemate, an epiphany landed in brain. Aunty Susan hadn't *asked* me if Chet was annoying: she had simply inquired as to whether he was a good boss.

"Yeah, Chet's a pretty good boss," I said, relieved to have escaped my moral dilemma.

"So do you like him?"

Damn her! Just like that, my implacable quandary was back and staring at me. An ugly image came to my imagination: Chet and Aunty Susan were walking down the marriage aisle—*ghostwriter have mercy.*

As you know, patient reader, years before, I was partly to blame for the same walk between my aunt and Bert after I had tricked them into sharing Aunty's Susan's phone number. *Surely, I wasn't arrogant enough to meddle a second time.* But then my imagination showed me Aunty Susan's Chet-marrying wedding face: she seemed to be smiling.

"Aunty Susan," I said, looking up at her, "are you *interested* in Chet?"

"Of course," she said, "well, no, not in *that* way," she added with a chortle upon seeing my skeptical smile. "I'm just interested in what you're up to and who's in your life."

"Oh, okay," I said, "because ...I think *he's* interested in you."

"You think so?" Aunty Susan said, fending off an unauthorized smile. "What makes you think so?"

"He asked me to give you his phone number."

At that point, the above-mentioned smile started really attacking my aunt's face. She tried to fight it off.

"No, no, no," she said, "that would be really weird for you, John."

"Why?"

"Well, he's your boss—I'm your aunt."

But, in truth, that was no issue: Chet wasn't the sort to hold a romantic grudge. If things didn't work out, the worst that would happen would be that Chet wouldn't invite me out so much (which, to be honest, wouldn't really be the worst).

I shook my head. "Aunty Susan, don't worry about that. Chet's a nice person—and he'd never …just don't worry about it."

"Really? You sure?" Aunty Susan said, now losing the battle with her smile.

"Yes, *really*," I said, and I took Chet's business card out of my pocket. "Call his work cell—he takes it home with him."

"You sure, John?"

"Of course," I said, my aunt's smile having defected to my face.

"It's just," she said, startling me with a suddenly faltering voice, "ever since Bert, I haven't really had a connection with anyone. And there's something about Chet—he's just so …"

'*Not Bert*,' I thought to myself, but I didn't say it. "I know what you mean," I said instead. "He's a nice guy."

"Yes," Aunty Susan said. "He is, isn't he? I feel comfortable around him, which is unusual for me."

So, within a few months, it was agreed that Aunty Susan and non-annoying Chet were a couple. They talked on the phone every evening; and, on weekends, one of them drove ninety minutes to the other's town. When they stopped by Chet's life, they sometimes visited me too, and I discovered that—as a member of 'Chet & Susan'—Chet continued to act as though he wasn't the most annoying person ever to roam a conversation. In fact, it turns out that a couple's collective personality gets half of its chromosomes from each person; and, apparently, for his half, Chet had contributed his non-annoying side. For instance, while Chet still told the same style of stories that he always had, he let Aunty Susan lead their conversations. Their unofficial rule was simple: Chet didn't discuss irrelevant topics unless Aunty Susan initiated them.

In time, therefore, I began to like Chet of 'Chet & Susan.' I only wished that Aunty Susan could also come to Ambiguity with Chet so that he could stop being annoying at work as well.

"Well, Johnny O," Chet interrupted my speculation on the matter right on cue. "She's perfect."

"That's great," I said, assuming he was referring to his car, which he'd told me about the day before. Indeed, I was about to ask if he'd gotten her an oil change as planned, but luckily he wasn't listening to me.

"I love my little plant admirer," he said. "And you know what that means, don't you, Johnny Gerard?"

"Um, it means you're not going to get a replacement for her?"

Chet laughed. "Not quite—it means I'm leaving you. I'm resigning my commission from Ambiguity. I'm putting in my notice today."

"Oh ...really?" I said, my stomach churning with an odd combination of shock, euphoria, and ...worry?

Chet shrugged boastfully. "Yup, the little lady has a more successful career in a less expensive town—and I'm a modern guy, so I'm going her way. Poor Elsje—she's going to miss our conversations."

"Right," I said, too lost in contemplation to notice Chet's outrageous claim.

Chapter 37
Dullard vs. Power Boss II

Bittersweet Than Never

Chet's departure from Ambiguity provoked a cascade of bitter-sweetness in your narrator. For the sweet part, the idea of working without the most painful conversationalist I'd ever known certainly had a nice ring to it. But, for the bitter part, I wondered if working at Ambiguity would be lonely and cheerfree without Chet's ever-present friendliness. Even though his visits to my office were usually redundant, they did make me feel that I was a valued member of Team Chet. It seemed unlikely that my replacement boss would take such interest in me.

As I rode the bus to work on the first morning of the post-Chet era, my thoughts were relatively relaxed. I did, of course, spend some nervousness on what was going to happen once I got to Ambiguity, but I didn't have enough information for my anxious introspections to go on just yet. Chet had only told me that Elsje and Glenroy didn't have a replacement for him ready and that Elsje, herself, would be "taking care of me for now"—which, in turn, had reminded Chet of his plants and the fact that he needed to phone my aunt to remind her not to pack up his greenery until he got home so that he could feed the little guys once more before their great voyage.

I smirked as I considered Chet's talent for distraction. In fact, as the bus stopped and welcomed a few more passengers, I even felt some nostalgia for Chet's inability to follow his own drift. *Was it possible that I would miss Chet's earnest belief in the importance of sharing his every passing thought?*

To that end, you'll be happy to know, sensitive reader, that—three days prior—Erik and I had given a little hallway party for Chet on his final Friday. We supplied all the cake and reminiscing that one could expect from co-workers on one's last day. I did worry that Chet might have expected more than the seven long-time colleagues, including Elsje, who dropped by to give their blessings for his departure; but, on the evening after the party—as I helped my aunt and future uncle pack—Chet reported only pleased feelings about his Ambiguous send-off.

"Well, that's satisfying," Aunt Susan had said. "I guess it goes to show that my nephew runs a good party, eh?"

"Definitely," Chet replied "Maestro Johnny Williams got everyone out—even Elsje was there."

Aunty Susan laughed and rolled her eyes. "Oh, the *wonderful* Elsje. You're lucky she's married—and you're leaving her to be with me—otherwise, I might think you were in love with her."

Chet and I giggled at that. "But I *am* in love with her," he said. "But she doesn't want me, and I couldn't take her rejection anymore."

"Well," Aunty Susan said, "maybe, if you told her how you feel, she might give you a chance. Have you even tried?"

"It's too late now," Chet then said, laughing a little harder than necessary. "I guess I'll just stick with you."

Aunty Susan shrugged. "If you're sure that's what you want. Wouldn't have been my choice, but it's your call."

I recalled that interaction with a smile as my bus dropped me off for the first time at a Chet-free Ambiguity. I was going to miss him.

When I got to my desk, I felt a murmuring of sadness in my belly as I clicked open my email (where I would normally find my day's Chet errands). To my surprise, there was a new message. *Perhaps Chet had sent a final farewell.* Nope, it was from Elsje Anders.

"Mr. Smith," she wrote. "As I'm sure Mr. Williams mentioned to you, I will be taking over as your supervisor until new arrangements can be made. I would like to start today. Please send word when you're ready to receive me."

I sent the word immediately and subsequently wondered what Chet's departure had gotten me into.

Letting Pride Get the Best of Me

Elsje Anders was the sort of boss who was polite with her staff just to be polite. My ghostwriter's research suggests that, if she had her druthers, she would dispense with politeness so that she and her underlings could get to work.

"Mr. Smith," she said, offering me an official handshake, "I look forward to working with you."

"Thanks," I said, "I look forward to working with you as well."

And that was it for pleasantries.

"May I call you *John*?" she said.

"Of course, and what should I call you?"

"You may call me Elsje or Mrs. Anders—whatever you're more comfortable with, but Elsje is perfectly fine since we'll be working closely together."

"Okay, sure."

"Now, John, Mr. Williams has done a good job of running this department. However, in my position, I have access to strategies that would have been difficult for him to employ from his vantage point in the company. So, in my time as your interim supervisor, I would like to assist you in taking advantage of various tools at my disposal, which should make this department more efficient. How does that sound?"

"Good," I said, not about to say anything else.

"Excellent," Elsje said. "So, to start, I'd like you to please Z-ate all of your Q with your W function."

"Oh," I said, confused by the irrelevant-seeming step, "with my *W*? Are you sure you don't mean—?"

"I'm quite sure, thank you."

"Okay."

Chet had never asked me to W-function anything. And I wasn't so sure how I felt about starting. But I did as I was told, and I took the results to Elsje, who was temporarily using Chet's old office.

"Good, thank you," my new boss said. "Now please Z-ate the Q results with your G function."

"*With the G function?*" I said, again not convinced that Elsje knew the elaborate consequences of her instruction.

"Yes please," she said, wearing a face that looked deeply uninterested in quibbling.

"Okay."

G function was another tedious tool that Chet had never imposed on me—and for good reason: it would only get us to the same destination that much simpler operations would have with less stress. I was tempted, therefore, to do the task the easy way, but an impressive fear that Elsje was testing my obedience in the presence of futile work scared the rebelliousness out of me.

Apparently Elsje was more settled into her role as my boss than her interim title implied. I grimaced as I considered that ominous thought. But then I smirked at it. Perhaps I was reaping the relativity of having had such an easy time of it under Chet. With a sigh in my walk, I travelled back into Elsje's office and handed her the results of her latest assignment.

"Good, thank you. Now I want you to start your L-figures for the day."

"Oh, okay, but—if I'm going to do the L-figures—I believe I'll have to do my F-figures first because the L-figures are based on the F-figures, aren't they?" I smiled, trying not to be condescending about my superior knowledge.

"Yes, they *are*," Elsje said. "But, by Z-ating your Q with your G, your F-figures will now compile automatically for you each day. You should never have to compile them manually again."

Never again compile my F-figures? My ghostwriter! Under Chet's command, assembling my F-figures was one of my most laborious daily chores. Elsje had provided a coup for my future productivity: she was suddenly my bossly hero. Indeed, I vowed never to doubt her orders again. Nor would I ever again question my old friend Tally's boasts about her former leader.

It didn't take long for me to confirm that Elsje Anders had an ability to make both Chet's department and me more efficient—which was an impressive thing for me to have noticed. In contrast, some members of Elsje's subordination were distracted by her harsh-seeming personality to the point that they would trick themselves into not noticing her talent for maximizing their work efforts. But, if you don't mind me congratulating myself, eye-rolling reader, I'm pleased to say that I was quickly enjoying Mrs. Anders's intelligence so much that I stopped being nervous around her gruff persona. And I was proud of myself for reaching that feeling.

Meanwhile, two weeks into my time with Elsje as supervisor, she arrived at my office with a woman who looked to be residing somewhere in her mid-twenties. I immediately diagnosed the newcomer as my new—non-interim—supervisor.

"John," Elsje said, "this is Khiron Gamir…Khiron, this is John Smith."

"Hi," I said.

"Hello," Khiron replied with a subdued voice, as though we were two members of detention.

Surely my new boss wasn't going to be so low in confidence. Indeed, I now guessed her age to be closer to her early twenties.

"So," Elsje said, "Ms. Gamir will be temporarily using Mr. Williams' old office since I won't be needing it as much for the next while. Khiron needs her own space to work on an important project."

Khiron nodded glumly.

"Sounds good," I said, now officially relieved that the grumpy visitor wasn't my new boss, after all.

Twenty minutes later—after Elsje had given my new neighbour and me our instructions for the afternoon and left us alone to follow through—Khiron stopped by my office.

"Hey," she said with a now engaged tone, "do you like it down here?"

"It's fine," I said, hoping not to scare her away from the diatribe that she was clearly planning.

"Feels like we're rats in a cage," she obliged. "How can you stand it?"

"I guess I'm used to it. What don't you like about it?"

Khiron sighed. "Elsje's got me doing all this stuff—at least up there I could talk to people. Here, I feel like I'm like the school troublemaker, and she's keeping me away from the other *bad* kids."

"That sounds like her," I said, trying a smile

"What a cow," Khiron concluded, rolling her eyes.

"Oh ..." I said, feeling ambushed by the remark. In fact, I wasn't sure what to do with it; polite conversation called for me to agree with my co-worker's complaint about our boss's alleged bovine tendencies, but my loyalty to Elsje required me to be offended. After a moment's panicked thought, I decided to go with: "Yeah, I guess she can be tough, but I like her."

Khiron stared at me. "Hmm. Maybe she's easier on guys. You know how some women can be bitches to other women but nice to guys?"

"Maybe," I said, resisting the desire to point out that Chet the non-woman had received his share of crusty treatment from Elsje.

Khiron nodded again, and then—without a word—she left for Erik's office where I could vaguely hear her retrying out her new theory on him.

Unfortunately, Khiron was likely right that Elsje had removed her from her more populated work area to help her find more time for her actual work; that wouldn't have been so unfortunate if it weren't for the fact that Elsje had good reason to make such a decision. Khiron, I would soon learn, was in a constant state of needing to debrief her thoughts with her co-workers. Thus, with only half an hour left to go in the workday—in which I was rushing to complete a finicky task—I heard a loud sigh from my doorway. I looked up to make sure everything was okay.

"Hey," Khiron said, sighing again. "Can you believe it's only 4:30?—I feel like I've been here for ten hours."

"Um," I said, not sure how I could possibly lead the topic to a prompt conclusion. "Maybe it's because it's your first day in this new location?"

Khiron seemed to ponder that. "Hmm. Could be. Maybe you're right: normally, me and Harald hang out around now. He usually has a joke at the end of the day. I miss Harald."

"Yeah, that's too bad," I said.

"Do you mind if I sit down for a bit?" Khiron said, already heading for my guest chair.

"Um, sure," I said.

GOSSIPY NOTE: You may have noticed, watchful reader, that Khiron was a woman-type within my age range, and you might have observed that, normally, I let you know fairly quickly whether I considered having a crush on such a person. Good point. Unfortunately, from the start, I found Khiron to be a little too whiney for my romantic affection; nonetheless, she was nice and seemed interested in talking to me, so I considered developing a crush on her. However, I discovered soon into our conversations that she already had a boyfriend, so I felt there wasn't much point in trying to stretch my already flat feelings into a crush on an unavailable candidate.

Now, as much as I was glad to have a new friend to talk to, I learned over the next few days that Khiron had a knack for arriving in my office, ready for a long-winded visit, just when I was feeling most in synch with my work. Consequently, my dear friend and apartment neighbour, Elizabeth, suggested that I be honest with my colleague and let her know when I was busy with work—which was an excellent idea, but, unfortunately, it didn't sound like something that I would ever do. Instead, I started accommodating Khiron's conversation needs by chatting with her as long as she wanted and then extending my workdays to complete my tasks.

"Elsje's got you staying late, eh?" Khiron said as she was leaving, one especially busy-for-me day.

"Oh, not really," I said, "I just wanted to get this done before I left today."

Khiron tilted her head. "Why don't you just to do it tomorrow?"

"Well, Thursday's usually my busiest day, and I wanna have this out of the way."

"But, if you don't get your Thursday stuff done on Thursday, do it Friday."

"But then I'll be behind next week."

Khiron chuckled at that one. "Don't you mean you'll be behind on *Elsje's* schedule?"

"No, a lot of this is stuff I've always done."

Khiron raised a well-manicured eyebrow at me.

"It's fine, really," I said, "she might have me doing stuff I didn't do before, but she's also—"

"Why do you always defend her?"

"Because I like working for her."

Khiron seemed to ponder that. "Hmm. No, I don't think so. Are you a mama's boy, by any chance, John?"

"I don't think so."

"I think you *are*," Khiron said, grinning. "I think you're one of those guys who doesn't believe in insulting any woman *ever* no matter how bitchy she is."

"No, that's not the reason. No, I defend Elsje because—"

"Okay, so say something bad about her."

"I don't *have* anything bad to say about her."

"You don't or you won't?"

"Both."

Khiron nodded and was suddenly headed for Erik's office. "John's a mama's boy!" she led with a laugh.

I put my eavesdropper on full power to get Erik's reply, but I couldn't make it out, so my thoughts drifted to Khiron's accusation. *Was I unduly biased in favour of Elsje such that I let her push me around with extra work?* Perhaps I *had* let my pride in my pride in Elsje's excellence go to my head to the point that I no longer registered how much work she was assigning me. Oh well, I was enjoying myself either way.

The next day, Erik stopped by my office for what he presented to be a casual visit. I was less nervous than I ought to have been when I saw him standing in my entranceway. Since Chet's departure, I had noticed that Erik's personality was generally less abrasive. That is, without Chet's wild babbles there to pique Erik's irritation, my office neighbour seemed to feel less urgency than before to lecture his colleagues about how they could improve their ethics with his own.

"Hey, Erik," I replied to his lean into my doorway. "How's it going?"

"Good—what are you doing there?"

"Oh," I said, helping myself to a false sense of security, "Elsje wants me to cull the supplier list for stale contact information."

Erik nodded. "You know you're not required to do that stuff, right? It's not in your job description."

"Oh, well, I don't mind."

"John, that's a red herring. Anders doesn't have the right to make you do discretionary tasks."

"Oh, okay. Thanks for letting me know."

I was hoping that—by thanking Erik for his advice—he'd leave me alone about taking it.

"You're welcome," he said instead. "So what're you gonna say to Anders?"

"Um, I was thinking I wouldn't say *anything* to her."

My words left both Erik and me cringing—Erik at my words, themselves, and me at his impending response to them.

"John, you *have* to say something to Anders. Otherwise she's going to continue doing what she's doing."

"Yeah, um, that's okay with me."

Once again, Erik and I were not happy with me.

"Look, John, if you don't stand up for yourself, no one else will."

"Oh, okay, I'm actually okay with that—but thanks for looking out for me."

Erik sighed. "Do you want *me* to speak to Anders?"

That question seemed to me to be unfairly inconsistent with Erik's earlier promise that, if I didn't stand up for myself, no one else would.

"Um," I tried, "like you said, I should fight my own battles."

Erik sighed at me. "John, you know what: sometimes it's okay to ask people for help."

Erik had made a good point, so I looked around to see if there might be someone nearby who could remove Erik from my back. But there was no one. So I decided that there was only one thing left to do: I had to tell Erik the whole truth.

"Actually, you know what: I'm actually kind of happy doing extra work for Elsje. I feel like I'm, I don't know, genuinely useful, which is unusual for me."

Erik was clearly not pleased with my use of the truth against him.

"You know what," he said, "I'm not telling you this for *my* benefit. Why should I care if Anders takes advantage of you? You can be her indentured servant if you want to be."

I was about to thank Erik for his understanding, but it was quickly apparent that he wasn't finished contradicting himself.

"The reason I care," he said, softening his tone again, "is because certain rights are inalienable."

"Sorry, what's 'inalienable' mean again?"

"It means the rights are yours whether you want them or not."

"But I thought you said I could be Mrs. Anders' *servant* if I wanted to be."

Erik's face hardened. "I was speaking *rhetorically*, John."

Erik seemed to have an answer for every contradiction. And so, just as in the Chet times, I felt overwhelmed by him. There was once again only one thing left to do: it was time to try a lie.

"Maybe you're right," I said, impersonating a smile as my words slid out through my teeth. "I think I *will* ask Elsje to cut my workload."

"*Okay*," Erik said, "now you're thinking like an individual organism with his own agency."

"Yes. Thank you for your advice, Erik."

We both smiled—it seemed we were both content with my non-truthful words: they had brought us together where my honest phrases had failed.

Now, interested reader, I've discovered that the problem with lies is that they are demanding. Once you give life to a lie, you constantly have to take care of it and make sure that nothing upsets it.

I did my best to keep my lie to Erik (that I would stop working hard) protected. I tried as much as I could to make it seem as though I had discontinued the silly business of working above and beyond the call of job description. So, while some employees might play computer games and then quickly transfer to important business as soon as a boss came around a corner, I found myself focused on work-related matters only to try to cover them up when my co-workers appeared.

It was a tiring battle that often continued past the confines of 9 to 5. On days that I would stay late—instead of admitting that I was going to remain behind for an hour or two to pay the company back for time visited with Khiron—I told my neighbours that I'd just be a few minutes behind them after they left the building.

A week or two into that deceptive existence, I was pleased with my success rate of getting things done without getting caught. As

I meditated upon that boastful conclusion on my bus ride home on a Thursday evening, we passed the poorest neighbourhood of the city; there, in the mouth of an alleyway, I spotted two women fighting. One of them reached her fist back and punched the other in the chest. Her victim grabbed onto her assaulter's arms, and the two of them became a violent clench until the first tried to get an arm free for another punch.

At that moment, I noticed my face heating up, and I realized that I was existing in the same time and place as the two women in my window.

I reached up and yanked the request-stop wire. I should have asked the driver to let me out closer to the battle, but, as ever, I was too timid to make such a simple request. So we continued on past the alley, and I lost my view of the fight. My heart rate increased; the danger to the participants seemed greater when I couldn't see them. A block and half later, I ran out of the bus. My adrenalin made me feel lighter of weight and head. I didn't know what I was going to do when I made it to the scene. I tried to slow my breathing so that I would be less likely to make a rash mistake, but that only seemed to make my heart want to move faster. I soon arrived at the corner, took in another futile deep breath, and turned into the alleyway. And there I found no one. They were already gone.

Even though I'll never know specifically what I would have done if I'd gotten to those two women in time to do something, I was pleased with myself for the sincerity of my effort. Yet, forgive the needs of my ego, embarrassed-for-me reader, but I felt a smidge disappointed that I was the only who knew that I had tried to intervene. I then scolded myself for sullying the sincerity of my initial impulse. That made me feel better, and I decided not to tell anyone about my phantom attempt to protect the two women from each other.

Strangely, the secret knowledge of what I had attempted to do provoked me to believe that I could be more confident when visiting with Erik and Khiron.

The next day at work—Friday—Khiron wandered into my office, plunked herself into a chair, and leaned in towards me for whispered conversation.

"Hey, do you know if Erik's gay?"

"Um," I said, nervous about providing Erik's answer. (I'd never witnessed him indicate any secrecy on the matter, but I wasn't sure if he would feel differently in a case where he wasn't involved in the conversation). "I think so—why?"

"I was thinking of setting him up with my friend, Pete—I think they'd totally hit it off."

"Oh, well, Erik's in a relationship, so—"

"Hey!" a loud-but-grinning Erik voice suddenly came around the corner. "What's with all the whispering? You guys talking about me?"

"Yes," Khiron said.

"Really? In what regard?"

"*In regard* to me trying to set you up on a date."

"Is that so? And with what gender?"

"This awesome guy in Head Office—"

"Okay, and how'd you know I was gay?"

"John told me."

"Um—" I said, panicking as Erik looked me over.

"Why'd you tell her that?"

"Um, because she asked me."

"Fair enough," Erik said, returning his eyes to Khiron. "So why didn't you come to me if you wanted to know?"

"Because I wanted the setup to be a surprise."

"You still could've asked, though, without—"

Khiron shrugged. "Oh well—it's all moot now. John says you're already taken."

"I'm afraid so. Out with it, please. Who'd you have in mind for me?"

"Peter Brookstarte from my old department."

"The full-figured guy with glasses?"

"No, that's Harald: he's straight."

"I don't think so."

"No, really, I helped him write his online profile—and it was for women."

"And you really think it's going to be that challenging for him to switch the genders after you've left his computer?"

"I guess not, but he would've told me."

"Coming out isn't as easy as it may look to you," Erik said with a smile. "You'd be surprised how many people don't tell all their friends."

Khiron shrugged.

"So which one's Peter then?" Erik said.

"Okay: Peter's kind of short, but he's really cute and really smart."

"Brown hair, dresses really well?"

"Yeah, he always dresses perfect."

"Not my type," Erik said, "but he might be Joshua's type, so I'll let you know if we ever break up."

"Okay," Khiron said laughing, only to take Erik seriously. "So are you guys thinking of breaking up?"

Erik gave a prolonged eye roll and sigh, but interrupted himself as a newcomer arrived in our conversation.

"Hello, Elsje," he said, smiling behind Khiron.

"Mr. Tham," Mrs. Anders said. "Ms. Gamir."

"Hi," Khiron said.

"How's it going?" Erik said, looking cheerfully at my interim boss.

"I am well, thank you," Elsje said, with a forced smile, before pausing for the appropriate amount of time necessary to give the sentiment its moment. "Well, if you'll excuse us, John and I have some work to discuss."

Erik nodded and took a step towards leaving. But, before he could let himself go, he decided he should remind Elsje of her own inalienable rights.

"You know, Elsje, you work too hard. I don't recall ever seeing you stopping and giving yourself a chance to catch your breath."

Elsje smiled to herself. "Thank you, Erik. It's nice to know that I don't have to work so hard—*what a relief.* There I was rather worried because the payroll department has discovered a glitch. I had thought I was going to have to work hard to fix the trouble—to make sure that everyone received their cheques on time for this weekend. What a relief that I don't have to worry about that. Thank you again, Erik."

Erik looked startled. "I wasn't aware of that—perhaps I can be of use?"

Elsje smiled, almost sheepishly. "That's all right, Erik. It's not in your job description to help me with payroll. I wouldn't want either of us to get in trouble."

"All right, but, if you come across a way in which I can be of service, please let me know."

As Khiron and a bewildered-looking Erik left my working area, Elsje smiled again at my dispersing neighbour. Once he was out of hearing, she looked with more interest than usual at my computer. She saw a screen that was no longer pointed at the assignment she'd asked me to focus my morning on.

"Was there a problem with the L figures?"

"Oh, no, it's just that Erik was here and, um ..." I needed a good lie to cover up the embarrassing fact that I was hiding my work from Erik. But nothing clever came to dull mind. "Sorry," I said instead, "I had to show Erik something."

"Erik was interested in your S-database?"

As I said before, recalling reader, creating a lie is a big responsibility. Once it's born, you have to be able to give it a proper upbringing. But I couldn't think of a way to justify why Erik—a non-database user—would want to see my S-database. So, right or wrong, I decided that the pressure was just too great, and I gave up my lie for detection.

"It's just that—even though I really *like* doing the work that you assign me—it can be, you know, a bit tiring trying to explain to my, you know, work neighbours why I'm doing it since it's not, um, you know, *technically* in my job description."

Elsje smiled.

I assumed, of course, that it was a sarcastic communication designed to mock my whining.

"It's not like I'm complaining about the work," I started babbling. "I've learned a lot from—"

"John," Elsje said, "you're one of a kind."

"Why?"

"You're the only person I'm aware of who would feel guilty that he was hiding how much work he was doing."

Wow. Using the truth on Elsje had worked much better than it had on Erik.

Chapter 38
Dullard in Transit II

The Math Suitor

I was in a pleased-with-the-universe mood after work that day as my bus picked up its tired but eager Friday evening commuters. I sat solo in a sideways-facing three-person seat with my canvassing supplies piled on my lap so that I could calculate the previous night's take, which I was planning to celebrate with Elizabeth over our Friday night game of Yahtzee.

The bus lurched to an aggressive impromptu stop just then, causing my canvassing nametag to jump from my legs to the floor; I retrieved the renegade item and then watched out the window as a pair of teenagers rushed to catch up to the waiting vehicle. Normally, their subsequently loud, giggling entry and lack of acknowledging of our driver for stopping out of our way would have irritated me, but, on this occasion, my good mood was too sturdy to be overtaken by a small bout of ungraciousness.

I have to admit, though, that my content mindset was a wee bit infringed upon when the teenagers (one from each sex) joined me in my three-seater seat as they continued celebrating their bus-chasing victory. They were so noisy that I had little choice but to eavesdrop on their shared babble, and I soon became embarrassed on their behalf as I discovered that they conversed with each other as if they were playing a game of football. Apparently, the object of their game was for each conversational contestant to carry the discussion for as long as possible without being stopped by the other.

"The thing is, Dmitri," the she-teenager eventually said, "I'm like fine with socials and English, but I can't do math. I don't know what's wrong with me."

She'd formulated her statement well, but, unfortunately, at the end of it, she'd made a fatal pause. Dmitri quickly spotted the error and intercepted the conversation.

"It's weird," he said, "because I'm totally good at math. I don't even have to study—I just always get good grades."

Tragically, Dmitri fumbled over his words just then, and so the she teenager took over again.

"I just think I'm too stupid to do math," she said, looking out the window with a sad tilt to her face.

Once again, her rival spotted the weakness immediately and regained the floor.

"I don't know why it is—I just don't ever need to study for math. I always get these awesome marks no matter what I do."

The game went on for a minute in that fashion until finally the crowd (namely me) nearly erupted at Dmitri, 'Can't you see that your friend's upset and that your unstudied-for A's just make her feel worse? Would it be so hard to take your head out of your ego and just listen for a minute?'

Of course, I didn't have the social courage to say any of that, but it was the thought that counted, and—when Dmitri finally got off the bus at his stop and waved back to his beaten opponent—I silently booed him.

While I was making my dislike for Dmitri unknown, a woman sat in his old spot. The remaining teenager didn't seem to notice her new neighbour; instead, she stared with bored fascination at her school bag. I silently consoled her to myself, but my unspoken words went unheard, and soon her eyes looked blurry with near tears. There was clearly nothing that could be done to revive the girl. But, strangely, a voice from the other side of her interrupted the hopeless moment.

"For what it's worth," the voice said, "I wasn't good at high school math either."

Those intriguing words provoked my eyes to fly around my neighbour: I discovered that the purveyor of them was a professional-looking woman near my age whom I recognized as a regular on the late-from-work bus.

"Really?" my teary-eyed friend mustered through her throat.

"Yup," the professional woman said. "And, not for nothing, but I'm now a research chemist for Nordmark Industries."

"Really?" the teenager said again, dabbing her eyes.

"*Really*," said the woman. "Math just wasn't for me in school. But the thing they don't tell you is that—once you leave high school—you don't really have to do much math if you don't want to."

"Seriously?"

"Yup, unless your job is math-specific, you don't really need the fancy bits."

"You serious?" the girl said. "You're making that up."

"No, I'm not that creative," the woman replied with a cheerful voice. "But—not to be nosy—but do you know what you wanna do after you graduate?"

"I'm gonna be a gym teacher."

"Great, so—forgive my ignorance—but whaddya need math for if you're gonna teach P.E.?"

'She needs it to get into college, doesn't she?' I asked internally.

"I need it to get into university, don't I?" the teenager agreed.

"Oh, well, sure, you need a decent *mark* in math to get into university—*sure*. But my point is you don't have to be *good* at math to get in."

"But," the teenager and I asked (me internally, her aloud), "don't you need to be good at math to get a good mark?"

"Not at all," the woman declared. "To get a good mark, you just have to learn enough tricks so you can do it. If you know the tricks, then even math-challenged people like us can do the stuff. You want me to show you a few of the tricks that got me through?"

"Yeah, that'd be awesome," the teenager said, opening her colourful knapsack.

Meanwhile, I didn't want to rush to judgment, but I couldn't help considering the possibility that the research chemist might be worthy of becoming my next crush. Even though I had no justification to introduce myself to her, she was a frequent fellow traveller on my bus route, so—with time—it was possible that we could form a familiarity with each other that might eventually lead to an introductory conversation about the weather.

SHALLOW NOTE: Oh, and in case you're interested, shallow reader, the research chemist was of median appearance and possessed an intriguing smile that comfortably put her within my attraction range.

"See what I mean?" our teenager friend said, staring at a text book that now identified her as *Jen*. "I totally don't get what I'm supposed to be doing with these."

"Oh, those're no big deal," the mathly woman said. "You're just combining agreed upon truths to prove not-yet-agreed-upon truths. Like here: working backwards, what would you need to *know* in order to prove that these two angles *must* be equal?"

"It's so retarded," her student said. "Why can't I just use the protractor?"

"Well, you *could*, but imagine if you were on a deserted island, and you *really* needed to know if two angles were congruent—but you didn't have a protractor—what then, my friend? What then?"

Jen and I giggled.

"Okay," our tutor/crush said, "so a proof is like an instruction manual—except, instead of step-by-step procedures showing you how to build an Ikea cabinet, you're creating, like, a step-by-step procedure for how we can *know* some mathematical fact."

"I don't get it," Jen said with well-practiced frustration. "The angles are *obviously* the same—why do we need a stupid step-by-step procedure to know that?"

"Well…" the math tutor said, "it's like this: your name is *Jen*, right?"

"Yeah, so?"

"*Prove it.*"

"Why?"

"Just try it—what evidence do you have that could prove your name's Jen?"

"Well, I have I.D.—my student card."

"May I see it, please?"

I smiled as Jen reluctantly took her school bus pass out of her bag.

"Nice picture," the tutor said, "but how do *I* know this picture's you?"

"Ah, it kinda *looks* like me."

"True, but how do I know that it's not your sister's picture—maybe she *also* looks like you."

"I don't have a sister."

"But *I* don't know that," the math tutor said with a smile.

Jen stared at my new crush. "Well, check out my neck—I have a little scar here, and you can see it in the picture."

The math tutor grinned. "*Okay*, now we're getting into evidence—that's a useful piece of information. But, first, how do I know you haven't painted the scar mark on your neck to make it look like your sister's real scar?"

Jen laughed. "I don't know." But then she licked her thumb. "See, it doesn't come off."

"All right," the tutor said, "so the *proof* that your name is Jen is this: (1) you have a picture of someone named Jen who looks like you—that's given. (2) The girl in the picture has a cute scar mark on her neck—that's also given. (3) You have what looks like a matching scar on your neck—that we know from sneaking a peek at your neck. And (4) we know that the thing that looks like a scar is real because it won't rub off—this we extrapolated from your saliva-on-thumb test."

Jen and I giggled again.

"So," the tutor said, "we may conclude—by the law of scar identification—that *you* are Jen."

"That's retarded," Jen said with a roll-of-the-eyes smile.

"True enough," the tutor said, "—but does it makes any sense? All you're doing with a proof is taking agreed upon facts to prove something not yet agreed upon. So, to prove that your name was Jen, you couldn't just *tell* me it was. You had to use facts that I could accept without having to take your word of it—does that make any sense?"

Jen shrugged. "I guess."

"You know, my friend," the math tutor said with a grin, "it's okay to just lie and tell me I've been incredibly helpful."

Jen and I laughed, but this time I accidentally went above private chuckle volume, which, in turn, led Jen to look at me with a sneer.

Normally, I would have pretended that my giggle was the result of a coincidental bit of internal humour, but Jen was staring at me, and I couldn't see her approving such a flimsy excuse.

"Sorry," I mustered instead. "I couldn't help overhearing."

Jen didn't seem impressed with that, so I glanced over at her tutor for a second opinion.

Apparently the instructor didn't like it either because she wore a smirking look of disdain.

"It's not nice to eavesdrop," she said.

"Sorry," I said, feeling my face drain itself of colour.

"That's okay," the math tutor said, before forcing a chuckle as I turned my attention back out the window.

I ignored the laugh and began rethinking my plan to marry its owner. Although, in her defense, she was probably right: I *shouldn't* have been eavesdropping—or, better put, I shouldn't have done something that would reveal it. So I decided that the little feud between us could be overcome, and I could hold onto my crush a little longer.

Not long later, though, the math tutor reached up and pulled the request-stop wire; as she did so, I spotted on her hand evidence of a wedding ring. Oh well. It was a fun crush while it lasted.

"Good luck, my friend," the woman said as she stood up.

"Thanks for helping," Jen replied with a smile.

As I watched that exchange with a stupid grin on my mouth, the math tutor—probably sensing the heat on her face from my eyes—glanced my way. Luckily, I anticipated her, and I looked away before she could confirm my stare.

After the math tutor's departure from our shared carriage, I watched Jen (through the reflection in the window opposite us) for the next few moments as she worked slowly through her homework. Clearly the mini-lesson that she had received would not instantly turn her into a mathematician, but Jen seemed to now realize that math wasn't some number-breathing dragon that was out to get her. And so, as ever, I wished for a personality like the math tutor's that would allow me to make such a dent in others' troubles.

Chapter 39
Dullard in Conversation III

Gossipping Success

In the week that followed my admission to Elsje of my Erik deception, she seemed more interested in me. Of course, she continued to make me work just as hard as always, but it came to be that she would usually talk to me for a couple minutes before she would assign me my work for the day. ("How are you today, John?" she might ask for no reason at all.) And her assignments started to seem more like suggestions than instructions—suggestions that had to be done, but it was my option *when* exactly to do them.

It was a fulfilling feeling. I felt as though I'd earned my boss's friendlier demeanour. Apparently, she didn't mind treating her employees like drones so long as her employees disliked her for it; but, since I was clearly a fan, she seemed to feel honour-bound to be nice to me.

At first, as I was getting used to Elsje's friendlier way with me, it was just she who asked me non-work-related questions, but soon I got bored of me, so I started asking Elsje about her Head Office existence. The result would scare the dullard out of me.

I'd had Elsje pegged as a hardnosed efficiency expert who ran her Ambiguous operation with pristine order. But, upon getting to interview Elsje, I came to realize that—underneath her tough presentation—there lay a squishy heart belonging to a five-time spoiling grandmother who spoke of her grandchildren with the sort of biased approval that could only be the result of genuine affection. Indeed, I was further surprised to learn that Elsje was planning to retire soon with grand hopes to visit more with her growing grand-family.

But that wasn't even Elsje's most startling revelation.

On a Thursday afternoon, she arrived in my office with a more serious tone than I had become used to of late.

"How are you, John?"

"Good, how are *you*?" I said, sensing that that was where the intriguing information would be.

"I'm well, thank you," she said with a wisp of a sigh.

I hesitated for a moment but then dove in. "Rough day in Head Office?"

"No, it's been okay, but I appreciate you asking."

Elsje was now wearing a serious smile, so I subdued my curiosity temporarily so that I wouldn't scare her away.

I waited until our next visit before I again inquired about life in Head Office. But Elsje was still evasive. The only detail I could obtain from her was that she had assigned a simple project to an underling, identified only as Mr. Litke. I flattered myself that I heard some irritation in her voice as she described Litke's interaction with his task.

"Litke," she concluded, "is going to have to be rather determined if he's going to manage the project effectively. There are certain obstacles to one's concentration involved in this endeavour, so I hope he'll be able to keep his wits about him."

I was nearly certain that Elsje did not respect Litke's wits.

I spent my Friday evening bus ride home feeling tentatively honoured that Elsje seemed to be on the precipice of including me in the details of her frustration.

Many minutes into those ponderings, the person next to me got off the bus, and someone else took the spot.

"Hey there," the newcomer said.

I looked over to find the face of the math tutor from the previous week.

"Oh, *hi*," I said.

She shrugged. "I think we work in the same building."

"Really? But ..." I was about to say that I thought she was 'a research chemist from Nordmark Industries,' but I preempted myself with a realization that such an observation would prove that, not only had I been eavesdropping on her, but also that I'd memorized a portion of her transcript. So, instead, I just offered a bonus, "*Really?*"

"Yup," she said with a sheepish-seeming face, "or, at least, I saw you leaving Ambiguity, so I just kind of assumed—I hope you don't mind?"

I wasn't sure if she was meaning to be funny, so I took her seriously. "Oh, yeah, no, you're totally right, I *do* work there—so you work there too?"

"Yup," she said, scrunching her lips in apparent thought. "But, yeah, um, you may have heard me telling that girl, Jen, last week that I'm a research chemist."

"Right, yeah," I said, activating my own sheepish face and voice, "sorry, I guess I *was* eavesdropping."

"Well, you shouldn't feel bad about that, my friend. It was my fault for being so interesting."

That made me laugh out loud.

The math tutor shrugged again with a half-smile. "Not for nothing, but I felt bad when I said *it wasn't nice of you to eavesdrop.* I was actually just trying to be funny when I said that."

"Oh, *how?*"

"Well, it's just that *I* had eavesdropped on Jen's conversation—that's how I got to talking to her in the first place—so I thought it was funny that I was telling *you* not to do the same."

"Oh, *wow*—I totally missed that. That makes total sense. Sorry, I didn't pick up on that."

"No, that's okay. Sometimes my humour's an acquired taste."

"Yeah, that must be annoying when people take you literally."

"Right?!" the math tutor said. "I always end up looking either like a complete bitch or a total idiot ..." she paused, perhaps recalling that I was the originating villain of our topic. "So that happens to you too?"

"Oh, not really—I'm not funny."

The tutor laughed.

That made me smile. "No, really, I'm not funny."

"Oh, you're serious?"

"Yeah, kind of."

"But ... so then—not to psychoanalyze—but how then do you know how annoying it is to have people take you literally?"

"Oh, yeah, fair question," I said, sending my eyes skyward to retrieve the answer. "Well, probably because of my brother. He jokes a lot, and a lot of people—including our own dad—think he's being serious a lot of the time."

"Hmm," the math tutor said, looking at me with eyes that seemed intrigued, "so, if you're not funny, then you're observant."

"I don't know about *that*," I said, delighted by the possibility.

"Well, it's gotta be one or the other."

"Hmm, that's a tough choice, then."

The math tutor laughed.

I felt a tingle to jump around my stomach.

And then, without warning, the woman offered me her hand. "I'm Jacklyn, by the way."

"I'm John," was my witty reply.

As I shook her hand, I was reminded of the wedding ring attached to it.

"So where do you work at Ambiguity?" Jacklyn the math tutor interrupted my pondering.

"Oh, um, I'm in Applications—how about you?"

"I'm in Development in Head Office."

"Really? But ...so you're not a research chemist *at all*, then?"

"Exactly," Jacklyn said, a smile starting at her chin and creeping up her face, "the thing is—well, the research chemist thing—that was actually, well, to be honest, that was a *lie*—I just made it up."

"Why would you make that up?" I said, not meaning to be so judgemental but too baffled to conceive of another question.

"Well, first of all, not for nothing, but I assumed that our mutual friend Jen would be more impressed by a bad math student turned chemist than what I actually do at Ambiguity, but also, um, well, yeah, that's it."

"But also *what*?" I said, feeling oddly comfortable interrogating the stranger.

Jacklyn sighed. "I shouldn't be admitting this to someone I don't know, but you seem, well, anyway, the fact of the matter is I have this little hobby where, every once in a while, I like to tell people things that aren't technically true, just to see how it feels."

"Oh ...*why*?"

"It's just there's something—I don't know—not to overly dramatize, but maybe it's the rush of seeing if I can get away it."

"But what about—"

"I know, I know," Jacklyn said, smiling, "it's bad to lie—*wash my mouth out with soap*—but it's so much fun. And it's not like I lie in the classically immoral ways—you know, to cheat someone or to get a job or something. I just enjoy making things up to see if I can pull it off."

"That's, um, unusual," I said, with few other thoughts to choose from.

"*Unusual* in a bad way?"

"Of course not," I blurted, not sure if I believed me. "It's just not something I've heard of before, so it seems strange."

"*Strange* in a good way, then?"

I laughed again. "Um, no, just sort of strange in a neutral way."

"That's fair," Jacklyn said. "*Neutral's* probably as good as I could hope for at this point." And then she sighed and smiled sheepishly at me. Evidently she thought it was my turn to say something.

I looked around frantically for inspiration, but—seeing only the bus—I went with, "Do you like this bus route?"

"Actually, I *do*," Jacklyn the math tutor said cheerfully as though I hadn't just asked a bafflingly boring question. "It's good for ..." and she mouthed the words, "*people watching.*"

"Agreed," I said. "*And eavesdropping.*"

Jacklyn laughed. "Exactly! Anyway, this is my stop. I'm sure we'll run into each other again on this entertaining route."

"Sounds good," I said, grinning stupidly.

As I walked home a few minutes later, I realized that—despite her wedding ring—I had no choice but to reinstate my crush on Jacklyn the math tutor. Don't worry, puritanical reader, I had no intention of trying to bring my crush to life. But it would be fun to have a fresh affection to contemplate; as my friend Tally had once argued, a crush is a great testing ground for one's hopes without necessarily being a literal impersonation of the future.

"So," Elizabeth asked me a couple hours later during a game of Yahtzee, "anything exciting happen today, dear?"

"Actually, yeah," I said, "I think Elsje's on the verge of cracking and may soon let me in on some gossip."

"What sort of gossip?"

"Well, I'm pretty sure that she doesn't like one of her employees—this guy named Litke."

"Well, that's unfortunate."

"Yes, but I kind of feel honoured that she's even hinting to me her dislike for someone. She's so professional and never talks badly about anyone."

"You're probably right, dear. That's definitely a sign that she values you and trusts you, but do be careful of getting mixed up in company politics."

That felt like a reprimand of my gossip enjoyment, so I reached for a legitimate topic.

"And also," I said, "I may have made a friend on the bus."

"Really?" Elizabeth said, her eyes perking up. "A young lady, perhaps?"

"Yeah, it's actually someone from Ambiguity. I didn't know she worked there. But she recognized me and started up a conversation."

"Really?" Elizabeth said, eyes and voice still perked.

"Yeah, but, for the record, she's married, so ..."

"Oh, too bad," Elizabeth said, reengaging her shields, "but it'll be nice for you to have a friend your own age to talk to."

"I guess," I said, offended on Elizabeth's behalf by her self-rebuking insinuation.

The following Monday, Elsje arrived in my office seeming cheerful.

"Good afternoon, John."

"Good afternoon. So how're things going up there today?"

"Very well," Elsje said with the slightest of smirks.

"Did something funny happen?"

"Oh, it's just Litke—his job, as you know, is to apply the technical aspects of the law that I lay down. And, to be completely frank, he's rather interesting to work with because, well, one never knows what he might lend to a project in the way of ... this is off the record, John."

"Of course," I said, trying not to look too eager. "So *one never knows what Litke might lend to a project in the way of...?*"

"Well, you see, Litke is the sort of gentleman who very much likes to celebrate his accomplishments. He is not particularly creative in the completion of the tasks I assign him, but, in the getting credit for them, he has more talent than anyone I've witnessed before."

I tried to camouflage my enjoyment of the description.

"Like how?" I said, as casually as I could.

"Well, since you ask: today, for instance, he spent the afternoon asking his co-workers to look over his work to make sure it was working—the fact that he and I had already tested it did not dampen his spirits in that regard. Instead, he was pleased to ask his colleagues to double-check his work to see how wonderfully it was working."

Without my permission, I felt myself chuckling at the description.

On cue, Elsje's face became serious. "Now, John, like I said, this is off the record. I only mentioned it because you are in a different department than Litke—I shouldn't have brought it up in the first place."

"Of course," I said. "I won't say anything to anyone."

I did not pry any further that afternoon.

I spent my walk to the bus feeling honoured that Elsje had officially included me in her chiding of Litke from afar. Elsje was as dignified a person as I knew, and it seemed to me that she would only share such a gossipy conversation with someone whose discretion she maximally trusted. I couldn't imagine a bigger compliment from my new mentor.

As I grinned goofily about that while I waited in line for the bus, a voice came up behind me. It was Jacklyn the math tutor again.

"Hey," she said.

"Oh, hi, how are you?"

"Good, care to share a bus?"

"Sure," I said as the lineup started to move.

We then had a hearty awkward silence as we boarded the vehicle and found a pair of forward-facing seats.

"*So* ..." I said, "how was life in Head Office Development today?"

"Good—actually," Jacklyn said, converting to a whisper, "not to namedrop, but [Jon Famous] visited Ambiguity this morning."

"Really? I like Jonathan Famous."

"Yeah, so did I. But you'll never guess who got to show him around Ambiguity."

"Was it you?"

"Oh," Jacklyn replied, looking disappointed.

"Sorry," I said, "—was that bad to say?"

"Well, it's just that I thought you wouldn't be able to guess."

I laughed. "Oh, sorry about that."

"That's fine. You can't help it if you're a good guesser."

"Right," I said, giggling some more. "So what was Jon Famous like?"

"You tell me—you're the one with all the guesses."

"Okay," I said, still giggling. "Was he nice?"

"Yes."

"Was he ...smart?"

"Yes."

"Funny?"

"No!" Jacklyn cheered. "So we're not as a great a guesser as we thought, are we?"

"I guess not," I said with a chuckle.

"Touché," Jacklyn said, which was a false accusation since my 'guess'-referencing reply was the result of coincidence, not wit.

"So, anyway," I said, "you were saying about Jon Famous ..."

"Right—Jon Famous: actually, he seems like a nice guy, but he seemed—you know that song by Jewel where she says something about her boyfriend being 'fashionably sensitive, but too *cool* to really care.'"

"No, but I like it."

"Me too," Jacklyn said, "and, not for nothing, but Mr. Famous seemed like he was trying *very hard* to say all the right things, but I just didn't get the sense that he was actually interested in anything I was telling him. Like I would slip in little jokes, and maybe they weren't funny, but he never really noticed that I was kidding. Instead, he'd just nod and say his usual, 'That's interesting' to something ridiculous."

"Yeah, that's so annoying," I said, feeling the words arrive on my lips without my mind testing them first. "I feel like sometimes people aren't stupid ...they're just ...lazy."

"Yeah, *maybe* ..."Jacklyn said, seeming to ponder. "That's a good point, actually. That's probably why it makes me so mad. He's being *lazy* in how he treats people."

"Yeah, exactly," I said, delighted to have played a part in provoking such a rant from my new crush/friend.

After Jacklyn the math tutor exited the bus, I realized that her wedding ring was allowing me to relax and be my least boring self around her.

On Tuesday afternoon, I decided to see if Elsje wanted to compliment me further with more gossip.

"So anything new today in Head Office?" I asked.

"*As a matter of fact,*" Elsje said. "As you may know, I'm retiring soon, and I believe we've chosen my replacement today."

"Really?" I said, suddenly discontent. "I didn't realize you were that close to leaving. When are you going?"

"As soon as I'm confident my replacement is ready."

"Right, I *guess*—so how long do you think that'll take?"

"Well, for now, I'll be auditioning Mr. Zhang; once I have an idea of which parts of his resume were exaggerated—and so require training to make up the difference—I'll set the date for my final departure."

"Right, that makes sense."

"And the exciting news is, once Zhang masters our systems, I think he'll point the department in directions that I would never have conceived."

As Elsje said so, I sensed sadness in her voice, so I decided to Chet us to a new subject.

"Right," I said, "so, um, did Litke do anything funny today?"

Elsje smiled. "You know, I greatly appreciate working with him—it's rather nice to collaborate with someone who never conceives his own ideas."

"Oh, but wouldn't it be better if he *did?*"

"Yes, were I the sort of person who could see the world from any other viewpoint than my own, then I'd love to have some other people's good ideas kicking about. But the fact of the matter is the reason I'm effective is because I do what I know. If I were to use someone else's ideas, I might have to adjust my entire methodology. I'm afraid I really don't know where that would take us."

"But … sorry, wouldn't your system benefit from other people's ideas, like, in the long run?"

"Certainly, but I'm afraid I'm set in my ways. And, as a consequence, Mr. Litke's lack of creativity is rather perfect for me. I don't have to worry about him challenging me with new ideas. And, to be completely frank, Litke is rather conceited and dishonest. But I can deal with that: so long as I assign him tasks that he thinks will impress his peers, and—so long as I give him credit for devising my ideas—he'll do exactly as I tell him. But, if he were inventing all sorts of innovative ways of doing things, I really wouldn't know what to do with him." Elsje paused just then to restate the obvious. "This is all off the record, John."

"Of course, but what about your replacement? He's innovative, you said."

"Yes, but he's *replacing* me. I don't require him to do things my way after I leave."

"Right, I guess," I said with a simulated chuckle because the re-mentioning of Elsje's exit had me selfishly wondering what was going to happen to *me* after she left. "So …" I said, "is Mr. Zhang going to come down and be *my* boss too?"

"No," Elsje said with a generous smile. "He won't be your boss."

"Oh, I guess not. I guess he'll just be working solely in Head Office, not on this small Applications' stuff."

My words were correct in the matter, but my thoughts were disappointed in it (Zhang, after all, sounded like a good potential boss).

"Zhang," Elsje said, "is not going to replace me in Applications because I've found someone *else* to replace me as your boss."

"Who?"

Elsje smiled.

I stared back at her.

"John," Elsje said, "*you* are going to replace me as your boss."

"How?" I said, too startled to be gracious.

"You already do all my interim work down here, John. I've just been supervising—as of next month, you will take over as your own supervisor."

"Wow, really?" I said, feeling a mixture of surprise and concern (that I'd misheard Elsje). "You think I'm qualified for that?"

"Of course you are. You'll do wonderfully—and you'll get a substantial raise for your trouble."

"Wow, thank you," I said, blushing pink.

"Don't thank me—you're the one who's earned it."

"Oh ...thank you."

Elsje laughed. "You're welcome."

After that meeting, I sat stunned in my office, which unfortunately was noticed by Erik as he walked past.

"Hey, John—everything all right?"

"Oh, yeah, thanks. How about you?"

"I'm fine, but you look like you've had an encounter with Hamlet's ghost."

"Oh, no, I was just surprised by something."

"Wanna talk about it?"

"Um, no thanks," I said (after all, I wasn't sure whether Erik would approve of my promotion).

"What's going on?" Khiron said, coming around the corner as she always did when Erik got clogged in my entranceway.

"Nothing much," Erik said. "We're just examining our weekend prospects."

Khiron had a lot of thoughts about that, so we spent nearly an hour comparing plans.

Chapter 40
Dullard vs. Regret II

For Old Times' Shake

On the bus ride home that evening, I noticed that my stomach was still squeamish with the news of my promotion. I decided to calm my valves by getting off the bus early to walk the second half of the commute. A few blocks along that calming plan, I spotted a short-haired woman. The short hair turned to the side and revealed a face that was similar to that of a less-short-haired girl whom I'd known and loved in elementary and high school. It was Ashley. She had a mild smile on her face and a fast pace on her feet that made her seem occupied with her life—she probably didn't have time to check in with a long lost admirer. Although—unless evil Jake was lying to me—she was married now. *What could I lose by talking to her?*

"Hey, Ashley!" I called out with a frog nestled in my throat.

A confused face turned and looked at me.

I smiled.

She squinted.

"It's John, from school," I said, suddenly wondering if I'd dreamt the whole thing.

"John—*of course*," she said, grinning to my relief before she went in for a hug.

"How are you?" I said once the cautious embrace was concluded.

"Great, how are you?"

"I'm okay. I just got promoted at work."

DEFENSIVE NOTE: Please understand, eyebrow-raised reader, that I didn't offer the above remark as a boast; instead, I was utilizing it as a means of filling my words with some sort of content.

"That's awesome," Ashley said. "Where do you work?"

We chatted casually for several minutes about our careers before exchanging email addresses. Ashley, it seemed, was not emotionally affected by my sudden reappearance in her life. She presented no awkwardness whatsoever. Perhaps she had forgotten about our wasn't-to-be relationship.

"Well," she said, "I'm actually late—but, yeah, let's make sure we catch up soon."

"Yeah, sounds good," I said.

Ashley smiled magnificently and started to turn away from me.

"Hey," I said, "can I just ask one more question?"

"Sure," she said with her famously playful smile, "—but only one."

"Is it true that you married Andrei?"

The playful smile turned surprised yet sweet. "I did, indeed. How'd you hear that?"

"Jake Richport told me."

Ashley shuddered from forehead to toe. "I almost forgot about that psychopath—I wish you hadn't heard it from him."

"Me too. Well, you have to go."

"Right, thanks, see you soon!"

As my never-to-be love smiled merrily in departure, I felt a constriction in my chest. The cheeriness with which she mentioned her marriage was proof to me that I'd never even been near her romantic contemplation.

IDIOTIC NOTE: My incorrigible ghostwriter, however, has just laughed at my reasonable conclusion above: he says that Ashley had had many years and a husband to get over her once 'obvious' feelings for me. But that's clearly a foolish argument: all the clichés I've ever read tell us that you never fully let go of your first love. To that, my ghostwriter says he never said Ashley was in love with me—just that she had a crush. But that's just stupid.

Not to worry, compassionate reader, it wasn't the worst feeling possible to come to the understanding that Ashley had never felt anything for me. In fact, the recognition reduced my regret levels. Now that I knew that she hadn't been a realistic candidate for me anyway, I no longer had to compare every woman I saw with Ashley's elite personality.

Perhaps that realization would make it easier for me to find a date. Not that there were all sorts of not-quite-Ashley women who had been offering me their company, but maybe now I would be more open to offering them mine.

Once I'd satisfied myself that I'd mined my meeting with Ashley for all the correct insights, I rehearsed my impending speech for my upcoming conversation with Elizabeth. The rules of modesty dictated that I not be too proud of my promotion, but, at the same time, Elizabeth deserved some positive reflections from me after being through so much with my self-doubt. So I prepared happiness instead of humility.

"Guess who's the new Ambiguous manager for my department?" I began when we'd settled in.

"Is it *you*, dear?"

"How'd you know?"

"You're the first person I think of when I think about Ambiguity."

I laughed.

Elizabeth smiled her widest. "Well, this calls for a celebration, wouldn't you say, dear? How about I make us some tea and hot chocolate, and you can tell me all about it?"

"Sounds perfect," I said.

Indeed, in spite of the simplicity of Elizabeth's celebration technique, the sincerity with which she pursued it warmed my existence.

Chapter 41

Dullard vs. Power Boss III

Riddle Management

The next day—one day into getting used to my new role as my own boss—Elsje reminded me that that wasn't exactly going to be the case.

"So," she said, "now that you're taking over Chet's position, I suppose you're wondering who you'll be reporting to?"

"Right, I guess I am."

"Well, at some point, you probably came across Glenroy Garrison?"

My pulse picked up its pace as I heard the name of Chet's former yelling partner. "Oh, um, yeah, I remember him. I met him when I first started here."

"Did he have any meetings with you?"

"Oh—just sort of an impromptu one. He told me to call him if I needed help with anything."

"And did you?"

"No," I said, sensing that each of my words were being inspected by Elsje. "Is that bad?"

"Not at all," Elsje said, slipping in a smile. "I would just like an idea of the extent of your working relationship so far—I think I'll bring us all together for a meeting."

"Okay," I said, convinced there were many messages being sent between Elsje's lines but not sure if I had decoded any of them.

"Very good," Elsje said. "How's tomorrow for you to meet with Mr. Garrison?"

I was nervous on the bus ride home that evening as I contemplated meeting again with the man who had seemed to threaten Chet's job in my first two weeks at Ambiguity. Elizabeth supported my anxiety.

"Be careful, John—I'm not sure I trust that Glenroy character. I think Elsje's trying to warn you to keep your distance from him, and I think we should take her word for it."

The next day at work, as I awaited the scary meeting, I noticed myself unable to get along with my computer. I repeatedly clicked the wrong icons and typed the wrong words. So I comforted myself with a reminder that at least Elsje would be at the meeting—that would give me both a buffer and hopefully a translator as to what was going on. Said contemplation then reminded me to borrow an extra chair from Khiron for the gathering. I chose Khiron over Erik for the request because I suspected she would be less likely to provoke my nerves further with an investigation of *why exactly* I was asking for the item.

"Hey," I said, "can I borrow your chair for a meeting?"

"Um," she said, with a smirk, "then what am *I* going to sit on?"

"Oh, sorry," I said pointing to her guest chair, "I meant your extra chair."

Khiron leaned over her desk to peek at the bonus seat as though she didn't know it was there.

"Hmm," she said, doubling her smirk, "but what if I have an unexpected visitor?"

"Oh, okay," I said, too nervous to play along with her joke, "I'll ask Erik, then."

Khiron chuckled. "I'm just kidding, silly. I don't have any visitors down here—well, except Erik. And I prefer to make him *stand* anyway."

"Oh, right, good one," I said, feeling like my dad trying to respond to a Per joke that he didn't quite get.

Despite the painful negotiation to acquire the chair, I noticed—as I was bumping the furniture through my doorway—that my irritation with Khiron had blended my anxiety with some general stress, which, actually, I thought was a tiny upgrade to my emotional concoction.

Thankfully, the meeting was set for the morning, so I didn't have to stumble through my work for too long. At exactly 10 a.m., I heard the voices of Elsje and Glenroy snaking their ways through the hallway towards me.

But Glenroy stopped the approach to serenade my office neighbour.

"*Hey, boss.*"

"Oh, hey, Glenroy," I heard Erik responding cheerfully. "How are things looking?"

"Up—always *up*," Glenroy replied with a laugh.

Erik laughed too. "Good to know."

"How about you, my friend?" Glenroy said.

"Actually, gentlemen," Elsje said, "sorry to interrupt, but Glenroy and I have a meeting presently—perhaps you could catch up afterwards."

"All right, duty calls," Glenroy said, and my heart thumped as he and our boss returned to travelling my way.

I focused my eyes on my computer screen and waited.

"Hello, John," Elsje said.

"Oh, hi," I said, turning to face Elsje and a grinning Glenroy. I stood up to receive him.

He gave me a nod that was an impressive combination of cheerful and assertive. "How are you, John?"

"Good," I said, surprised that he remembered my name. "And you?"

"Marvelous."

"So," Elsje said as she sat down, "I wanted to meet to ensure that we're all on the same page as John takes on this new role."

"Whaddya need to know, boss?" Glenroy said, looking at me.

I hesitated, not sure if he was talking to me.

"Um, well—"

"Well, so far," Elsje said, "since effectively taking over for Mr. Williams, John and I have been collaborating, and—in that context—we have worked to make RQB a self-sufficient department."

"Excellent," Glenroy said.

Elsje nodded with a near smile. "So here's the situation, gentlemen. There are a few things at Ambiguity on which I would like to leave my stamp. The RQB department is one of them."

"Really?" I said.

"Quite so," Elsje said, and I realized, by the flat tone of her voice, that she did not necessarily appreciate my interjection. "But, as you know—upon my retirement—I will no longer have direct influence on the goings-on here."

"Well, *Elsje*," Glenroy said, turning up the volume of his smile, "if I may speak for all of us, you have left such an impression on this place that I'm sure your influence will stay with us for a long time."

"Thank you, Glenroy," Elsje said with her same horizontal tone. "That's very kind. Nevertheless, I would like to codify that flattering notion with a plan of action."

"I see," Glenroy said, a tiny smirk on his breath, "that sounds extremely helpful. But I worry a bit that these plans of yours—while brilliantly crafted, I'm sure—could, you know, lose their potency without you there minding the store."

Elsje nodded. "Precisely my concern, Mr. Garrison. And, for that reason, I have spoken with both Mr. Wilson and my replacement, Mr. Zhang, and both of them have signed off on my plan for this particular store. Does that help to clear up any trepidation, gentlemen?"

I wasn't sure if I should reply, but Glenroy offered an, "Of course," so I followed up with my own squeakier version.

Elsje smiled and handed each of us a small booklet. "I appreciate that, but, of course—as we get busy—such best laid plans can fail us. Thus, I have taken the liberty of creating a modest manual depicting how I expect things to go. As I say, both Mr. Wilson and Mr. Zhang have signed off on it."

"I see," Glenroy said, grinning, "that's very helpful of you, Elsje. So what've you got on the menu for us?"

"Right. John, I expect you to run the day-to-day operations of RQB, utilizing the discretion I've witnessed you employing these past few months. You will continue to anticipate and then tackle problems as they arise. If, however, you are unable to suss out a solution, or, if you require additional resources, then please report your concern to Mr. Garrison."

"Yup, ring me any time, mate," Glenroy said.

Elsje nodded. "And, Glenroy, if you don't have access to the necessary resources to solve the matter, don't hesitate to contact Stephen Wilson. John, you should be aware that, as of my departure, Glenroy will be reporting to Mr. Wilson instead of Mr. Zhang—we felt that, considering the diverse roles in Glenroy's portfolio, it would be prudent for him to work with someone of greater experience within the company."

Glenroy shrugged with a hearty smile. "I know too much."

Elsje nodded. "Now, Glenroy—if I may make a suggestion— in working with Mr. Smith, I have discovered that he functions very well independently. If John is completing these tasks on time, there should be no need to intervene."

"Is it okay if I say 'Hi' to him in the hallway?" Glenroy said.

"I'll leave that to your discretion," Elsje replied.

I forced a smirk at the interplay. Glenroy did not.

Uh oh, Glenroy clearly didn't enjoy being patronized by our boss as much as I did.

Elsje looked us over. "So, gentlemen, are we all clear?"

I deferred to Glenroy to give the first reply, but—in lieu of speaking—he looked back at our boss without expression. She returned the blank face.

After watching the silent tennis match for an extremely long second, I could endure no more.

"Yes, I think so," I said, trying to sound calm. "I'm to be self-sufficient in making sure I get everything in here done. If I have any problems, I should contact Glenroy for help?"

Elsje shifted her eyes to me and offered a tiny smile. "Precisely. And you, Glenroy?"

"I think I got it, thanks Elsje."

Elsje turned her eyes slowly back upon Chet's nemesis. This time, her look seemed to wrap itself around her target.

"So long as we're clear," she said.

As I watched the exchange, I realized that Elsje despised Glenroy. Whereas Chet and Mr. Litke annoyed her, Glenroy boiled her insides. And, by the similar look on Glenroy's face, I sensed that the loathing was mutual.

As soon as the meeting was done, I decided to send an email to my old Ambiguous mentor, Tally, asking her what the deal was between Glenroy and Elsje. But, as I started typing, I heard Khiron and Erik walking and talking my way. It was no time to be interrupted, so—grabbing onto a whim—I picked up my phone and dialed the long-distance number of my former lunchtime companion. After a few nerve-provoking rings, Tally answered in her business voice.

"*Tally*," I interrupted, "it's John."

"John . . .?" she hesitated. "As in my old friend, John *Smith*?"

"Yeah—sorry to call you at work."

"That's okay—I like getting paid to talk to my friends."

We exchanged a few questions and answers about how we were, and then—out of deference to our work locations—I itemized the reason I'd called.

"*Well*," Tally's ever-cheerful voice said, "I thought you'd never ask. I never gossip unless provoked, but—now that you've inquired—let's see what we can do. Are you ready?"

"I think so."

"I hope so 'cause you can't put gossip back in the ketchup bottle."

I laughed. "Okay, I'm ready."

"Good. All right, here goes: so, as far as I could tell, Glenroy and Elsje never liked each other—mostly, I think, because Elsje was one of the few people who saw through him right away. I'm sure you did too, John, but most people get caught up in his charm."

"Did *you*?" I said, grinning.

Tally chuckled. "I cannot answer that on the grounds that I may incriminate myself. But I *do* know that Elsje didn't fall for his B.S. And Glenroy didn't like that."

"Yeah, I could see that."

"Exactly," Tally said, "they would've been fine, though, if they'd just been content with hating each other. But you know Elsje: she expects everyone to do as good a job as she does. So, if you work hard for her, then she's awesome to work with, but, if you're Glenroy—who likes to get *other* people to do his work for him—then you can feel her watching you."

"Right," I said, nodding emphatically as if Tally could see me.

"So," she continued, "the thing with Glenroy is he's like a professional schmoozer: he's managed to stay in the organization for like ten years just taking people out for lunch and charming them until he's got them doing his work and even errands for him—I may have picked up his dry cleaning for him once or twice before I realized, '*What the hell?*'"

"Really?"

Tally laughed again. "More or less, *yes*, but this is not about embarrassing stories—it's about the dirt. So the thing with Glenroy is that, if anything goes wrong, he'll turn on you in a second. And the brilliant part is: after he's secretly gotten you in trouble, half the time, he'll actually make you believe that he was actually *secretly* your best advocate."

"Wow, that's horrible."

"If you think that's horrible, think how Chet felt."

"Why?"

"Well, you see, Chet was one of Glenroy's favourite playthings. They used to be the best of friends. But then—just before you got there—Glenroy needed a scapegoat for something, and he thought Chet wouldn't notice, but Chet was smart enough to see that Glenroy was hanging him out to rot, so Chet started fighting back. The top boss, Steven Wilson, was tending toward taking Glenroy's side, and it looked like Chet was going to get the axe, but then Elsje stepped in and proved that—even if Chet had been the one to have made the call on the offending action—Glenroy should've been aware of it. So he was either complicit—Elsje's fancy word, not mine—or incompetent. Either way, she convinced Steven to let Chet off with a warning *and* to give Glenroy one too."

"Wow," I said, "I had no idea it was that bad."

"So Chet never said anything about it to you?"

"No, I overheard Chet and Glenroy arguing, but that was it."

"*Well*," Tally said, "first of all, why wasn't I informed of *that* gossip? And, second, the fact that Chet never said anything about it should've been your first clue that it was serious."

"That's true," I replied, not sure if we were making fun of Chet.

"Anyway, whatever you do, John, don't let Glenroy get his tentacles in you. Be polite, but always tell him you're busy when he tries to take you out for lunch. If he senses he can't charm you, he'll give up and seek out other prey."

I immediately agreed to the strategy, so Tally moved on to explaining that—after rescuing Chet's job—Elsje replaced Glenroy as his de facto supervisor, and, in doing so, she rapidly discovered that he was much less competent than she would have liked for someone whose position she had saved. That apparently mortified her, and so she did everything she could to fix Chet, but—upon discovering such renovations to be impossible—she began looking for legitimate means by which to relieve Chet of his role with the organization. Tragically for Elsje, though, Chet left Ambiguity—of his own romantic accord—before his boss was able fulfill her dream of redundancy redemption.

With that revelation, Tally was apparently empty of details, so I thanked her for her wisdom, and we agreed to communicate more frequently in the future.

Once off the phone, I pondered Tally's information. It was all so startling, and yet I felt as if I had been on the verge of guessing much of it.

I now had the direct or indirect recommendations of Elsje, Tally, Chet, and Elizabeth to keep my distance from Glenroy's schmoozing. That caused me to have a moment of ego-supported delight since it seemed to me that I had been following the advice long before receiving it. Indeed, I was pleased to accept Tally's diagnosis that I—like Elsje above me—was one of the few who had seen holes in Glenroy's charm on first meeting him. Although, I smirked to myself, I couldn't take all the credit for my schmooze-detection skills: I had been trained to see through all forms of schmoozing by the schmooziest of them all, the great charmer himself, Bert Hardelean.

"Well, Mr. Smith," Elsje said a day later. "It's been a pleasure working with you and getting to know you."

"You as well," I said, feeling my throat tightening. "So this is it?"

"Yes, I don't think there's anything else we need from each other, is there?"

"No, I guess not," I said, sad that our association was concluding with such an unglamorous moment.

"I don't think so either," Elsje said. "But, if you're up for it, John, I'd love for you to attend my retirement dinner."

Oh. "*Of course*. I'd be honoured."

Elsje smiled. "Funny, I think you actually mean it."

I laughed.

"See you there, John. There'll be an email with the details."

Chapter 42

Dullard in the City II

A Mingling Sensation

As I pondered Elsje's self-exile from Ambiguity, I decided that having such an excellent boss had been a muse for my confidence. When you know your leader is brilliant, you can experiment with your aptitudes, assured that your boss will tell you when you've traveled too far the wrong way.

Yet it seemed unlikely to me that such self-improvement could sustain the loss of the motivating benefactor indefinitely. That distracting thought had me doing my work at a slow, autopilot pace.

"Hey," Khiron interrupted morosely from my doorway with half an hour to go in our workday.

"Hey, how's it going?" I replied, not even annoyed as I awaited the open-ended consequences of my question.

Khiron obliged with her usual complaints about how much work she was expected to do on such a small salary. Erik joined in twenty minutes later to provide support and then to lead Khiron to the exit as soon as 5:00 arrived.

"You coming, John?" he said.

"Just about," I said, providing my standard lie about needing just *a few* more minutes.

"All right," he said. "Don't forget—if you can't get your work done today, they do provide us with tomorrow."

"Right," I said, chuckling as if I hadn't heard him say that before.

Upon arriving at my bus an hour later, I spotted Jacklyn the math tutor already on board, so I decided to try a turn approaching her.

"Hey," she said when she noticed me. And she seemed so clearly to be making space for me in the spot next to her that I didn't second guess myself.

"Hey," I said, sitting down.

"How's your day?" she said.

"Good, yeah, sort of sad. It was my last day with my interim boss, and I really liked her, so ..."

"Who's your *interim boss*?"

"Elsje Anders."

"She was my boss *too!*"

"Really? Wait, is this another of your—"

"No, no, this one's true, I promise. I know I said I enjoy inventing stories to see if I can get away with them, but I try to only do that with, you know, newcomers to my presence."

"Oh, okay," I said, trying to show amusement at Jacklyn's strange ethics.

"Wait a second," she said, "so you work for Elsje in *Applications*?"

"Yes."

"So are you, by any chance, the famous Mr. Smith from the RQB Department?"

"Um, yeah, that's me—*wait*, how am I famous?"

"She's mentioned you a couple times—apparently your work habits are obsolete."

"Oh," I said, confused by why the compliments had suddenly gone bad.

Jacklyn laughed. "Sorry, poor choice of adjective. Let me try that again: she seemed to be making the case that your work style is, um, *less common* these days among her younger colleagues because, unlike many of us under her charge, your first, you know, *loyalty* seems to be about getting your work done to meet her specifications—instead of, you know, constantly trying to show off your own superior way of doing things. Does that sound better?"

"It *does*," I said with a laugh that was half amusement and half ego-sponsored catharsis. "But, um—"

"But now you're wondering if I made that all up to cover for her calling you 'obsolete'?"

"Um," I said, grinning, "that *wasn't* what I was going to say, but I guess I *should* be worried about that, eh?"

Jacklyn shrugged with a pretend grimace. "I'm afraid so, my friend."

I giggled and rolled my eyes. "So do you like her as a boss?"

Jacklyn shrugged again. "Yeah, I adore her. I realize she's not always cute and cuddly, but she's so calm and clear in what she expects of us that you never have to be anxious about whether you need to be anxious about anything … Or does that not make any sense?"

"No, no, it *does*," I said, trying to camouflage my delight at our matching appreciation for our boss, "yeah, that's a great way of putting that."

Quite rightly, we spent the rest of the bus ride comparing compliments of Elsje.

Once Jacklyn left the bus, I discovered myself to be in a good mood. It seemed I now had a premium-level work friend in Jacklyn the math tutor. It was like having Tally back—except now Chet and Bernice weren't there to water her down.

Two weeks later, I arrived at Elsje's retirement party, which was set in a high-end hotel ballroom. After proving my identity to a guard at the entrance to the room, I discovered inside a gathering of well-dressed Ambiguous dignitaries who were, for the most part, strangers to me. But I wasn't as anxious as the situation suggested. You see, popular reader, when you're solo most of your time, you're not afraid of having no one to talk to at an event; it's your natural setting to be surrounded by people you're not speaking to.

Soon after I entered the room in search of safe patch of wall at which to stand, I felt a tap on my shoulder. It was Jacklyn the math tutor.

"Hey there," she said, "I didn't know you were coming to this."

"Oh, yes," I said, suddenly feeling like an imposter, "um, Mrs. Anders and I worked together a lot in the last few months, so …"

"Oh, *right*, of course. So do you know where they have you sitting?"

The question confused me for a millisecond until I realized there was a seating a chart on the opposite wall. Strangely, I didn't want to acknowledge my lack of prior knowledge of the sitting guide.

"I'm not sure," I said, feigning calm. "They probably just randomly threw me in somewhere. I don't really know anyone here."

"Well, you know *me*, John," Jacklyn said. "Maybe we can do a little tinkering and move you to my table. I say we check the board."

So I followed Jacklyn to the seating chart with my nerves firing. I was not pleased with the thought of being a seat fraud. But, with Jacklyn the math tutor's sometimes unfastened personality, I had no doubt of the sincerity of her plan.

"Yeah, *see*," she said when we arrived at the intricately crafted seat map. "I know Ketoy, Anton, Derrick, and Harald, but we're also stuck with some guy named John Smith."

"That's *me!*" I said, too relieved to spot Jacklyn's humour.

"Oh, okay," she said, "well, my friend, would you *mind* giving up your spot to you?"

Finally, I laughed. "I guess, just this once."

Shortly after we sat down, Glenroy Garrison approached our table. I was appropriately startled to realize so; and, in case that wasn't clear to anyone nearby, my eyes widened to take in my boss's approach. You see, Glenroy-free reader, if there was anything to be held against Jacklyn and me for our interdepartmental friendship, Glenroy Garrison would surely grab onto it with both hands.

"Hey, troops," he said, grinning at his discovery. "I didn't know you guys knew each other."

"Um—" I panicked.

"Yeah," Jacklyn took over with a smile, "John and I are on the same bus route, so—"

"I see. So you guys forming a secret committee to take over Ambiguity?"

Jacklyn laughed without a hint of the anxiety I was feeling. "Yeah—that too."

Glenroy smirked. "Well, have a great time tonight, gang."

Next to arrive at our table was young man of questionable confidence.

"Hi, Jacklyn," he said with a soft voice.

"Hi, Ketoy," she replied. "How are ya, my friend?"

"Oh, I'm fine, just you know ...I'm trying to figure out the social dynamics of this place."

"Cool, what've you got so far?"

"Well, it's like the bosses and us plebeians have switched sides. Normally, it's our job to ingratiate ourselves to the bosses, but *here* it's like they're all smiling and pretending to be happy to see everyone, and it's like they're worried that *we're* judging *them* and whether they can show us a good time or not."

"Yeah, yeah, you're totally right," Jacklyn said, looking around. "It's kind of like, as bosses, they're competing to be the best host."

"*Right,*" Ketoy said, his voice lifting, "yeah, I think that's right. I couldn't figure it out before, but, yeah, it's like, at a gathering like this, being a good host is like a demonstration of their power and influence. They wanna show off how many employees *like* them or something."

"Interesting," Jacklyn said.

Ketoy was wearing a smile now, which slipped away as a man in a manual wheelchair and an expensive-looking suit manoeuvred himself up to the table.

"Why, Ms. Chapman," the newcomer said, "is this the guy we haven't been hearing about?"

"Hello, Derrick," Jacklyn replied

"Howdy," Derrick said, staring at me, "and this is Mr. Chapman, I presume?"

"Nope," Jacklyn said. "Mr. Chapman's out of town on business. This is John. He works at Ambiguity too—John, this is Derrick. He works with us in Development."

"Hi," I said, smiling as best I could at the sharply dressed ambusher.

"Hi," he said, looking me over.

INTROSPECTIVE NOTE: Isn't it an odd feeling, social reader, when someone whom you've just met is transparent with their contempt for you? Ordinarily, of course, when a person is obvious about disliking you, it's your job to feel wounded. However, in the case where the person detesting you has just met you, it's difficult to take the disapproval seriously: even if you have an impressive assortment of villainous traits, how could the disliker yet be so sure of them? And so you're able to step out of your overly sensitive mind and watch the disliker's dislike of you with an objective curiosity.

"So, John," Derrick said, as he picked up his beverage, "what do you do at Ambiguity?"

"I'm in Applications."

"Which department?"

"RQB."

"I know *RQB*," he said. "You guys've come in handy for me a few times—although I'd like to see you work on your efficiency."

"Oh, what's wrong with our efficiency?"

"Come to my office sometime. I'll give you some tips."

"Oh, okay," I said, trying not to be irritated, "but can you just give me an idea of what you think's wrong?"

Derrick chuckled. "Don't worry, you guys are doing fine. There's just a few things I'd love to see done with more precision."

"That's fine, but now I'm curious: what part of the department is inefficient?"

Derrick smiled. "There's no one big problem, John. There's just a plethora of little issues."

"Name one," I snapped, more out of embarrassment that Jacklyn the math tutor was watching me being picked on than from an actual injury to my pride.

"Like I said," Derrick said, "there's nothing specific."

"*Derrick,*" Jacklyn said, "it's gotta be pretty frustrating for John when you claim there's something *wrong* with his department without telling him specifically what you mean. John's got a right to confront his supposed flaws."

That made me grin: with a thousand typewriters, I couldn't have described my situation so well.

Derrick laughed. "All right, if you insist, let me see; first of all, you guys really need to work on your productivity: you should be able to get much more done with your allotted time."

Jacklyn and I stared at Derrick.

"Um," Jacklyn said, "thank you, my friend, for *defining* efficiency. But—not to get technical—but I think what John wants to know is *how specifically* you think he can get more done with his *allotted time.*"

Again I couldn't have worded the point better.

Derrick forced another smile. "Specifically, um, well, *for instance*, I've looked at your inventory procedures, and they're not as well organized as I'd like them to be."

"In what *way?*" Jacklyn said, almost laughing.

"Well, here's an example: it's like Jean in RST ..." Derrick then described Jean's inefficiency, utilizing several computer words that I didn't know. He chortled when he reached his conclusion. "It's a staggeringly inefficient system."

Jacklyn raised an eyebrow at my new nemesis. "Derrick, I'm very sure that's a great example of inefficiency, but it's not a case of *John's department* being inefficient."

"No, I'm aware of that. I was just giving you a specific instance of inefficiency—*per your request*, Jacklyn."

"Awesome. So now that you've proved you know what efficiency *means*, do you have an example that actually relates to our friend here?"

"Absolutely, but, Jacklyn, you seem to be hung up on examples. I can show John all the tricks that he wants, but—ultimately—his system needs an overhaul before I can help him with the details."

Jacklyn's forehead contracted delightfully. "Wow—so now you're contending that John's system needs an overhaul even though you can't produce a single example of what's wrong with it?"

Derrick laughed. "Yeah, *that's* what I said."

Jacklyn looked at me and raised her hands as if to surrender.

I smiled back. I was over it now. It seems that, when someone defends you against an obnoxious accuser with words that you couldn't have said better yourself, you can feel vindicated even if the villain is not officially retired.

"Well, anyway," I said, "thanks for offering to help, Derrick."

"No worries, bud. People usually realize—once they put their egos aside—that I'm just trying to help them out."

I smiled back at Derrick. I'd given him a small victory; if he wanted a large one to go with it, he could have it.

"You know, Derrick," Jacklyn interrupted the ceasefire, "it's funny that you say that people always see things your way because— *it's odd*—I don't remember Faisal seeing things your way."

"*Faisal Singh?*" Derrick said, putting on a face of amusement.

"That guy's an Orwellian drone. He makes my senile grandmother look like Alan Turing."

Jacklyn smiled. "You might be right, my friend, but didn't that particular Orwellian drone teach you a few things not too long ago?"

"Funny, that's not how I remember it," Derrick replied.

Ketoy laughed, but—upon receiving a glaring glance from Derrick—he quickly stifled the evidence of his amusement.

"Anyway," Derrick said, moving away from the table, "I think I'll mingle before dinner."

"Fair enough," Jacklyn said. "See you soon."

"I hate mingling," Ketoy said once Derrick was away.

And soon we were having an interesting discussion regarding the power dynamics contained within the pastime of mingling.

Dinner was good, but the speeches were better as various high-powered characters with high-powered voices shared funny stories about Elsje Anders and her obsession with excellence. (My enjoyment, however, was mitigated by Derrick who critiqued each of the speeches while they were in progress. According to the tone of his voice, his commentary was brilliant, but I was too distracted by the disruptive volume of his snarky play-by-play to appreciate any of his exquisite content.)

"And now, without further ado," the MC, Steven Wilson, said, "I believe it's time to hear from our guest of honour, your friend and mine, Mrs. *Elsje Anders*."

"Hello, friends and colleagues," Elsje said. "I can't tell you what a great pleasure it is to have all of you here with me tonight to celebrate my freedom."

We all laughed; indeed, Elsje's speech was funnier than I'd expected as she teased various Ambiguous characters. Although, I sensed that it was only the people she liked who were hit by her wit; I surmised so after noticing that her old staring-contest rival, Glenroy Garrison, was absent from her roasting. Admittedly, I was spared too, but I didn't take that personally because, if Elsje *had* satirized me, only a few people would have known the person she was mocking about. Plus, during her closing remark—in which she said it had been *a joy* these past few months to get to know better the Ambiguous talent who would be taking over various

Ambiguous reins in the future—I'm 80% confident that she sent me a smile.

"Hey," Jacklyn half-whispered to me as the event neared its closing bell. "Not that it'll make up for … *you know* … but I can give you a ride home, if you want?"

"Oh," I said, not sure if it would be polite to accept such politeness, especially since I wasn't sure to what the 'you know' was referring, "um—"

But Jacklyn raised her forehead at me as though I was disrupting something covert. I, therefore, suspected, that the 'you know' was related to her co-worker's earlier mistreatment of my department and me.

"We're going the same way," she said, adding squinting eyes to her foreheading expression. "It's no problem."

"Oh, okay, thanks," I said, relieved to have agreed.

"All right, follow me," she said. "*See you, Derrick.*"

"Ms. Chapman," he replied, still in mingle mode.

Once we were out of the building, Jacklyn glanced back at the entranceway.

"Sorry, by *ride*," she said with a shrug that indicated a cab parked in the hotel roundabout, "I meant I'd have my driver drop you off on our way."

"Okay," I chuckled before following Jacklyn's scrunching lead into the vehicle.

"Hey," she said to the operator once we landed on our soft chairs. "I'm new to this: is it okay if you drop one of us off and then the other, and I pay for both trips?"

"Of course," the driver said. "What's the first address, please?"

Jacklyn turned her forehead on me again.

I supplied the necessary information.

"Perfect," Jacklyn said, "he's closer, so we'll go there first, if that's okay?"

"Of course," the driver said, swiftly activating the vehicle.

"Thanks," I said, lowering my voice just for Jacklyn, "but *you* don't have to pay."

"*Really?*" she said, putting on her sheepish face. "I'm pretty sure that's a condition of the service, isn't it?"

"No, no, I meant …" I started to say with a panicked voice

before realizing Jacklyn was trying to humour-manoeuvre me into submitting to her generosity. I chuckled as I searched my unwitty mind for a way to indicate that I was neither humorless nor cheap.

Jacklyn grinned at my conundrum. "Honestly, not to be all First World about it, but I **really** don't care about money. You can't take it with you."

"Neither do I—" I tried.

"*Except,*" Jacklyn caught me with that forehead again, "I do enjoy flaunting my cash, so—if you let me pay for the ride—you'll be doing *me* a kindness."

I assure you, judgmental reader, ordinarily, I would not have let such a comedic manipulation trick me into neglecting my financial obligation, but—in this case—Jacklyn's humorous expression seemed to be financed by something serious.

"Okay," I said, "I guess I can do you that *kindness.*"

"Thank you," Jacklyn said, laughing as though I hadn't just joked within the lines that she had drawn.

"So," I said, "was that whole thing to do with Derrick?"

"Um, which part?"

"Sorry, that you were giving me a *ride?* It sounded like you meant your *own* car. Was that, um, implication somehow for Derrick's benefit?"

"Right, yeah," Jacklyn said, her face back to sheepish, "sorry for the subterfuge—hopefully Derrick isn't as perceptive as you."

I chuckled back to hide my enjoyment of the compliment.

Jacklyn took in a shake-of-the-mouth sigh. "Not for nothing, but I've never actually told him I have a car. It's just that it would never occur to him that someone *wouldn't* have a car, so my hope is that—well, so long as I create the appearance that I'm a car person—I won't have to worry about him offering me rides home." Jacklyn shuddered. "I can handle working with him because I know, at the end of the day, I can turn him off and go home. But, if I were in the same car with him …" Jacklyn grimaced. "Not to be hyperbolic, but he's the most patronizing and narcissistic person I've ever met."

I laughed. "You don't feel bad insulting him?"

"Why would I feel bad about that?"

"Because, you know, he's—"

"Socially inept. No, I think he reaps what he sows there."

I laughed. "No, but I mean he's in a wheelchair. Doesn't that make you feel some compassion for him?"

"Compassion, sure. But carte blanche to be an ass, no. I've known lots of disabled people who are perfectly lovely. Hardship is not a licence to intrude on everyone else's happiness."

"Yeah, I guess you're right."

Jacklyn shook her head. "Sorry, my friend: you're not going to make me feel bad about this. Your view is condescending. Mine treats everyone like an individual. If his disability means he needs help with something, I'm happy to do so, but—"

"No, no," I said. "I actually agree with you. I was just kind of feeling guilty about disliking him, so—"

"So you tried to make *me* feeling guilty in order to placate your own guilt?"

I laughed. "I'm afraid so."

"Fair enough," Jacklyn said. "I would've done the same to you if I'd thought of it."

I giggled. "So what is it that you dislike so much about working with him?"

"Other than him being a pompous ass?"

I giggled again. "Yeah."

"Well, not for nothing, but he constantly asks about my ..." she indicated her wedding ring, "even though I clearly don't want to talk about my personal life with him. Know what I mean? I don't get why he can't leave it alone."

"So do you feel like he's harassing you, or...?"

"No, nothing like that. He's just so—he's one of these people that's never able to do the gracious thing. He's always either self-promoting himself or trying to make people feel uncomfortable. So I don't think he has a thing for me or anything. I just think he realizes I don't like talking about my personal life at work, so he *digs*. It's uncanny how he always knows which buttons to stomp on."

"Wow, that's obnoxious."

"Yup."

"So how did that Faisal guy you were talking about make Derrick look like a novice?"

"Oh, right, glad you asked," Jacklyn said, suddenly grinning. "You know how we recently overhauled the ATS?"

"Yeah, I love the new design."

"*Really?* What exactly do you love about it?"

"Um," I said, sensing that Jacklyn was trying to trick me again, "it was really easy to switch over to from the old system."

"Thank you, my friend: I was in charge of setting it up."

"Really?"

"Yes, sir. Now I bet you feel bad about saying such nice things about it, eh?"

"No, ma'am," I said, beaming.

"*Oh,*" Jacklyn said, with a mock frown that made me chuckle. "Well, anyway, I'm glad you say it was easy to adapt to: when I started on it, I hadn't been here long, and I didn't want us to lose any, you know, particularly handy functionality from the old ATS, so I stole Faisal from the LYN department to give me a guided tour of how he actually used the system, so—"

"That was smart."

"I thought it made sense, but Derrick was not pleased. He was certain no one from Applications would be of any use to us. But, unfortunately for our friend, Derrick, Faisal turned out to be great: he pointed out all sorts of useful intangibles that we should keep from the old ATS. But, as you witnessed tonight, Derrick's not the type to let being wrong get in the way of being dogmatic, so he made some far-fetched arguments to back up his point—arguments that, sadly, were quickly refutable with a quick search of the records. I almost felt bad for the guy."

"So you *do* feel guilty!" I said, trying to be funny.

"Touché," Jacklyn said. "I guess it is hard not to feel *a little* bad for him. He thinks so very highly of himself—*he's totally smitten*—and yet he's so completely misinformed about his skills. Not to be cruel, but sometimes it's hard to resist the urge to let him know he's fallen in love with a witless windbag."

Jacklyn's words were both funny and nostalgia-inducing. I'll let you work out the funny part for yourself, funny reader, but the nostalgia provocation had to with the fact that talk of Derrick's misinformed ego reminded me of Elsje's description of her underling—Mr. Litke—who—just like Derrick—had a confused self-image.

"Wait a minute," I said, staring at Jacklyn. "I just realized: is Derrick's last name *Litke?*"

"Yeah, so?"

"Oh, it's just that Elsje told me about him: he drove her nuts. Oh, *wait*, I wasn't supposed to tell anyone that."

"*Really?*" Jacklyn said, sitting up. "I've never heard Elsje gossip—at least, not negatively—about *anyone*. How'd you get this out of her?"

"Well, um, Litke and I are in different departments, so she probably thought it was safe to tell me. So please don't tell anyone what I said."

"I won't," Jacklyn said, her face now in ponder mode. "I see what you're saying about the different departments. That might be part of it, but—still—you managed to get gossip out of a stone. Impressive. I'd better be careful around you."

"Okay," I said, chuckling.

"Speaking of gossip," Jacklyn said, "I wanted to ask you earlier: how do you know our friend, Glenroy?"

"Well, he's technically my boss."

Jacklyn raised up her eyebrows. "*Technically?*"

I was pleased to unleash the complete Glenroy-Chet saga onto my friend (under continued promise of confidentiality), and she appeared fascinated with every twist of the tale.

"I heard about some of that," she said.

"Oh, did Elsje tell you?"

"No, it was just a friend of mine."

Jacklyn seemed uninterested in exploring her own gossip sources, so I segued to an investigation of Jacklyn's experience with Glenroy, which—amazingly—turned out to be less entertaining than mine.

It's Better to Have Used a Platitude and Lost than Never to Have Used a Platitude at All

The following Monday morning, I decided to go into Ambiguity early to catch up on some neglected work. Much to my approval, Jacklyn the math tutor landed on the same trip. But the conversation was awkward, which startled me; after all, Jacklyn's and my previous feature-length discourse had been so natural—and full to the brim with gossipy goodness—that I had felt as though I could talk with her indefinitely. My ever self-assured ghostwriter claims not be surprised by that result: he says that, when a post-natural meeting is begun, it sometimes seems strange to leap into the old topics, and so one does not know what to say. Apparently it is an especially difficult time for new friends, who have come to know each other too well for small talk but not yet well enough to rush into big talk. Consequently, Jacklyn and I needed some sort of conversation-starter device.

"Is, um, have you got a busy Monday scheduled?" I tried.

"No, it's not too bad. You?"

"Fine," I said. "I'll just be busy with my usual stuff." I was attempting to be vague about my work so that I wouldn't have to bore Jacklyn with elaboration, but—oddly—Jacklyn mistook my vagueness for job dissatisfaction.

"You find your work boring?"

"No, no, I love my job …" I said, hoping that would be sufficient.

But, once again, Jacklyn pointed her truth-provoking forehead at me.

"Um," I babbled in reply, "I guess one of the things I like about it is that it's so repetitive. It's kind of cool because the more I do it, the better I get at it—and I actually like feeling like I know exactly what to do at all times."

"Wow," Jacklyn said, "I never thought of it that way—I think I'm jealous."

"Why?" I said.

"Well, because I'd like to *always know what to do* in my job too."

"Right," I said, smirking.

"What?"

"Well, your job is a little more complicated than mine."

"Not really—"

That made me grin. "Jacklyn, the reason you don't always know what to do is because you're one of the people who comes up with the stuff that the rest of us do—like when you redesigned the ATS—you had to come up with new procedures. How could you have known what you were doing until you did it?"

As you can read, paying attention reader, I was on a roll. Jacklyn was my superior in every way except at assessing her own talents.

"But—" she tried.

"Plus," I said, "I was looking at the new ATS again the other day—it's so ...perfect."

"Thanks, but I had help."

"From Derrick, yeah, great help there."

"No," Jacklyn said, switching to a whisper, "Derrick was mostly an irritant, but there was four of us—it was a group effort."

"Saying modest things," I quickly retorted, "will do nothing to help you hide from admiration."

Wow, I had made a remarkably clever rebuttal—a strange thing for a dullard to do. It was unintentional, I assure you, startled reader. The perfect words just happened to fall from the situation onto my lips.

"Well, anyway," Jacklyn said, rolling her eyes, "we're not talking about me—we're talking about you, my friend, and I'm wondering, um, what else do you like about your job?"

"The new ATS," I said instinctively.

Jacklyn rolled her eyes again.

Wait a ghostwritten minute: she seemed *annoyed*. My chest froze as I awaited confirmation of the scary possibility. But then Jacklyn gave me a smirk, and I breathed again.

With relief on my mind, I was in a good mood when I arrived at my desk that morning. My workload was hefty for the week, but I had come to find that it was exciting to be the sole proprietor of my operation. I felt as though I were a workflow artist who had to use my well-practiced instincts to prioritize my requirements with precision in order to stay ahead of the demand.

Halfway through the day, Erik leaned into my office. "Hey, Kiron and I are going for lunch. You wanna come?"

"Oh, thanks," I said, "but I should keep at it."

"Tell him we promise to let him go after half an hour," Kiron called form across the hall.

I laughed. "Okay, thanks, I'll join."

On the following Monday, I once again landed on the same bus ride home as Jacklyn the math tutor.

"So how was Head Office today?" I asked.

Jacklyn glanced around the bus and switched to a lowered voice. "As you know, my colleague Derrick Litke's never made a mistake in his life."

"Right," I said, giggling in anticipation.

"What do you mean by *that*?" Jacklyn said.

"That I agree with you that he's never made a mistake."

"Good," Jacklyn said, "I thought for a second you were only agreeing *sarcastically*—but Derrick's worked too hard on his reputation for being perfect to have *you* questioning it."

"No, no, I *know*," I said, trying to play along without giggling out loud, "that's why I never *would* question that he's infallible."

"Okay," Jacklyn said. "So, in taking his vow of never making a mistake, Derrick, therefore, has no reason to ever take the blame for anything *ever*."

"Makes sense."

"Right, so, when I ask him to check something *before* the weekend, and he declines because he checked it a year ago—but then the item breaks down over the weekend—who do you think Derrick sees fit to blame?"

"*You?*" I said grinning.

"Close, my friend. No, he explained with his smuggest, smirk-faced delivery that we needed to have a conversation with *Faisal*, who obviously hadn't alerted dear Derrick to the problems that would've made it reasonable to check things before the weekend."

"Wow, seriously?"

"Yup. The fact that I'd listed my reasons for wanting everything checked before the weekend was not relevant because I'm a novice in these matters. Instead, he was basically just like, '*If only Faisal had done his job.*'"

"Right," I said, suddenly distracted: just outside the bus window, there was a pedestrian who looked a lot like Stacy, my old Sweet On You co-worker who—you'll recall, recalling reader—had once tried to reward the crush she assumed I had on her. She and the bus were stopped at the same red light, so I had a good-sized moment to stare at her to confirm her identity. She wasn't as attractive as I'd remembered her describing herself, but she was still very pretty and was making adept use of physique-complimenting fashion.

"Do you know her?" Jacklyn said, peering over my shoulder.

"Oh, sorry, yeah, I think so."

Just then, the Stacy-look-alike looked our way, spotted our staring, and returned it with a glare.

I offered a wave, but she glared again and began walking.

"Yeah, I definitely know her," I muttered as the bus started up in tandem with my former co-worker.

"Good friend?" Jacklyn said.

"Not so much," I said, still reeling from having been caught in the stare. (My brain was frantically trying to determine whether Stacy's unpleasant response was the result of her recognizing me or simply the consequence of her perceiving that a stranger was giving her a creepy look. Both interpretations seemed consistent with Stacy's personality, so I knew there would never be a way to choose between them, which meant I would have to spend the rest of my existence suffering from the embarrassment of both.)

"So what's the deal with her, Mr. Pensive?" Jacklyn said.

"Sorry," I said. "I interrupted your story."

"No, no," Jacklyn said, "this sounds more interesting. Who is she?"

"Um, well, I used to work with her. She was quite, ah, confident in her looks. She thought every guy was into her."

"Were *you*?"

"No," I blurted.

"I'll take that as a 'No,'" Jacklyn said, giggling.

"That's what I said."

"Exactly, that's why I'm taking it as a 'No.'"

I smirked. "Fine then."

"Okay," Jacklyn said, "so why weren't you into her?"

"She was just kind of arrogant and would interrupt people a lot."

"You didn't find her attractive?"

"She was attractive, but I wasn't attracted to her."

"Nice distinction," Jacklyn said with smile. "So you weren't into *her*—was she into you?"

"Not really."

"I'll take that as a 'Yes.'"

I smirked again. "No, it's just that someone might've told her I'd said I wasn't into her, so I think maybe she wanted to prove me wrong."

"Oh, wow," Jacklyn said with a chuckle, "so what happened?"

"Oh, um, it's a long story."

"It's a long bus ride."

"Okay, well, she invited me to her place, and, I don't know—"

"Did you go?"

"Yeah."

"Why?" Jacklyn said, smiling.

It was a wonderfully generous smile, devoid of any eye-roll-style judgement; instead, it seemed to assume that I had a reasonable explanation for my contrary claims. Nonetheless, I was nervous.

"I guess—I don't know, I had no friends, and she said her friends were going to be there, so I thought it might be worth a try to, you know, make friends."

"So I'm assuming her friends *weren't* there?"

"Right."

"Wow," Jacklyn said, grinning with a shake of her head. "Okay, so what happened? Did she try to seduce you?"

"Sort of—she just kind of got really close to me."

"Okay, and what'd you do?"

"Well, I just kind of told her that I'd heard that someone at the bakery was into me—which I *had*—but that I didn't think we'd be a good match."

"Very bold, my friend. Nicely done."

"I guess—but Stacy didn't appreciate it too much."

"Well, yeah, of course not. She doesn't sound like the sort of girl who'd ever heard 'No' for an answer."

"True."

"Still," Jacklyn said, "she *is* beautiful. That's some pretty good will power on your part, my friend."

"I guess," I said, too embarrassed to admit that I had been tempted, but had turned Stacy down partly to prove to her that I could.

Meanwhile, as Jacklyn and I continued to chat about Stacy, and later about some similarities of ego between Stacy and Derrick, I strangely felt better about having been caught staring by my old co-worker.

Now, I don't want to alarm you, skittish reader, but my crush on Jacklyn the math tutor was growing without my permission. It seemed that Elizabeth suspected as much because she responded to one of my Jacklyn tales with:

"Be careful, dear. Sounds like she's a lovely person, but let's not forget that's she not available."

"Oh, no, I *know*," I replied. "But that doesn't mean I can't admire her as a friend."

"Of course, dear. But be careful with your heart, John. It's the only one you've got."

Perhaps Elizabeth was right: perhaps the smartest thing to do was to avoid Jacklyn the math tutor ...

But, wait a minute, *why couldn't I fall for Jacklyn?* The only problem I could really see with losing my balance for Jacklyn was that she was unavailable to catch me, which meant that I would break my heart when I hit the ground. *But, really, was a broken heart that big a deal?* I'd often heard that to love and lose was not actually the worst thing that could happen to a relationship pursuer—apparently, to have never loved *at all* was even worse. And what luck! I, myself, had never loved at all, which meant that the heartbreak of favoring an unavailable woman was, by definition, going to be an improvement on my life.

UNWARRANTED NOTE: My ghostwriter claims my benefiting-from-a-*new*-broken-heart-experience reasoning is flawed because I was in love with *Ashley* back in high school. But he's whining up the wrong tree. I was certainly in awe of Ashley, and I couldn't resist thinking about her for many years, but I never really knew her well enough to claim that I was in love with her.

Despite my impeccable solution to the conundrum of whether maintaining my crush on my married friend would make me happy, I realized that there was another question that needed an answer. *Would it be ethical to fall for Jacklyn?* It has been well-documented that romantic affairs with married people are moral no-nos, but I wasn't sure about the rules in regard to unmarried people falling secretly in mono-directional love with wedded types. After a long deliberation on an evening stroll, I concluded that—so long as the one-way love thoughts were to be kept just between me—there could be no real objection to them. With that solution in mind, I walked with a smile on my face.

Wait a ghostwritten moment, my mind interrupted the fun as an over-noisy motorcycle grumbled past me. *What about Jacklyn's husband?* If I was going to be friends with Jacklyn, then surely I would eventually have to meet the selfish Jacklyn-heart stealer. Rationally, of course, I was aware that Jacklyn the math tutor's approval of her spouse recommended him with the highest honour, and yet I discovered myself to be unintentionally rooting for him to be a bit of a jerk—not enough to make Jacklyn unhappy, of course, but enough to make her secretly wish she'd picked me instead. Since that fantastical result was unlikely, I hoped I wouldn't have to meet Mr. Math Tutor and prove my preferences wrong.

Chapter 43
Dullard vs. Power Boss IV

Good Schmooze

On the following Friday afternoon, I discovered an email from my faraway friend, Tally.

> *'Dear John,' she wrote,*
>
> *I've always wanted to write a* Dear John *letter, but don't worry, I'm not trying to break up with you. ;)*
>   *It's been a while again since we've talked. What are you up to? Any problems with Glenroy? Your old friend Tally is still loving school (and work, to a lesser degree). I'm so glad I did this. And Hank's doing well with his job also. So let me know what's going on!*
>
> *Cheers,*
> *Tally*
>
> *P.S. I miss our conversations.*

I was nervous as I wrote my response to my former idol. I told her how smoothly Elsje's departure had gone and that I'd had no communications with the Glenroy the Schmoozer since. But, in regard to what I was up to, I decided it would best not to elucidate my crush on someone whose return affections were reserved for someone else. (Even though Tally was the one who had told me it was worthwhile to test one's romantic preferences by having crushes, I was still embarrassed by the married nature of my choice.)

A few minutes later, my office phone rang.

"RQB Department, John speaking."

"Very official, John," a cheerful male voice replied. "I like it."

"Thanks," I said, trying to decipher the man's voice. "I do what I can."

"That's what I like to hear," the man said. "So how are we doing?"

"I think … *good*," I said, not sure how much information I should give the possible stranger yet strongly suspecting that we knew each other.

The nameless caller laughed. "That doesn't sound as confident as I'd like."

"Well, you know how it is," I replied, now feeling my neck muscles clench as I searched my ear's memory for the identity of the inquisitor.

"*Do I now?*" replied the rogue caller with a chuckle, which had me savagely feeling that he was purposely tormenting my ignorance. "Well, I gather you're wondering to what you owe the pleasure of my call?"

"Um, yeah," I said, and I considered asking *to whom* I owed my delight as well, but it was too late for that kind of question now.

"Well, it seems to me," the caller replied, "that we haven't done an employee evaluation since you came under my charge."

"Oh, I think you're right," I blurted with relief. I now knew that he was my phantom boss, Glenroy Garrison—although, I supposed it could also be *his* superior, Steven Wilson. I was technically under his *charge* too.

SMUG NOTE: My ghostwriter says it was obvious that it was Glenroy—and not Steven—since Glenroy's boss would have had no reason to contact me directly, but I would like to point out that it's easy to be that confident in one's speculations when you're not the one who's going to embarrass yourself if your arrogant assumption goes wrong.

"Okay, good," Glenroy or Steven said with a chuckle. "I've never had an employee so excited to be evaluated before."

"Yeah, I guess I just like evaluations," I said, fearing that Glenroy/Steven was on to my confusion.

"Well then," he said, "you'll want to get right to it, then—how's this afternoon for ya?"

"Sure, that's fine."

"Excellent—let's make it a late lunch meeting. I'll pick you up at your office when it's time to go."

That comment reminded me of Glenroy's reputation for collecting lunches with colleagues, so I helped myself to the belief that I recognized Glenroy's distinct voice and pretension. Although, I then recalled from Steven Wilson's emceeing of Elsje's retirement party that his voice was somewhat similar to Glenroy's.

ANOTHER SMUG NOTE: My ghostwriter once again boastfully contends that Steven wouldn't have been so familiar when calling. In reply, I again politely point out that it's easy for my ghostwriter to loftily assume anything he likes when there are no mortifying consequences looming for him should he be wrong.

As I rushed my mind through the above Glenroy-or-Steven speculations, my evaluator-to-be included *my name* in his goodbye salutation, which tempted me to go for glory and exit with a reference to him being Glenroy—but the nauseating thought of accusing Steven Wilson of being his underling scared me into a conservative, name-free good bye.

So my mini-work afternoon before my second lunch for the day was spent on full nerves—not, as one might hope, because I was anxious about being evaluated by one of my bosses, but instead because I feared that my confusion about which of them was coming would provoke an incomplete reaction to the one who *did*.

Of course, cruel fate had my work hallway much more populated than usual that day, which had me lighting my eyes up for each passing stranger just in case they were Glenroy or Steven. It was an exhausting exercise both for my eyes and for my stress system, and so, when Glenroy Garrison finally did stroll into my vicinity, I had only a blank look available for him.

"Hello there, stranger," he said.

"Hi," I said, waiting for him to give proof that he was the man from the phone.

"How's your work treating you, boss?"

"Pretty well."

"Good, are we ready?"

"Um, yes?"

"You gonna come with me, then?" Glenroy said, chuckling.

"Oh, yeah, sorry," I said, randomly clicking my mouse. "To lunch, then?"

"That's the plan."

"Okay, great," I said, breathing in a full helping of relief. Indeed, all of the time spent worrying that Glenroy might be Steven had continued to distract me from the anxiety that I should have been feeling about my evaluation. Instead, I was relaxed and cheerful as Glenroy serenaded us with chatter on our way to the restaurant.

A FINAL SMUG NOTE: Meanwhile, my ghostwriter is helping himself to an extra-large helping of arrogant vindication that he correctly anticipated that my boss's boss, Steven Wilson, would indeed never have invited me for lunch. I can only reiterate my retort that it's not difficult to make prescriptive predictions in which one has no stakes.

After we ordered our sandwiches, I asked Glenroy when the evaluation would begin (since I wasn't sure what else to say to him).

"You really *are* eager," he said.

"I guess I'm just curious."

"Right you are," Glenroy said, opening a file and calmly looking over its contents. "Good," he concluded. "Now, first of all—how do *you* think you've been doing?"

"Um, I think I've been doing a decent job. I've completed all of my tasks on time, I think."

"True," Glenroy said, looking again at the file as though he were peering through reading glasses, "your assignments have been completed effectively and on time—for the most part," he slipped in brilliantly. "I'd like to look also, though, at the presentation of the reports that you send me every week."

"Okay, is there something you want me to do differently?"

Glenroy smiled and waited for a moment.

"Um—" I filled in the dead air.

"Presentation," he interrupted, "leads to perception, and you know what they say about perception and reality, don't you?"

"I think so, but they're just internal numbers—who, um, whose perception am I trying to change?"

Glenroy chuckled. "You're dressed in business-casual wear today, are you not?"

"Yes."

"And yet all of your Ambiguous interactions are *internal*."

"Yeah, I guess. But, given that my reports are just numbers, what do you want me to do to improve their presentation?"

"*You tell me*," Glenroy said. "Let's make that a goal for our next evaluation."

"Okay, sure, but—"

"'But' is a very overrated word, John," Glenroy said.

"Okay, but—or it's just that I didn't design the reports, so I'm not sure what—"

"You know what," Glenroy said, "change is not always a bad thing. You may be surprised by where it takes you."

"Okay, I'll give it a try."

"That's what I like to hear. So, overall, John, I'm quite pleased with your work."

"Thanks," I said, waiting for details.

Glenroy again opened his file, which I was surprised to notice had very few papers in it.

"So," he said, pulling out an envelope, "I've approved you for a raise in salary."

"Oh, thanks," I said, accepting the envelope. I wasn't sure, at first, if I was supposed to open it right then, but the parental smile on Glenroy's face told me he was expecting to witness my reaction. So I broke into the envelope and pulled out a letter that stated that I was to receive a 2% improvement in compensation.

"Oh, thanks," I said, trying to hide my confusion—for it was very much like the letter I received every year that told me that I was getting a 2% cost-of-living upgrade in payment. In fact, now that I thought about it, we were currently residing in the approxi-mate time of year that I usually received the good news.

"Congratulations," Glenroy said, "you've earned it."

I returned to my office wearing an amused smile: Glenroy's sneaky attempt to portray himself as my hero made him less formidable. To that end, I retroactively realized that his request for me to improve the presentation of *my* reports was just a random assignment meant to demonstrate to me that he had much to teach me. All I really needed was one or two cosmetic changes to those reports, and he would be placated—at least until he needed to make a follow-up presentation of his leaderly ways

Chapter 44
Dullard in the City III

The Undershare

Upon locking down the epiphany that concluded our last chapter, I opened my email and found a message from Tally; oops, with all my meeting anxiety, I'd forgotten to anticipate her response to my reply to her.

'So,' she wrote, 'I notice that you conveniently left out any details about your love life. Can I assume this means you're still unattached and available to be snatched up by some lucky girl?'

I laughed at her biased flattery and wrote back that—while she was correct that I remained unattached—I saw no evidence that there were 'lucky' girls out there waiting to collect me. That was my attempt to be funny, not self-pitying, but, after I sent the message, I re-read it and realized it probably came across as the latter. Oh well, it would be interesting to get Tally's reaction.

With half an hour left before the end of the day, Tally showed up on my screen again. I clicked her message open with a nervous rattle in my chest.

'Hello, Mr. John,' she said, before going straight for the heart of my matter and asking whether there were any lucky girls on whom I at least had my eye. I laughed again at her lofty-by-proxy imagination. But I wasn't ready yet to name my inappropriate crush on Jacklyn the married math tutor. Instead, I reported back—with a matter-of-fact tone in my typing—that there were always interesting women around, but, as ever, they tended to be already booked up.

The moment I sent *that* empty message, I realized that I was disappointed that I was wasting the opportunity to ask Tally whether I should avoid furthering my friendship with Jacklyn, given my ulterior emotions. Thus, I decided that, if Tally's next reply probed again, I'd finally relent and itemize Jacklyn and the problem with my affection for her.

I smiled at that noble conclusion and stood up with a nervous stretch: it was time for my daily walk to the bus stop and my accompanying hope that I might run into my favourite bus-time companion.

Fifteen minutes later, I arrived at the bus time that most often coincided with Jacklyn's travels. A minute later, I spotted her walking towards me. I smiled as unobtrusively as I could; nevertheless, I noticed that I felt extra nervous seeing my unrequitable crush on a Friday evening.

"Hey," she said when she got close enough.

"Hi."

Jacklyn sighed as she pulled up beside me. "Not to be all philosophical, but don't you think it's funny how the mood in the Friday bus line feels different?"

"*Yeah*, I agree!" I said with more enthusiasm than was required. "I've noticed that too. I bet, if you didn't know what day of the week it was, you could still work out that it was Friday, just from, I don't know ..."

Jacklyn nodded with a polite smile. "Exactly, my friend. Even in a seemingly tranquil lineup like this, there's still something about the Friday air of anticipation, isn't there? I kinda love it."

Jacklyn's face seemed to turn introspective, so I stupidly decided to intervene.

"Um, so are you anticipating something fun on the weekend or something?"

Jacklyn frowned at me.

"Oh, is that a bad question?"

"Well, no, it's just that ..." and Jacklyn paused for one perfectly timed second. "Well, yeah, it *is* a bad question."

I laughed.

Jacklyn smiled. "There's just always so much pressure on people our age to *do something* with our weekend. But, for my part, I don't do a lot—"

"Me either," I said.

"Well," Jacklyn said, shrugging, "that's nice of you to say, I'm sure, but I have a strong suspicion you're just saying that to make me feel better."

"No, really," I blathered with maximum grin. "My weekends are like the most boring ever."

Jacklyn looked me over. "All right, my friend, let's compare boring plans, then. Not to be competitive, but we'll see who makes the *least* of their weekend."

"Sure," I said, smiling my widest, "I've *literally* got nothing to hide."

"Touché, my friend, but we'll see about that."

The bus line up took flight just then, which allowed us to individually strategize as we paid our fares.

When we got to our shared chair, Jacklyn looked at me seriously. "Care to go first?"

"Sure, but how exactly—"

"Excellent question ..." Jacklyn said with a wink in her voice. "As I see it, the best way to assess who has the most boring weekend is to list the things we *don't* do on our weekends and then see who has the better list."

"I see," I said, glancing around for inspiration. "Okay, well, I've never gone on one of those long bike rides with a group of friends."

Jacklyn shrugged. "Go fish—neither have I. In fact, I've never even been tempted."

"Fair enough," I said, unable to resist chuckling at her faux earnestness. "Your turn."

Jacklyn seemed to drop into a ponder. "Okay, my friend. For my part, I've never been partial to spending my weekend shopping for sports cars. I mean (A) I can't afford one and (B) I don't *like* sports cars."

I shrugged sheepishly. "Sorry, I've never even been shopping for a regular car."

"You're lying!" Jacklyn said with a delightful frown. "I bet your go shopping with your butler for luxury automobiles every weekend."

I giggled. "Nope, not even once."

Jacklyn nodded, but then her face seemed to turn serious again. "All right, my friend, how 'bout this? Have you ever spent a weekend secretly giving money to strangers for no particular reason?"

"Nope, never even occurred to me."

"Oh, damn," Jacklyn said, "I guess you win then."

That stopped me in my laugh track. "Oh ... wait ... so you *do* secretly give money to strangers?"

"Well, if I did, would you impersonate a stranger just to get the money?"

"No," I said, giggling at my friend/crush's elite comedic timing—even though her tone still seemed serious. "I don't *think* so."

"Really? You're not just saying that?"

"No. I'm pretty sure I wouldn't impersonate a stranger just to get money out of you. So you really give money to strangers?"

"I'm afraid so."

"Why?—Or do you mean it's like for charity or something?"

"No, it's not a charity thing—it's just for strangers."

"Why would you do that?"

"Um, actually, I'd rather not say."

"Oh, I'm sorry. I didn't mean to pry."

"No, don't be sorry—*I* brought it up. I just meant that I'd rather not say because it's the sort of thing that's easier to show someone than to describe."

"I see," I said cautiously.

"So," Jacklyn said, "you busy tomorrow?"

"No," I blurted before realizing I should soften my enthusiasm. "I think I've established, through our little contest, that I'm not usually busy on the weekend."

"Right," Jacklyn said with a smile, "I guess we made that clear, eh? So, my friend, in lieu of your usual *not*-busyness, would you like to be my assistant in a day of giving money to strangers?"

The answer was in the question, and so the plan was set. I was to meet Jacklyn at 9am at a coffee shop that we guessed lived about equidistance between us.

"Oh, and here's my number in case you need to cancel," Jacklyn said.

"Thanks," I replied, impressively resisting the urge to mock the outrageous suggestion.

Now, obviously the discussion between Elizabeth and me that Friday evening was focused first on why Jacklyn wouldn't want to spend her Saturday morning with her husband.

DISCRETE NOTE: Against my ghostwriter's better instincts, I have a hypothetical confession to offer you, non-judgmental reader. At the time, I *may* have enjoyed speculating in my spare time that Jacklyn's wedding ring was some sort of ruse—perhaps a private protest for gay marriage rights, which hadn't at that time yet arrived in Canada. However, given my neighbour's moral prudishness, I decided it would be best not to inform Elizabeth of my secret, subversive imaginings; consequently, she didn't officially object to my pending romance-free adventure with my married colleague.

The best Elizabeth and I could invent to explain Mr. and Mrs. Math Tutor's odd set up was that he was either on another business trip, or he wasn't interested in Jacklyn's hobbies. I secretly rooted for the latter option.

Hidden Acts to Grind

At 8am, on that cold Saturday morning, I decided to go for a nerve-expunging walk before the big meetup with Jacklyn the math tutor. Twenty-five minutes into the endeavor, I came around a corner to find Jacklyn gliding towards me on a bike. A pony-tail was adorably presenting itself from the back of her oversized helmet.

"Hey," she said with a half wave when she got to me, "you're out early."

"Oh, um, I guess I just wanted to go for a walk before—"

"Yeah, me too," Jacklyn said, patting her bike like it was a horse, "I love starting my day with exercise—endorphins and all that good stuff."

"Right," I said. But, oddly, I noticed that Jacklyn did not look like she was on an exercise mission as stated; she wore neither exercise wear on her person nor sweat on her brow; instead, she displayed casual (non-sporting) clothes that looked unscathed by perspiration.

"All right, fine," she said, "I don't usually go for morning exercise. I was actually just kinda nervous about letting someone join, um, this that we'll be doing—so I decided to go for a bike ride to relax my nerves."

That was shocking news (that Jacklyn the math tutor could be nervous).

"Oh, what are you nervous about?"

"I don't know," Jacklyn said, irritation seeping into her voice. "Anyway, since we're all here, do you wanna just start early?"

"Oh, sure."

"Great, we just have to go to my place to drop off my bike—as well as my *marvelous chapeau*," she added, raising her eyes boastfully at her helmet, "—and then pick up the stuff...if you don't mind a quick detour?"

"No, sure, that's fine," I said, realizing immediately that I'd betrayed myself. After all, *Mr.* Math Tutor could easily be *at* Jacklyn's place, and—upon seeing me cheering on his wife—he would surely realize that my admiration included sadness that he existed. In theory, it would be a good reminder to me that my little crush could only qualify as morally neutral if it was fully hidden beneath my surface so that it wouldn't irritate Jacklyn or her teammate. Thus, I should have been glad to meet Mr. Math Tutor so that I could prove to myself that I could comfortably present as comfortable around him. But, tragically, I have always found it impossible to *plan* to be calm: the more I covet serenity, the more it thinks we're playing a fun game of hide-and-seek.

In short, on the walk to the home of Mr. and Mrs. Math Tutor, I was annoyingly anxious. "Um..." I said, grasping for an easygoing topic, "so what sort of stuff are we doing today?"

"Oh, right, good point, I guess I can't keep the details hidden forever. Um..." she said, helping herself to a long sigh, "so, most simply put, we'll be doing a series of these lovable exploits that I call HAKs."

"Okay, and ...what are *HAKs*?"

"You don't know what HAKs are?" Jacklyn said with forehead and smile tilted crookedly in my direction.

"Um—" I began.

But the delightfully accusatory forehead overpowered me

again. "You should really know what HAKs are if you're going to let yourself be invited to take part in them."

That made me chuckle through my nerves. "Fair point. I'll remember to check before you invite me next time."

"Exactly," Jacklyn said, "is that too much to ask?"

"Nope," I said, chuckling again.

My friend shrugged with a grin. "So, to answer your crude question, obviously, HAK stands for Hidden Act of Kindness."

"Right, *of course*," I said, this time faking my chuckle. "So is this the same thing as *random* acts of kindness, or…?"

"*Ah*," Jacklyn said, suddenly switching to an exaggerated teen-aged cool girl voice of dismissal, "*I don't think so*, my friend. Hidden acts are *totally* different from random ones."

"Right…how come?" I said, trying not to grin.

"*Um, I'm sorry, but we're just not gonna give out random kind-nesses which could randomly land in the hands of someone we don't particularly care for.*"

"Right, fair point."

"I should say *so*," Jacklyn said, switching back to her more mature condescending comedy voice.

"Fair enough," I said, my nerves ruining my fun by reminding me of our untoward direction of travel. "So, um, what's our first step in the process?"

"It's a good question," Jacklyn retorted, almost sounding serious. "Not to be overly dramatic, but the thing I should tell you in advance is…"

I turned to face the apparently genuine revelation. For a wafer of a moment, Jacklyn's eyes looked at mine.

"Um," she said, her tone rising like a barber's chair back to jokeful, "so, yeah, the first thing we're gonna need for you is a code-name—just in case you get caught."

"Who might catch me?"

"Um, one of our *victims*, obviously."

"Victims?" I said, too distracted to offer a less boring response.

"Yes, as in the people we give the money to. Poor things—now they're stuck wondering where it came from."

"Right, got it—so what's my codename?"

Jacklyn and helmet turned to consider my face. "For *you*, I'm thinking…John *Smith*."

I subdued my giggle so that I could play along. "Um, isn't that kind of similar to my actual name?"

"Wrong, it *is* your actual name."

That one made me laugh out loud. "So, but, um, wouldn't a codename work a little better if it was different from—"

"That is where you are wrong, my friend. Ya see, if you tell someone your codename is Smith, I guarantee they'll assume you're anyone *but* Smith."

"Got it," I said, offering my most bemused chuckle. "So, in the meantime, um, how does a HAK actually work?"

"It's pretty easy. We just find people we think we'd *like*—or at least people who seem to be having a crappy day—and we try to sneak them a HAK."

"And what's in the HAK?"

"Usually just money. That way, they can buy what they want—since I don't know their hobbies."

"Oh, okay," I said, as we paused at an intersection, "but how do you, you know, afford that?"

"Wish I could tell ya, my friend, but it's classified."

"Right," I said as we followed the directions of the walk signal to move again, "so ...when do we start?"

"Actually, anytime you're ready. You're my first protégé, so—"

"Really?" I said, beaming at the news.

"Actually," Jacklyn interrupted, "before we start, I should warn you: there are some nasty risks involved in HAK."

"Oh, like what?"

"Well, first of all, like I said, our victims have been known to catch us in the act."

"Right ...and that's bad?"

"Of course it's *bad*," Jacklyn snapped to my full nervous amusement. "These are *hidden* acts of kindness—they're supposed to be anonymous. When you play Secret Santa, do you usually write your name on the card?"

"I see your point," I said, stifling another giggle.

"Exactly, my friend—just wait till you experience the mortification that comes with getting caught."

"Have *you* ever experienced it?" I said, but my amused face turned to an instinctual deep breath as I noticed that Jacklyn was leading us down a pathway to an apartment building. 'Hi, nice to meet you,' I practiced saying in my head. 'Yeah, we both work for Ambiguity. But I don't work directly with your wife. How come you're not joining for the HAKing?'

"Once again ...*classified*," Jacklyn said to my autopilot chuckles as she pulled out a key to the building—and, in turn, to my full nerves.

"Okay," I said, as Jacklyn led us onto an elevator—which showed no indication that it might break down to spare us our destination. But then, shockingly, Jacklyn hit a button to go *down* towards the parking.

"You live underground?" I said, unable to fathom any other possibility in that moment.

"No, not usually," she said with a grin. "But, sadly, that's where our bikes have to live."

"Right, of course," I said, pretending not to have spotted the silliness of my question. "So, um, what are the other things that could go wrong during the, um, HAK ...stuff?"

"Well, let's see ...right ...as well as being caught in the act by your intended victim, a HAKer can also be caught by a *bystander*."

"And that's bad too?" I said as the elevator landed on our new level.

"Well, *yeah*," Jacklyn said as we stepped out, "once again, your HAK's been exposed. Not as bad as having the mark, themself, catch you, obviously, but *still*."

"I see," I said as we walked through an ominous hallway. In theory, the journey a thousand leauges *under* the Math Tutors' apartment should have made me less nervous, but, of course, I imagined that Mr. Math Tutor might also be doing some below-sea-level work that morning.

"Okay," Jacklyn said, "so it feels pretty bad if you get caught by a victim or a bystander—*though that's not as big a deal*—but one of the worst things that can happen is when you're *rejected* by your intended target."

"Okay," I said as Jacklyn took us into a large room of storage lockers, "and, um, what's that mean?"

"Well, in that situation, you've left your HAK in the path of your mark, but they refuse it and just leave it there."

"Ouch," I said, pretending to care as we stepped up to a specific storage locker.

"*Ouch* is right," Jacklyn said with unnecessary calmness as she spiraled in the code for her combination lock. "It's very troubling, my friend. But no point in getting ourselves worked up about it—it's just a risk we have to be aware of."

"Right," I said with another forced laugh as I peered through her now open storage room doorway, readying myself for stilted introduction.

But the squared-off space caged a few boxes but no humans.

After placing her bike and safety hat against one side of the mini-room, Jacklyn came upon a little table that was placed next to the entrance as though it were the intro desk to an office. From there she picked up a purse-backpack hybrid.

I offered the item a stare-faced greeting. *Did its presence here mean we didn't have to look for it upstairs?*

Jacklyn smiled. "Yup, this is the holder of the magic, my friend. I keep it here when I'm not doing the HAK-thing—that way, I'm less tempted to take it out more than I should."

"Right, okay. That's good," I said.

"*Good?*" Jacklyn said, activating her comedy forehead. "Some might says it shows great restraint and, you know, spiritual wisdom."

"Right, you're right," I said, pretending to laugh.

"So," I said, as we left the nerve-saving room, "um, what happens if you leave a HAK out for someone, but someone *else* gets to it first?"

"Oh, yeah, good catch, my friend—it *can* happen. But, you know, it's not the end of the world unless you specifically *don't like* the person who steals it—admittedly, that feels pretty crappy."

"Right," I said, my anxiety still holding out fear that our errands weren't yet done.

"Now," Jacklyn said, "there's one more big risk that we face—probably the worst one of all. You think you're ready for it, my friend?"

"Yeah, yeah, of course," I said, "I'm sure I'm ready for it."

"No," Jacklyn said as she walked us down that basement hallway back to the elevator that would announce our next destination. "I don't think you're ready."

"I'm pretty sure I'm ready for it."

"It's very unsettling—you're not gonna like it."

"I'm ready," I said, annoyance now sneaking onto my tone.

Jacklyn giggled as we got on the elevator. "All right, there are situations where,"—she put her hand to my shoulder—"where we can be *conned* by a victim."

"How?" I said, looking at the elevator buttons wondering why Jacklyn hadn't announced our intentions yet.

My friend finally (but slowly) clicked the awkwardness-saving LOBBY button.

I felt a gentle breeze spread across my insides. Indeed, I was so relieved to have escaped without introduction to Mr. Math Tutor that I promised myself that next time I would be prepared to meet him with full serenity on board. In fact, I instructed myself to ask Jacklyn friendly questions about her husband as soon as I could find a casual moment to do so.

"Well," Jacklyn continued with an amusingly exaggerated sigh, "there are times when a person'll *seem* nice—so nice that we'll sneak them a HAK. But then—inexplicably—they'll turn horrible."

"Wow—in what way?" I said, suddenly interested again in the topic as the rescuing elevator returned us to street level.

"Well, for instance," Jacklyn said, comically sighing again as we exited the carrier, "this one time, I sat next to this guy on the bus, and he told me all about how his life was off the rails—his boss was mad at him; his kids were mad at him—and so, being the sweet person I am, I decided to cheer him up with a HAK."

"Oh, but how could you be, you know, surreptitious when you were in such a confined space?"

Jacklyn gave me a boastful shrug. "Yeah, when you're in close quarters, you have to be quick—like, as soon as you see an opening, you have to go for it. So, when he reached up to ring the [request-stop] buzzer, I snuck an envelope into his grocery bag."

"Brilliant," I said as we left Jacklyn's building into the soothing morning air.

This time, Jacklyn's shrug was sheepish. "Yeah, well, he then preceded to yell at the driver for missing his stop. Our guy actually rang the buzzer too late, as far as I could tell, so it was actually *his* fault but that made no difference to him, and he let loose with a cascade of four-letter words on the poor driver. So, needless to say,

I didn't feel so good about donating money to such a loudmouth cad."

"Wow, yeah, that's unfortunate," I said. "But, um, you don't think sometimes *loudmouth cads* need cheering up too?"

"Nope," Jacklyn said, "not my jurisdiction. But I wasn't about to say to the cad, '*Excuse me*, Mr. Cad, I just slipped some money in your bag, but—now that I see you're so unlikeable—I'd like it back, please.'"

"Right," I said, chuckling to the full extent of my now relaxed nerves.

A few minutes later, we arrived in a neighbourhood of houses.

"All right, Mr. John Smith—*codename, John Smith*—now that I've briefed you on the perils of HAK, I think you're ready to try one out."

"Really, you sure?"

Jacklyn looked me up and down. "Yeah, I think so."

I laughed. "Okay, what do I do?"

"All right, my friend. So the first thing I'd like you to do is pick a house around here that hints at the sort of people you'd like to give a HAK."

"Um, okay, how about *that* one?"

"*That* one *there*? Really?"

"No, of course not *that one*," I said, hiding my giggle. "How 'bout that one?"

"If I didn't know any better, my friend, I'd say you were picking houses randomly."

"I *am*."

Jacklyn laughed.

"Sorry," I said with a sheepish grin, "I didn't really know what you were looking for, so I figured I'd just guess."

Jacklyn nodded. "I'd've done the same, but—for the record—it's not about what *I'm* looking for—I'm just asking you to identify a house that suggests people *you* would like."

"Um, sorry, how can I tell that from the outside of a house?"

Jacklyn's face turned serious as she panned the area with her gaze. "Okay, see the first house you pointed at?"

"Yes."

"See the garbage bins in their garage?"

"Yes."

"And the recycle bins?"

"Yeah ...um ...*no* ...where?"

"Exactly—so, if you're an environmentalist, that might not be a good sign for *you*—maybe you always want a high, you know, ratio of recycling to, um ...garbaging."

"Okay, fair enough."

"I'm not saying that *is* your priority—I'm just using it as a *for instance.*"

"Right, no, that makes sense."

"Okay, and see the house next to it? We should *all* be opposed to that one because of the sports car out front."

"Oh, okay ...*why?*"

"Well, I'm sure some sports car owners are nice, but—not to be judgmental—but it's best to avoid people who are obsessed with the sociopathic concept of going menacingly fast."

"Okay," I said, not sure if Jacklyn was serious, "well, what about *that* house? No sports car, and there's no garbage or recycling *at all*, so maybe the recycling thing breaks even?"

"Right, but it's just that there's newspapers built up near the front door—"

SOCIO-TEMPORAL NOTE: At that time of that interaction, young reader, newspapers were almost exclusively found in paper form and were delivered daily to the doorsteps of home-owners who had indicated an interest in reading them.

"I see, so they're lazy? We don't like lazy people?!"

Jacklyn laughed. "Actually, I was just thinking they might be on vacation, so they probably don't really need, you know, our mood-enhancement services."

"Oh, I see, yeah, that makes sense." I looked around again. "*Oh*—how about *them?* They're *Block Parents.*"

Jacklyn shrugged with a smirking smile. "Yeah, I guess—*if you care about keeping kids safe*—then that could be something. So you wanna give them a try?"

The invitation made me so nervous that I forgot to chuckle at Jacklyn's humour. "Okay, so what do we do?"

Jacklyn opened her purse-backpack hybrid and produced a

crisp light blue envelope that read sharply on its cover, HIDDEN ACT OF KINDNESS. She handed it to me with a smile.

"Now, my friend, all you have to do is put this in their mailbox without getting caught."

"Is it likely I'll get caught?"

"Well, I don't see anybody around, so you should be fine. Just walk super casually up the path. Pretend to knock on their door—that'll keep the neighbours from getting suspicious—and then, if there's no answer—"

"Wait, why would there be an answer if I'm *pretend* knocking?"

"Well, there's always a chance they'll see you in the window and intercept you. But, trust me, the risk's part of the fun."

"I guess," I said with furrowed brow.

Jacklyn chuckled again. "So, when and if there's no answer, put the envelope in the mailbox and come back here."

"Okay," I said, taking a deep breath.

I entered the driveway and was soon on the pathway to the front entrance. One step, two steps, and the door opened! I stopped in my dullard tracks.

A woman came rushing out of the house. She stopped when she saw me. "Who are *you?*"

My first thought was to go for Jacklyn's joke and introduce myself as 'Codename Smith,' but, luckily, I realized in time that—from the stranger's perspective—that would seem more *creepily* mysterious than humourously so.

"Um, sorry," I said, "I'm John Smith, and that's my friend Jacklyn, and we deliver surprise gifts to strangers." I held out Jacklyn's envelope for her.

"What's that?"

"It's, um, a hidden act of kindness?"

"And what's that?"

"Um, basically it's money."

"I don't want your money," the woman said, moving again to her car.

I gulped my embarrassment as I turned to look at Jacklyn. She offered me a cringing grin. It was the perfect blend of playfulness and compassion—in fact, it was so well articulated that my shame nearly vanished. But I didn't let on as I walked back to Jacklyn.

"I was caught *and* rejected," I told her.

Jacklyn held her amused grimace as the woman drove by glaring. "There was nothing you could do, my friend—there's just no guarantees in our business."

"So," I said as we continued walking, "can I review?"

"I look forward to it," Jacklyn said with a smile.

"Okay," I said, hoping to be funny, "so, so far, we're against people on vacation, sports car drivers, people who don't recycle—"

"Don't forget the Block Parents. We're against them now too."

"Really?"

"Okay, fine, we'll give the Block Parents one more chance."

I laughed. "That's nice of you."

Jacklyn offered me a sheepish shrug. "It's not like we're judgmental. It's just that—as HAKers—it's our job to determine who's worthy and who's not."

I smirked. "Right, I get it."

Jacklyn smiled. "Actually, the way I see it is—since we're giving up our own money—we get the fun of including people we like and *snubbing* people we don't like. And, for me, that means I get to exclude sports car people." Jacklyn paused, her face contemplative again. "Sorry, I just see sports cars as a symbol of senseless speed. And, well, I don't like them for it."

"Right," I said cautiously. The sudden seriousness of Jacklyn's mood had me wondering if the dangerous speed of a Ferrari driver had impacted her past. I glanced around at the cars parked along the street, hoping I could find something meaningful to cheer up the moment. "Hey," I said, "whaddya think of *that?*"

Jacklyn looked up to find a parked tow truck with a bumper sticker that stated:

IF YOU'RE DRIVING DRUNK...
HONK TWICE. I'LL GIVE YOU A FREE TOW.

"That's cool," she said.

"Yeah," I said, "it's like, it's not about blame—it's just, 'You're a danger behind the wheel, so I'll give you a ride home.'"

"Well, I wouldn't go *that* far," Jacklyn said. "Unlike you, I guess, I'm into blame. I can't think of anything more selfish than driving a massive hunk of glass and metal when you're mentally and physically impaired."

"Maybe, but don't you think that sometimes, when people are being stupid—"

"Not *stupid*—utterly selfish."

"Okay, but don't you think that—when people are being selfish—sometimes it might be better to, I don't know, to offer them our help instead of yelling at them?"

Jacklyn shook her head and glared at the air. "I'm okay with offering them help, but that doesn't mean I have to stop blaming them for their sociopathic crimes. They made their evil choice."

I winced at that. Jacklyn almost seemed angry with me for my faulty perspective. That surprised me almost as much having the opinion in the first place; I'd never articulated it before, which made Jacklyn's sudden rebuke particularly off-putting. Nevertheless, I tried to hide my disillusionment.

"Anyway," Jacklyn said, "I think we agree that Bumper Sticker Guy is trying to do something nice. Shall we make a contribution to his cause?"

"Really?" I said, suddenly smiling without intention.

Jacklyn shrugged her own smile as she looked back at the truck. "His window's open enough to get *that* inside," she said, gesturing to the envelope still in my hand.

So I walked to the truck, and I felt a flutter in my hand as I reached it to the opening. The moment I released the envelope, a surprising feeling of fulfillment cascaded through my chest. It seemed that I had officially joined Jacklyn's strange club.

After a five-minute walk, Jacklyn and I sat in a mega-sized coffee shop at a table with good sight lines. I was pleased with myself because I'd managed to pay for our beverages.

"Now we wait," Jacklyn said. "Keep your eyes open for a good victim."

My open eyes were privy to a wide assortment of women attached to baby strollers.

"What about *them*?"

"Hmm …coffee-shop moms are tricky."

"How so?"

"Well, not for nothing, but coffee-shop moms often suffer from a certain baby-producing, um, let's say, *self-assuredness*."

"Oh—"

Jacklyn shrugged with a grin. "It's a known fact, my friend: coffee-shop moms are more important than the rest of us. *Just ask them.*"

"Okay," I said, chuckling while simultaneously feeling sorry for the cheerful-looking parents.

"You know," Jacklyn said a few minutes into our wait, "familiarity is a strange little creature—don't you think?"

"Um, sure, I guess …well, how so?"

"It's just interesting to me the way familiarity seems to make significant things seem, I don't know, ordinary. Like, have you ever—is there anything that you do all the time now that used to scare you but doesn't anymore?"

"I guess so."

"Like what?"

"Um, well, I don't know if this is a good example, but I was intimidated when I first came to Ambiguity."

"Why?"

"I guess it seemed kind of chaotic and that, like, I don't know, any stranger could come up and talk to me."

"Anyone still *could* come up and talk to you."

"Yeah, but now I feel like I'd know what to say."

Jacklyn smiled. "Well, I don't know, then, if that's an example of what I'm getting at, but maybe part of the reason you feel more comfortable walking around Ambiguity is just because you've done it so many times now that it's no longer exciting enough to make you nervous. Maybe it's not that it's stopped somehow being chaotic or whatever you found intimidating—maybe it's just that, I don't know, you don't pay attention to the chaos anymore."

"Maybe," I said.

Jacklyn laughed. "Maybe not. Maybe, in that case, you just realized you *could* handle big crowds. But I think, in so many instances, we have no other option but to hang out with our demons, so we don't necessarily kill them: we just kinda get used to being around them all the time."

I nodded, still wondering what Jacklyn was getting at. "So familiarity is a *good* thing, then?"

"Well, that's my question—I don't know if it is. Maybe it's good to get used to things that scare us. I don't know. But what worries me is when people get used to the things that are supposed to, you know, be important to us."

I nodded vacantly again.

"Like, for instance," Jacklyn said, dropping to a whisper while she pointed with her forehead muscles at a tranquil family at the other end of the coffee shop, "I've heard so many stories of how people get super inspired—beyond their greatest expectations—by the birth of their children. And yet—not to be melodramatic—but some parents seem bored or even irritated. There they are with the supposedly most precious people in their lives, and they don't even look that *interested*."

"Right," I said, "and yet, I'm sure, if they ever lost, you know, a family member, they'd wish, you know ..." I couldn't find the right words to complete my overwrought sentence.

Neither apparently could Jacklyn. Yet she seemed fascinated by my clichéd offering. Her gaze became focused on the table. Perhaps she was thinking of the victim of the sports car driver.

"Sorry—" I said, hoping to apologize for turning her speculations dark, but she waved me off with a closed-eyes, scrunched-nose shake of her head. My instincts thus informed me that she neither wanted her gloomy reflections to be ignored nor discussed. So I looked around for something to distract her from them.

"Um," I said, "I think I see someone who might deserve your next HAK."

"*Who?*" Jacklyn said, her face magically morphing back to cheerful as though it had been there all along.

"That girl behind the counter, cleaning the glass."

Jacklyn took a hearty look at my barista target. "I agree. She's a sweetie, but she looks super sad when she thinks no one's looking."

I nodded. "So how do we do it?"

Jacklyn scanned the coffee shop. "We need some place that customers won't be snooping around."

Just then, our intended victim's supervisor asked her to clean the coffee shop washrooms.

"Back in a sec," Jacklyn said.

One hundred seconds later than she'd promised, Jacklyn returned with a hefty smile.

"Now we wait, my friend—I put the HAK in the washroom."

We didn't have to wait long; soon, our victim came out of her backroom and walked gradually toward the washrooms. Her timidity was in stark contrast with an assertively moving woman who entered the coffee shop just then.

"Hi," the newcomer said, interrupting our mark on her cleaning mission, "before you do that, can you put my order in? I need a large Frappuccino, no whip."

"Oh," our startled friend replied so softly it was hard to hear. "Okay, I guess," [we surmise] she said.

"Thanks," the assertive woman said, "mind if I borrow that key there while you're doing that?"

"Oh, okay," the shy barista replied, handing over the washroom access.

I sent Jacklyn a look of concern. "Will she find it?"

Jacklyn stared back at me with a scrunched forehead. "I just taped it to the back of the door."

I giggled. "I thought you were going to put it where a customer couldn't get it?"

"I know, but I was trying to hurry—and I thought Miss Sad Barista would be the next one in there, so ..."

"Right, *too bad*," I said, with my best sheepish shrug.

Miss Sad Barista, meanwhile, had slowly walked behind the counter to let her co-worker know about the assertive woman's order. And, before she could return to her washroom duties, she was caught by a bubbly customer inquiring about a product.

"All right, quick," Jacklyn said, handing me an envelope and a piece of tape, "she'll be finished with that any second. Can you grab the other key and put this one in the men's washroom?"

"Okay," I said, seizing the loot.

I returned a minute later feeling impressed with myself.

Jacklyn and I smiled as we watched the melancholy barista reach down to pick up her cleaning supplies again.

"I'll get a large coffee," announced a loud man suddenly arrived at the drink-ordering area. He scattered some change on the counter before turning to the opposite till. "I'll take that," he said, grabbing the men's washroom key ahead of our sad friend's reaching hand.

"That's not for *you*," Jacklyn whispered.

"Oops," I said, my chin stretched into a full cringe.

Soon after, the first troublemaker exited her washroom, sporting a pleased expression on her face—and a helpless envelope in her hand.

Jacklyn glared at her.

But the enemy customer didn't notice and instead collected and paid for her beverage and sat down with a smug smile.

Not much later, the second enemy of etiquette came out of his washroom with his own envelope-induced grin. He picked up his drink, and—*holy ghostwriter!*—he sat next to the first stealer of HAKs.

"Look what I got in the washroom," the man said, holding up his thievery.

"I got one too," his partner said, and they merrily took to discussing what they apparently perceived to be some sort of new marketing gimmick designed by the coffee shop chain.

Jacklyn shook her head with strained cheek muscles. "This *sucks*," she said. "All right, let's dispense a HAK on that evasive girl, and then let's get the hell out of this cursed place."

"Okay, but ...*how?*"

"All right, let's see," Jacklyn said, scanning the room. "If we put it next to that tray of dishes over there, it should be safe."

"But what if she's not the next one to clear them?"

Jacklyn took in a sigh. "That's a risk we're gonna have to take, my friend. But at least," she said, glancing at the assertive, HAK-stealing couple, "we know Mr. and Mrs. Brashness won't get it."

"Thanks," Miss Sad Barista's soft voice said from behind the counter as Jacklyn deposited our cups and secret donation.

"See you," Jacklyn replied before raising delighted eyebrows at me.

But I wasn't so confident.

Jacklyn and I next entered a giant mall where we found a large selection of meandering people from whom to choose.

"Only problem with this place," Jacklyn said, "is people move quickly in here. So we'll have to think quickly."

Thinking quickly wasn't going to be a problem for Jacklyn the math tutor; within moments of entering the mall, she had spotted our first victim—a man in a pet store buying a flashy light to attach to a collar, presumably so that the collar wearer would be safer during nighttime walks.

"That's cute," Jacklyn said. "Let's give him a HAK."

We scurried to the nearest exit where a large but cheerful-looking canine sat people watching. As Jacklyn pet the creature with her left hand, her right hand subtly snuck an envelope under its collar. Her movements were so quick yet soft that the animal seemed unaware of the reverse pickpocketing. We then reentered the mall and walked past the dog's presumed human companion, who was now on his way out. We turned back around and followed him.

On the outside, man and dog greeted each other with great tail-wagging joy. The human looked at the canine's collar and took hold of the HAK underneath. As Jacklyn and I walked by, the man looked curiously at the envelope Jacklyn had delivered. He squinted with apparent confusion as he examined the money inside. He looked around for a moment and then finally smiled.

"I guess somebody likes us," he said, petting the ears of his doggy friend.

Jacklyn shrugged a smile at me. "And *that*, my friend, is first our confirmed sale of the day."

"That was cool," I said, trying to quell my own smile. "Can we try another one?"

"Of course," Jacklyn said with a tiny additional lip curl.

Yet, despite her diminutive expression, I sensed that she was pleased with my enthusiasm.

As we looked around the mall for our next victim, I decided to accidentally ruin the fun by overanalyzing it.

"I really admire that you do this," I said.

Jacklyn nodded blankly. "Thanks, but it's really not a big deal. Who am I really helping?"

"All the people you're giving the HAKs to—you're making their day."

"Maybe," Jacklyn said. "I guess it's possible someone might appreciate it. I hope so—it's hard to say. But, if I really wanted to help, I'd give the money to a cause that *actually* improves people's lives. But I'm too selfish to do that. I'm—not to be melodramtic—but I'm very much attached to doing it this way. I need the rush. But, if I were a truly good person, I'd put my money towards something much more important instead of—"

"But," I tried, "most of us keep *all* of our money for ourselves. You're actually doing something nice for other people with yours."

Jacklyn half shrugged and rolled her eyes. "Anyway. Thanks for the nice …sentiment. Let's keep going."

Jacklyn next led us into a photography shop where we spied a gregarious, senior-looking customer at the photo counter.

SOCIO-TEMPORAL NOTE: At that time in entrepeneurial history, small photoshops were a common way of turning the undeveloped images recorded on one's non-digital camera into tactile photographs. Indeed, at that very time, my ghostwriter worked at such a place. In fact, don't be alarmed, easily startled reader, if my attention-seeking ghostwriter makes a cameo in this scene. Look for someone who's tall in both stature and ego.

"So," the senior said, "have you had any luck with the photos yet?"

"Actually, Mr. Henderson," the diminutive girl behind the counter said nervously, "sorry, there was a problem with the machine. Your photos aren't quite ready yet. Is it okay if—"

"Oh, that's no problem," Mr. Henderson said with a grand smile that calmed all nerves within a ten-metre radius, "I have plenty of errands to do in the mall. When should I come back?"

"Is fifteen minutes okay?"

"No problem," Mr. Henderson said with another smile as he went on his cheerful way.

Jacklyn raised her forehead at me. "Okay, my friend," she whispered, "we've got fifteen minutes to come up with a plan."

"Um, maybe we could get the photo shop people to help us?"

Jacklyn squinted at me with a half-mouthed sigh. "I don't know: it's risky to involve civilians."

I laughed. "Oh, okay—"

"Although," Jacklyn said, "if we *could* gain access to Cashier Girl, she could give us unobstructed access to our victim's photo envelope. Very interesting. Give me a moment to consider your proposal."

I chuckled again at that. But, just as Jacklyn began considering my idea, a better one arrived on her desk. A tall photo lab technician came out of his backroom.

"Oh, hey, Kanika," he said to his tiny co-worker with a boastful shrug, "I fixed the jam quicker than I thought—here's Mr. Henderson's pictures in case he comes back sooner." He then put the photos on the counter and returned to his backroom.

"Okay," Jacklyn whispered to me. "I'll distract *Kanika*—here's the HAK—put it in the photo envelope when she's not looking ... *Excuse me*," Jacklyn then said, suddenly approaching Kanika, "do you have any scrapbook photo albums?"

"Yeah, I'll show you," Kanika said, and she walked Jacklyn to a faraway area of the store.

With Kanika and Jacklyn away from the front till, my heart began to thump. There Mr. Henderson's photos sat—unguarded— on the counter. I walked to them and then glanced back at Jacklyn and Kanika; they were laughing at something; clearly Jacklyn had the enemy firmly distracted.

I slowly reached my hand to the counter—my heart was beating so loudly that you'd think Kanika would have heard it. I took hold of the photo envelope, opened it, slipped in the HAK and then put the envelope back down as quickly as I could. Relief spread across my stomach as my red hand was freed of its incriminating evidence.

'SUDDEN VOICE FROM BEHIND ME!'

I yelped in surprise.

"Sorry," the voice said as I turned around to discover that Kanika was approaching me at a rapid pace. "Just wondering if you needed some help?"

That was a clever question, for it implied another. *What was I doing standing in front of the counter so suspiciously?*

"Um," I said, scraping my mind for assistance. "Thanks, um, I just wanted to check if my photos were ready?"

"Oh, sure. What's your last name?"

"Smith?"

Kanika walked behind the counter and looked in the S section of her photo files.

"Hmm," she said, "I don't see anything ready yet under that name. Are you sure your photos are due back today?"

This Kanika was a keeper! She'd rescued me from my own lie.

"Actually, I think you're right. I forgot: the photos are due back tomorrow, not today. Sorry about that."

"Oh, that's okay," Kanika said. "I can check to see if they'll be ready early—"

"No, no, that's okay, I'll come back tomorrow."

"Oh—okay then. See you tomorrow."

"Sorry, my friend," Jacklyn said outside the store, "I thought I had a handle on her."

"No, that's okay. It was fine," I said, not sure if I believed me.

Jacklyn flickered into a smile. "Not for nothing, but—if you're ever trying to be inconspicuous—one thing you can do is purposely do something *conspicuous*."

"Really?"

"Yeah, as I see it, trying to be inconspicuous can actually *be* conspicuous. So I purposely draw attention to myself—like by, say, knocking something over—and then my theory is people'll look at me—draw their conclusions—and then they'll leave me alone because they think they *know* what's happened."

"That's brilliant."

"Thanks," Jacklyn said, rolling her eyes, "but it's just something I noticed by accident."

"Really? How do you *notice something by accident?*"

"Well, one day at a grocery store, I accidentally knocked over this huge cereal display. It was funny because a lot people stared at me, but—once they'd determined I was just a klutz—I don't think they wanted to embarrass me, so they stopped staring pretty quickly. So it's not like I had some great insight into human nature. I just noticed it because it happened."

I smiled at Jacklyn's attempt to dimpress me.

"What are you smiling at?" she said.

"Oh, just your *accidental* observations. How come I never make accidental observations that are that interesting?"

Jacklyn again rolled her eyes in reply. Indeed, without a viable defense against my assault on her modesty, Jacklyn was forced to change the subject back to our HAK responsibilities.

We then spent two hours taking turns being in charge of running HAKs. Although, in truth, when I was the captain, Jacklyn ever so directly helped me come up with my plans. You see, disappointed-in-me reader, all I could think to do when I was leading the HAK was to try to copy Jacklyn; whereas all Jacklyn could think do when she was steering us was to invent creative new HAK tactics. For instance, after I'd had one of my turns, Jacklyn spotted a stroller-mom in a clothing store. I had assumed that Jacklyn's apparent prejudice against coffee-shop stroller-moms would apply to mall stroller-moms as well, but one should never attempt to predict what Jacklyn the math tutor is going to do.

Jacklyn nonchalantly started a conversation with the stroller-mom; apparently, the contents of the stroller-mom's stroller— an eleven-month-old human—was a cute sight to see.

"What a happy baby," Jacklyn said.

"Yeah," said the stroller-mom, "she *is* a happy little girl."

Jacklyn nodded. "I bet that takes some skill and patience on your part."

The stroller-mom laughed. "With babies, it's just the luck of the draw, I'm afraid."

Jacklyn smiled back. "Is she your first?"

"No, Chelsea here has two older brothers."

"And were *they* happy babies?"

"Actually, yeah," said the stroller-mom, "we've been very lucky."

"What a *coincidence*," Jacklyn said—and then she smiled at *me*.

Her expression punched me in the face. Jacklyn had taken *my* method of modesty removal and used it on the stroller-mom! A distinguished non-dullard was actually copying a dullard. It was an occasion for the dullard history books.

"No *really*," the stroller-mom said, "I've seen lots of great parents have really cranky babies—and lots of not-so-great parents have little angels. It really is just the luck of the draw."

"I'm sure you're right," Jacklyn said, grinning.

The stroller-mom shook her head with a surrendering laugh.

"Well, Chelsea," Jacklyn whispered to the stroller's contents, "keep up the good work."

As Jacklyn and I left the stroller area, I was about to say that it was her turn for a HAK, but my friend beat me to my words.

"You're up again," she said.

"I thought it was *your* turn," I replied dumbly before realizing what Jacklyn meant. "Wait, you sure a parent would want you introducing a foreign object to their baby?"

"Yeah, probably not," Jacklyn said, "so I put it in the back pocket of the stroller."

"How?" I demanded. "I don't remember you being anywhere near the back pocket."

Jacklyn shrugged her shoulders like Michael Jordan after making an astonishing shot.

I laughed with a full eye roll.

"All right," my friend said, "break time."

I was pleased to hear it. (For it turns out—and don't tell Jacklyn that I said this—but being a HAKer can actually be energy-draining and thus hunger-inducing.)

Chapter 45
Dullard in Conversation IV

Truth or Share

Jacklyn bought us a couple of snacks and beverages, and we sat outside on a sun-warmed park bench.

"So," she said, "you having a good time, my friend?"

Was I having a good time? Of course I was having a good time! Was Jacklyn stupid?

But that seemed like a startling way to respond, so I decided instead to hide my overly dramatic feelings within some comedy. Unfortunately, I didn't have any of my own humour available, so I resolved to steal some of Jacklyn's.

"Wish I could tell ya," I said, "but I'm afraid that's classified,"

Jacklyn looked startled by her words. "Oh …it's been that bad?"

"Oh, no, no, it's been great. I just meant, you know, that—"

Jacklyn grinned sheepishly at me.

"Oh, you're joking?"

"I'm afraid so. You have a right to keep your feelings classified—so long as you have a good reason."

"Oh—well, I *do*."

"All right, let's hear it."

"Well," I said, clawing my mind for some wit of my own. "Well, the thing is, if I told you how much I'm enjoying HAKing, you might get a big head."

"Good plan, my friend. I know how I get."

"Exactly," I said.

Jacklyn nodded that forehead. "So, just so I'm clear, the more you enjoy the HAKing, the *less* you're gonna say about it—is that about right, my friend?"

"Right, so I guess I won't say *anything* about it."

"What a sweet thing to say."

I laughed.

"No really," Jacklyn said, "if I'm understanding your code, you're essentially saying you *love* the HAKing."

"I *do*."

"*Oh* ..." Jacklyn said, tilting her head, "and, by that, you mean that you *don't* like it."

I laughed again. "That's classified."

"Really? You mean that?"

I shrugged. "*Classified.*"

"That's so sweet," Jacklyn said, grinning right at me.

I became nervous at that point that I might mess up the humour, so I ventured to make like a Chet and change the subject.

"Um, so, anyway, what made you start HAKing?"

"Oh, good question," Jacklyn said. "It's ... for sentimental reasons."

"Oh, sorry—would you rather not talk about it?"

Jacklyn's forehead scrunched for a moment, and then she smiled again.

"What?" I said.

"Well, ordinarily I wouldn't tell a friend about this, but, strangely, I feel I like could tell you pretty much anything ...is that silly?"

"No, of course you *can*," I said, suddenly nervous about whether I could live up to the compliment.

Jacklyn nodded. "So the thing of it is: I started this whole HAKing hobby to honour my parents and my little brother." She paused again. And then looked at me. "They all died a few years ago."

Oh no. "I'm so sorry."

"It's okay," Jacklyn half-whispered.

"I'm so sorry."

"Thank you," she said, taking a deep breath. "It's been a long time since it happened—I guess I'm a lot better now."

"I'm so sorry," I said once more.

"It's okay," Jacklyn said.

"Um," I said, "so, um, how'd you get through that? How'd you keep going?"

"I don't really know. I almost didn't. You know, for a while, you just think, 'What's the point? Nothing matters anymore.' It's like the most important...the people you cared about the most have been taken away from you. And you just think: 'I'll never care about anything again.'"

Those words wedged themselves in my throat.

"So," Jacklyn said, "my gran kind of forced me to get on with life. She'd lost her son, so I guess she put her heart and...energy... into me. She kept telling me—you know that song where the girl says something about how she'd let her little brothers—who died young—live through her?"

"No, I haven't," I said, suddenly guilty about my ignorance.

"Well, anyway, my gran kept telling me pretty much that. And she kept saying that—as long we remembered them, and we let the memory of them keep us company—they would never be completely gone."

"That's nice," I said, hopefully.

Jacklyn smirked. "Well, I have to say, my friend, I thought it was BS. But I also felt like—for my grandmother's sake—I had to pretend like I believed what she was saying. And, after a while—I don't know, when you pretend to believe something for long enough, you sometimes forget why you didn't believe it in the first place. And now it's funny because, if I'm having a crappy day, or, if I can't solve some tricky problem, I just kind of—this is going to sound silly—but I imagine my family's watching me. And it's like I want to be at my best for them. I know it sounds silly, but it actually works—it totally motivates me—because I want them to be proud of me."

"That's amazing," I said.

Jacklyn smiled. "The funny thing is I don't really believe they *are* watching me, but I can still say they're helping me because— if I couldn't imagine them watching me—I couldn't keep going sometimes. That probably sounds silly, doesn't it?"

"No, not all, it sounds brilliant...well, not *brilliant*—"

Jacklyn waved off my panic with a smile. "No, I know what you mean. Thanks for saying that."

"Um, yeah, of course, so, um, can I ask what your family was like?"

"Hmm ...good question."

"Sorry, would you rather not talk about it or...?"

"No, it's okay. I like talking about them ...So my dad was—in my totally objective opinion—the funniest person ever. He had so many funny facial expressions and ...Well, like, this one time, I asked him if I could borrow five dollars—it's weird that I remember this so clearly—but, so I asked him, 'Hey, Dad, can I borrow five dollars?', figuring it was no big deal, but he responded with this look of horror at the idea of lending me *all that money*." Jacklyn suppressed a chuckle as she imitated her father's shocked face.

I laughed.

"Exactly!" Jacklyn said. "You can't help but laugh at it, but, when *I* laughed, Dad said, 'If you're going to laugh at me, I'm not going to lend you all that money.'"

I giggled again.

Jacklyn smiled introspectively, which made me nervous.

"So what about your mom? Was she funny too?"

"Definitely. Actually, I think she was comedically brilliant too—excuse the bias again, but whaddya expect?"

"Yeah, be as biased as you like."

"Thanks, yeah. So, anyway, she wasn't as laugh-out-loud funny as my dad. She was more, like, witty than funny. She just had all these clever phrases, but she was always deadpan, so—if you just listened to her tone—you'd be convinced she was completely serious."

"That's cool. Um, so do you have an example?"

"Well, it's like, when she and Dad disagreed about something—and, on the rare case she thought he'd proven his case—she wouldn't say he'd proven her wrong; instead, she'd be like, 'I'm glad to see that you've improved on your opinion. With those modifications, I see no further reason to disagree with you."

I laughed again, but I was afraid to linger on the story. "That's funny. Um, what about your brother? I'm guessing he was pretty funny too."

"Um," Jacklyn said, "not really—and it's funny because Geoffrey didn't think my parents were particularly funny either. He tolerated their jokes, but he was never much for laughing at them.

And yet—not for nothing—but he was the sweetest little guy you could ever meet. He hated to see anyone unhappy. Like, if someone looked at all sad, he'd go up to them—complete stranger or not—and he'd try to cheer them up."

"Wow, that's so ... I don't know ... that must've been fun to watch."

"Yup, he'd be like, 'Excuse me, why are you sad?' Of course, the person would usually lie and say they *weren't* sad, but little Geoffrey wouldn't be convinced, and he'd ask them if they wanted a hug. No one could turn down a hug from little Geoffrey—and, once you got a hug from him, it was impossible not to be cheered up at least a little."

"Yeah, I bet."

"He was just so sincere. You could tell he was genuinely upset that you were upset. And you felt like—for his sake—you had to stop being sad."

"Yeah," I said, my hair tingling to the moment.

Jacklyn took in a large breath. "So you may have guessed it was actually Geoffrey who gave me the idea for this whole HAKing thing."

"Oh—how old was he?"

Jacklyn smiled. "I guess he performed his first HAK when he was only eight years old."

"Wow ...how?"

"Okay, so we were on a road trip, and we were at a gas station. My parents were in the store, and my brother and I were outside getting fresh air, and Geoffrey noticed a teenaged girl sitting in front of the store, looking sad, and he asked me if he could cheer her up. I said he could, so he went over to the girl, and, like always, he made her smile right away. But then he came running back to the car, and—I'll never forget—he climbed into the front seat and very seriously told me that the girl was upset because she couldn't afford to go to a concert with her friends, and he wanted to give her something to dry her tears—he said it so seriously, as though eight-year-olds do that all the time. So, of course, I was greatly entertained, but I didn't let on, and, instead, I very seriously authorized his plan—*as though I had a choice*—and he grabbed a napkin from the glove compartment and ran it back to the girl. The girl, of course, was totally smitten, and Geoffrey returned to the car rather pleased with himself."

"Wow," I said.

Jacklyn shrugged. "Yeah, well, then Mom returned with less traveling treats than usual—she said she'd forgotten her wallet in the car and so had just used spare change. That's foreshadowing, if you care to notice it."

"I *do*," I said with a laugh.

"So, anyway, twenty minutes after we left the gas station, Mom looked in her wallet and realized her last twenty-dollar bill was missing—and so, you know, she asked us if any of us remembered her spending it. And, um, so Geoffrey said *he'd* spend it—snuck it into that napkin he gave the girl—said he was trying to help her get to her concert."

"Wow, did your parents mind him taking the money?"

"Um, well…no, well, a little, but, you know, they knew he was doing it because, you know, they'd praised him when he'd cheered people up, so they couldn't really be mad at him. Of course, they told him not to take money out of their wallets again without asking, but—"

"Did he ask again?"

"Um…yes, sir, and—every once in a while—Mom'd let him put some money in a charity box to curb his predilections."

"So your own *predilections* all started because of—"

"Yup—all because of Geoffrey," Jacklyn said, suddenly sounding irritated. "That was actually the last road trip we went on together. We used to go on them every year. But, for the last one, I said I was too busy at university, so they went by themselves."

I nodded as softly as I could.

"What's the matter?" Jacklyn said, coldly.

"Oh, um, I guess it sounds sad—it seems like you're foreshadowing again."

"Yup. Sorry I don't mean to be…I just have trouble talking about it, but, yeah, they were on a road trip without…you know. And an animal ran onto the road, and this poor guy named Grant Linde swerved instinctively to avoid it." Jacklyn paused again. "I can only imagine what story my mom was telling when it happened…but they all died…Mr. Linde…my mom…my dad… and perfect little Geoffrey. They all died."

"I'm so sorry."

Jacklyn looked at me again—her eyes seemed tired from thinking about it. "You know," she said, "it's funny ... you're the first person in a long time that I've told the truth about that."

"Really? Like, which part?"

"About how—you know, the animal on the road. Usually I tell people it was a drunk driver. I know it's silly, but I just get so angry when people are killed needlessly that I like to—I don't know—I like to use my own experience to fight against the recklessness. It was so awful, and I have so much anger for anyone who would knowingly add to the risk on the roads when there's already so much risk out there for people, so ... I *lie*. It's my private stand."

"Wow, that's—"

"Does it seem silly to you?"

In truth, I was a wee bit morally shocked by Jacklyn's failed truthfulness around something so significant, but I hope you'll understand, empathetic reader, that I wasn't going to admit that to my grieving friend.

"No, not at all—tell people whatever you want. And maybe you're right. Maybe it'll make a difference."

Jacklyn nodded. "And yet ... I didn't feel like lying to *you*, my friend."

"Oh, thanks, but—" and I was about to lie and tell Jacklyn that I wouldn't have minded if she'd lied to me.

"Don't *thank* me," Jacklyn interrupted.

"Oh, why?"

"Well, not for nothing, but part of what I told you about Geoffrey *was* actually a lie. God, I'm awful."

"No, you're not," I snapped back. "Jacklyn, honestly, when you've been through what you've been through—"

"That's no excuse—you're my friend. I don't know why I do that."

"Well, maybe it makes you feel better to keep some things—"

"No excuse."

"Okay, well—if it makes you feel better—why don't you tell me now? What wasn't true about Geoffrey?"

Jacklyn took in a long breath. "The whole thing about Geoffrey being my inspiration for the hidden acts of '*kindness*' ... that was a lie. I don't know, I just liked the idea that he was a HAK prodigy.

But what actually happened was he just brought that girl an empty napkin—he really did just want to give her something to dry her tears. But he didn't take twenty dollars with him."

"Did he still give her the hug?"

"Yeah, that was true—he did love to cheer people up with his hugs—but he never conceived of sneaking money to anyone."

"But that was still a HAK, then, wasn't it? All except the *hidden* part."

"True, I guess, but he wasn't the reason I started the whole HAK thing."

"Oh, okay—so what *was* the reason?"

"Well, since you ask, the other true thing about my story is … my mom *was* missing twenty dollars from her wallet. That was true too."

"Okay."

"Ya see, Geoffrey hadn't taken the twenty dollars from Mom's wallet—*I* had. I had this klepto phase for a while. It wasn't that I wanted stuff—I just wanted to see if I could get away with taking things. I don't know what it was. I guess it was a rush. But I'm convinced—or, at least, I've convinced myself—that I would've given my mom's money back if she hadn't noticed it was gone right away. But, once she spotted the hole in her wallet, I didn't have the heart to say I'd taken it." Jacklyn shook her head. "I so wish I'd told her, but I didn't want her to give me that disappointed-mom face. You know that face?"

"Yup."

"Right, so, anyway, I felt so guilty about taking the money from my mom that I decided to give up my klepto habits. And I *did*. For the longest time. But then …" Jacklyn paused. She looked at me with a half-smile before a tear crawled down her face. "When I lost my family—nothing seemed to matter anymore, and I decided I may as well start stealing again to entertain myself. But I couldn't get myself to do it. I felt too guilty—not about the stealing—but about having stolen from my mom. So that's when I started doing the HAKs. I mean, I'd taken twenty dollars from my mom without her knowing it—and I decided I wanted to give twenty dollars back to her without her knowing it. HAKing seemed like the only way to do it."

"Wow," I said as Jacklyn took another lengthy breath. "So, um, what was your first HAK?"

"Well, I found this—and this is the truth this time, I promise—I found this teenager on the bus, and he looked super sad, so I slipped twenty dollars into his backpack—and it was such a rush. I hadn't expected that, but it was exactly like stealing, except I didn't feel any guilt about it. You know what I mean? It was the same deception I'd had with stealing—except, in this case, I was being deceptive to try to do something nice."

"Wow that's …amazing."

"*Amazing* in a bad way?"

"No, just amazing—you're so creative in how you deal with things."

Jacklyn smiled as she guided the tear off her cheek. "I guess I'm going to have to tell you the truth more often."

"It's your call. I enjoy the lies too."

Jacklyn laughed—which had quickly become my favourite sound in the world.

An hour later, after a couple of lackadaisical HAKs, Jacklyn the math tutor and I sat on a bus for home. Given our earlier conversation success, I decided it was a good time to finally inquire as to why Mr. Math Tutor was not along for the HAK ride.

"Hey, Jacklyn," I said, "can I ask you a question?"

"Of course, questions about me are my favourite."

"Okay, well, does your husband like your HAKing, um, hobby?"

"Good question. I wouldn't say so, no."

"Why?"

"I think…probably sees it as waste of time and money."

"Oh, does that bother you?"

"No, I think I agree on that one. Plus, I only do it when, you know, he's out of town, so we rarely talk about it."

"Hello, *Jacklyn*," a woman in the seat behind us suddenly said.

"Ms. Roberts!" Jacklyn squealed back. "How are you?"

"I'm very well," the woman said. "I'm Ms. Kari now."

"Oh, what was wrong with Roberts?—Tired of people not being able to pronounce it?"

The woman chuckled. "No, I married someone named Kari."

"Yup, that's another good reason."

Ms. Kari and I both laughed.

"So," Ms. Kari said, "may I be introduced?"

"Right, this is my good friend, John. John, this is my favourite English teacher from high school."

Ms. Kari smiled and offered me her hand over the seat.

"Not for nothing," Jacklyn said, "but Ms. Rob…Kari was a two-time favourite teacher of mine."

"That's quite right," the teacher said. "Jacklyn was a blank slate of curiosity when I had her Grade Eight, and then—when I got her back in Grade Twelve—I'm sure I learned more from her than the other way around."

Jacklyn laughed. "Not likely."

We all chuckled at that before sharing a nice awkward pause together.

"So," Ms. Kari said, "how are your parents, Jacklyn?"

"You met my parents?"

"Of course—don't you remember when you weren't doing your work in Grade Eight? I had a meeting with them."

"Oh yeah …*yeah*. What happened with that? What'd they say?"

"They were funny."

Jacklyn laughed.

Ms. Kari smiled. "Your dad was taking it quite seriously, but your mom insisted on making jokes."

"Really, like what?"

"Hmm," Ms. Kari said, tilting her head into memory mode. "Let me see … oh, I remember I was telling them that you had trouble following directions on your assignments …"

Jacklyn chuckled and looked over at me with a sheepish smile.

"Your dad," Ms. Kari continued, clearly straining her memory muscle, "he was—yes, I remember him being very concerned about your unwillingness to follow directions. But your mom evidently thought it was all very funny, and she blamed your dad."

Jacklyn exploded a laugh.

"*What did she say?*" Ms. Kari whispered upwards at her memory. "She said something like—that your dad had told you that directions were optional."

Jacklyn laughed louder than I'd ever heard her. "It's true—when I was little, Dad and I'd play basketball, and he almost always did something illegal to be funny. So, of course, I whined about him not following the rules, but he was just like, 'Oh, the rules are just suggestions.'"

As Jacklyn presented that brilliant story, I had to force my laugh since I was internally strategizing. I was not going to let the conversation return to the question of what Jacklyn's parents were *up to*. She seemed to like talking about her parents, but I suspected that—while we were on a public vehicle—she wouldn't want to tell Ms. Kari that her favourites were no longer with us. And nor did I get the sense that she would want to lie to her former teacher about them.

I decided that my best bet to disrupt further talk of Jacklyn's parents' status was to make like a Chet and change the subject to an unrelated topic. The thought of being my own worst annoyance wasn't particularly pleasing to me, but, unfortunately, it was the only secret plan I could think of, so I reconciled myself to it.

For a few moments, I nodded at Jacklyn and Ms. Kari's conversation as I searched my brain for a specific interruption to use. By the time I'd made my disruptive selection, Jacklyn was finishing up a story starring her as young girl playing cards with her parents.

"My dad," she said, "was in charge of our cards. And I was in charge of going over to my mom and giving her a hug and then taking a peak at her cards so that I could report the intell back to my dad."

I giggled at the image of a young Jacklyn being a spy in her father's card battles.

Ms. Kari, though, seemed to be trying to cover up her displeasure at the thought of a child being taught to cheat.

"What did your mom do in response?" I said, annoyed at the alleged judgment.

"Sometimes she'd laugh, but then she'd usually trick me into giving my dad the wrong info."

"Right," Ms. Kari said, "so, anyway, how *are* your paren—"

"Hey, by the way," I rushed in, "you might interested to know, Ms. Kari, that Jacklyn works at Ambiguity now."

My words were so sudden and so far off topic that Chet would have been proud.

Oddly, Ms. Kari did not seem perturbed by the intrusion. "That's wonderful," she said. "What are you doing at Ambiguity, Jacklyn?"

Several bus stops later, Ms. Kari pulled the request-stop wire for herself.

"Well, Jacklyn—you're just as clever as I remember."

"Thanks, Ms. R. So are you."

Ms. Kari laughed at the reflex compliment, claimed it was nice to have met me, and then exited the bus and blended into the pedestrian traffic.

Jacklyn presented me with a smile.

"What?" I said.

She shrugged. "Thanks, I really didn't feel like talking about it on the bus."

I was so startled and honoured by the appreciation that I didn't have the will to try to deflect it.

"You're welcome," I mustered instead. "Any time."

Jacklyn smiled again. "So what're you up to the rest of the weekend?"

"Um, oh, my neighbour and I are going to watch *The Princess Bride*—she's never seen it."

"Never seen *Princess Bride*? What kind of a neighbour's never seen *The Princess Bride*?"

I giggled. "Yeah, it's hard to fathom—but I guess she just didn't realize how good it was when it came out."

"I don't know," Jacklyn said. "I would be careful. Someone who hasn't seen *Princess Bride*? I mean what *else* hasn't she seen?"

Chapter 46
Dullard and the Neighbour II

Storming the Weather

After I handed a bored-looking video store clerk my choice, she grinned.

"*This*," she said, "is my favourite movie of all time."

"Yeah," I said, "it's one of mine too. I'm watching it with my neighbour. She's never seen it, so—"

"Lucky her," the clerk said. "The first time you see it is the best."

As I left the store, the clerk's unbridled approval of my selection reminded me of Jacklyn's, and then suddenly it occurred to me that I ought to have invited my orphaned friend to watch with Elizabeth and me. Her husband was out of town, so she was going to arrive home to a solitude-filled apartment after an emotional day. Perhaps she would prefer some company.

When I got home, I dialed Jacklyn's number. Of course, the thought of mingling two of my favourite friendships worried me, so my fingers were clumsy-nervous as I punched in Jacklyn's digits.

"Hey," Jacklyn's smiling voice answered, "we're out right now. But remember: to call is human ...to leave a message is divine."

I did my duty, and Jacklyn called back twenty minutes later explaining that laundry work had cost me a response earlier.

"No worries," I said. "I had to do laundry last week, so ..." At that moment, I let my voice fade out as I realized that I was making a palpably boring point.

"*Thank you*," Jacklyn said, sparing me the mocking voice I

deserved. "No one seems to get that. When there's laundry to do, life must be put on hold."

I laughed. "Anyway, I know you said you had some work to do this weekend, but—if you feel like a break—you're welcome to join Elizabeth and I for *Princess Bride.*"

"Oh, thanks, that's nice of you—but you two go ahead."

Strangely, I sensed that Jacklyn was turning down the invite more for Elizabeth's sake than her own.

"Okay, if you're sure. But Elizabeth's very friendly. I'm sure she wouldn't mind."

Jacklyn laughed. "One thing about women—just because they're friendly to *you*, doesn't mean they're gonna be friendly with other women."

That made me chuckle. "Um, Jacklyn …" I said with my own teasing voice.

"*What?*" she said.

"Trust me—she won't mind."

"How do you know? Is she single?"

"Yes."

"And she comes over to visit you all the time?"

"Yes."

"Then how do you know she's not *into* you?"

"Trust me," I said, now much less nervous about Jacklyn's possible meeting with my neighbour.

A couple hours later, Jacklyn the math tutor and I were sitting in my apartment awaiting Elizabeth's arrival.

"How do you like it here?" Jacklyn said.

"It's nice."

On hearing those words, Jacklyn's forehead instantly activated. "Now, not for nothing, but—when you say, 'nice'—do you mean you *actually* like the place, or are you just giving that sort of empty, noncommittal 'nice'?"

"Um, yeah, sorry, I'm not sure what you mean by—"

"Well, you know how, like, when you find someone to be a little, let's say, *dull*, but you don't wanna sound mean, so—when your friend asks what you thought of them—you're like, 'Oh, they're *nice.*'"

I laughed. "I suppose you're right. I don't really have much of an opinion about my apartment."

"Ahah! So you admit it! You *were* using the empty, noncommittal 'nice.'"

"Yeah, is that bad?"

"No, I guess not, but—just so I'm clear—why'd you sugarcoat your answer?"

"Um, how was I *sugarcoating*?"

"Well, when you describe a boring *person* as 'nice,' you're sugarcoating because you don't wanna sound mean. But, when you're talking about your *apartment*, I don't think it cares if you find it boring."

"True, but—"

"Wait, maybe you were sugarcoating because … this isn't a *haunted* apartment, is it?"

I laughed. "No … I don't think so."

"Good. Haunted apartments make me nervous."

"Me too," I was in the middle of saying when the apartment door made a knocking noise.

"Did you hear *that*?" Jacklyn said.

"It's just my neighbour," I said with a roll-of-the-eyes smirk as I moved to the door.

"Whew," Jacklyn said.

I laughed again before opening the door to Elizabeth.

"Hello, dear—am I early?"

"No, not at all. Come on in."

"*Hello*," Jacklyn said with a slightly startled voice when she saw my senior citizen friend.

That pleased me greatly.

"It's so nice to meet you," Jacklyn told Elizabeth as they sat down.

"It's nice to meet you, dear," was the reply. "John's kind enough to tell me about his friends—so I've heard a little about you."

"*Really?*" Jacklyn said as Elizabeth put her tea supplies on my coffee table. "If you don't mind my asking, what's John said about me?"

"He says you're a very nice person."

Jacklyn raised her eyebrows. "So, my friend, you think I'm *nice*, do you?"

I laughed.

Elizabeth looked confused.

"Sorry," Jacklyn said, "it's just funny because John and I were just talking about how sometimes—when someone's not very interesting—people'll cover up their bored feelings by calling them, 'nice.'"

"Oh, well, I don't think John meant *that*, dear."

"Right, sorry, no, I'm just teasing him."

"Oh," Elizabeth said, clearly resisting the urge to ask *why*.

Jacklyn smiled. "It's just that it's fun to tease John since he never defends himself."

I laughed at that.

But Elizabeth still looked confused.

"It's not that I'm *sadistic*," Jacklyn tried again. "It's just that I like to watch him squirm."

I laughed again.

Elizabeth did not.

And so there was a small pause in the conversation.

Clearly, I needed a topic that could bridge the personality gap between Jacklyn the math tutor and Elizabeth the dullard neighbour. Nothing came to dull mind, though, so I was forced instead to widen the divide by bringing up a dullards-only subject.

"So, Elizabeth, it looks like it won't be a great day for your walk tomorrow, eh?"

"No, it looks like it'll be a downpour. I imagine I'll have to take my umbrella."

"Yeah, that's too bad—and I think it's supposed to rain for a few more days."

"Yes, unfortunately."

The weather talk continued for several sentences. I was well aware that its dull content was excluding Jacklyn's non-dull mind, but I couldn't think of a better way to save the conversation from an awkwardness divide.

"Not for nothing," Jacklyn said, "but sometimes I *like it* when it rains."

"Why?" two startled dullards replied.

"Well, no, I mean …*sure*, a nice sunny day is prettier and easier to get around in than the rain, but it's kind of boring, don't you think? Sunshine is just so bland. Nothing interesting happens when it's sunny. But …when it's raining or snowing—or hailing!—half my childhood memories have to do with weather incidents."

"Interesting," I said. "Like what?"

"Well, like, once, we were at the park with my little brother, and we got caught in a hailstorm. My dad found us this tiny little coffee shop, and my mom told us this great ghost story while we waited out the storm all huddled up around a heater. And it's still the only ghost story I know."

Elizabeth smiled. "My sister used to tell us stories when we sat by the fire to warm up from the snow—before we went back out again to play in it some more."

"Right?!" Jacklyn said. "And, not to be overly Pollyanna, but I doubt that would've been as much fun if it was sunny out. Who warms up by the fire with a cup of hot chocolate on a sunny day?"

Elizabeth smirked, apparently caught in a memory.

"So," Jacklyn said, "by 'us,' you mean you had other brothers and sisters with you, or…?"

"Just one sister, actually, dear. But she often had her school-mates over to the house. They were a few years younger than me, but she was much more socially precocious than I was."

Just then, I saw a wee smile on Jacklyn's face, and I knew that she'd officially taken the conversation under her protection.

Within two hours, Jacklyn and Elizabeth had traded several tales of childhood. The stories fit together so well that I almost believed that my two friends had had similar upbringings. Each had an anecdote to match the other in every category. (Of course, Jacklyn's offerings were funnier than Elizabeth's, but I found Elizabeth's adventures to be nearly as entertaining.)

"So," Jacklyn said, after concluding a story, "how long have you lived here, like in this building, Elizabeth?"

"Let me see, dear … it was two, maybe three months after I retired."

Now, considering that Jacklyn did not know *when* Elizabeth had retired, Elizabeth's response to Jacklyn's question was not much of an answer.

"What are you retired *from*?" Jacklyn redirected.

"I was a nurse, actually, for many, many years."

"I bet you were brilliant."

"Thank you, dear. I like to think I meant something to my patients. It was the right career for me since I wasn't bright enough to be a doctor."

"Of course you were!" Jacklyn and I overlapped.

Elizabeth smirked. "You remind me of my sister: she had me convinced that the only reason I wasn't in medical school was because of the patriarchal establishment. At the time," she said, looking at Jacklyn, "there were many fewer women doctors. But I've long since recognized that, with my particular aptitudes, I was best off being a nurse."

"I don't know about that," Jacklyn said, "but I bet you have a very high emotional intelligence—to be able to help people cope with everything."

"I don't know if I'd go that far, dear," Elizabeth said. "But I believe my gift to my patients was that I never looked ahead. That was their doctor's job—looking ahead and deciding whether surgery was required and what medicine to give and such. But the best care for the patient in the long term didn't always make the patient feel best in the short term."

"Right, I guess *so*," Jacklyn said, "—so, like, in the case of surgery?"

"Exactly, dear. So, as nurses, our job was to focus on *the present*. I tried to never look past what was happening to my patients in any moment I was with them. My job was to make them comfortable no matter what their doctors needed to put them through. As such, I tried not to think about the long-term health of my patients."

"It wasn't your jurisdiction?" Jacklyn said.

"Exactly, dear. And I think, after I realized that, I was a better nurse for it."

"That's really great," Jacklyn said. "I never thought of it that way."

"Me too," I said.

Elizabeth smiled back and went on to tell us some more fascinating details about her nursing career. Some of the tidbits were familiar to me, but others were new, so I felt as if I had found an extended version of a favourite book.

"What about *dating*?" Jacklyn said. "If you don't mind my asking?"

"What about it, dear?"

Jacklyn switched to her comedy face. "Well, it's just that, based on what we see on TV—which I'm sure is *totally accurate*—there's a lot of interoffice romance in hospitals, so—not to pry—but I'm just wondering if you ever met anyone who…?"

"Only once, dear."

"Really? Care to share any details, or …?"

"Well, it was someone I worked very closely with for about a year—another nurse."

I suddenly found myself staring at Elizabeth. *Did she mean a female nurse?*

"So what happened?" Jacklyn said as I frantically reviewed my previous conversations with Elizabeth for any indication that she preferred her love interests to be female.

"Well," Elizabeth said, no longer looking in her audience's direction. "She was a couple months behind me when we first started nursing, and she wanted some help with some of the duties. So we started going around like a couple of school girls at lunch and after work. And that was all it took."

"That's so romantic," Jacklyn said.

"Yes it was, dear. But then she had to leave school because of an illness in her family. We wrote letters for a while, but it wasn't the same—she was too adventurous a girl to keep her mind occupied with drab old me."

"I doubt *that*," Jacklyn said.

"That's nice of you to say, dear, but I'm satisfied that that's what happened."

"Right," Jacklyn said. "I think I know what you mean."

Meanwhile, I sighed heavily without meaning to. I dearly wanted to ask Elizabeth why she'd never told me that she'd lived her life as a participant in a non-visible minority, but I didn't want to put her in an awkward position about her awkward position. So I was left to my paranoia. *Perhaps her secrecy was the result of her realizing that it had never occurred to me that she might be gay.*

"Do you find it a sad to tell that story?" I asked my neighbour.

"No, not really, dear. There was a time that it would have, but now I'm able to cherish the memory of being in love once. Thank you both for asking. It's very generous of you to take such an interest in my old stories. Maybe we could talk about something else now."

"Of course," Jacklyn said. "Hey, what's *this*, by the way?"

"My bookshelf?" I replied.

"Right, but what's this *Official Canvassing Diary*?"

"Oh, that's nothing—just something Elizabeth and I are working on."

Strangely, I felt an intense inclination to hide the diary—and I had no conception of why.

SPECULATIVE NOTE: My ghostwriter contends that I was feeling retroactively guilty for having formerly had some impure hopes for canvassing (that it might help me find a love interest). He further surmises that setting those improper hopes next to my improper crush was overwhelming my guilt. Seems like a bit of a wild guess, but you do you, wild ghostwriter.

Unfortunately, Elizabeth was not on the same hide-the-page.

"John's a canvasser for the Green Cross," she said. "We have a wonderful time keeping track of his collections."

"Oh, that's very nice," Jacklyn said.

"*Nice?*" I jumped in.

Jacklyn laughed. "Oops, I guess I shouldn't have told you how to translate that."

Not too many minutes later, Jacklyn and I dropped Elizabeth off at her apartment, and then I dropped Jacklyn off at the elevator.

"I have to tell you something," she said.

"Okay," I said, my heart revving up.

Jacklyn scrunched her forehead. "I already knew that you were canvassing for the Green Cross."

"Oh, okay, how'd you know?"

Jacklyn took in a sheepish-seeming smile. "I saw you with your canvassing supplies on the bus back before we met."

"Oh, what's wrong with that?"

"Well, I just didn't want you to think I was spying on you."

"Oh, okay," I said, pleased with the thought.

"Anyway," Jacklyn said, "so I happened to notice your canvassing supplies at some point when we didn't know each other, and it made me think. So it kinda stuck with me."

"Really? Why? What'd it make you think?"

"About my whole HAK project. I've decided to quit. No more HAKs for this girl."

"Why?"

"Well, I wanna do something more, you know, *useful* with my money—so no more HAKs."

"Oh…okay."

Jacklyn giggled at my serious face. "Now, my friend, I don't want you thinking you did anything *wrong* during our HAKing expedition today that made me wanna quit."

"Oh, okay."

Jacklyn giggled again. "Hadn't occurred to you that you might be to blame, had it, my friend?"

"Not really."

"Well, maybe it *should*."

I laughed. "All right, I'll give it some thought."

"Actually," Jacklyn said. "Thanks—*really*—for coming with me today. I think I needed to have someone witness it before I could give it up…does that seem silly?"

"No, of course not! I'm…honoured."

Jacklyn smiled. "Thank you."

The Meddle Ground

That late evening, I pondered my friendship with Elizabeth. If I had been the good friend that my Jacklyn-inspired ego was claiming I was, I would have discovered Elizabeth's past romance—and its distinct genre—long before. So I spent a few minutes insulting myself for requiring the curiosity of Jacklyn the math tutor to get at Elizabeth's most significant memories. After ten minutes of scolding, I was exhausted, so I turned on some comfort TV; and, of course, the first sitcom I came upon featured a guest-starring character who was aiming to come out of his own closet.

POMPOUS NOTE: My smug ghostwriter says he's not surprised by my TV's perceptive offering. He claims that one of the great talents of TV shows—and sitcoms, in particular—is that, within their exaggerated scenarios (along with the commercials that divide them), they're always able to provide at least one character or plot point that will remind you of whatever happens to be weighing down your mind at the time of your viewing. If, for instance, you're considering quitting your job, there will either be a character thinking of leaving their particular sitcom profession, or there will at least be a between-scenes advert for a product that 'does the *job* on tough grease.' In any case, my ghostwriters contends that it will always seem as though the TV has read your mind and is empathizing with you about whatever you're going through. Unfortunately, I must admit that I see my ghostwriter's arrogant point on this one.

To my surprise, the TV character who was hoping to evict himself from his closet received some kind support from the most unexpected of sitcom characters. That was an instructive point of analogy: suddenly, I had no choice but to consider the possibility that it wasn't too late for me to let Elizabeth know that—despite my previous lack of inquiry—I was interested in her hidden stories.

A few evenings later, while Elizabeth and I were in the middle of a particularly good game of Yahtzee, I found myself nervous about the topic I'd chosen to initiate my investigations.

"You're quiet today, dear," Elizabeth said as she assessed the roll of her dice.

"Yeah, sorry …actually, can I ask you something?"

"Of course, dear, once you're finished rolling."

"Right, okay, so," I said, scattering the dice with only a tiny shake of them, "so I was just thinking about your sister …"

"Dorothy?"

"Yeah—unless you have another sister?"

"No, just Dorothy."

"So, yeah, um, you said that—when you were first training to be a nurse—she helped you study even though she wanted you to be a doctor?"

"Yes, good memory."

"Thanks, so did she ever try again to get you to go to medical school?"

"Why do you ask, dear?"

"Sorry, I was just wondering, actually, why … um … why you never tell any stories about her from *after* you first started nursing."

"Well, there's a very good answer to that, dear." Elizabeth marked her roll into the scorecard and then looked at me. "She and I haven't spoken for a few decades now. We send letters occasionally, but we're not a part of each other's lives anymore."

"Wow, that's …sad?"

"Yes, it is sad."

"Okay, so, um, if you don't mind my asking, what happened?"

"I don't mind you asking, dear, but there's not much I can tell you. She couldn't accept me for who I was, and I wasn't willing to change, and that was that."

Elizabeth's face had turned melancholy. I wasn't sure if she wanted any more questions, so I waited silently for her cue. She, in turn, became focused on the game. For a few minutes, we just rattled away.

"I miss her," Elizabeth finally said before another of my rolls.

"Yeah, of course …" I said nervously. "So have you ever thought about calling her?"

"Of course—*every year*. But it was she who didn't accept me for who I was, so I believe etiquette says it is she who should call me."

On my way to work the next day, I again pondered my neighbour and her sister. Obviously, Elizabeth missed Dorothy, but—in an impressive case of mutual stubbornness—she was not going to make the first move where justice required the other to grovel. That seemed reasonable to me: Elizabeth was not the sort to hold a grudge unless she was entitled, which meant that her sister's unwillingness to accept my friend for who she was must have been in regard to a matter of significance. And, given the sisters' generation (and the era in which we were residing), my internal stereotyper told me that the unacceptable feature of my neighbour might have been her penchant for falling in love with women.

Yet long-term residents of our planet can surprise you. While it seemed clear to me that seniors of my then time were disproportionately opposed to like-gendered people falling for each other, many golden-agers also seemed to have an open-mindedness below their years. So, if my speculation was right that Dorothy had not accepted her sister as an early adult, maybe she had softened with age.

"Whaddya think I should do?" I asked Jacklyn the next time I saw her on the bus.

"Well, not for nothing—" she started to say.

But I realized that—before she articulated whatever brilliant advice she had in mind—I wanted to try to bias my jury.

"I just think that maybe—if I could find out what her sister's like *now*—maybe she's changed, and maybe they could be friends again."

"Yeah, why not?" Jacklyn said. "Worst that can happen is they still don't get along, and their grudge stays, but at least now they won't have to have any regret about it."

That made me smirk. "Okay, but how do I find her? Other than sneaking around Elizabeth's apartment looking for her sister's address."

"Oooh, I like that," Jacklyn said. "That's what I'm voting for, but, if you're skittish about, you know, *breaking and entering*, you could always just search for the sister online."

Said wise and obvious plan was immediately approved.

The next day at work, I set a course for the internet and typed Elizabeth's sister's name and suspected province into a search engine. The results were impressive—or, at least, there were a lot of them, and it only took the boastful search engine .12 seconds to come up with them. I clicked on the first one, but I was pretty sure that the Dorothy Braun I was seeking wasn't currently a competitive water-skier, so I moved on. The fourth click proved intriguing as I was sent to an article about a seniors' centre in our city. There, in reference to the title, 'Volunteer Recruitment Coordinator,' sat the near face of my neighbour. Under her picture, was the name, 'Dorothy Braun-Low.' Yup, I had found the sister I was looking for.

I scanned the article, but it didn't tell me much of use about Dorothy. The fact that she worked for a seniors' centre was good evidence that she would be able to accept her sister's *senior* status, but I still had no indication of whether she would be willing to approve the rest of Elizabeth. I needed to meet with Dorothy in person.

As I came to that terrifying realization, my office neighbour, Erik, dropped by for an uninterested check-in. I decided to forego investigating whatever impressive movie or book he'd taken in last; instead, I asked him what he thought about my predicament.

He frowned at me in reply. "I'd be careful there, John. People don't like meddlers."

I nodded. "Yeah, but it's just that it seems like she misses her sister, but she doesn't wanna make the first move. So I just thought, if I could find out if her sister's still—"

Erik shook his head. "I know your heart's in the right place, John, but you have to let people make their own decisions. You can't rescue people from their problems. You can be there to support her every step of the way—but she's the one who has to take those steps."

"But she's not *going to* because she thinks her sister doesn't accept her—I just wanna see if that's still true."

Erik sighed. "What is it she thinks her sister doesn't accept about her?"

"Oh," I said, suddenly nervous, "well, she likes women—my neighbour does—so I don't actually know what the problem is, but I think it *might* be that—"

"She's a lesbian? Oh, then *definitely* ...if she came out and was met with homophobia from her own sister, then you can't intrude on that."

"*Intrude* on what?" Khiron suddenly arrived to my annoyance.

"John wants to try to reconnect his friend with her long-lost sister. And, as far as I'm concerned," Erik said, turning his intensity back to me, "your friend's right: it's up to her sister to come groveling back."

"But it's been decades. Don't you think maybe one of them could use a push?"

"No, John. You cannot rescue people from their problems. The homophobe sister has to—"

"But," I said, "what if she doesn't feel the same way anymore? That's all I wanna find out."

"No," Erik replied, "this is coming from someone who was locked firmly in the closet: when I finally came out, I didn't have any time for those who couldn't accept me for who I was. You're toying with something very delicate here. And, if your friend's sister is reformed—and is now open to all races, creeds, and sexualities—it has to be *her* who makes the decision to act. Or it won't mean anything."

I wasn't sure what would be so heinous about casually pointing one of the sisters in the reconciliation direction if indeed it did turn out that the rift that had kept them apart for nearly half a century was not actually there anymore. But I could see Erik's point about the dangers of tinkering with other people's bitterness. So, overall, I was disillusioned.

Two days later, I shared another bus trip with Jacklyn the math the tutor.

"Hey, by the way," she said part way through our journey, "what happened with Elizabeth's sister? Any luck finding her?"

"Oh, yeah, I found her—she works at a seniors' centre."

"Great—so what're you gonna do?"

"Oh, well, I was talking to Erik, and he was saying I shouldn't meddle; I should let them, you know, deal with it themselves."

"But they've had forty years! Not for nothing, but maybe it's time to do something to wake one of them up."

"Really? You don't think it's bad to meddle? Shouldn't I let them make their own decisions? Erik figures that they're the only ones who can help themselves—"

Jacklyn shrugged her way into my sentence. "I don't know—this crap about people being the only ones who can help themselves... You know, if no one ever helped anyone else, it'd be..." Jacklyn laughed. "I don't know—it'd be anarchy. I'm not saying people can't make their own decisions, but sometimes I appreciate it when someone gives me a nudge."

"Fair enough," I said. "So whaddya think I should do?"

"Okay, well, why don't you go to the seniors' centre and meet up with sister Dorothy and see what she's like?"

"But how would I justify meeting with her?"

"Couldn't you say you're interested in volunteering?"

"I guess, but then I'm wasting her time."

"No you're *not*—you might be reconnecting her with her sister."
I pondered that. "Okay, I'll try it."

It was not even a false claim. Indeed, the moment I heard Jacklyn's advice, I realized that it matched what I wanted to do.

So, the next day at lunch hour, I snuck out of Ambiguity, took a short bus ride, and—after circling the block a few times—I walked into Dorothy Braun-Low's seniors' centre as if I weren't doing the craziest thing in my history.

"Hi," I said to a non-senior-looking receptionist.

"*Hello,*" she replied cheerfully but gently.

"Good, thanks," I said—and, for a moment, my nerves attacked my memory, and I forgot what I needed to ask. "Um ...I ...um ..."

The lady smiled patiently, apparently accustomed to people with memory troubles.

"Sorry, I was just interested in volunteering, so ... is that possible?"

"Oh, okay, you can just fill out an application form, and then—"

"Oh, um, yeah," I interrupted with panic in my heart, "um, I wasn't sure yet if I wanted to volunteer. I was just wondering if I could, sort of, talk to someone about what sort of volunteering you have here. Would, um, would that be okay?"

"Oh, I guess—usually we have you fill out the application, and then we have you come in for an interview."

"Right, but—because I wasn't sure if I wanted to volunteer—I just wanted to talk to someone and see if it would suit me."

"Okay, one sec, I'll see if Dorothy's available."

My heart started to beat at full steam as I watched my plan working exactly as intended. The receptionist peaked into an office around the corner.

"Hey, there's a young man who's interested in volunteering. He wants to talk to someone about—"

There was a hard-to-hear reply.

"I know—I told him, but he says he wants to talk to someone first."

There was then a nonverbal reply, which didn't sound too friendly to me.

The receptionist returned. "Okay, go ahead in."

"Thanks," I said. My adrenalin was starting to overtake me. I walked as slowly as I could, but there wasn't quite enough friction in the air to stop me, and I was soon rounding the corner to Dorothy Braun-Low's office.

There she was, looking just like her sister, except she was dressed in work clothes.

"Hello there," she said. "Have a seat. I understand you have some questions about volunteering. What would you like to know?"

"Oh, um, well, I'm just wondering what sort of programs you have?"

"Okay, well, we have a resource library; we have social outings, including game nights; we have support groups, including one for lesbian and gay seniors who—"

"Oh, *really?*"

"Yes," Dorothy said, looking at me seriously, "seniors are just as likely to be lesbian or gay as anyone else."

"Oh, yeah, of course, I just—"

"Are you uncomfortable with homosexuality?"

"No, of course not—I just think it's great that you have a program like that. How's it—is it effective?"

"Well, these matters are not easy for seniors. They're marginalized enough when it comes to sexuality, let alone homosexuality. Most people assume that seniors are non-sexual beings—you can imagine how sons and daughters feel about their parents admitting their true selves."

"Yeah, that sounds really hard. It's great that you have that program."

"Thank you," Dorothy said. "So what else would you like to know?"

I now knew all that I needed to know, but I asked a few more questions to justify my visit and then left the building with a never-to-be-activated application in hand.

That evening, I went to Elizabeth's apartment with intent to inform her that I'd inadvertently run in to her sister at the seniors' centre and that I'd discovered that Dorothy was so far from being heterosexist that she'd actually tried to guilt me into thinking I was homophobic. But, when I saw Elizabeth, my beating heart trampled on my nerves. I was suddenly terrified of Elizabeth's opinion of me snooping around her private family life. Therefore, quite understandably, I cowarded out.

"I thought you were gonna talk to her right away?" Jacklyn said, the next time I saw her.

"Yeah, I know."

Jacklyn laughed. "Don't feel bad, my friend. It's not like anyone expected you to do it on your first try. It took you—what?—two weeks to actually talk to the sister? As I see it, you're on a two-week delay."

"Very humourous," I said. "Okay, fine, I'll say something tonight."

"So," Jacklyn said a few days later, "if you don't mind my asking, what did our friend Elizabeth say about your meeting with Dorothy?"

"Um, she didn't say anything."

"She was too stunned to say anything?"

"Yeah, that's it."

Jacklyn laughed. "Don't feel bad. You're still on—what?—day eight of your two-week procrastination plan? You've got plenty of time."

"I won't need it, though. Tonight, I'm gonna tell her."

"*Aww*," Jacklyn said, "you really think you will, don't you?"

"Maybe."

"Well, I'm totally sure you will."

I laughed. "Okay, this time it's happening. I'm definitely going to tell her tonight—or tomorrow night at the latest."

Jacklyn smiled her most condescending smile. "I totally believe you, of course, but I tell you what—*just in case*—meet me for lunch tomorrow, and we can strategize."

"All right," I said, delighted that I had been authorized at least one more day of procrastination.

The next day, I arrived in the Ambiguous Head Office to retrieve Jacklyn for lunch five minutes earlier than assigned, which resulted in much enjoyment on my behalf as I sat in the waiting area where I could vaguely witness Jacklyn interacting brilliantly with her job.

"Hey," she said when she saw me. "I'll be another five minutes—you mind waiting?"

"Sure, no problem," I said a little too eagerly. "I'm just reading my book anyway."

As it turned out, Jacklyn's five minutes took ten, but I didn't notice because—while I was pretending to read my book—I continued to be riveted by Jacklyn's work life.

"Jacklyn, m'dear," said a handsome woman approaching her office with a chuckle, "correct me if I'm wrong, but I thought you were going to sign off on these."

"I'm afraid you're wrong about that," I faintly heard Jacklyn retort, "but, since you're here, do you mind if I sign off on those?"

The handsome woman and I laughed.

"Actually," Jacklyn said, "if you wouldn't mind grabbing the—"

Someone rolled up next to me. "Hi, John."

I was both startled and irritated by the interruption to my show; nevertheless, I tried for a smile as I looked over to discover Derrick Litke smirking at me.

He shrugged. "You're a long way from your natural habitat, aren't you?"

"I guess. How are you, Derrick?"

"I'm fine—so whatcha doing here? Can I help you find something or someone?"

"Oh, no, thanks. I'm, ah, just waiting for Jacklyn."

"What for?"

"Um, we're friends."

"Oh, really?"

"Yeah, we're on the same bus route."

"Oh, I see, that makes more sense—*environmental charity*. I knew there had to be a reason."

Worry not, offended reader, I still didn't care enough about Derrick's good opinion to be troubled by his contempt, but, just then, I heard another laugh coming from Jacklyn's handsome co-worker, and I was deeply wounded to have missed its cause.

"A *reason* for what?" I said, staring at Derrick.

"Well, you know, Jacklyn's a busy woman, but—if she thinks she's doing a good deed, like taking transit—she'll appear to have unlimited time."

"Oh, I see," I said. (And, I must admit, I was impressed by

Derrick's ability to insult between his lines.) "You're probably right."

Derrick shrugged his approval of my concession.

"So," he said, "do you want me to let her know you're here?"

"That's okay, thanks—she knows I'm here."

"All right, just give a holler if you need anything."

As Derrick left, I perked my ears up for the rest of the entertainment between Jacklyn and handsome colleague, but it was all over now, so I sighed and pretended to continue my reading.

"Hey," Jacklyn said, standing in front of me five minutes later, "thanks for waiting—I'll make it up to you with some gossip at lunch."

I laughed as though I weren't craving the service.

"Hey, by the way," I said whispering as we sat down at our lunch location. "I had a run-in with Derrick."

"Really? What happened?"

"Well, I'm pretty sure he was trying to make me feel like I was unworthy of being your friend. You know, like, *Jacklyn's very busy. Could he take a message for me?* That kind of thing."

Jacklyn smirked. "Such a creep. He loves to poke at people if he thinks they're hiding something."

"What would I be *hiding*?" I said, suddenly nervous that my crush on Jacklyn was about to go under the microscope.

"Oh, sorry, not you—no, he senses *I* have something to hide."

"Like that you don't actually own a car?—Sorry, I told him we're on the same bus route, but I think it's okay because he seemed to think you were just taking the bus for 'environmental charity' or something like that."

Jacklyn laughed. "Perfect, no that's fine ... No, I think he actually suspects something deeper."

There was a sheepishness in Jacklyn's expression that made me think she wanted me to explore it.

"Oh, okay," I said, "and, um, do you think he's ...*on* to something?"

"I'm afraid so, my friend. And I'll tell you what it is if you promise not to tell anyone."

"Of course."

"And you can't be mad at me for not telling you sooner."

"Of course."

"No, no, that's not fair. You're allowed to be mad if you want. But don't tell anyone, okay?"

"Deal," I said, smirking.

"Okay, fine, I'm stalling," Jacklyn said with chuckle. "Here's the thing. You know *this*?" She indicated her wedding ring.

"Yeah?"

"It's not real."

"Oh, okay, that's—"

"No, I mean it's *real*—it was my mom's—but there's no guy attached to it."

"What? So you're—?"

"Not married."

"Oh, so you and your husband—or guy, or whatever—are just common law, or…?"

"No," Jacklyn said, half chuckling, half looking sheepish, "my husband's a figment of my invention. There is no guy."

My face was warm as it emptied itself of colour. "What? Why?"

Jacklyn took in a nervous-seeming sigh. "It's just—sorry, this is gonna sound weird; I apologize in advance—but it's just that, after my family died, I really wanted nothing to do with romance ever again, but people love to ask each other about their personal lives. So, when I started working at Ambiguity, I decided to wear my mom's ring full time. And then, whenever somebody asked where Mr. Chapman was, I'd just say he was out of town on business. And it nearly worked: most people—if they see you're not interested in talking about your personal life—they'll leave you alone about it. But obsessive-curious Derrick obviously sensed that there was something I was hiding, so he kept prying."

I nodded, trying to keep my facial muscles calm. "Right, I'm sure that was annoying, but *I* wasn't bugging you about it, was I?"

"No, no, and I'm sorry I didn't tell you sooner, John. It's just that you and I became friends gradually, so there was no obvious point early on for me to tell you, and then—once we became, like, actual friends—I felt like it was too late."

"Right, yeah, I guess that makes sense," I said. Although, in reality, compassionate reader, I was too mystified to know whether I was offended or not.

"So," Jacklyn said, looking at me with wide, adorable eyes, "are you mad at me for lying to you?"

"Um, I don't think so, but I'm a bit stunned right now, so ..."

Jacklyn nodded assertively. "Yeah, yeah, take your time, my friend. You've earned the right to delay telling me off till the timing is right."

"Right," I said, half-smiling. "Thanks."

That evening, I decided to go for an early evening canvass to have a good pondering about Jacklyn's marriage annulment. My brain did wind sprints back and forth between excitement—that maybe I had a chance at Jacklyn romance, after all—and then back the other way as I realized that, if she'd had any feelings for me beyond friendship, she surely would have told me of her false marriage sooner. That harsh thought occupied me as I canvassed my territory. It distracted me so much, in fact, that I forgot to canvass my territory. Instead, I walked my way out of my canvassing area and into the city. At that point, I realized that I'd traveled out of canvassing range, so I decided to walk through the city and into an unauthorized territory that I recalled had an interesting aesthetic.

By the time I got to the neighbourhood I sought, the time left in the evening was getting sparse, so I determined that it was best that I get to my canvassing. I picked the nearest residence, walked up the pathway, and knocked on the door.

"Hello," an oldish man said through a screen door.

"Oh, hello," I said, trying to activate my canvassing spiel. "Um, would you like to give us some money?"

The man frowned at me. "I don't think so."

"Sorry, I should introduce myself. I'm John Smith; I work for the Green Cross. Would you like to give *them* some money? It's a good cause."

The man's frown lightened, but his words didn't. "I don't think so."

So I let him be. Evidently I needed to refocus myself and put some professionalism back into my delivery. I spent a few moments aligning my breaths, and then I knocked on another door.

"Hello," said a youngish woman with annoyance in her tone.

"Hi, I'm John Smith with the Green Cross. How are you?"

"Busy, what's up?"

"Well, I just thought that maybe perhaps you would like to donate some money to the Green Cross. We're trying to—"

"No thanks," the woman said. "*Maybe perhaps* next time."

That one landed. My canvassing powers were clearly out of order, so I packed them up for another day.

An hour later, I arrived at Elizabeth's door.

"Hello, dear," she said, "to what do I owe the honour of such a late visit?"

"I have to tell you something."

"What's the matter, dear—are you all right?"

"Yes, I'm fine; it's just that I found something out about your sister, and I hope it's okay that I found it out."

"What do you think you found out, dear?" Elizabeth said as we sat down.

"Well, um, it's just that you know how you said that Dorothy wouldn't accept you for who you were? I think that might have changed."

"I'm sorry, dear, but how did you find things out about my sister?"

"I'm sorry—I just wanted to see if there was any chance for reconciliation. So I looked her up on the internet, and it turns out that she works at a seniors' centre, so I went there, and I told her I was interested in volunteering—don't worry, I didn't say anything about *you*—I just asked her some questions and, um ..." I stopped as I noticed a stunned look on my neighbour's face.

"If you don't mind my asking, dear, what did you ask her?"

"Oh, um, I asked her about what sort of volunteer work I might be able to do—and one of the things she told me about was this gay and lesbian seniors' support group, so I asked her about that, and she was very, um ...like, she seemed really pushy that, if I had any problem with someone being gay, then I couldn't volunteer there." I looked hopefully at Elizabeth.

A smirk surfaced on her face. "I'm sorry, dear, but what is it that you think my sister wouldn't accept me for?"

"I thought it was because you were, you know, not into men?"

Elizabeth laughed. "I'm afraid not, dear. That pushy woman you described—that's my sister, all right. She was always that way. She never had a problem with me liking girls—I felt like she knew before I even told her. And, when our parents found out, she was angrier than I was when they weren't supportive."

"Oh, so then, um ..."

"What is it that she wouldn't accept me for?"

"Yeah."

"That's very personal, dear."

"I'm sorry, I shouldn't have—"

"That's all right, dear. I'm touched that you cared enough to ask. But, if you don't mind, I'd rather not talk about it."

"Oh, okay, um—"

"So, other than that, how was your day?" Elizabeth said.

I would have preferred *any* other segue, but—after Elizabeth had let me off her hook so gently—I wasn't going to argue. So I sighed and told Elizabeth that the rumours of Jacklyn's marriage had been greatly exaggerated.

Elizabeth shook her head. "That girl needs psychiatric help."

"No, no," I said, "I could see why she did it. She was trying to get people to stop bugging her about dating, which she's not interested in."

"That may be, but there's no earthly reason that she needed to lie to you about it."

I exited the conversation feeling a healthy helping of self-contempt. Being enamoured with Jacklyn while she was married had been honourable because it was just a wistful dream, but adoring her while she was suddenly single was cruel because it was an embarrassing overreach of my ego.

Chapter 47
Dullard vs. Cupid II

Opportunity Mocks

I arrived at work on Monday morning to find on my desktop an email from my faraway friend Tally. That overpowered my thoughts as I remembered that I'd promised myself that—if she again pursued information about my alleged romantic life—I'd tell her about my complimentary thoughts towards a then unavailable woman. *Would I hold myself to that now that the unavailable woman was technically available?*

So I took in a sigh and opened the message.

Oh. Tally had made no effort to investigate the dangled-in-front-of-her topic; instead, she had tangented to an old one.

'Hey,' she wrote, 'remember when I wanted to set you up with that cousin of mine? She's still single. And I still think you guys would get along. I know you said you didn't want me to pressure her since she already declined, but she really was having a tough time at the time. I'll tell her it's all my idea. What do you say?'

Oh my wow.

"Hey, John!" Khiron said, peering into my office. "Did you watch *Conan* last week?"

"Um, I don't think so."

"Well, *I* did," Khiron said as she slumped into my guest chair, "and I don't think he's that funny anymore."

"Oh yeah?"

Khiron was undeterred by my hollow retort; she began babbling whole-mouthedly about the basis for her squabble with Conan. My ears and mind were not in the discussion. As you may have spotted, observant reader, Tally's email had left me in a blizzard of emotions. Indeed, the mention of Cousin Tally reminded me of the dreariness I'd felt after her heartfelt anonymous rejection of me, but, oddly, the harsh results of her previous repudiation had disbanded over time. Instead, I was now re-enchanted by the tangible possibility of going on a date with the clearly complicated cousin of one of my favourite people.

"Yeah, good point," I said to Khiron, noticing—by her cadence—that she was at the end of a sentence.

Hmm, perhaps going on a blind date would help me to recover from my ridiculous crush on Jacklyn.

"Right!" I said, faking a chuckle at what looked to be a Khiron joke.

But how could I go on a date with Cousin Tally, given my now morally allowed *appreciation for Jacklyn?*

The answer was obvious. Jacklyn was not interested in me, but Cousin Tally *could* be (at least until she met me).

With that clarification in place, I rejoined Khiron's conversation already in progress. But, at that moment, she was apparently satisfied that I fully understood her musings, so she left to teach Erik the same curriculum.

I quickly then turned back to my keyboard and accepted Tally's offer of a date with Cousin Tally. After I pressed send, I noticed that I was more excited about the future than usual.

On my way home several hours later, I decided that I needed to dislodge from myself any hurt feelings that Jacklyn hadn't told me sooner about her phony matrimony. While discovering myself to be on the wrong side of that fabrication had been startling to me, her reasons for putting me there were understandable at every step.

I received a positive reply from Matchmaker Tally the next morning, and—after ping-ponging a few more emails over the next couple days—the set up was set. Cousin Tally and I were to meet for coffee after work on Friday.

During that anticipation-packed week at Ambiguity, I noticed that the two interactions I had with Jacklyn the unmarried math tutor were somewhat strained. Even though neither of us was mad at the other for having been lied to about Jacklyn's marriage, it seemed as though we were both still unsure of what to do with the news. I suspected that Jacklyn suspected my feelings for her, and so—without a sham marriage to protect her—she was surely worried that I would ask her out.

As I reached that conclusion, Erik peaked into my office.

"Hey John, what's up?"

"Oh, I'm fine, I was just—"

"Yeah, you *look* fine. Anything you could use an Erik's perspective on?"

With my high level of introspection, my defences were in exile, so I didn't deny Erik's accusation.

"Well, there's this girl—"

"*Girl* or *woman?*"

"Right, um, woman. And I have pretty strong feelings for her."

"Okay, good so far."

"But I'm pretty sure she's not interested in me."

"Ahah—that explains the melancholy face."

"Right, but I wonder if it would be good if I told her how I feel so that at least she would *know*, just—you know—just in case."

Erik sighed. "Well, I don't know whether she's carrying a reciprocal torch for you or not, John, but I would say, if you're confident that she *doesn't*, then do you think she would *want* you to tell her? If not, then maybe, leave her be."

"Right," I said, relieved yet disappointed by that surprisingly compelling argument.

"I'm not saying you *shouldn't* tell her," Erik continued. "I'm just saying it might be easier to decide if you consider how it'll affect *her* and thus your friendship."

"Right," I said again, but I was already convinced.

On Thursday night, I told Elizabeth about my Friday evening date with Cousin Tally. As always, my friend provided all the enthusiasm I could hope for in a confidant; yet I felt squeamish talking so openly about my betrayal of my affection for Jacklyn the math tutor.

When the topic was vanquished, Elizabeth smiled.

"I have some news of my own," she said.

"Really? What?"

"I've become reacquainted with someone."

My eyes widened. "With who?"

Elizabeth smiled again. "I should think you would be able to guess, dear. I have just come from tea with my sister."

"Wow! How'd *that* happen?"

"Well, I decided that forty years is a long time, and I wanted to see my sister again, whether she should have called me first or not."

"Wow—and how'd it go?"

"It was like we'd never been apart. We laughed and giggled, and she was just as bossy a little so-and-so as she ever was, but I love her dearly."

I felt an influx of endorphins. "So are you going to hang out again?"

"Of course, dear. We're *sisters*—why wouldn't we visit with each other all the time?"

I laughed out loud at that.

Elizabeth smiled. "Thank you, dear."

"Oh, what for?"

"For inspiring me to see my sister again. You made me realize that, if you were willing to do what you did to get us back together, well, I was just being a stubborn old woman."

"But you *weren't*. She's the one—"

"You're right, she was, dear, but it takes two to keep a feud going that long, and I wish I'd ended it a long time ago. So thank you for helping me to do something about it before it was too late."

"You're welcome," I said, too honoured to deny the compliments any further.

On the following fateful and dateful Friday morning, any nerves that had relaxed the night before reawakened. It occurred to me that I, alone, was to be meeting Cousin Tally. I wonder if people who frequently date feel anxious during first encounters with *their* prospects—maybe only when they think that the possibility has especially impressive potential. In which case—since I felt that *too*—the butterflies in my stomach were flying around so incessantly that, as I rode the bus to work, I thought I might be ill.

Later, as I went through my morning work, I noticed that the simplest tasks required double and triple checking. Moreover, when Erik came by to ask me a question, I noticed myself staring at him and not replying.

"Something wrong, John?"

"Oh, no, no, sorry, I think my hearing's a little off today—could you repeat the question?"

"How late are you here tonight?"

"*How late am I here tonight?*—I don't know, 5:30?"

"Oh, great, could you do an Erik a favour and receive a package?"

"Sure—*you're* Erik, though?"

Erik laughed. "Yeah, sorry, third person. Josh hates it when I invoke the third person, but he's the one who taught me *Seinfeld*."

"Oh—does *Seinfeld* use the third person?"

"Yeah, the George character seems to always be invoking the third person: 'George is getting upset!'"

I faked a laugh, but not well.

"You don't appreciate the *Seinfeld*?"

"Oh, um, no, I *do*—sorry, I'm just a little distracted."

"Work or leisure?"

"Leisure, I guess."

"Good choice. So is it a hot date or that woman you told me about or...?"

I felt my veins tighten. "Um, actually, I'm kind of nervous about it, and talking about it makes me more nervous, so do you mind if—"

"Yeah, no worries. Can I give you one piece of advice, though?"

"Okay."

"You're the one and only person who can be the person that you are. So just be yourself."

I nodded and smiled sincerely. Even though Erik's advice was a familiar truism, his earnest delivery made the hair on the top of my head stretch out with feeling.

"Okay, thanks," I said.

As Erik left, I sighed much relief that I'd avoided his more extensive counsel. Somehow I'd expressed exactly the right emotion to persuade my co-worker to spare me just this once, but I was aware that that was a rare and lucky break: I should never have put myself in that position. So, for the rest of the morning, I instructed myself to concentrate my thoughts away from the

Cousin Tally distraction. I was of course unsuccessful in the task, but it was a cute idea.

Five minutes before the official end of the workday, the voices of Khiron and Erik approached my office.

"Hey there, worker bee," Erik said. "Oh, by the way, that package came in already, so don't worry about waiting for it."

"Oh, okay, thanks," I said, retroactively relieved because I'd forgotten about it.

"Okay, John," Khiron said, hopping into my office, "can you settle a debate between me and Erik?"

"Sure, I'll try."

"Okay, so...he thinks [Janis Famous] only got famous because of that sex tape that got all over the internet, but I think she's totally beautiful. What do you think?"

"Oh, um..." My date-anticipating nerves had no opinion on the matter, but I scanned my brain anyway. "Probably both."

Erik laughed. "He's probably right. The elicit video likely wouldn't have provoked so much hype if she wasn't already on the high attractiveness spectrum."

"But I still think she would've been successful *anyway*," Khiron said, looking at me with urging eyes, "she's so beautiful. Don't you think she's beautiful?"

"Sure," I said, hoping to show respect for Khiron's good opinion, while also not agreeing too generously with it, which would have then allowed Erik to pronounce that my looks-based approval was sexist.

Erik laughed. "Another ringing endorsement from our resident fence-sitter."

I smirked back at my accurate accuser.

"Anyway," Erik said, "we're done for the day—I suppose you've got another of your standard *half hours to go*?"

"Oh, actually," I said, pleased that I could show Erik an occasion where I was not overworking, "I'm just about to go too."

"How very un-John-like of you. Do you want a ride somewhere?"

"Oh, thanks—um, where are you going?"

"Where are *you* going?" Erik replied. "Wait, is this the date you wouldn't cop to earlier?"

"Um, yeah, I guess."

"Then we're definitely driving you."

"So, John," Khiron said as we left Ambiguity, "what's this girl like?"

"Um, I don't actually know a lot yet. It's a blind date, but I know she's—"

"Oh, *fun*—I love blind dates. Okay, so we don't know what *this* girl's like, but what type of girl's normally your type?"

"Um, someone funny, I guess."

"No, but what does she *look* like?"

Erik laughed. "You know: as in *the most important* part of who she is."

I smiled at that. (I was pleased to diagnose that, through their friendship, Khiron had drawn a previously underutilized sense of humour out of Erik. He, in turn, seemed to have unearthed a cheerier disposition within her.)

In response to the friendly inquisition, I decided to describe my long lost love, Ashley, as my ideal looks mate since I wasn't about to offer a composite of Jacklyn, which could then be used against me if she and I were ever Khiron-spotted hanging out.

"Sounds *pretty*," Khiron said as we got into Erik's environmentally considerate car.

"Sounds *specific*," Erik added. "Is that an ex-girlfriend, per chance?"

"No," I said, smirking at my transparency. "But she was an ex, you know, *wished*-she-was my girlfriend."

Erik and Khiron laughed, and we soon segued off to Erik's preferences.

"Well, if I must choose," he said, "I'll go with a Janis Famous doppelgänger."

"Be serious," Khiron said.

Erik shrugged. "Well, I think Josh is as handsome as they come, so I'm actually all set."

"That's so sweet," Khiron said. "I feel the same way about AJ." She paused at the nice sentiment and then added, "But I wish he was a couple inches taller."

When we got close to our destination, Erik glanced back toward my backseat position.

"How's your confidence?" he said.

"It's okay."

"Trust me," he replied. "Just be yourself, and—"

"Don't tell him *that*," Kiron interrupted. "A girl likes a guy who puts in a little effort."

"*Please*," Erik said. "So it's your testimony that a woman wants a guy to impersonate the guy he *thinks* she wants?"

"No, but she wants him to show her that the date *matters* to him."

"Hmm," Erik said, nodding, "I *suppose*. All right, John, be yourself, but set to eleven."

I laughed at that. "Okay, thanks, guys. I'll see you next week."

As I got out of the car, and waved to my deliverers, I was pleased to note that their conversation had dulled my nerves. And, as I walked the final block to the coffee shop, I realized that—whatever happened with Cousin Tally—I was glad to be taking a leap of possibility with her. Indeed, I'm sure it seems melodramatic to say so, judgy reader, but going on a date with Cousin Tally was, for me, not just meeting a woman for coffee: it was taking a weight off my heart as I allowed myself to hope for someone other than Jacklyn the math tutor. Of course, it was likely that Cousin Tally would not approve me for further courtship once she met me, but that was not relevant to the fact that my hopeful intentions could not be retracted. By choosing to meet with her, I was choosing not to try for Jacklyn.

Hmm, that was a powerful thought to impose on my brain right before a date. But having gotten my ride there, I had extra time to examine it. *Was I sure that I wanted to give up on Jacklyn?* No, I *wasn't*, but I was confident that she wasn't interested in me. *Why else would she have waited to tell me about her marriage-faking hobby?* Hmm, maybe she was telling the truth when she said that she felt obligated to the lie when she first met me and subsequently felt awkward undoing the deception when we became friends.

So I sighed and began to survey my few failed loves. I had once been glad to determine that I had never really had a shot with Ashley. *But did that really make me feel better about never having taken that shot?*

Maybe not, but this wasn't just about *my* feelings. As Erik had asked, *would Jacklyn* want *me to tell her about my out-of-league crush?* I saw no evidence of that.

And *yet…was it possible that Jacklyn was hiding her* own *emotions because she didn't want to betray her grief and admit that she was ready to return from her self-imposed romantic exile?* Instead of lamenting how long it took her to tell me about her unmarriage, maybe I should have been considering the fact that she was taking *even longer* to tell everyone else. *Was it possible she wanted me to know about her unbetrothal for reasons other than friendship?*

Probably not, of course, but…*maybe.* Either way, maybe it was worth stepping over my embarrassment, *just in case.* Indeed, when I considered Jacklyn's advice on matters not related to herself, she always seemed to promote the most proactive option. And Erik *had* told me to consider Jacklyn's opinion *first*, so…

I found a pay phone and dialed Jacklyn's number. She probably wouldn't be home from work yet anyway—

"Hello?"

"Hi, Jacklyn. Sorry to bug ya. It's John from—"

"Oh, hey, John. What's up?"

"Um, sorry to bug you, but I have a serious conundrum. Do you have a minute?"

"Yeah, sure, what's—what's going on?"

"Um—so I'm about to go on a date."

"Oh, cool."

"Okay, so you think it's *cool?*"

"Yeah, um, dates are usually meant to be fun, aren't they?"

"Right, well, that maybe answers my question, but I'm going to ask it anyway. Um, is there any reason you wouldn't want me to go on the date?"

Jacklyn paused. "How do you mean?"

"Well, our friendship is very important to me, so I would appreciate if you could spare me saying more than, you know, necessary to get my point across. I'm just wondering if you would rather I *didn't* go on the date because, you know, um, yeah. Do you know what I mean?"

"I think I do," Jacklyn said. "That was a beautiful thing to say."

I sighed my relief. At least she wasn't yelling at me for breaking our friendship code.

"And? Do you think I should go on the date?"

Jacklyn paused. "Yes," she said (and, for a wonderful moment, I thought the 'Yes' was in my favour), "um, I think you should go on the date, my friend."

My face went white. "Okay, if you're sure?" I said, not meaning to ask again, but needing something to say.

"I'm sure," Jacklyn said.

I nodded out a gulp, but forced a smile onto my voice. "Okay, I have to go."

I felt a soft breeze travel through my face. But it wasn't a sad sensation. It was adrenalin-fueled. I had slayed my fear of stilted, post-rejection conversation, and I was okay. In fact, very soon, I would truly be letting go and meeting Cousin Tally.

A moment later, I walked into the dateful coffee shop. I was still twenty minutes early, so I ordered a coffee and found a comfy chair. I felt that marvelous blend of anxiety and excitement.

Ten minutes later, the door to the coffee shop opened, and I looked up instinctively to see ... *Jacklyn the math tutor.* Oh my awkwardness.

"Hey," I said, gulping as she landed in my location. "This is quite the coincidence."

Jacklyn smiled. "Not necessarily."

"Oh, how so?" I said. Indeed, I was baffled in the fullest sense of the word as I had no conception of a guess as to what Jacklyn meant.

She shrugged. "May I explain while you're waiting for your date?"

"Um—"

"I'll take that as 'Yes,'" Jacklyn said, sitting down in the opposing comfy chair. "So imagine, if you will, a stubborn girl who had sworn off dating for rest of her life because her whole family had died, and she couldn't imagine pursuing romance ever again."

"Right, yes, I remember."

"Well, imagine that was all going very well, and then one day her favourite and most cherished cousin told her about this sweet guy she'd befriended at work."

That sound you hear, perceptive reader, is of all my cells crashing into each other at once.

"Wait, are *you* Tally's cousin?"

Jacklyn smiled. "Please save your questions till the end."

"Um, okay, sure."

"Now, not for nothing, but Tally is *not* one of those people who makes a hobby out of playing Cupid. If she thinks you're a good match for someone, it's because she *sees* something. So I was tempted. But my blackened heart still wasn't ready to rejoin the dating pool, so I politely declined."

"Wow, Tally didn't explain it quite like that."

"Yes, well, that's because I forbade her. But then, one day, a job came up at Ambiguity, which Tally thought I would be perfect for, and she recommended me to our old friend, Elsje Anders. I got the job, and—while I was working with Elsje—*she* happened to mention this *John Smith* character's name a few times."

"Right, yeah, I remember you saying that."

"Yup, she said you were this incredibly down-to-earth, sincere guy, so—not for nothing—but I felt a few pangs of regret that I hadn't met you. But I left it at that until we started riding the same bus together, and I spotted you with your canvassing stuff out, and I noticed your nametag, so I was pretty sure you were *you*, so I watched you for a bit."

"You were watching me?"

"Yeah, it wasn't creepy, I promise. Just, you know, people watching with a one-person focus."

I laughed.

Jacklyn shrugged that adorable shrug. "And you were fascinating. I've never seen someone looking at the world so intensely. You seemed to care so profoundly when you saw people unhappy."

"Wow, really? But maybe that was just my face."

Jacklyn laughed. "Yeah, I *did* think of that. Some people *do* present their faces all gloomily all the time, but then—remember that day those two women were fighting in the alley, and you ran off the bus—I assume to break up their fight?"

"You saw that?"

"Yup…so I presumed that your face wasn't just making stuff up: you really did have a soft spot for the rest of us."

"Wow, I thought that was a totally anonymous gesture. It's amazing to think you were there."

"I *was*," Jacklyn said with another perfect shrug. "And I decided

I wanted to meet you. But I still wasn't looking for romance—at least not that I would acknowledge to myself—which is why I kept wearing my mom's ring … so I wouldn't have to admit to myself that I might be interested in more."

"I'm baffled," I said.

Jacklyn grinned. "I know, and I'm sorry. But I have to get through this. So do you remember Jenny? The girl on the bus who was struggling with math?"

"Yeah."

"Well, I saw you studying her sad face, so I decided to try to introduce myself to you by showing off and cheering her up."

"Seriously? You did that for my benefit?"

"Well, I hoped it would benefit Jenny too, but, yeah, I probably wouldn't have done it if I hadn't noticed you watching Jenny and trying to console her with your eyes."

"Wow, I'm … baffled."

"But then," Jacklyn said with a laugh, "I accidentally insulted you by saying you shouldn't eavesdrop or something like that—"

"Right, I remember."

"So that's when I realized I had to introduce myself to you properly, which I did the next time I saw you on the bus."

"I'm … um … is there anything else?"

"No, I think that's it."

"Um, okay, so what about Tally and this date I'm supposed to have with—?"

"Right, sorry, so—after a while of hanging out with you on the bus—I admitted to Tally that we'd made friends. She begged me to tell you who I was, or to let her tell you, but I forbade her again. So she asked me if she could investigate whether you had feelings for anyone. I said she *could*, and I said that—if you said you had, you know, a positive disposition towards me in that way—I'd be willing to break my romance prohibition, but only if it was *your* idea." Jacklyn laughed. "I was so stubborn. I was convinced it would be a failing of my grief if it was my idea."

"Wow," I said, "yeah, I remember Tally sending me emails about whether I was interested in anyone. *What did I say?*"

Jacklyn pointed that wonderfully accusatory forehead at me. "You were *totally* unhelpful. You wouldn't admit feelings for *anyone.*"

"Wow, I truly…I was totally in the dark about all of this."

Jacklyn giggled. "I take that as a compliment of my elite deception skills. So then I decided I should let you know about my pretend marriage and see how you reacted."

"And how *did* I react?"

"Impossible to read! You seemed hurt, but I couldn't tell if that was because you were interested in me. But then Tally went rogue and sent you a message asking again if you wanted to meet, you know, her cousin. I was so mad until I found out you agreed to it, at which point I decided to go along with her scheme to finally bring everything into the open. But I truly had no idea whether you'd be disappointed or not. And then, half an hour ago, when you called me to see if I wanted to stop you from going on the date, I was pretty sure I'd cracked the enigma of my friend, John Smith."

I laughed and noticed as I did so that my eyes were warming with tears.

"I'm sorry, John," Jacklyn said. "I'm sorry I put you through all my craziness. I just needed a protective, you know, bubble around myself for a while in order to get here. I'm sorry, that probably sounds silly."

"I don't know if it's *silly* or not," I said, "but, for me, it's probably the best thing I've ever heard."

Jacklyn smiled and put her hand on mine.

"So," she said, "if you'll permit me, I lied when I said I was okay with you going on a date with another girl. Because *I* want to go on a date with you."

Wow. That took my heart beat away.

"Me too," I said.

"You want to date *you* too?"

"Well, can you blame me?"

Jacklyn laughed back. "*No*…so do you wanna go for a walk and see where it takes us?"

As we walked, my stomach was alert with the pitterpatter of butterflies, but—in that moment—I was not nervous.

Chapter 48
A Predictable Boring Ending

The Last Name

Fifteen months later, Jacklyn and I sat in her apartment.

"Hey Jacklyn," I said, "have you ever thought about what we would call ourselves if we ever got married?"

"Um—" she started.

"Because," I said, "I think we should take your name, in honour of your family."

Jacklyn smiled at me. "Are you asking me to marry you?"

"No," I said, not opposed to having proposed but realizing that a proposal was supposed to be much more romantic. "Just wondering what you'd want to be called if we *did* get married."

"I see."

That made me panic that she might think I had any hesitation about wanting to finally legitimize her wedding ring.

"If I *were* asking you to marry me, I'd be much more romantic about it, of course."

"*Of course*. So how might it go?"

"Oh, well, how would you *like* it to go?"

"Well, not for nothing, but I think the most romantic thing is sincerity. So I would—*hypothetically, of course*—just want you to ask however you felt like asking."

I loved Jacklyn's 'hypothetically, of course,' which allowed there to be some theoretical doubt as to my intentions. So I sat down next to her, smiled, and unleashed a standard, boring proposal.

So, patient reader, we are now nearly at the end of the autobiography of John Smith.

LEGAL NOTE: You might be wondering, critical reader, why the alleged autobiography of my life is concluding at my marriage. Good point, wise reader! In fact, in spirit, you're right, but—as per usual—my ghostwriter has found himself a loophole to your profound objection. You see, with the pending marriage of John Smith to Jacklyn Chapman, John Smith was to become John Chapman in honour of her family, and so John Smith was to be no more, and thus, technically, his autobiography would indeed be complete. But first we have one final piece of eventfulness.

You Guest It: A Wedding

ARTISIC LICENCING NOTE: Two of the interactions included in this wedding vignette claim to illuminate my 'first' follow-up visits—after the eventful events of the preceding chapter—with (A) a certain conning character (Matchmaker Tally) and (B) a certain conned character (Dorothy Braun-Low of the never-to-be-volunteered-for seniors' centre). In reality, my initial reunions with those two women occurred *before* this gathering. Nevertheless, my ever-untrustworthy ghostwriter insisted on presenting those two reconnections within the upcoming wedding reception because, he says, their dramatic tensions are more artistically suited to that time and place. I can only say in partial defence of my deceitful ghostwriter that he has not altered the spirit of those first meetings; he has only changed when and where they happened.

Many months after my boring proposal, there was a dullard-Jacklyn wedding, and it was—I'm told by many observers—a beautiful sight to see.

SNARKY NOTE: My ghostwriter says that *every* wedding is described as 'beautiful,' but that's not my problem: I heard 'beautiful' so that's what I'm reporting.

Per was the Best Man, and I was touched by the enthusiasm with which he performed the role. For instance, when it was time for him to deliver Jacklyn's wedding ring to me (the very one she'd worn when I first met her), he reached into his pocket but seemed to find nothing in there, so he padded his jacket before suddenly finding the prize behind my ear. We all laughed at that.

My mother seemed especially delighted: she was clearly proud of the Best Man and his brother.

Meanwhile, Elizabeth—who brought her sister, Dorothy, with her—spent the festivities smiling with what seemed a lot like pride. I would have better enjoyed the sentiment if I hadn't been busy pleading telepathically with her sibling to have a bad enough memory to forget my phony visit to her seniors' centre. But no such senior luck.

"Hello there," she said when my neighbour officially introduced her to me at the receiving line, "I guess you decided not to volunteer with us, after all, eh?"

"Right," I said, "um, yeah, I just ended up volunteering for the Green Cross instead."

"Good for you," Dorothy said. It was clear that she didn't believe me, but apparently she was impressed enough with the speed of my lie that she was willing to leave me alone about it. "Well," she concluded, "they're a very good organization too."

Meanwhile, sitting at my parents' table at the reception were Uncle Chet Williams and Aunty Susan Williams, along with my new mini-cousin, Chet Williams Junior. Uncle Chet and Aunty Susan cheerfully told my parents about how proud they were of me. But one can only talk about one's pride in a dullard for so long; eventually, Uncle Chet and Aunty Susan switched topics and told my parents about how pleased they were with little Chet Jr.

And then there was Tally. (She'd called me after my discovery of her cousinly relationship with Jacklyn, but I hadn't yet seen her in person.) During the pre-meal mingling, she spotted me by myself for a moment at the head table.

"Hello," she said, smiling sheepishly as if she'd accidentally spilled her wedding reception beverage on me.

"Hey," I said, pretending not to know what she was feeling guilty about.

"Are you sure you're not mad at me?" she whispered.

"Yes, I'm *sure*," I said, glancing at Jacklyn the math tutor, who was mingling nearby. "It was *her* fault."

"Right?" Tally said, going in for a hug.

I grinned as I received her.

"I guess you're right," Tally said as we unbraced, "if you could forgive *her* enough to marry her, then *of course* you could forgive me enough to still be my friend."

"Well, I wouldn't go *that* far."

Tally laughed. "Fair enough. I guess I was being a bit greedy there."

I giggled. "You know," I said, "I was just thinking—"

But I was interrupted by the arrival of a handsome yet friendly face.

"John," Tally said, "this is my husband, Hank."

"Great to meet you," I said.

"You as well," he said with a smile. "I've heard a lot about you."

At that moment, Jacklyn moved in on our conversation. "So, Hank, I've been meaning to ask you: were you in on the matchmaking conspiracy that caused all the trouble?"

Hank looked aghast at the accusation. "I was *not* involved, I swear—it was a lone shooter."

"Wow," Jacklyn said, shaking her head at Tally, "all that devious matchmaking, and it was all because of you alone."

"Well," Tally said, stifling a grin, "I would love to continue this inquisition, but my friend John here was about to tell me about an interesting thought he was having."

The trio looked at me.

"Right," I said, "well, um, I was just thinking it's funny that the first two people I met at Ambiguity were Chet and then you, Tally, and now Chet's my uncle, and you're my cousin."

"Wow, yeah," Jacklyn said, "you've really turned Ambiguity into a family business, John."

Hank laughed.

"I see Hank's point," Tally said (causing me to laugh out loud), "I think it's best if we refer to each other as cousins-*in-law*. If we were genuine cousins, then—since Jacklyn's *my* cousin—you'd be marrying, like, your second cousin."

Hank and I laughed again.

Jacklyn stared at me with her most comically judgmental face.

"I agree with Tally: I think it would be weird for you to marry your cousin, my friend."

"Yeah, *good point*," I said, without even hesitating as I pointed my thumb merrily at Tally, "but, don't forget, *she's* the one who set it up."

Jacklyn laughed.

Just behind her, I spotted my dad watching our banter. He smiled at me for a moment and then rotated his attention back to his own conversation.

The Boring End

THE BORING CREDITS

GHOSTWRITTEN AND DIRECTED BY
Seth McDonough

COVER DESIGN BY
Calum McDonough

FORMATTING BY
Michelle Arglye via Melissa Williams Design

NARRATED BY
John Smith

STARRING
(in order of appearance)

You
as the loyal reader

Ghostwriter Seth
as himself

John Smith
as the dullard

Jacklyn Chapman
as the math tutor

CO-STARRING
(in order of appearance)

CLARIFICATION NOTE: By 'order of appearance' we, of course, mean the chronological order in which the characters appear in the book, not the preferential order of the characters' physical appearance. No offence, good-looking reader.

Per Smith
as brother dullard

Paul & Mary Smith
as father and mother dullard

Aunty Susan Smith
as the favourite relative

Ashley Anonti
as the first love

Jake Richport
as the sociopath

Amy the co-worker
as the babbler

Stacy the co-worker
as a beautiful ego

Bert Hardelean Jr.
as the charmer

Nicolette & Noelle
as the positivity sisters

Annette the MC
as the first girlfriend

Chet Williams
as the segue artist

Miss Elizabeth Braun
as the favourite neighbour

Tally
as Cousin Cupid

Erik Tham & Khiron Gamir
as the work neighbours

Rayann the receptionist
as the training crush

Glenroy Garrison
as the schmoozer

Mrs. Elsie Anders
as the favourite boss

and Derrick Litke
as the irritant

No animals were killed or injured in the writing of this book.
(Although, a few keyboards may have been damaged.)

This book was written to keep people company. So, friendly reader, if you're ever feeling lonely, please consider visiting us again. We'd be delighted to renew our conversations. Either that or do something social: people, after all, can occasionally be a cure for loneliness. But, if they let you down, we'll be here, waiting to make fun of them with you.

THE BORING ACKOWLEDGMENTS

A Boring Book has been a two-decade project that has required support, inspiration, and skepticism from friends, family, and other servants. The author's gratitude flows to Marg 'M' McDonough (for your ever-present inspirational talent and for reading Jane Austen to us as kids), Tom 'Wait, let me start that again' McDonough (for your ever-present wit even when you forget the punch line to your joke and for reading Charles Dickens to me without the other kids), Tarrin 'Bloody foot while teaching karate' McDonough (for first proving to me that a civilian could be a comedy writer), Violette 'Tricked by Seth into believing an editing machine was alive' Baillargeon (for so bountifully cheering on my first writing inclinations), Erika 'Letters from Asia' Eineigel (for travelling with a draft of *ABB* and leaving it in India for someone to "discover"), Amanda 'Trekker not Trekkie' Davies (for reading a draft of *ABB* and, like Gene Roddenberry to our future, always finding the best version of every joke), Claudia 'R' Costa (for reading a draft of *ABB* and, despite your apparent expectations to the contrary, admitting that it "wasn't that bad"), Tamsen 'I don't know what they're talking about' McDonough (for learning so much from me during our debate-filled writing collaborations and for always saluting *ABB* as a perfect work of art regardless of what other commentators might say), Sorrel 'Tweak!' McDonough (for co-producing—with your 'amazing' computer's assistance—books of family anecdotes with me and for somehow convincing me you liked my writing even while you cut two thirds of it away), Candida "Miss Deeds" Moreira for your unquenchable enthusiasm and support of my rival writing efforts, Brenda 'The Best Cousin (Other Than Seth)' Jones (for relentless support and for introducing me to Margo Bates), Margo 'Author of *P.S. Don't Tell Your Mother*' Bates (for generous encouragement and introducing me to Bernice Lever), Bernice 'Colour of Words' Lever (for editing suggestions and for sending me to the Surrey Writers' Festival), Robin 'Author of *Dead Politician Society*' Spano (for kindness to a stranger at the Surrey Writers' Festival and inviting me to join your Off The Page Writers' Group), my friends in the Off The Page Writers' group, who have provided elite feedback on *ABB*—including Louvain 'I'm not a writer' Chalmers (for teaching me to enhance my words out loud), Erik 'The Scribe' D'Souza (for so generously interviewing and supporting all of us soon-to-be famous authors), Lily 'The Poet-Biologist' (for always seeking the best for our words), Eric 'The Wise' Mason (for seeing connections we writers may not even see in our own works), David 'The Comedian' Haines (for being so generous in both comedy and laughter), Sheilagh 'My Rival' MacDonald (for being so good-natured about losing every writerly debate with me), Patrick 'The Entertainer' Cotter (for agreeing to pretend to be me when it's time to read *ABB* in front of an audience), Katie Ormiston 'The singer-storyteller' (for, in case Patrick's not available, teaching me to present my words with a wink at the audience), Franci "The Haiku Laureate" Louann for teaching me to see the poetry in story, Dr. Olga 'Read Dumas before she was seven' Thierbach-McLean (for elevating the brainpower of our meetings)—Aram 'The Most Interesting Cousin in the world' McLean for swapping editing ideas across the Atlantic and for letting me publish my books first to spare me one more competitor, Wendy 'The Facebook Whisperer' Anderson for your elite propaganda efforts in supporting my writing career, Calum 'It's Right Here, bud' McDonough (for uncompromising and uncompensated cover design and for providing me with a permanent funny place to go in my writerly mind after you boasted that you'd found the tennis ball we were seeking in a little green bag, only to note, "Eww!" because it was actually the dog's bounty that you had reached in to discover), Michelle 'Melissa Williams Design' Argyle (for your skill and patience and more patience), Natalie 'Wait, so you're actually *related* to Jane Austen?' Anderson (for expert grammar services, inspiring this writer with your elite comedy every day, and for not running off with that tour guide on our Austen-themed honeymoon when you found out he was a great nephew of our favourite author), and Jamie 'Name Pending' Anderson McDonough for letting us read Jane Austen and Charles Dickens to you in the future.

www.ingramcontent.com/pod-product-compliance
Lightning Source LLC
Chambersburg PA
CBHW050843210726
48290CB00004B/1066